They'd never gotten along as children, but would his brother really *kill* him?

"Where is she, Gabe!?"

"Go home, Nick. Go home to your little life in Arizona, whatever you have left of it. Run away again. Just like you did before. Just like you always do."

Nick refused to back down. Not this time. "Tell me where she is.*"*

"Go to hell!"

Nick's hands clenched. It took everything he had to restrain himself. So filled with rage, anger, and fury, he was ready to tear his brother from limb from limb. "I'll find her." He glimpsed the dead man, knowing he should feel a sense of loss but it was difficult. His eyes returned to his brother's icy stare and he reaffirmed his objective. "I'm going to find Brandi." He turned his back on Gabe.

Nick had barely taken a step when the clunk behind caused him to halt. Regrettably, it was a sound he was becoming familiar with—a hammer being cocked. He pivoted, looked at the firearm in his brother's hand. "You going to shoot me?"

"Get the hell out of town and forget Brandi. I'll handle this. Just like I always have. You just run away. That's what you're good at. Running."

With resolve, Nick advanced closer to the weapon. "Brandi's coming with me, Gabe. You want to stop me? Then you'll have to kill me."

Click.

Nick recoiled.

Click. Click. Click. Click.

Gabe continued squeezing the trigger, forgetting he hadn't reloaded since emptying his handgun into Brooke Lauser thirty minutes earlier.

Nick's heart thudded in his neck. The fact that Gabe was ready—willing—to kill him, indicated nothing remained between the Garrison siblings other than contempt. Nick walked away, determined to never again turn his back on his brother.

Nick Garrison had two goals in life. He longed to survive high school and then quickly flee the dead end town in western Pennsylvania to pursue his dreams across the country. Never looking back, he says farewell to friends, family—and his high school sweetheart, Brandi Conrad.

Decades later, Nick returns home a failure. But with a secret to share. As he catches up with old pals and confronts decades-old animosity within his family, he realizes something is amiss in Avalon Hills. Everything appears untouched by the passage of time. But Nick quickly discovers looks are often deceiving. When he begins inquiring as to the whereabouts of Brandi, he inadvertently sets in motion a deadly chain of events. While shadowed by a mysterious figure, he realizes a countdown has begun.

Because Nick is not the only one with a secret.

ACKNOWLEDGEMENTS

Writing is a solitary journey. Luckily, however, I've had the good fortune to have several people who've been more than influential and significant in helping me reach the finish line. I'd like to thank them.

I am forever indebted and grateful to Kristin Harmel. Despite her unyielding hectic schedule, she found time to extend both a helping hand and critical eye. This book and my dream would not have happened if it wasn't for your guidance. Thanks for helping me achieve the life intended.

More than seven years ago, due to our shared passion for writing and baseball, Joe DeCaro gave a chance to a stranger. To this day, he continues to be my mentor, my Yoda, my pal-o-mine. Thanks for standing by me, Brother Raccoon.

For a quarter of a century, Brian Wright has been a giant of a friend who's accompanied me for this entire ride. I wouldn't be able to call myself a published author if it wasn't for him. You're a true pal. Literally.

There are still good kind-hearted people in the world and Michelle Wargo is proof. She went above and beyond what I ever could have dreamed of. Thank you for helping me navigate the traffic and complete this journey.

When I reached a crossroad, unsure if I should keep pushing forward, Bonnie Vaughan appeared. Thank you for your help, assistance, and information. And for taking lunch when you did.

Of course, Faith, LP, Lauri, Jack, and the entire crew at Black Opal Books for putting up with the questions this newbie author had.

Plain God

Rob Silverman

A Black Opal Books Publication

DEDICATION

No one could tell a story like my dad. I like to think I possibly inherited some of that from him. He's not here to see my dream come true, but I'd like to believe he still knows.

My mom continued to believe in me long after I stopped believing in myself. She countered my barrage of self-doubt with her encouragement, reassurance, and praise.

This book is for them.

Chapter 1

1987:

Nick Garrison's first seventeen years were predictable and uneventful. Then he witnessed a murder. Hours after the sun was absorbed into the blackness of night, Nick's path in life would be forever altered.

From the outset he knew this evening would be memorable, a turning point in his existence. He just had no idea of the severity.

A week after graduating high school, he was chomping at the bit to get his ass out of this hellhole. Avalon Hills offered two paths in life: factory work and more factory work. Neither befitted Nick. He'd be the one to break free, to live his dream, and not turn into his father. His sentence in northwestern Pennsylvania would end.

Summer was blooming and the high temperature spiked with unrelenting humidity was enhancing Nick's miserable state. It added to his hunger to get as far away as fast as humanly possible.

From up in the charcoaled hills the town resembled a modern day Netherworld. A scimitar moon hung low, the refraction shone on the layer of iron smog that perpetually blanketed the hamlet. The nearby factory belched gray toxins into the air. People were working and generally happy. The strong economy brought with it extra shifts. But extra shifts meant extra pollution. Unlike Nick, the townspeople had grown oblivious to the stench that choked the city.

Sitting in a clearing Nick glanced north. Atop Aliquippa Mountain, out where the streets had no name, he scrutinized the alternating red blinking lights of the TV towers. Right.

Left. Right. Left. He'd been watching these damn lights since childhood. As a young boy, peering at them through his bedroom window, they lulled him to sleep. Now, they taunted him, his entire existence passing by one blink at a time. He smirked at the towers. Just like that, he'd been trapped another minute.

The land sloped downward and, in the valley beyond the thicket, he detected the gentle rustling of the Acheron River. The blue-black waters flowed peacefully, the moonlight shimmering off the surface.

River, my ass, Nick told himself. It was a piss-filled stream. He and his buddies hadn't fished there since second grade.

The shallow waterway snaked around the factories, meandered the foothills, and streamed through the center of town. Nick once heard that the Acheron fed into the Allegheny on the far side of the Appalachian Mountains and ultimately to Washington DC, Chesapeake Bay, and out into the Atlantic. It made sense. Even bodies of water got the hell away from Avalon Hills.

Nothing and no one would keep Nick imprisoned. Not even Brandi Conrad.

But the way she sparkled angelically this night Nick knew it would be tough not to surrender.

Their biology professor made them lab partners during junior year. Thanks to dissecting frogs, Nick was teamed with one of the hottest girls at Avalon High.

Brandi radiated confidence beyond her years. And sexuality. She was a living breathing conundrum. A tomboy wrapped in the body of pure femaleness, a girl with a brain and a body. She was perceived as *unapproachable* but her personality was welcoming.

She preferred hanging out with the guys and, as such, had been labeled *easy*. At first, Nick believed he would also get laid by Brandi. Why not? Everyone else had.

But as their friendship grew and graduation neared, *that* didn't happen. Sure, there was some intense petting and making out. But Nick never made it past second base. He wondered what was wrong with him. Brandi supposedly gave herself to every other guy, so why not him?

She'd been involved in an on-again off-again relationship with a much older guy. Nineteen. Gino was the town badass. He'd been arrested for burglary and carrying a concealed weapon. Rumor was he even once killed a guy over the border in Ohio.

Gino was now out of the picture, serving time in Somerset Correctional Facility after a grab-and-dash turned ugly. That particular evening, Brandi was waiting outside the convenience store with the engine running. Pot-bellied Gino marched in. He'd grab a couple six packs and haul ass. They had been successful numerous other times. What they hadn't counted on was a hero making minimum wage.

The overzealous clerk retrieved a baseball bat from behind the counter. When Gino refused to halt, the middle-aged clerk turned into Pirates slugger Willie Stargell, leaving the kid with three broken ribs, two broken arms, and one trip to the hospital. Gino was sentenced to six to eight. Brandi drove away and never looked back.

Tonight, she wore tighter-than-usual acid-washed jeans that were tucked into her pristine white boots. Her red V-neck top exposed slightly more cleavage than she typically displayed. Her jet black hair fell just below her shoulders, framing a perfectly rounded face with flawless features and high cheekbones. Her sienna complexion fed rumors in school that Brandi's heritage could be traced back to the Lenape Indians. Her deep-set chestnut eyes were mesmerizing and mysterious while laced with a hint of vulnerability.

Brandi had said farewell to Gino. She wouldn't say farewell to Nick.

Legs stretched out and ankles crossed, she rifled through the backpack she'd brought into the highlands. She tilted the pack, using the moonlight to illuminate its contents. She smiled sheepishly at the condom and then started to lift the small bag of pot she got from a friend. She hesitated for a beat, choosing instead to remove two bottles of *Bud.* Tonight she and Nick would at long last consummate their relationship. She wanted to remember it and not be stoned. A beer or two would settle the nerves and take the edge off as their friendship would be taken to the next level.

Wearing Levi 501's and a Whitesnake T-shirt, Nick slanted back. With his palms pressed into the pink blanket he couldn't help but smile. Brandi twisted off the cap and handed him a bottle. Not ladylike, but sexy as hell.

She raised her bottle. "To our future."

They clinked, they sipped. Some foam nearly trickled over the lip onto her jeans but she gulped it down. Dabbing her thin lips with the back of her hand, she winked. Leaning closer, she planted a few tender kisses on Nick's mouth. Her lips were soft, engaging, and tasted of Budweiser.

Brandi gently parted Nick's lips with the tip of her probing tongue. The passion intensified. Her right hand cupped the back of his neck, pulling him deeper into her mouth. She placed her left elbow on his shoulder so that her hand could gently tousle his hair as they smooched. Nick loved when she did that. A major turn on. He shifted himself, his hand now cupping her hip.

He was unsure how long they continued. As always, time stood still in Brandi's presence. When she unexpectedly pulled away, Nick wailed "Hey!"

She retrieved a second blanket from the backpack and draped it over them like a tarp. It was a warm night. Nick realized it would make things more intimate. Seconds later, the two seventeen-year-olds picked up where they left off. More passion, more thirst.

Like all boys his age in Avalon Hills, Nick went through middle school with a crush on Brandi and senior year of high school wanting her. Now they were adults. High school graduates. This was no longer a childish infatuation. Tonight would be the night. *Their night.*

It'd better be tonight. Nick was going insane.

When she abruptly stopped again, Nick frowned. "What?"

Brandi replied with only a smile.

The moonbeam shone from behind. Nick did a double take as the moonlight created a halo-like effect behind her head. His male insecurity kicked in. "Did I do something wrong?"

Brandi tenderly tapped his face as she spoke, one gentle poke for each word. "You. Don't. Have. To. Go."

Nick swallowed hard. Repositioning himself slightly and

readjusting his suddenly restrictive jeans, he would have agreed to anything at this point: Sabotaging the Space Shuttle the previous year, blowing up the Marines barracks in Beirut four years ago. He didn't care. He needed Brandi. He craved her. He'd do anything to, at long last, be with her. But he could never lie to her. "I can't stay."

"Sure, you can."

He drew his eyes away, staring off toward the valley. "No, I really can't." He paused, added, "I've got nothing here."

"Thanks a lot," she said, playfully smacking his chest and realizing it was true: Girls did mature quicker.

"I d—don't mean it like t—that," he stammered and stalled by swigging his beer.

"This place isn't *that* bad." Her tone lacked enthusiasm.

Nick opened his mouth, started to speak, stopped. His eyes broke contact and he spoke to the pollution that veiled Avalon Hills. "I've got a scholarship, Brand. Am I supposed to throw that all away? It's my ticket outta this dump."

"San Diego State?" she bellowed. "Could you have possibly gone any farther?"

"It's a good school, a great opportunity."

Brandi's smile faded for an instant. Hopelessness crept into her voice. "Baseball, Nicky? It's almost impossible to make the majors."

"It's my dream," he stated philosophically. "My purpose."

"It's such a long shot."

Nick blew out through his lips. "Thanks for your optimism. Some encouragement would be nice."

"I *am* optimistic. If anyone can make it, I know you can. You're great. You've got the talent. But—" Her words trailed off.

"But what?"

She moved her head in a yes-no fashion. "But there are plenty of talented kids out there." She waved her arm like Vanna White. "Why not…I don't know…stay around here? I mean, this way, if things don't work out—even though I'm sure they will—but if things don't work out, you'll at least be home."

Home? This place? He cupped her face, her head falling into the warm touch. "Baby, this is football country 'round here. Baseball is like, I don't know, soccer. And what's wrong with going after my dream?"

"California is so…far."

Brandi recognized her appearance made her popular with boys and hated by their girlfriends. Her provocativeness garnered backstage passes when *Van Halen* and *Bon Jovi* played down in Pittsburgh. Her World History professor let it be known he'd be willing to give her an *A* if it was mutually beneficial. One of her father's co-workers, some old married geezer who was pushing forty, offered a weekend getaway to the Catskills. But when Brandi looked in the mirror, she didn't see it.

She was sexier than some, less sexy than others. Her eyebrows were too thick, too dark. She saw breasts that were a bit too small and hips a bit too wide. Numerous times, be it high on cocaine or drunk on Jack Daniels, Gino had advised she was *fat*.

But California?

Brandi saw those videos on MTV. She knew what girls out there were like—lean, tall, blonde, blue-eyed model types with implants. *Bitches.* And now her Nicky would be among them. She finally responded. "There's nothing wrong with going after your dream. But you have to be realistic."

"Mike and Wolfsie are going after theirs. You think their girlfriends are giving them a guilt trip?"

She cupped his knee. "I'm not trying to make you feel guilty. I just want you to realize what you're up against." She paused for effect, then flashed her most seductive smile. "And think of what you're giving up."

Nick's anger subsided as he lost himself in those brown eyes. Brandi truly was faultless, impeccable. They had trekked half a mile into the woods and her pristine boots remained white as snow. Who else could manage that?

She was an angel in the hell known as Avalon Hills. There was no doubt Brandi was blessed with good looks. Nick adored the way her dark features contrasted with her olive complexion. But below the stunning perfection was a girl, a simple girl, insecure in her own skin. And he found that more addicting than her physical appearance. As radiant as she was on the outside, she was faultless on the inside.

He considered her statement. His future and his dreams awaited him on the opposite end of the continent. California might as well be Pluto. He'd be alone, far removed from everything he knew. He heard himself say, "Come with me."

"Huh?"

Nick took her hands in his. "Yeah, come with me. You said you wanted to take a year off before starting college anyway. Come. Maybe you'll like it out there. And we'll be together."

Brandi furrowed her brow, an unsure expression crossing her face.

Nick was excited. "We can ride off into the sunset together."

Brandi snickered. "Oh really?"

"Sure, why not?"

Brandi cocked her head. "You watch too many movies."

Nick was so enthusiastic about his idea he didn't hear the sound.

"What was that?" Brandi asked, looking nervously through the brush.

Nick followed her gaze. "What was what?"

A brief silence. Then Nick heard it, too. The tranquil waters were being disturbed.

"That," she murmured. Brandi sprang to her feet and moved stealthily away.

Nick took a gander at her butt in those jeans before following.

Cat-like quiet, the pair proceeded out of the clearing and entered the foreboding forest. The desiccated ground and deadened branches cracked under their feet. The sound seemed to rattle the hills. Brandi led the way, stooping under low hanging branches that reached out like skeletal arms. After twenty or so yards, she stopped, stuck out her hand.

Nick sashayed alongside, draped his arm over her shoulder. "What—"

"Shhh." Gingerly easing aside some limbs, she squinted. The sound came louder. Closer. "There." She pointed.

Nick angled closer, resting his chin on her shoulder, and

examined the reedy banks of the Acheron River. The valley was dimmed by the night. If it wasn't for the shimmering reflection in the moonlight, one would be hard pressed to differentiate between land and water.

They watched a figure stagger forth from the shadows. He collapsed to his knees in the shallow water. Splashing. *The sound they heard.* The man was well-dressed in a suit but his shirt was partially torn, his tie hanging crookedly. Nick and Brandi could detect labored breathing.

Brandi flashed a curious glance at Nick, mouthed, "Drunk?"

Nick cocked his head, studied the scene. He wondered if it was Haggerty, the town bum, who supposedly got messed up in Viet Nam. But Nick never recalled seeing the vet in a suit.

"We should help," Brandi claimed. "He seems hurt."

She began to move but felt Nick grasp her shoulder and hold her in place.

A second figure appeared from obscurity. This man seemed taller, leaner. The moon's glow failed to illuminate the silhouetted shape. His clothes were dark black. The only thing that stood out in his appearance was his footwear. His boots were olive-colored snakeskin with thick heels, heels that sank a few inches into the marshlands. He walked with purpose, a confident gait, approaching his injured prey.

The terrified man placed his hands together as if in prayer. "No, please." His voice was tinged with dread and weakness.

Nick and Brandi watched as the booted individual wrenched the man to his feet. He pulled him closer, their noses almost touching. He appeared to speak in a threatening manner.

Like a caged animal, the injured man threw his arms about in all directions. His spasmodic motions enabled him to break free. He turned, staggered, and again fell to his knees in the river. Water splashed everywhere.

The man with the peculiar boots advanced on his victim. He contorted his body in a strange way, almost as if trying to avoid ruining his odd footwear. He towered over the man for a moment, jeering him.

Two quick flashes of light. *Gunfire.*

The man collapsed face down in the Acheron.

Brandi instinctively screamed before Nick could cup her mouth and silence her. The killer scrutinized the hillside, scanning where he thought he detected a sound.

Nick moved his mouth to Brandi's ear. "Be quiet and don't move," he breathed.

They peered down at the riverbank and watched the movement of the killer.

❦❦❦

Half a block from home, Nick killed the lights on his eleven-year-old Chevy Nova. He eased onto the driveway, pleased the house was dark and his parents were asleep. As Bruce Springsteen's latest single, "Brilliant Disguise" emanated through the tape deck, Nick replayed the events of the night. After the song finished, he started to exit the car. Then, remembering his mom would be going to church tomorrow and not wanting to block her in the garage, he reversed and parked curbside.

Upon entering the noiseless home, Nick was relieved everyone was asleep. He was an adult. He'd be in college in a couple months. He didn't see why he had to be home by a certain time. But, as his father repeatedly admonished him, "My house, my rules."

Nick was a few feet inside when he heard a familiar jangling. "Hey, Scrappy," he whispered happily and took a knee.

The West Highland Terrier scampered cheerily down the hallway to welcome him home. Scrappy placed his front paws on Nick's knee and slobbered his face. Nick feverishly scratched behind the dog's ear, effectively turning Scrappy's tail into a propeller. Nick made his way to the kitchen, the Westie at his heels. A pair of excited little yips caused Nick to turn and glance nervously toward upstairs. No lights. *Whew.*

Opening a pantry, he removed a Milk Bone. Scrappy then performed the one and only trick he knew, something taught to him by Nick's father. As Nick held the treat in a closed palm, the animated canine rose onto his hind legs and spun in a clockwise circle exactly three times, front paws dangling.

He rewarded the Westie. "Good boy."

Nick went upstairs and skulked to his room. His parents' bedroom door was open. He noticed strange flashes dancing on the wall, indicating they'd fallen asleep with the TV playing. Going past his younger brother's closed bedroom, Nick overheard the familiar voice of an MTV Vee-Jay.

Closing himself in his room, he stripped down to his boxers and slipped into a faded and tattered black shirt with gold lettering that proclaimed, *We Are Fam-a-lee.* The shirt commemorated the Pirates World Championship eight long years ago.

Once in bed, Nick stared at the ceiling. His mind was clicking on all cylinders and sleep did not come.

The bizarre scene that had played out on the banks of the Acheron River could not be shaken. He tried to convince himself that maybe it wasn't a murder after all. He must've been mistaken. Avalon Hills was a lot of things but crime, especially homicide, was not commonplace.

Then again, if it was, in fact, a murder, it only solidified his desire to get out of this town.

He and Brandi had remained stone-like in their secreted location for a good ten minutes. As the booted killer—if he really was a killer—focused his attention on hauling the man away, Nick and Brandi fled. During the drive home, conversation was sparse. They were too wrapped up in their own thoughts.

Something about what they witnessed seemed…familiar. He couldn't quite place it. He decided to go to the police tomorrow morning and file a report on…whatever it was.

He'd hoped his girl would accompany him to corroborate his story. But Brandi was not warm to the idea. Her refusal to back him up was perplexing.

Mike was going to New York with his band. Wolfsie was going to Penn State to become a lawyer. Nick wondered if their girlfriends were giving them as much grief for following their dreams.

Brandi.

What was with her anyway? They'd been together more than a year. They made out a lot but, even though she had slept with guys prior to Nick, she had not slept with him. *Why?*

Then, finally tonight she seemed ready. It irritated him. She was using her body to convince him to stay.

He liked her—a lot. She turned him on plenty. But he wondered what caused him to blurt out *come with me.* Like going to the police tomorrow, she was not receptive to that idea either.

Part of him hoped she'd up and leave town with him. The two of them would discover San Diego together. At least he wouldn't be alone. On the other hand, the way she'd been acting, perhaps it was best they went their separate ways.

Nick would be in Cali-friggin'-fornia. Sun, sand, and surfing. Beaches, blondes, and boobs.

As his eyes grew weighty, Nick accepted that Brandi was his past, a high school crush. His future was in southern California. He'd leave behind this town, he'd leave behind his family. And he'd leave behind Brandi.

There *would* be other girls.

There would definitely be others.

Nick was seventeen.

Chapter 2

Present Day:

Suffocating.
Choking.
Unable to breathe.

Nick sprang upright in bed, coughing, gasping for air. His head pounded. His brain pulsated within his skull. His shirt collar wrung with perspiration.

"Bad dream?"

The voice came from the foot of the bed. Blinking away the cobwebs of sleep, he watched in silence as Gwen slipped into her sheer black skirt.

She looked into the mirror, giving Nick a cursory glance behind her before admiring her own appearance. In her stocking feet, the shapely woman with indigo eyes, blonde hair, and killer legs, stepped left and slid her feet into a pair of new black pumps.

Not fully cognizant, Nick blinked several times. "Huh?" His eyes fell upon her unbuttoned blue blouse that brought out her eyes.

Gwen buttoned her shirt. *Faster than usual,* Nick thought.

"I asked if you had that dream again." She turned around looking for her earrings, not waiting for an answer.

To her back, he replied in a scratchy morning voice, "No. No, I don't think so. I don't remember." He always found it intriguing how dreams could be so vivid, so powerful. And then so quickly forgotten and shoved aside. He craned his neck, winced. "This headache's killing me."

Gwen checked herself in the mirror one final time. Turning right, then left, she seemed pleased with the way her heels accentuated her ass. Ignoring—or perhaps unconcerned with Nick's headache remark—she stepped to his side of the bed. "I'm off to work."

Nick straightened, puckered his lips. Gwen offered a cheek. "Tootles," she said and walked out.

By the time Nick wished her a good day, she was already gone.

He sat a beat, massaging his neck, and eyed the nightstand clock. *Shit.* Had he forgotten to set the alarm? Why didn't Gwen wake him?

Swinging his legs out of the bed, hand still clasping his neck, he shot a contemptuous snarl at the pillow. He struggled to his feet and stretched his stiff muscles. The room spun. When his equilibrium returned, he headed off to shower.

Sauntering across the room, he sensed Gwen's perfume lingering. She always wore too much he thought. He wasn't too fond of the scent but she liked it. And in the relationship they had, Gwen's happiness was all that mattered.

Between the bed and the dresser, Nick caught sight of something in the mirror. He turned, looked directly into it. And saw what resembled his father staring back at him.

Nick leaned closer. His eyes were not as sharp as they'd once been. His skin less taut. Crow's feet began making inroads to his face. He slid his hand through his bed hair and thought about renewing his driver's license. Would he still get away with listing his hair color as brown? The few strands of gray that had slowly crept in were spreading like locusts across farmland. Nick curled his lips. His *father* in the reflection did the same. Kneading his lower back, Nick sighed and lumbered to the bathroom.

The vanity was littered with oils, lotions, bath powders, perfumes, nail polish, moisturizers, and the rest of what Nick referred to as "woman stuff." Gwen never appreciated that remark.

In the midst of her beauty supplies, he noticed a note. A small Post-it with *Try this* followed by *xoxo* was attached to a box of Grecian Formula.

⌘

Nick turned right and drove onto the grounds of Scottsdale Memorial Gardens. He slowly eased by the well-manicured lawns, headstones, and mausoleums and found his usual parking spot. Wearing tattered sneakers, tan trousers, and a light brown workman's shirt, he stepped into the blistering Arizona heat and entered the office. "Is Peter around," he asked the receptionist.

Before she could answer, Peter Smoak thundered down the hallway. With a disapproving glare, he pointed to his wristwatch. No words were needed.

Dressed in a neat black suit, white shirt, and perfectly knotted tie, the funeral director looked the polar opposite of his clientele. Whereas his customers were ashen and pale, Smoak looked like he just stepped out of a tanning booth.

"Sorry I'm late. My alarm didn't go off."

Smoak stepped closer, violating Nick's personal space. He flashed his professional smile at some grieving family members sitting on a sofa and then herded Nick to a remote section of the lobby. Tranquil piano music filtered gently across the foyer, the impact of losing a loved one apparently lessened by Yanni.

Hands folded before him, Smoak began. "Aren't you leaving early today?"

Nick nodded.

"Come in late, leave early? Interesting."

Nick contemplated cancelling the appointment but he needed to find out what was wrong. "I'm not able to reschedule, Mr. Smoak. I can make up the hours next—"

"You're already negative eleven hours," Smoak retorted. "And that doesn't include—" This time he looked at his watch and didn't tap it. "—these seventy five minutes."

Peter Smoak was a hard-ass, one who believed your job is your life—an interesting dichotomy for a funeral director.

Nick had no defense. He had been missing a lot of work recently due to the headaches. He was about to offer another apology when Smoak waggled his head. Judgmentally, he waved his hand in the air, muttered something, and walked away. Nick was left alone in the far corner of the lobby, just himself and a bronzed metal casket on markdown.

Moments later, Nick made his way to the rear of the building. He clocked in and removed his supplies from the storage room. Stepping into the scorching relentless heat he ambled beyond the Pool of Reflection and traipsed to the markers in the Garden of Tranquility.

Observing a gathering of mourners across the lawn huddled under a green tent and a priest standing alongside a coffin, Nick dropped to his knees and started polishing his first headstone of the morning.

Just another day at the office for Nick Garrison.

୧୨୧୨

It was now Nick and not Peter who was looking at his wristwatch. More time passed him by.

He gazed around the waiting room, sizing up the other patients. To his gratification, most seemed older. He contemplated what they were all here for, what was ailing them. One elderly man sat hunched over, eyes half mast, an oxygen tank at his side. His wife wore a pained expression while mechanically patting his back. Nick looked away.

He glanced at the wall-mounted TV. The sound was barely audible. A handsome clean-shaven man with a white coat and a stethoscope draped around his neck was babbling on about reducing cholesterol. His image was replaced by a generous portion of scrambled eggs, then a juicy bacon cheeseburger sitting on a greasy paper towel. Nick's mouth watered and he realizing he hadn't eaten all day.

He again looked at his watch and purposely emitted a loud sigh. When the receptionist behind the glass window failed to acknowledge his restlessness, Nick moaned again and perused the magazines: *Men's Health, Women's Health, Family Health, Senior Health, Health and Fitness,* and *Time.* He opted for the only non-medical periodical. The cover photo presented an unhealthy looking heart under the headline, *Non Evasive Bypass: The Future is Now.* Nick flung the magazine back onto the table.

And continued waiting.

He'd read that, in the course of one's life, the average person spent more than six years simply waiting: Waiting on hold, waiting in traffic, waiting in a doctor's office. Waiting. Nick was in his late forties and, based on average life span, he loosely estimated he'd wasted three and a half years of his life, doing nothing—nothing but waiting.

Three and a half years.

Almost as long as high school.

Upon hearing his name called, he stood. Forcing a smile and a greeting, he followed the nurse who seemed about twelve years old through the maze of hallways before entering an exam room. She took his vitals and made mention that his blood pressure was slightly elevated. *I've been waiting for an hour. What do you expect?* But he kept that thought to himself.

"The doctor will be right in," she announced before departing.

Alone in the chilly environs, Nick again found himself waiting.

The oldies station that wafted into the room was a pleasant departure. After being subjected to images of diseased hearts and cholesterol clogged arteries, Nick found his toe tapping to "My Sharona" by The Knack. The respite was only temporary. The disc jockey with the annoying voice spoke. "Going way, way back to 1972 for this classic from a one-hit wonder. By special request, here's Looking Glass performing 'Brandy, You're a Fine Girl.'"

Nick grinned as rueful memories flowed over him. In the car or the few times over the last several decades when he'd heard the song, he'd change the station. The recollections of Brandi were too painful. Despite the passage of time, the endless sleepless nights of playing what-if, he wondered if fleeing Avalon Hills and leaving the only girl he ever loved was the right decision. He looked around the exam room but could find no dial to switch stations.

Nick was brought back from decisions of the past when Dr. Rajagopal knocked once and entered. Nick liked the guy. He was always upbeat, smiling, and had a pleasing bedside manner. Nick had been his patient for years. Once, the doctor alluded to his son playing shortstop on his high school team. Nick advised him of his own short-lived career as a left fielder, a career that ended sophomore year at San Diego State. In passing, they'd discussed Nick mentoring the young boy. But nothing ever came from it.

The broad smile always exhibited on his face was nowhere to be found. The normally positive physician appeared sullen, troubled, and at a loss for words.

ↄ◌ↄ

As usual, dinner conversation that evening focused on Gwen. Nick was updated on some probate case one of the other partners was embroiled in. He heard Gwen's supposition that Christine was sleeping with one of the senior partners, a married man thirty years her senior. Nick listened half-heartedly as he was regaled with an excessively descriptive detail of the conference room being refurnished. The only time Gwen stopped talking was to read or respond to a text.

He normally had no qualms about listening to her day at work. After all, working as a partner in a law firm offered better dinner conversation than being a headstone polisher at a cemetery. Or *marble engineer* as Nick jokingly called himself.

Finally, Gwen brought the conversation to Nick, but in a roundabout way. She studied him a moment, then asked, "Did you try that Grecian I bought you?"

Nick shook his head and aimlessly twirled the pasta with his fork.

Gwen sounded wounded. "I left it right there on the counter where you'd see it. I even attached a note. Why didn't you?"

"I was running late." He paused, and then in an attempt to douse her simmering anger, added, "I thought gray makes men look more distinguished."

Gwen arched a skeptical brow and then responded to a text.

They were the same age but Gwen looked at least ten years younger. Apparently all that woman stuff was beneficial. Nick, on the other hand, looked beyond fifty. He felt part of it was due to their opposite career paths. She worked inside an air-conditioned office, whereas he worked outside in the searing Arizona heat.

Nick calculated Gwen. She was a physically captivating

woman. She was smart and successful. They'd been together five years. At the time, it was nothing more than a financial arrangement. Nick had been sharing a place with a roommate who took a job out of town. Unable to afford his own place on his pathetic paycheck, he needed someone to split expenses. Gwen was working as a waitress full-time at a sports bar Nick frequented. She'd just come out of a messy divorce and was fulfilling her dream of becoming an attorney. As she put herself through law school, she, too, needed a place to stay. Nick moved in with her, the roommate status became physical. However, when Gwen graduated and began earning close to six figures, Nick became expendable. She was stunning, successful, and self-reliant. She had no need to lower herself to being with a loser who tidied up tombstones.

Gwen smiled at her phone, a smile Nick hadn't seen in quite some time. "I'm thinking of taking some time off," he announced. "Going home for a while."

She wrinkled her brow as if he'd started speaking in tongues. "Hmm?" she said. Then, "Wait," and she read her text, smiled again.

"Who is that you're texting?"

"This? Oh, it's just…Vanessa…ya' know, from the firm."

"Uh huh," Nick responded doubtfully.

"You're thinking of going away you said?"

"I haven't been home for a while and I—I probably should."

She rolled her eyes. "Back to Babylon Hills?"

"Avalon. Avalon Hills."

"Whatever."

She obviously could care less. Nick pressed on, for some reason feeling a need to explain his decision. "My parents are getting older and…well…maybe meet up with some old buddies. Check out the old neighborhood."

Gwen displayed a formal smile she held in reserve for clients. "I think some time apart would be good for us."

It was now Nick who felt wounded. "Oh?"

She leaned forward, elbows on the table, phone like an appendage. "Nick, we know things have been…how should I say?…dead for a while. We've fallen into the routine of an old married couple. And I don't want to be an old married couple. Hell, I don't even want to be married."

"You've been thinking about this, I see."

"What's to think about?" she replied. She tucked a few strands of blonde hair behind her right ear. Nick used to find that sensual. "We've become roommates again. This relationship—and I use that word loosely—is nothing more than a financial arrangement. Plus, lately it seems like you're not really here."

Nick lowered the fork and leaned back. His immediate feeling was to defend himself, to blame their dying relationship on her. She was a workaholic. She lived, breathed, and shit that damn job. She was also a narcissist. But any counterclaim would be weak. He realized she was correct. "Not here?"

"Right. You're somewhere else. I don't know if you're thinking of being somewhere else or being *with* someone else. Look—we've had this conversation more times than I can count. I'm tired of trying to break down these walls that you put up."

Nick bowed his head, unable to shield himself against the verbal bullets he knew were true. He opened his mouth to speak but once again Gwen stuck up a finger and looked at her phone. This time, she laughed. After typing a response, she looked into Nick's eyes, the smile gone. "When are you planning on going?"

"Soon." *Tonight if I could.*

"Okay." She stood and disappeared into another part of their home. Nick remained behind with the leftovers.

Chapter 3

Brooke Lauser didn't flinch in response to what sounded like a gunshot. She peered at the stairs, perked her ears, but was greeted only by deathlike stillness. Reaching for the remote, she moaned and regrettably muted the rerun. One Kardashian was debating getting implants, another was irate because the majordomo of the exclusive Beverly Hills restaurant didn't have her table ready, and a third was disappointed she'd have to push back her weekend in Vail.

Brooke cried out, "Mike!"

Silence.

Louder now. "Mike, you all right?"

Answered by discomforting silence, Brooke stood, crossed the room, and ambled up to their bedroom. She again called her husband's name as she closed in. When reaching the doorway, she froze, her mind not registering what her eyes viewed.

"Oh, God," she hollered through her cupped mouth and flew across the room.

They'd been having financial problems for some time. First his hours had been cut. Then his position had been cut. They'd been bombarded with collection calls. Mike's car had been repo'd two weeks ago. Brooke had to swallow her pride and ask her parents for money to keep the lights on. She knew Mike had been depressed. *But this?*

His body lay twisted in an unusual angle. Feet on the floor, torso crooked. His eyes stared blankly into a void of nothingness. Blood and brain matter oozed from where his temple had been. The revolver was clutched loosely in his hand.

"Mike! What have you *done*?"

White foam trickled from between his lips. Knowing it was

pointless, she lifted his hand anyway. No pulse. She placed her ear to his chest. No heartbeat. She looked at the unresponsive expression on his face. No reaction.

Brooke dove across the bed and picked up the receiver to call the police. She pressed nine, one—and then stopped. Looking at the nightstand clock, she raced out of the room where she nearly trampled over their daughter.

"Mommy, what happened?"

Brooke stiffened when seeing four-year-old Janis in her gi-raffe-covered jammies. She scooped up the little girl. She didn't want their daughter to see what Daddy had done.

"What's wrong, Mommy?" Janis asked. Picking up on her mom's frantic actions, the young girl began sobbing.

"Nothing, baby," Brooke replied weakly. "We're going for a ride."

"What about Sammy?"

Brooke had forgotten about their eight year old. "Where is he?"

"Sleeping."

Raising her arm, checking her watch beyond her daughter's little shoulder, Brooke responded. "Let 'em sleep. We don't have time."

Janis's tears stopped. Going for a car ride without her older brother could cheer up anyone.

∽∾∾

The older vehicle, long overdue for maintenance, barreled around the corner. The screeching tires were loud enough to wake the sleepy town of Avalon Hills. Brooke nearly overcor-rected when the Ford fishtailed. She glanced at her daughter in her car seat. Janis was enjoying the speedy ride. Brooke shot a nervous glance at the dashboard clock, snarled.

Jamming on the brakes, she skidded to a halt. The car was half on the street and half on the driveway of the Garrison home. "Wait here!" She bolted from the car.

Brooke stumbled, falling to one knee as she scurried across the recently watered lawn. Righting herself, she sprinted to the front door and began pounding. "Open up! Please."

It was only a few seconds but to Brooke Lauser it was an eternity.

The door opened slowly.

Despite being in his mid-seventies, Lloyd Garrison maintained a fit, healthy appearance. Standing at six three with broad shoulders, he was built like a linebacker. Brooke had once heard that he played college football. His build made it plausible.

He removed his half-framed black reading glasses and beheld his visitor. "Brooke?"

Uninvited, she grabbed Lloyd's arm and stepped into the home. "You have to help me. Please."

"Where are your children?" His authoritative tone went well with his full head of white hair and commanding cobalt eyes.

"Janis is in the car, Sammy's home. Lloyd, please—"

Undeterred, Lloyd peered out at his driveway. "You really shouldn't leave your daughter in the car. It's hot this evening."

Brooke frantically tugged on his arm. "It's Mike."

"What's all this ruckus?" Eve, Lloyd's wife, materialized at his side. "Brooke, good evening."

Lloyd scowled disapprovingly and began sidestepping Brooke. "I'm going to get Janis out of that car."

She tightened her grip on his arm, preventing him from moving, and shifted her glance between Lloyd and Eve. "You have to help me."

Concerned, Eve stepped closer. "What's wrong, honey? Did something happen to your husband?"

Brooke recognized her voice but couldn't accept her words. "Mike killed himself."

Lloyd said nothing.

Eve stepped closer and placed a comforting hand on Brooke's trembling shoulder. "By accident?"

What a stupid question. "No, not by accident," Brooke scoffed. "In the head." She pointed to her left temple as if the Garrisons didn't know where the head was.

"Oh my word," Eve bellowed.

Lloyd asked condescendingly, "You keep a firearm in a home with small children?"

"They're locked up. Please, help."

"Did you call an ambulance?"

"No. I—"

"Don't you think you should have?" His tone was patronizing.

Brooke had no answer.

Lloyd looked at his wife, rolled his eyes, and tilted his head at their houseguest. Sighing, he announced he would make the call.

He started walking away but was again held in place by the grip of a panicky woman. "I came to you instead." She checked the time on her watch. "I beg you, Mr. Garrison."

Lloyd contemptuously looked at the way she clutched his arm. He nodded once and displayed a brief but reassuring smile. "Come with me," he said, the authoritative tone now fatherly.

As Lloyd steered Brooke out of the anteroom, Eve announced, "I'll get the little girl out of the car."

"Just keep her outside," instructed Lloyd. "I don't want her in here."

Moments later, Brooke sat on the opposite end of an old-but-still-comfortable sofa with a flowered pattern. She leaned forward, moved her head in a way that said *Let's get moving.*

"Why do you think Mike would do something so drastic?"

Brooke couldn't concentrate. The only thing in her mind was the haunting image of her husband lying cockeyed and lifeless on their bed, brain matter strewn across their linens. "What?"

Again. "Tell me why *you* think Mike would shoot himself." Seeing the distraught woman struggling with the enormity of the situation, he demanded, "Focus!"

She took a few seconds, calming herself as best she could. In the distance, she heard a car door close and the exuberance of her daughter, *their* daughter. "He's been—depressed lately."

"So I've heard. And why do you think that is?"

"He lost his job. The bastards—sorry—took his car. My parents had to loan us money, though I'm not sure when we can even pay them back. Money's tight. We're struggling."

Lloyd pulled on his rugged chin and pointed to the window.

"Everyone's struggling nowadays. But not everyone puts a bullet in their head."

Brooke shrugged. She had no time for Lloyd's psychobabble bullshit and carnival logic. "I'm asking for your help."

"What is it you want me to do?"

"You can help, sir." *Sir.* Perhaps showing respect would motivate Lloyd to get his ass moving.

Lloyd angled back and slapped his knees. "My dear Brooke, I appreciate your kind words and your reverence. But I'm the mayor, the mayor of a small town. Population thirty-one hundred and seventeen. And we both know the position is just a title, a designation if you will."

She started waving it away but was interrupted.

"Let me ask this. What happened with Mike's desire to become a musician?" His baritone voice was irritating.

Brooke cocked her head like a fly was buzzing around. She mumbled something, looked impatiently at her watch.

Lloyd smiled, not bothering to repeat the question.

"He just…I don't know, gave up on it. It was just a dream of his."

"From what I heard, he sacrificed his dreams fairly quickly."

The clock was ticking, seconds becoming minutes. Time was passing. But she needed Lloyd and would therefore have to play his cat and mouse game. "They went to New York and tried. They played some gigs here and there. But it was the late eighties. There was lots of competition. By the time they started developing a following and making some headway, Grunge came around. The type of music Mike and his band played died out."

"Grunge?"

"Nirvana? Kurt Cobain?"

Lloyd pursed his lips, taking a moment to recall the name. "Oh? Oh, yes, that young man who took his own life. Pity people do that." He paused, refocused on Brooke. "You were in New York with Mike, yes?"

"Yes." She stopped. When it became clear Lloyd wanted more, she continued. "We lived in this—this rattrap." A smile flitted across her face at the memories. Two young kids with their entire lives in front of them and all the time in the world to achieve their dreams. "Seven of us crammed into a small two bedroom down in the Village."

"That's when you became pregnant, yes?"

"Yes." The brief smile faded at the memory of what followed.

"The baby was stillborn, yes?"

Decades had passed but the pain remained. She bowed her head. "Yes."

"It was during your pregnancy when you convinced Mike to get married and quit the band, yes?"

Brooke became defensive as well as growing irritated with his leading questions. "It was a mutual decision. *We* married each other."

"Semantics. So he came back and ended up working in a transmission shop, yes?"

She nodded, eyed her watch.

Lloyd noticed her foot tapping impatiently. "Is it not true that he was arrested twice for DUI and once for disorderly conduct? I've also heard through the grapevine as they say that both you and he strayed during your marriage. As a matter of fact, some in town question if Janis is his daughter."

Kissing Lloyd's ass was distasteful enough. But having her life called into question by this judge, jury and, yes, executioner, was becoming unbearable. "Will you help me or not?"

Lloyd knitted his brow. "And what is it you think I can do?"

"I've also heard things around town," Brooke shot back, surprised at her defiance.

"No matter what you may have heard, my dear, it's not true anymore."

"Bullshit!"

"Please refrain from vulgarity in my home, Mrs. Lauser. You may have no qualms using profanity, but I refuse to allow that language in my Christian home."

Brooke jumped to her feet and indignantly paced. She again heard childlike jubilation out front and decided on a different angle. "We have two children. If not for me, if not for Mike, then at least do it for them."

Lloyd waffled for a moment, weighing his options. He leaned back and stared across the room at nothing, running his hands through his schlock of white hair. He listened for a beat to the young girl's laughter from his lawn. "I'm sorry. I can't."

"You can't? Or you won't?"

Lloyd said nothing.

Brooke stood stone-like, unsure what to do. The walls of the Garrison home closed in around her, smothering her. She couldn't breathe. She couldn't erase the image of Mike's corpse. She couldn't imagine raising two children on her own. "Who gave you the right, you son of a bitch?"

"*Excuse me*?" Lloyd snapped.

"No one gave you the right to be playing God."

"Again, semantics."

Chapter 4

Nick finally exhaled when wheels touched down just after nine p.m. He loathed flying but, now that he was on the ground, he felt relieved at cheating death. He looked at the indentations in his palm, a result of fisted hands across three time zones.

With sensation returning, he retrieved his phone from his pocket. He debated a moment then decided to send a text rather than getting involved in a lengthy phone call.

As he typed away, a heavyset woman leaned over and removed a suitcase she'd stuffed into the overhead. A smaller valise fell and brushed Nick's shoulder.

"Sorry," the woman muttered in a less than sorrowful tone.

Nick flashed a courteous grin. She'd been unaware she stepped on his foot so he assumed the apology was due to the falling luggage. After typing *just landed c u soon,* he turned off the phone and waited for first class to deplane.

Pittsburgh International had made numerous upgrades since Nick's last visit. Not since the bat mitzvah of Wolfsie's daughter Rebecca three years ago had Nick set foot in Pennsylvania. The airport seemed resurrected.

For decades, starting in the late 70s really, the city became the butt of jokes. Pittsburgh was to Pennsylvania what Cleveland was to Ohio. Nevertheless, as Nick walked through the terminal, what he'd heard was true. The steel city was making a comeback. Several Hollywood movies were filmed here. Tourism was up, crime was down, and even his beloved Pirates were again good. For the time being, at least, Nick felt good to be home.

Wheeling his suitcase across the car rental company lot, he shifted his glance between the ticket and the space number then pursed his lips. He momentarily considered taking the Jitney back and asking the girl at the counter for something else—anything else—but decided against it. It was only a rental car so what the hell. A Hyundai something or other, but the off yellow made it resemble a jar of mustard on wheels.

His peaceful sentiment faded each minute he approached Avalon Hills. By the time he found himself on Main Street an hour later—yes, the main thoroughfare in town really was named Main Street—his serenity had morphed into restlessness.

Bouncing over the railroad tracks, he drove across the rusted bridge that traversed the Acheron River. The somnolent town was gloomy, soundless. After all, it was the ungodly time of ten-thirty.

He cruised along at fifteen miles per hour into the *heart* of town, realizing nothing had changed in three years since Rebecca's bat mitzvah or since he graduated Avalon High School. Hell, nothing had changed since the Woodrow Wilson administration.

Main Street was two lanes in each direction. No median, no turning lane. Old-fashioned gaslight lampposts lined the sidewalks. Nick wondered if they'd ever replaced kerosene with electricity.

The brick storefronts lining the main drag were typical small town America: a quilting store, a bank, a gas station, an auto parts dealer, a closed down Friendly's, an office for the local cable company, an ice cream parlor, a funeral home, a place that sold second-hand paperbacks. Above the businesses were mostly vacant units, though some now served as offices for lawyers and accountants.

Nick had always heard people claim "I remember everything being bigger," when returning to their childhood haunts. He never agreed. The only feeling he got was how small and cluttered everything was. The buildings, schools, and homes did not seem smaller, the streets seemed narrower.

Every few blocks a traffic signal hung above the intersection, blinking yellow. Nick noticed a police car facing the street in the lot of a Jamba Juice. "Jamba Juice," Nick said to himself. "Business here is a-boomin'."

Passing the old-fashioned Arby's, the roof still in the shape of a cowboy hat, Nick brought his car to a stop. Main and Fourth, the only juncture in town that housed a working four-way traffic signal.

He could hear the cicadas as he peered around. Set back from the street was a two-story ramshackle motel. The motel's lot was deserted. The marquis boasted *Int rne Acc ss* and *C lor TV*. Sizing up the decrepit Olive Tree Motel, Nick was grateful he chose not to stay there.

While he sat in the empty intersection, waiting an interminable amount of time for a green light, a recollection of childhood made him grin. He'd been a small boy at the time, eight, maybe nine. His father, Mayor Garrison, had proposed changing the name from Main Street to Avalon Boulevard. *Boulevard* conveyed bustling business. And since his father was trying to lure a K-Mart into the structure where a furniture store had filed bankruptcy, *boulevard* was more enticing than *Main Street*. Ultimately, the townspeople chose to stay with their small town motif.

Moments later, Nick couldn't help but snicker when he read the road sign: *You are now entering the Avalon Hills Cultural District*. The four corners were comprised of two churches, the local public library, and the Avalon Hills Dance Troupe.

It took just seconds until Nick was through the so-called cultural center and found himself in the *seedy* part of town. *Kitty's Kustom Designs* sold what many referred to as questionable nightwear, appealing to the sinful women who cowered in the darkened corners of the town. There was also Texas Jack's where residents could imbibe in the devil's drink. And the corner drug store. Nick and his pals had spent many evenings huddled in the far corner, excitedly paging through *Hustler*.

A mile farther, Nick stopped in the center of an intersection. He looked left down a shady lane. He recalled that west of Main the streets all bore the names of flowers: Tulip, Rose, Daisy. Chrysanthemum was too many letters for the financially strapped town. To his right—east—the streets were named after trees: Maple, Fig, Oak. The generic names were a far cry from the vivid images conveyed back home in Mesa, Arizona—Crystal Waters, Babbling Brook, Shimmering Fountain.

There was no traffic at this late hour so Nick sat motionless in the crossing. He gazed deeply down the leafy side street. His stomach tightened. He glanced at his watch. He still had time. By instinct, he looked for traffic in his blind spot and mumbled, “Why not?” Turning right, he proceeded deeper into the night.

The rented Hyundai crept along the lane, barely inching forward. The only sound was the click-click-click of a pebble that became ensnared in the tread of the right front tire. His head throbbed, but it was a different throbbing than he’d experienced back home.

Nick switched off the headlights and turned left.

Hickory Circle was an insignificant cul-de-sac. There were only five homes situated on the street. They were older tri-level weather-beaten clapboards that sat on large three acre lots.

No houselights were on. The street was dark, tomb-like quiet. A porch light from one dwelling provided no illumination. Older cars sat in driveways. Not jalopies, but pretty close. Unlike Arizona, residents of northwest Pennsylvania were more concerned about practicality than impressing their neighbors.

A short *bzzt* sound was heard as a mosquito was zapped to death.

A transformer tower stood behind the anchor house of the street. The power lines which wafted gently in the breeze resembled a pseudo-security system, a warning to keep trespassers out of an unseen land.

Nick stopped in the center of the cul-de-sac. He powered down the window, rested his chin in the crook of his arm, and stared nostalgically at the second of five homes.

His throat tightened, his breathing pinched, and his stomach knotted as he studied Brandi’s old residence.

Memories.

More than a quarter of a century had passed. The house was slightly more worn, but mostly untouched by time. The cement bird fountain was still positioned in the center of the lawn. A white pick-up sat in the driveway, a frayed Steelers pennant filling the rear window.

Nick slowly exhaled through his surprisingly parched lips. He studied each window. Although the white curtains were drawn, he could still *see* the room in his mind. Looking into a memory, he could feel it, could sense it. He recalled the way the furniture was set up. Even the way the house smelled. He always found it a bit musty, almost damp. At the time, he didn't like the aroma. Now, he longed for it. He could almost taste it, sense it in his nostrils.

Nick continued examining the place, his eyes moving slowly from the location of the living room on the main floor to the bedrooms on the second floor. When his gaze reached the far window at the end of the upper floor—Brandi's old bedroom—he felt his body shudder in a nervous euphoric feeling.

So many great times. Laughing and joking and making out. He was young, with his entire life ahead of him—his life limited only by the restrictions he'd placed in his own mind. He had so much he wanted to do. And all the time in the world to do it.

Shortly after Nick had ventured to the opposite end of the country, Brandi's step-father suffered a massive heart attack. Two years later, her mom followed, having drunk herself into an early grave. He'd heard that Brandi kept the house, but he wasn't sure.

The last time he saw her was when he had flown home after his sister-in-law gave birth and he met Brandi for breakfast one morning. Twenty years. But he still recalled exactly what she wore, what they chatted about, and the music playing in the IHOP.

He hadn't talked to or seen her since.

The world around Nick now closed in. Tunnel-vision. Like a laser, he fixated on the bedroom. He almost expected to see a younger version of himself peering out. He recalled the view looking out of that room. Of Brandi's room.

He reflected, thought back, wondered *What if.*

☙❧

Nick was unaware how long he was parked motionless in the road. As always, time stood still when it came to Brandi. He finally vacated Hickory Circle and switched his lights on.

He saw a slow moving vehicle coming in his direction. The motorists were temporarily blinded by each other's bright glare. As the vehicles passed one another, Nick instinctively glanced over.

He noticed the raven black hair.

He observed the deep-set chestnut eyes.

It was an instant, a flash. But long enough to identify the driver.

"Brandi?"

His foot found the brake, his eyes darted to the rear view. Several car lengths behind him, brake lights came on. She had stopped also.

Nick paused. What could he do? What could he say? He'd just arrived back in town not even twenty minutes ago and his first stop was to the home where his old girlfriend once lived. Borderline stalking, anyone?

Nick cruised forward, reached the crossroads, and drove away.

Chapter 5

Before Nick killed the engine, his mom bounded through the front door, arms waving frantically as if he'd just pulled up in a *Publisher's Clearing House* van.

Eve wore fuchsia pants, a green embroidered top, and, for some reason, a bright pink sweater in summer.

"Let me have a look at you," she cried, bear hugging her son. Her smile widened as she stepped back. "You look great, Nick. A little thin. Have you lost weight?"

"Maybe a couple pounds."

"It's wonderful seeing you," she said and again embraced her son. "I've missed you."

"I have, too."

Nick fiddled for the appropriate buttons on the unfamiliar key fob, opened the trunk, lifted his suitcase, and figured out how to lock the vehicle.

Eve Garrison had been a homemaker her entire life. But she fired questions as if she was an ardent member of the White House Press Corps. How was his flight? Had he eaten on the plane? What was new with Gwen?

Taking the three cement steps, his mom at his heels, Nick entered the home where he'd grown up. His nostrils twitched as a pleasing aroma of something cooking drifted from the kitchen. The rust-colored shag had been replaced with tiled floors. But other than that, the Garrison home was exactly as Nick remembered. "Looks the same, Mom."

Nick's father emerged from around the corner, extending his arm in a ceremonial manner. "Hello, son."

Nick pumped his father's hand, remembering to make eye contact just as he'd been taught by the patriarch of the family. "Hello, sir."

Lloyd eyed the luggage. "I'll take this up to your room."

"I can—"

But his father had already begun his trek out of sight.

Being ushered into the living room indicated his homecoming was indeed a special occasion. The formal living room was primarily used for entertaining guests. The furnishings as well as the slightly stale odor that hung in the air created a museum-like ambiance.

The sofa was surprisingly soft, considering its age. He sat in the center, his mom at his right. When his father returned from bellhop duty, Lloyd elected to sit in a chair across the room rather than sitting beside his son.

Idle banter started. Nick told his parents about the flight, the weather back home, and his job, though nothing ever changed in the world of marble engineering. When Eve asked about Gwen, Nick glossed over it. He'd returned home for another reason, not to piss and moan about yet another failed relationship.

Within moments, his father became disinterested. An out-breath, a shift in his body language, and a reach for the remote.

"Lloyd!"

He depressed the volume arrow. "It's low."

Nick eyed the Plasma TV. ESPN was broadcasting tennis highlights.

For the next fifteen minutes, his mom controlled the conversation. She updated her first born on the town gossip, her volunteering at the library. A distant cousin, one Nick hadn't seen since he was a boy, had gotten divorced. Aunt Trudy down in Florida was having problems with her hip again. Nick became uncomfortable when hearing about how wonderful things were going with his brother and his family.

"Things always go well for Gabe," Nick heard himself spit.

He thought his father grumbled judgmentally but perhaps not. "We'll have Gabe and Yolanda over in the next night or two. They'd love to see you."

Sarcastically, Nick said, "Can't wait."

Eve decided not to tell her son about Mike Lauser's suicide. Tonight was for catching up. Nick could wait to learn about his childhood friend taking his own life. She patted his knee and sprang from the sofa like a woman half her age. "Lloyd," she said, "why don't you tell Nick about what happened last week by the river. I've got something on the stove."

"My lord, woman," Lloyd snarled. "The boy's going to be here several days. We don't need to update him on *everything* tonight." Not pulling his gaze from the set, he asked, "Just several days, yes?"

"Yes, sir." Nick feigned a smile at his father who never took his attention away from *SportsCenter*.

With his mom busying herself in the kitchen, Nick and his father stared blankly at the idiot box, not uttering a sound or exchanging a glance. The silence was a deafening thunder.

"Thanks for taking the suitcases to my room." *My room.* Nick sounded like he was in high school again.

Lloyd said nothing.

Either his father had become the world's number one tennis aficionado or simply had no interest in conversing with his child. Desperate to break the stillness, Nick matter-of-factly inquired, "How's your health been?"

This time Lloyd did respond, but not right away. He waited a few seconds before declaring, "I woke up early this morning. Think I'll turn in."

"Sure. Okay. Have a good night, sir."

Lloyd dipped his head, muttered something unintelligible, and disappeared upstairs.

Nick moaned and hoisted himself from the sofa. In the kitchen, Eve had just set out some food. "*Mom?*"

"I know airline food is terrible nowadays. Here, sit." She eased back a chair—not his father's seat. "It's homemade bean and bacon soup 'cause I know you like that. And I picked up some corned beef from the deli especially for you."

"Oh, *real* corned beef." Nick's mouth watered. There was almost nothing he missed about the east—except for the food. If Nick had never left, he'd weigh four hundred pounds. Although the sandwich was thick and juicy and the soup delighted his senses, Nick tried to blow it off. "You didn't have to do this, Mom."

"Nonsense. How often do you come home?" She paused, added, "Not often enough if you ask me."

Looking at the late night snack, he laughed. "Mom, really? You cut the ends off?"

"You don't like the ends."

"Yeah, when I was a boy."

Eve patted his shoulder. "You'll always be my boy."

Nick heard a rapid patter along the tile. He smiled as he saw an eager fur ball scampering toward him. "Hey, boy." Nick slid his chair back and the Westie hopped onto his lap, his wet nose twitching toward the sandwich. "He looks just like Scrappy."

"Your father's always had a soft spot for West Highland Terriers. I wondered what took you so long to smell the food, Four."

Nick arched a brow. "Four?"

"Scrappy Four."

Nick had been the one to name the family puppy when he was a boy. Scrappy was short for Scrap Iron, the tough-as-nails second baseman of the 1979 World Champion Pirates Phil Garner. His childhood dog had apparently become Scrappy One, followed by Scrappy Two, Scrappy Three, and now, Four. Nick started to tear off a piece of bread. "Is it okay?"

"Sure," Eve responded. "Had I known Four would come down, I'd have left the ends on for *him*."

"Oh," Nick deadpanned, "more worried about him than me?" The small dog gingerly took the food from his fingertips. "Scrappy Four, huh?"

"Your father always liked the name Scrappy."

"At least that's one thing in my life he's agreed with."

"You know how your father is," Eve said, rubbing behind Four's ears. "He's not easy to please."

"Tell me something I don't know."

Nick took a few more bites and then broached the subject. He pointed his chin at the stairs. "How's Uncle Hank?"

Eve did a good job of showing strength. "He has his good days and his bad days. Today was a good day. Maybe he sensed you were coming."

Hank was only three years older than his sister Eve but he'd been battling health issues his whole life. It seemed as if all the family history of medical problems came down on Hank's side of the ledger. He suffered his first heart attack shortly before turning thirty, his second one coming just a few years later, after his wife, Martha, choked to death.

When he was young Nick assumed Hank was his mom's father, not brother. He looked that much older.

Three years ago, Hank suffered a debilitating stroke that left him incapable of speech and paralyzed on his right side. No longer able to take care of himself and totally alone in the world Hank had been moved in to the Garrison home to live out his remaining days.

Nick always liked Uncle Hank. Growing up, he'd felt bad that he was without Aunt Martha. His memories of them were vague but they seemed happy and in love.

Nevertheless, Nick had never been thrilled with Hank residing here. Although his mom was healthy, she was no spring chicken either. Taking care of an enfeebled individual was draining, both emotionally and physically. A nurse came in a few hours a week but the bulk of caretaking fell on Eve. She was the one who bathed him, fed him, cleaned his bedpan, changed the IV bags and kept on top of the meds. "Does he even recognize you?"

"Oh most definitely. I can see it in his eyes."

Nick thought the response was too quick. He'd only been home a short time and didn't want to push too hard. But he felt a need to clear his conscience. "It's a lot of work for you, Mom."

Eve waved it away.

"You're not getting any younger. I don't mean anything. Hank's a great guy. I always liked him—"

"And he was always fond of you."

"—but don't you think he'd maybe be better in a nursing home? You know, they can probably keep a closer eye on him than you."

"He's my brother."

"I know, Mom." Nick stalled, took a bite of the sandwich and searched for the proper words. "It's just that I worry about you."

"Those nursing homes are a nightmare."

"I'm sure they're not *that* bad."

Eve closed her eyes, shook her head. "Besides, the closest one is just this side of Pittsburgh. That's a long drive, at least seventy five minutes away." She paused, added, "No, too far. Won't happen."

Nick decided to drop the subject for now. Since she knew the location of one, perhaps she'd already researched it.

They chatted until almost three in the morning before deciding to turn in. Eve sluggishly took the stairs. Sliding her hand along the brass rail for balance, Nick followed behind, questioning why his parents didn't sell the house for a single story. He wondered how they managed to get Uncle Hank down these stairs for doctor appointments and whatnot. Unless they never did.

"I'm just going to check on him," Eve stated. "Did you want to say hi?"

Nick vacillated. Between jet lag, the time difference between Arizona and Pennsylvania, and the three hour layover in Atlanta, Nick had been awake close to twenty-four hours. He longed for sleep. However, he felt obligated to see his uncle. "Sure, I'll pay my respects."

Pay my respects. It was a strange choice of words, a comment reserved for a visit to the cemetery. Perhaps, in his mind, Nick already had his uncle in the ground.

Standing in the doorframe of what had been his parents reading room when he was a boy, Nick was immediately overcome by the stench of urine that lingered in the air. He watched his mom walk over to Hank, unaware of or simply accustomed to the reeking.

The bariatric hospital bed appeared massive. Or maybe the room was smaller than Nick recalled. Side and foot rails walled the bed. Metal bars circled the bed making it appear to Nick like a horizontal cell. A thirteen inch TV rested atop Gabe's childhood dresser. Uncle Hank sat in a tattered orange chair. An insignificant reading lamp provided little light. A wicker basket on the nightstand overflowed with prescriptions bottles.

The entire scene was depressing as hell.

Eve displayed an overly broad smile for her vegetative brother. "Hank," she announced, tousling his few remaining silver hairs, "look who came to see you. Nick. You remember Nick, don't you?"

"Hey, Uncle Hank," Nick said, stepping into the stench. His voice was as artificial as his mother's smile.

He shouldn't have been surprised by the lack of reaction, but he was. Hank sat there motionless, oblivious to everything around him. He was a prisoner of his body and of his mind. Or what was left of them.

Hospital booties were on Hank's feet. His emaciated legs were contorted in an angled position. Had he been alert and functioning, he'd surely be hurting from the abnormal slant. From shins to shoulders, he was draped in a thin blanket. His neck was craned, seemingly unable to support the weight of his head. His face pointed at the floor, eyes focused on nothing. Lips were hooked, the right side of his mouth, droopy, exposing what appeared to be diseased gums. Even from several feet away Nick detected halitosis.

Nick felt even more adulation for his mom, now seeing first-hand his uncle's condition. He applauded her bravery and fortitude. But he wondered why God would allow someone to suffer in such hell.

Eve retrieved a few baby wipes from nearby and patted away the spittle from her brother's chin. She bent at the waist, putting her face in his line of sight hoping for recognition. None came.

The small table alongside Hank housed a framed picture of himself and Aunt Martha, probably when they were in their thirties. Nick recalled seeing that picture as a boy. There was also an outdated rotary phone on the bedside stand.

The TV was on but muted.

"Animal Planet?"

Eve said, "I've read that sometimes observing animals can help stroke victims. I've tried to get Four to come in but he cowers and runs away."

Can't blame him.

Eve tenderly washed away some of the crust from her brother's eyes. "They say music helps, too. And Hank always liked Doo-Wop music. " She gazed into her brother's distant stare. "Isn't that right, Hank?"

Nick hadn't noticed nor heard the portable CD player situated next to the TV. Music supposedly *could* heal, but Frankie Limon's "Why Do Fools Fall in Love?" seemed out of place.

Nick offered to help his mom, but was relieved when she said, "No, I've got it."

She stepped back, sized up the motionless thing her brother had become. "He seems comfortable. I think I'll leave him in the chair. Is that okay, Hank? Do you want to sleep in the chair?"

Nothing.

"The chair or the bed? Up to you."

No reaction.

"Okay, the chair it is." Eve kissed her brother on the top of his scabby head. "Tomorrow I'll wash your hair." And she walked out, maintaining her composure.

Moments later, Nick found himself in his old room. The remnants of his youth were now relegated to boxes. His Phoebe Cates and *Miami Vice* posters, his baseball signed by Pirates' greats Willie Stargell and Manny Sanguillen, his picture with Pirates skipper Chuck Tanner, his high school diploma—all of it gone and buried in the dank garage.

Nick closed the door, stripped down to his boxers, and collapsed onto bed. The frame was the same but the mattress felt new. And surprisingly comfortable.

He waited for sleep to come, the familiar sounds of childhood a distant memory. It was as if he'd never before slept in this bed or this house.

Nick couldn't help but feel sorry for his mom. She catered to her brother, feeding him, patting away dribble, and wiping his ass. And she did it all, clinging to a miracle, hoping that somehow her brother would break free from the binds that trapped him.

Seeing his uncle was heartbreaking. Nick had been fairly close to him as a young boy. But Hank's visits became less frequent after Martha died. Still, the guy was so fried and so out of it, he didn't even know where he was. Probably better that way.

Nick thought of his father. They hadn't been close since Nick was a teenager. To him, it seemed like the father never forgave the son for teenage rebellion. Nick was not that much more of a hell raiser than his brother. But Nick always believed his father favored Gabe.

And what about Brandi? Was that her in the car? It *had* to be. The jet black hair was as full and prominent as years ago. Those enthralling brown eyes were as radiant and sharp as in high school. Was she still living in that same house? She must be. Was she married now? Did she have a family?

Why hadn't he stopped, turned around, said hi. Was it *that* strange that he was back in town and immediately went to the home of the *one that got away*? The one he never should have left behind.

Nick still felt that connection. Maybe tomorrow he'd work up the nerve to knock on her door. Or perhaps, the day after. He couldn't wait too long, though. Time was fleeting.

He turned over and readjusted his pillow. His eyes looked through the verticals and, in the distance, just as in his youth, he viewed lights at the summit of Aliquippa Mountain. Blinking. One second at a time. Flickering away the years, just as they had since he was a boy when he still had plenty of years ahead of him.

Chapter 6

Nick woke rejuvenated. His restful slumber was capped off by the scintillating whiff of bacon. Instinctively, he reached for Gwen. Swinging his legs over the side, Nick sat motionless and prepared himself. He rose cautiously, like a man twice his age. For a while now, he'd lift himself slowly, kowtowing to the headaches that greeted him every morning. To his wonder, there was no throbbing sensation today.

Slipping into a pair of running shorts, he exited the bedroom. He did a double take at Hank's room, debating saying good morning. Instead, he followed his nose downstairs.

"Sleep okay?" asked Eve as she moved away from the stove to hug her son.

Not yet fully alert, Nick confirmed he had.

His mom was genuinely pleased. "Scrambled and bacon will be right up, biscuits are almost done, and coffee is fresh."

Nick poured some caffeine and lowered himself at the table. "Good morning, sir."

His father grumbled something and continued reading the *Pittsburgh Post-Gazette*. After serving her husband and son, making sure all the condiments were in place, Eve allowed herself to sit down. "Eat before the eggs get cold."

"Thanks for breakfast." Nick took his first bite and kissed his fingertips. "Delicious as always."

"Thanks," Eve responded. Facing her husband, she asked, "Everything taste okay?"

"Everything's just wonderful," Lloyd clipped.

Undeterred by her husband's acerbity, Eve faced Nick, "If you moved back home, I could cook for your more often."

"As tempting as it is, I can't."

"Why not?"

Lloyd finally joined the conversation and not in a good way. "Yes, why not, son? Arizona hasn't cornered the market on dead people, have they? Plenty of graves here you can buff."

Nick curled his lips while holding his tongue. Twelve hours and already the tension between father and son hung in the air like a guillotine.

"I almost forgot." Eve stood, retrieved a note, and handed it over. "Ed called for you this morning."

"Wolfsie!" Nick cried out. He had e-mailed his friend he'd be in town for a while.

"He said he'd like to meet you today. I took his number in case you needed it."

Nick thanked his mom. His elation at seeing his childhood friend was quickly soured when his mom added, "I'm having Gabe and his wife over tonight for dinner so don't have a big lunch."

Opposite ends of the spectrum. An afternoon with a life-long buddy followed up by an evening with his brother.

☙❧

The Jordan Turnout?

After a delightful breakfast, Nick contacted Ed. He assumed they'd meet at Texas Jack's or one of Avalon Hill's many mom-and-pop diners. Perhaps even the one and only Starbucks in town. But the Jordan Turnout?

Normally, one would refer to this area as being *out in the sticks*. But, in all actuality, the entire village of Avalon Hills was *out in the sticks*.

Nick turned left and began bouncing over the uneven gravel path. The dashboard of the rental car shimmied and knocked. The trail was seldom used by vehicles and not maintained. The harsh Pennsylvania winters had torn up the route. The long forgotten road was practically indiscernible as tree roots encroached, lifting the narrow path to unevenness. Boughs scraped the top and sides of the Hyundai like claws. Nick wondered if his auto insurance applied to rentals.

After a jolting and jarring mile and a half off-roading, the overhanging forest opened like a curtain, presenting the Acheron River. Mud, slush, and reeds bordered the waterway. A hundred yards south, he noticed a vehicle parked. And a man leaning against the hood, facing the Acheron.

Wolfsie.

Nick honked his horn and waved as he approached. The Hyundai's tires struggled to find traction in the damp marsh.

Nick drove over. He noticed his pal make a visor with his hands to verify who had showed up, as if he might be meeting someone else. Confirming it was Nick, Wolfsie approached. "Nick fucking Garrison!"

"Ed fucking Wolfe!" The two pals man-hugged, foregoing a fist bump or a complicated handshake reserved for kids half their age. "How you doing, Wolfsie?"

"It's good seeing you, my friend."

"You know," Nick began, smiling broadly. "The whole ride out here I wondered if I'd ever done something to piss you off."

"Why?"

"Out here, middle of nowhere? Perfect place to hide a body."

Wolfsie ignored the comment. "Beer?" He walked to the passenger's side of his car and presented an ice chest on the front seat. "I've got Bud, Bud, and Bud."

"Still a Bud man, I see."

Wolfsie handed one to Nick, kept one for himself. The two pals clinked bottles. "To old friends and good times."

"Amen, brother," replied Nick.

Wolfsie looked fit. He was one of those whose eyelids sloped as if perpetually sad. Still, just like in high school, he wore his blond hair cropped close. He always joked about one day enlisting in the Marines, but wanted to start slow. The closest he ever got to Camp Lejeune was the haircut.

Standing at six one and a svelte one seventy-six, Wolfsie maintained a robust appearance. His tan shorts and red tank top revealed a healthy physicality.

Nick realized, thanks to the ever increasing gray and slight paunch, he came off looking older than Wolfsie. But they were pals and appearances didn't matter. Taking a swig, Nick nodded at the vehicle. "Nice ride."

"Chevy Traverse," Ed confirmed. "Around these parts gotta drive American." He looked over his shoulder. "What's with the jar of Mustard?"

"It's just a rental car." Nick added in a whisper, "Hyundai."

He studied his childhood friend. It'd been a while since he'd seen his old chum. Wolfsie's wife Karri did something or other in real estate and attended a convention in Phoenix. Wolfsie took advantage of the opportunity and tagged along to visit Nick. "It's been almost two years, man."

Wolfsie nodded. He extended his arm and gave Nick a reassuring squeeze on his left shoulder. His always-sad countenance seemed more prominent. "It's really good seeing you." His words were soft.

Nick furrowed a brow. "You're not going to kiss me, are you?"

Wolfsie raised the bottle. "Maybe after the second." The laugh that followed, like the smile, seemed forced.

A few moments later, Wolfsie made his way to the front of the SUV. Lowering his butt on the front fender, he placed his elbows on his knees and stared emptily across the Acheron.

It wasn't just Ed's face that was saddened. Slouching forward his entire body rang of torment.

"Life," Nick mumbled and lowered himself alongside Wolfsie. *Life.* It was strange how things worked out. Or did not.

The Three Amigos, as they called themselves after a popular movie at the time, all had dreams. They'd keep in touch after graduation, no matter how far they fled from Avalon Hills.

Wolfsie got his law degree and became a defense attorney for a huge firm across the state in Philadelphia. He'd been doing well and was being considered for a partnership. Somehow, he and Karri and their family ended up back here in Bumfuck, PA. Wolfsie had forsaken his criminal justice career and now worked as a wire tech for the phone company. Nick had never pried for an explanation. Wolfsie would share when he was ready.

Nick got his ass out of town immediately after graduation. He wouldn't come back here until he was the Pirates' left fielder. So much for that. His dream was as dead as those whose headstones he now polished.

The third member of their inseparable trio was destined to become the next Tommy Lee or Alex Van Halen when he ventured to New York with his band in the late eighties. "How's Mike?"

Ed cocked his head. "I thought that's why you came back. You didn't hear?"

"Hear what?"

"He's gone, man."

"Gone?" Nick cried. "He moved?"

Wolfsie paused for a minute. His friend didn't know. "Stupid bastard ate a bullet."

Disbelief. Nick heard the words but they didn't click. He, Wolfsie, and Mike were an indissoluble team. They'd remain friends until the end of time. The thought of Mike being...*gone*...was incomprehensible. The end of time came earlier than expected. "What—happened?"

"What happened? The guy reached his breaking point and threw in the towel."

Nick stammered. "I mean—why, when?"

Wolfsie hiked his shoulders. "Beats me. I know they'd been struggling. He'd been pretty depressed the last several months. Guess he lost hope." Wolfsie took a huge swig, swallowed. "I was sure you'd heard."

Nick bowed his head and tried to come to terms with his buddy's suicide. After a moment of silence, he breathed, "Damn."

"Why *did* you come back then?"

His mind enveloped in a fog of questions and confusion, Nick chose not to respond to Wolfsie's query. "He should've called me. Shit, why didn't he just call me? Maybe I could've talked him down."

"I live here, Nick, and he didn't even call me."

Nick stood and began pacing away the inconceivable news. He finished half the Bud in two large gulps. He thought of Mike's widow, Brooke, and of their kids. He tried to picture in his mind's eye where it happened, how it looked. He thought of Dr. Rajagopal out in Arizona. "Sure is a lot of death going around."

"Ain't that the truth," Wolfsie confirmed plainly.

Several moments of unforeseen reverence passed between Nick and Wolfsie. Their unbreakable trio now reduced by one third.

Nick asked details and Mike shared what he knew, which was not much. For some reason Nick felt personally affronted when he learned Brooke had decided on cremation and no service. "He should've stayed in New York."

While Wolfsie continued staring blankly across the river Nick thought out loud. "Mike was a good drummer. He gave up on his dreams too quick."

"Look who's talking."

Slightly taken aback, Nick raised an eyebrow.

"You could've rehabbed the shoulder."

"Believe me, I tried." Nick closed his eyes tightly. "It was stupid. *I* was stupid."

It was the third game of the season during his sophomore year at San Diego State. His Aztecs were trouncing their opponents, 12-3. The entire team had turned it up a notch that afternoon. Scouts from both the Cubs and the nearby Padres were in the stands due to the promising young phenom on the mound.

Nick and his teammates, however, were determined to garner their own attention.

As soon as Jimmy Dellatorre connected, Nick took off from second. He ran through the sign of the third base coach and raced for home where he was met by an unyielding wall of bricks. The collision at the plate rattled his skull. His bones felt as if they'd been redistributed within his body.

The last thing he felt before unconsciousness was a piercing pain in his left shoulder and numbness tingling down his arm. When he came to, his shoulder and his dream had been destroyed. *Up by nine late in the game? Stupid, stupid, stupid.*

"Why'd you come back, Wolfsie?"

"Whadaya mean?"

"You were pulling in six figures in Philly. Why did *you*

give up on your dreams and come back here?" Nick extended his arms. "To this shithole?"

"Why?" He opened his palms as if saying *How can you ask?* He peered into his friend's eyes. "This is my home."

Nick pondered the reply. He wanted to feel some connection to Avalon Hills, to the place where he grew up. But he'd never been able to. From his earliest memories, Nick had dreamt of getting the hell away. San Diego for college, then winding up in Phoenix due to the cost of living in southern California. There was only one positive in Avalon Hills and her name was Brandi Conrad.

Feeling not enough reverence had been paid to Mike's passing, Nick decided to wait a touch longer before inquiring about Brandi. He stared across the tranquilly flowing waters of the polluted Acheron.

Nick lost himself in the outcropping across the banks. The shoreline on the opposite side was thick with elms, sycamores, chestnut oaks, and eastern white pines. Thick, menacing, and somewhat ominous, even in the early afternoon, they appeared to stand sentry, warding off evil that dared encroach upon their domain. An impenetrable barricade.

Nick observed a chain-link fence, topped off by coiled barbwire, partially submerged in the reeds. Every twenty yards, a placard warned of danger. *No trespassing.* His eyes followed the fence that shadowed the shore for at least two miles in each direction. To his left, he noticed a narrow bridge, not much wider than a walking path, extending over the river.

Had this area been marked when he was a small boy, Nick would have been unable to resist the temptation. Surely the place must be haunted. Making conversation and pointing with his chin, he asked, "What happened there?"

It took Wolfsie a moment to catch on to what his friend was referring to. "Chemical spill. Members of the Department of Energy and Nuclear Regulatory Commission all came out with their funny little hazmat suits and cordoned off that whole area."

"What'd they find?"

Wolfsie stood and removed another pair of bottles from the ice chest. Handing one to Nick, he returned to the front fender.

"Some carcinogens. Mostly benzene is what they told us. Other crap too that causes babies to be born with three heads and twelve fingers."

Nick found the news disturbing. He was surprised by Wolfsie's blasé outlook. "From where?"

Wolfsie stared upriver. "The Tri-Delta Plant."

After shooting a glance north and remembering the plant from childhood, Nick asked, "They still operating?"

"No. They got fined and the fed shut 'em down. Word around town is they changed their name and relocated out in Nevada or someplace."

Nick's entire childhood flitted across his mind. He recalled growing up in the grimy cloudbank that perpetually blanketed the entire town. He could still recall the odor that hung over the city many nights, smelling like a combination of ammonia and singed hair. The water supply for Avalon Hills came from the Acheron. As he took a swig from the fresh bottle, his throat burned. Or was it psychosomatic.

"How long had they been dumping?"

"Since the forties, I believe. What I heard was that they unloaded some atomic waste from the Manhattan Project here and up in New York at Love Canal."

Nick vaguely recalled the toxic disaster just outside of Niagara Falls. In the 1970s, the amount of miscarriages and babies born with defects skyrocketed in the upstate New York neighborhood of Love Canal. From 1974 through 1978, more than half the babies delivered had at least one birth defect. Everything from deafness and nerve disorders to cleft palates and mental deficiencies plagued the children. Cancer rates soared.

"Was what happened here a result of the crap from the Manhattan Project or from Tri-Delta?"

Wolfsie shrugged. "Probably a little of both."

"But it didn't get into the water supply?"

"Supposedly not. Apparently whatever chemicals were dumped flowed down the Acheron and were caught in the tide pools around the island there." He pointed across the river.

Nick couldn't help but wonder what kind of mark Tri-Delta had left on residents of the city. Perhaps the side effects were not purely physical. Could whatever poisons cloud one's mind, cause them to act irrationally, and perhaps go as far as committing suicide? His thoughts drifted to Mike Lauser, then he glanced at Wolfsie who appeared lost in thought, staring at the other side of the waterway, as if in prayer.

Crestfallen, Nick gazed downriver. Around the bend and out of sight lay Avalon Hills. Yes, he'd wanted to bust out as far back as he remembered. He hated that dead-end town. But still, it was his home. It was the place where he was born, where he grew up with his brother, where he fell in love. Learning that a company called Tri-Delta Industries had infected and invaded *his* turf left Nick feeling violated.

He again looked at Wolfsie, who appeared defeated. Nick assumed that Wolfsie, like Nick, felt infringed upon by the unscrupulous factory. But when Wolfsie muttered the next words, Nick realized he was dead wrong.

"It's my wife. Karri found a lump."

Chapter 7

Unsure how to respond, Nick heard himself utter, "Jesus, man."

Wolfsie spoke in a detached tone. He informed Nick on her status as if he was talking about a stranger. He kept to the facts, his voice lacking emotion. The oncologist in Pittsburgh had diagnosed Karri stage III. Tests determined the cancer had spread to nearby lymph nodes in her chest wall. They'd begun treating it with biological therapy, mainly Herceptin and Taxotere.

"Surgery?"

Wolfsie shook his head. "She only wants to do that as a last resort. Karri's always been afraid of being put under. She freaked out years back when they pulled her wisdom teeth."

"Back in Phoenix they have some real good doctors and a great cancer center," Nick advised. "Maybe you—"

Wolfsie cut him off. "She doesn't want to travel. I mentioned Sloan Kettering and Johns Hopkins. I found online there's some place down in Houston that's been making some great strides and doing great things."

"But she won't go?"

"Nope. She says if it's going to end, it's going to end here. At home."

"Want me to talk to her?" Nick blurted out, then wondered why he did. He'd always gotten along well with Karri. But if her own husband couldn't convince her, how would he be able to.

"Talk to *her*? Why not talk to me?"

Nick furrowed his brow. "Huh? I am talking to you."

"You're talking at me, Nick, not to me." Wolfsie downed more beer.

Unsure where his pal was coming from, Nick attributed it to the duress he was under. "The offer's on the table. Maybe hearing it from an outsider will help. You guys could stay at my place while she's getting treated. We *can* make it work."

"Thanks." Wolfsie's tone seemed curt, abrupt.

Nick wondered what he'd said wrong. He fully anticipated spending the afternoon reminiscing about the good ol' days with his friend. Sure hadn't worked out the way Nick planned. A minute later, Wolfsie uneventfully declared he needed to get going.

Nick was surprised. "Um, sure, okay."

As the two men pumped hands, Wolfsie peered into Nick's light brown eyes, peered *through* him.

"What is it?"

Wolfsie appeared as if he was searching for words. Finally, he voiced, "You can help."

"Of course. I'd love to. Want me to talk to Karri?" Wolfsie met his stare. The lack of response resulted in a follow-up. "I'm serious about you guys staying at my place if you want to bring her out."

That wasn't it either.

"How long will you be in town for?"

"Not sure exactly. A week, maybe less."

"We'll talk." And with that Wolfsie lumbered to his SUV and drove away.

Perplexed and left behind, Nick watched the Chevy U-turn and get swallowed up by the impenetrable forest. Nick's stomach churned. It'd definitely been an eventful fifteen hours back home. His father was still distant, holding a grudge about God-knows-what. His mother had become caretaker for her brother. One of his best friends put a bullet in his skull. The wife of his other best friend was battling breast cancer.

Nick had hoped to press his friend for information on Brandi, but the opportunity never presented itself.

He got into the rental car, checked his watch. With time to kill, he decided he'd cruise by Brandi's old home again. Maybe he'd even go up and knock on the door this time. Not that he had any clue what to say. Bringing the engine to life, Nick instinctively glanced into the rear view.

The lurking figure caused him to do a double-take.

He pivoted, looked over his shoulder. The being was gone.

Nick exited and scanned the gloomy sinister woodlands. He was sure he saw someone standing in the tree line thirty or so yards away. All he saw—or *thought* he saw—was a ghostly face in an endless screen of blackness.

He scanned the area, now realizing it was not far from this exact spot. All those years ago, the night he was sure he and Brandi would consummate their relationship, when they witnessed a possible murder. That following morning, he did the right thing. He talked to the sheriff, told him what he saw. And it never went further. Time passed and that macabre incident became a distant and fading memory. A mystery of youth.

Nick stood soundless, suppressed his own breathing, and searched unsuccessfully for the spectral figure prowling the forest.

❧❧❧

Whereas the afternoon had not played out as he hoped, the evening proceeded exactly how Nick feared. The novelty of seeing his brother wore off in about three seconds. Gabe seemed more eager to engage their father in conversation than he did to converse with his seldom-seen brother who lived across the country. Even Scrappy Four's stubby tail wagged excitedly at Gabe's entry.

As Nick watched everyone interact, he felt like an outsider in his own family. He was treated like an unwelcomed guest. Observing Gabe in action, Nick's neck warmed. He'd never been close to his younger brother. Even growing up, they simply tolerated each other. They had different interests, different friends. Yet, for some reason, even though they'd never gotten along as children, it troubled Nick they still did not as adults. Communication between them was non-existent.

Nick watched his brother babble on and work the room. He even paced while relating a story about his job as if he was some great actor performing on stage.

The self-righteous prick.

Gabe was one of those who did not handle stress well. He'd

always seemed unable to multi-task, unable to handle more than one issue at a time. And whatever was front and center at that particular moment was always earth-shattering and life-changing. With those traits, Nick wondered how his brother managed to keep his job, considering the work he did.

"He sure loves the attention, doesn't he?"

"Always has," responded Nick to his sister-in-law's spot-on observation.

Although Nick did not know Yolanda that well, he liked her. In all reality, he felt closer to her than his brother, even though that wasn't saying much.

She was friendly, intelligent, and attractive. She was dressed to the gills, outfitted more for a job interview than a family dinner. Both their children were successful. Their oldest, Alex, had just graduated college and was working for a Congresswoman in DC. Chelsea would be starting her junior year in the fall.

Leaning over, Nick asked, "Where's Chelsea going again?"

Yolanda beamed. "Ohio State."

"That's great. You must be proud."

"We are, we are."

"Excuse me," Gabe snapped. "Do you mind?"

"Sorry," Yolanda said.

"Where was I? Oh, yeah. So anyway…" And Gabe continued his diatribe. No one else was allowed to speak when Gabe Garrison had the floor. He took it to be a personal affront.

Whispering, not wanting to interrupt her husband, Yolanda patted Nick's knee. "We'll catch up after dinner."

As proud as Yolanda was of her children, Lloyd seemed equally enamored with his youngest. Gabe was clearly the pride of the family. He was successful, well respected in the community. He and his wife had given him two upstanding and respectable grandchildren. On the flip side was Nick, never married, no kids, and spent his life polishing tombstones.

Perhaps it was an ironic twist of fate that younger Gabe stood at six-three, a few inches taller than Nick. He clearly lived in his kid brother's shadow.

For seventeen years, Nick was imprisoned in Avalon Hills. He lived in a home with little affection and less communication. His father had grown up in a different time. Blacks and whites stayed at different hotels, drank from different water fountains, had separate rest rooms. Lloyd was not prejudiced in any way. He was just a product of the times. *You stay with your own* was never spoken but was implied.

Yet, in spite of Yolanda being African-American, Lloyd had no recriminations about welcoming her into their clan. Yolanda was treated more like a Garrison than Nick.

As Gabe blathered on, Eve excused herself. She went to the kitchen, checked on dinner, and then retreated upstairs to feed her incapacitated brother.

Nick debated assisting. As depressing as it was to be around his uncle, it was intolerable being around his egotistical brother.

Nick wasn't sure where he belonged.

☙❧

Dinner conversation developed into an unmelodiousness of muted sounds and distant laughter. Gabe did not shut up the entire meal. Nick was amazed he even had time to eat, since he was using his mouth for jabbering.

Feeling like a fifth wheel, Nick snuck a peek at his watch and wondered what Brandi was doing at this moment.

After the main course was finished, Nick and Yolanda cleared the table and began loading the dishwasher. When he reached for his brother's glass, Gabe snapped. "I'm still drinking that. Some coffee would be great, though."

Nick clipped. "What am I, your waiter?"

It was the first time since his brother's arrival that the house became silent. "No, you're a dude who works at a cemetery. My bad."

"I'll get the coffee," Eve proclaimed, extinguishing the simmering fire.

Before Nick could respond and let his holier-than-thou brother have it between the eyes, Gabe turned to their father and picked up where he left off. Nick was now not just a *dude who works in a cemetery.* He was irrelevant.

After Eve served up the coffee and lowered some freshly

baked oatmeal cookies onto the table, she spoke. "I'm going to bring Hank his dessert and put him in the tub."

"I'll help, Mom," Gabe announced and flew out of his chair.

"When you're done, come see me out back," Lloyd called out. "We need to discuss some things."

"Okay, Pops." And the good son scampered away.

cɔƹɔ

Father and the good son retired to the back yard. Nick sauntered out to partake of the conversation but was quickly waved away. "This doesn't concern you," his father instructed.

Feeling like a little boy, Nick dropped his shoulders and lumbered back inside. With his mother upstairs bathing Uncle Hank, he found himself alone in the living room with Yolanda.

She smiled at her brother-in-law and politely lowered the magazine she'd been perusing. "Finally, we can catch up. How have you been doing, Nick?"

Nick had travelled across the country for one reason only, something he had yet to broach with his immediate family. He briefly considered sharing the news with Yolanda first. She was welcoming, outgoing. Overall, a good-hearted person. Still, for some strange reason, he felt obligated to have his parents hear it first.

As Four hopped into Yolanda's lap, he updated her on his life. As he spoke, he realized he really didn't have much to share.

"How are things with you and Gwen?'

Impressed that Yolanda remembered her name, he advised her they were taking some time apart.

"Think you can make it work?"

Nick hemmed and hawed. "Maybe, but probably not. We are just too different and want different things."

"If you want it to work out, then I hope it does. If not, you'll find someone else."

Nick strained a smile.

Yolanda continued. "The lord has a way of leading us to our soul mate. You just need to put your faith in Him."

Nick had forgotten his sister-in-law was strongly religious. "Is Gabe your soul mate?" As he spoke, he fretted sounding sarcastic.

"He's not perfect. Only one perfect man has ever walked the earth and Him they crucified. My husband has his faults. As do I. As does everyone, especially your father." She chuckled. "Life's a journey to come as close to perfection as we can. And eventually He guides us to the one we are destined to take this journey with."

Destined. Brandi's face flashed into his mind. The opportunity to discuss Brandi this afternoon with Wolfsie never materialized. Yolanda was insightful and grounded. And she could provide a woman's perspective. Nick wanted to open up. But rather than diving in, he dipped one toe in the water. "Do you really believe we are truly predestined for only one person?"

"I most certainly do."

"And…well, does someone just sit and wait for a superior being to bring you and that person together or take the initiative and do it on your own?"

"I know it's a cliché, Nick, but if it's meant to happen, it will happen."

Resorting to his own cliché, he chortled. "The Lord works in mysterious ways."

"He most certainly does."

"I'd prefer He work in a plain and simple way that's easy to understand."

Yolanda laughed. A moment later, a look of genuine concern appeared. "I'm sorry to hear about your friend, Mike."

"Apparently I'm the last to know."

"Rest assured, he's in a better place now. He walks with Jesus."

Internally, Nick cackled. He'd resented Gabe getting all the attention this evening. Now that conversation was focused on him, he felt strange in the spotlight. "How have you been doing?"

Reading between the lines, Nick determined that Yolanda was having a hard time being an empty nester. Their children were grown and out of the house. It was bewildering to him that Yolanda, who was the same age as he, three years older than Gabe, had two adult children. Meanwhile, Nick was still trying to find his own way.

"You've got a degree in Political Science. You're a smart woman—"

"I appreciate that."

"Just seems like, I don't know, such a waste you're sitting home all day.

"I blog here and there about the political landscape," she countered. "And every other Saturday I volunteer down at the VA Hospital in Pittsburgh."

"I know it's an hour south and the commute's a bitch." Nick stopped, wondering if he'd burn in hell for saying *bitch* to someone religious. "But your talents and your mind are being…well, not fully utilized here."

With an endearing smile, she replied. "Nick, this is my home. This is where I belong."

This is my home.

First, it was Wolfsie. Now, Yolanda. Home or not, Avalon Hills was a shithole, a shithole where a company had been dumping chemicals and carcinogens.

What am I missing?

Chapter 8

People were always caught flatfooted when first meeting Frannie Fitzgerald. The name conjured up images of an old maid, a spinster perhaps. A grandmotherly type, knitting in a rocking chair, shawl draped over frail bony shoulders, hair in a bun. Paradoxically Frannie was only forty years old but looked ten years younger.

Restless, Frannie kneaded her stiff neck and decided to stretch her legs. She vacated her dreary gray cubicle, traversed the maze of identical workstations, and ambled over to the expansive window. Looking out, she viewed C Street from her office on the third floor in the Department of Commerce.

The streets of Washington DC were filling with government employees slipping out for an early lunch. The unpitying heat and pounding humidity of the nation's capital withdrew for a couple days. Eating outside was *almost* tolerable.

11:40.

She still had twenty minutes to get through, followed by a tedious afternoon. She couldn't wait for this day to be over. On the other hand, she was in no real hurry to get home to her so-called life.

Two decades earlier, Frannie was living in south Florida, a stone's throw from where she was born. She had just turned twenty when her life began taking form.

As corny as it sounded for the old-fashioned girl with the old sounding name, she got stung in the heart by Cupid's arrow. She and Tom met, dated, and fell in love. They married seven months later. Frannie then gave birth to their daughter. A short time later, they were blessed with a second daughter. And then, just like that, Tom was gone.

Too quickly.

He habitually devoted the second Saturday of every month as a boy's night out. From what the police informed her, this particular evening his blood alcohol was just a smidgen over the legal limit. Their sedan leapt the guardrail. Tom not only killed himself but took a pregnant woman and her four year old daughter with him.

The Fitzgerald name was poison in the small community.

A single mom raising two children, she needed extra money and volunteered to work on the decennial census. Her hard work resulted in a full time job offer a thousand miles away inside the beltway. She now worked as a statistical analyst III for what was officially titled The Bureau of the Census under the umbrella of the Commerce Dept. After all these years she'd never learned the difference between a stats analyst I, II, III, and IV. But III paid well, so that was all that mattered. This career started seventeen years ago.

Too quickly.

With her life gradually coming together a second time, her children growing, and her career taking hold, there was only one thing missing: A man. Fearing being unattached at the ripe old age of thirty, Frannie entered the mystical world of dating. Like with Tom, things with Davis moved swiftly. The wedding occurred just a week prior to the big three-oh.

Frannie had recently turned forty. Where did the time go?

Davis had no qualms about her maintaining the Fitzgerald surname as a tribute to her daughter's father. Frannie Fitzgerald-Zerbe didn't flow easily from one's tongue.

By their one year anniversary, she and Davis had fallen into the routine of being an old married couple. Twelve years her senior, Davis came from old money and was a big shot over at the State Department.

It became obvious their marriage was nothing more than a mutual arrangement. Frannie's children would grow up with more financial security than she could ever achieve on her own. She performed her wifely obligations, both in the bedroom and at unending functions. And Davis had a younger wife to display. Frannie had already decided that when her youngest turned eighteen, she would file for divorce. The birthday, like five o'clock, couldn't get here fast enough.

Returning to her desk, she decided to finish compiling the analysis report and take a late lunch. It would make the afternoon less than four hours. She glanced at the photos of her girls. There was none of Davis or proof that he even existed.

It was at that moment when something caught her eye.

Two hours later, foregoing lunch, an invigorated Frannie rapped her knuckles on the open door of her boss, a supervisor *VI,* whatever that meant. "Got a minute?"

Dennis Linebrink had been sitting at computers so long his shoulders had permanently rounded. A heavyset man, who hadn't seen his toes in two or three censuses, he less-than-enthusiastically signaled for her to enter without lifting his eyes. He much preferred dealing with numbers than with people. Seeing who it was, he instinctively used his hand as a makeshift comb.

Frannie related her findings. At first, her boss seemed disinterested. He asked generalized questions, solely to keep the young and cute Frannie in his presence. At his age, after a dreary and unremarkable career, the only bright spot of coming to work anymore was to see Frannie and get a whiff of her body wash. Eventually, he became intrigued. "These numbers can't be right."

"They are. I verified them with Social Security and ran a Monahan evaluation as well. The figures are valid, Dennis."

He looked across his desk, removed his reading glasses. He took a quick gander at Frannie's small but perky breasts before delving deeper. After a few moments of grunting and groaning like an old locomotive chugging up a steep mountainside, he spoke. "Run the numbers again. Verify them against local data. Don't forget to check the content validity of these figures. Track two scenarios of the Cohen Integers. Oh, and check for Asymptotic Efficiency as well."

"I'm on it."

"Get back to me by Tuesday."

Next Tuesday came three hours later. When Frannie reentered the office just before five, Dennis was wrapping up his day playing Free Cell. He had just uncoiled and was hoisting his sagging slacks to cover his expansive belly. This time, Frannie just walked in. "I've got it."

Dennis sighed miserably. He checked the wall clock. He checked the time on the computer. Then he checked out Frannie's petite five-two frame. And plopped down. The chair groaned under his girth.

Frannie immediately noticed that the man who'd spent his career working with stats and figures was titillated as never before. She'd prepared a detailed analysis that went far above what her boss suggested. Almost forty pages in all, loaded with graphs, charts, logarithms, tables, and grids. She even threw in some bright colors to make the boring numbers come to life.

They played point-counterpoint. Dennis continually proposed why these figures were impossible. Frannie successfully rebuked every claim. "As you always say, numbers don't lie."

He arched his brow. "Maybe this time they are."

Frannie leaned forward and winked in that irresistibly innocent way that always caught Dennis' eye. He never knew if it was a wink that said *I'm onto something* or a wink that said something else.

Thirty minutes passed quickly. Dennis seemed fascinated, somewhat excited, and not due to Frannie's company. A smattering of co-workers stuck their heads in and wished their boss a good evening before clocking out.

For a fleeting instant, Dennis considered offering to discuss this further over dinner. But tonight that wouldn't work. His ball and chain had requested his attendance at some bullshit charity function out in Reston. "Let's look into this tomorrow with a fresh perspective."

"I'd like to go there and see what's going on."

The expression on Dennis' face said *You are joking, right?*

Frannie pushed. "Stats only tell us so much. I'm sure it's a glitch but if numbers truly don't lie, then we need to see what's happening." She tapped the report. "We both know it can't be true. But yet, here it is."

Dennis's mind shifted gears. For the next week he had a lot on his plate. But perhaps, if he could stall, he'd tag along. He and Frannie, together, on a little investigative road-trip. And all funded by the taxpayers. Before he could make that suggestion, Frannie continued.

"I really want to see it firsthand, see what's up." She added what she'd heard her husband say numerous times over the years, "Nothing beats boots on the ground."

Dennis vacillated. "I just don't think now would be a good time. The GAO is watching us. Nowadays, all those political watchdog groups scrutinize every plum nickel the fed spends."

Her marriage was in a free-for-all. Her teenage daughters were at that age, thirsting for space and freedom. The timing made sense. Frannie announced vehemently, "I've got unused vacation time I've been carrying over for years. I'd have to live to be a hundred to use it all. I'm going, Dennis." She stood, placed her hands on her narrow hips.

"Frannie, please."

"You *really* want to stop me?" Her resilient tone seemed unable to come from such a small person. As surprised as Frannie was by her own insistence, her boss was equally taken aback.

Dennis caught the hidden meaning. As a man who worked with stats his entire life, he had no difficulty reading between the lines. Over a period of several months last year, Dennis e-mailed Frannie crude jokes and questionable pictures some might find offensive. There was the double entendre used in the cafeteria and the Saturday afternoon he got drunk at the department barbeque. Frannie might be two hundred pounds lighter, but she was the one who had him over the barrel.

Dennis scanned the massive detailed report, flipped a few pages. "Where is this place, Avalon Hills? Never heard of it."

Chapter 9

Nick lurched upright, gasping for breath. He gazed at the blackened room, strangled by the walls that tightened around him like a noose. He was not claustrophobic but the murky room and confining space created a sensation of being buried alive.

It must've been the dream. No, a nightmare. Even in the unrelenting stifling dim, the vivid images jumbled together and slowly drifted away. All he recalled were flashes, glimpses: Barbed wire, the Acheron River, his sister-in-law Yolanda wearing a cap and gown, a car being driven by a smiling Brandi as blood poured from a massive knife wound in the center of her beautiful face.

It was 5:42. The faint green hue of the nightstand clock provided the only light. Sliding his hand along the rear of his clammy neck, Nick was surprised at the amount of perspiration on his T-shirt collar. In spite of the unexplainable dream and the way he jerked up in bed, he felt no pain in his head. Since arriving in Avalon Hills, the throbbing in his skull had ceased.

And that's when he sensed a presence. Like someone—or something—was observing him. The nape of his neck tingled. It was July, but Nick felt chilled. He muffled his breathing, listened.

He heard it: a muted conversation. Nothing intelligible, words unclear. It sounded like a gentle guttural moan of someone in pain but unable to cry out for help.

Nick lifted himself from the bed. He chose to leave the lights off, electing instead to rely on the indistinct shadows of morning light that slithered through the home and illuminated the upstairs in strange angular shapes of a soft gray-white. The night had yet to fully surrender.

Nick perked his ears. He heard it again, though he couldn't discern its origin. No welcoming aromas wafted through the gloomy corridors. His mom was still asleep. The only other possibility was Uncle Hank.

The hallway seemed menacing, a macabre ghoulish path to uncertainty.

Nick was a child again, a frightened boy, afraid of the monster under his bed and the boogeyman in his closet.

He contemplated waking his mother. She'd probably be getting up soon, anyway. Plus, she was the one who took care of Hank. If his incapacitated uncle needed something, Nick wouldn't know what to do.

He decided to first check out things on his own. Awakening his mother would surely cause his father to stir. As it was, Lloyd already thought of his eldest son as less than a man.

Nick padded along the corridor. Beads of sweat formed on his brow. His shirt collar was now damper than a minute ago when he woke.

The reflection of TV images danced on the door to Hank's room. However, the utterances Nick heard were not from a program. The TV was muted. And Frankie Limon had apparently answered his own question.

Nervously, Nick peered into the room while keeping his feet planted safely in the hallway.

Hank looked dead. He sat slumped over in his chair, head hanging, shoulders slouched forward. The stench of urine was stronger than ever.

Nick scanned his uncle's body. The rotary phone sat on his lap. Reflections from *Animal Planet* slithered across his face swiftly, too swift for Nick to determine if Hank's eyelids fluttered. Nick scrutinized Hank's chest for a rising. Not fully awake, he strained his eyes. After the longest twenty seconds of Nick's life, he heard a deep soft groan coming from his uncle's shell. The man dry coughed twice, a globule of spittle falling from the corner of his wilted lips.

Uncle Hank was okay. *Okay* being a relative word.

As Nick turned to exit, his eyes swept across the room and he caught a glimpse through the raised verticals of an image across the street, staring up at the Garrison home.

Nick slithered across Hank's room, stood alongside the window, and peeked out. The being lurked in shadow, dressed in head-to-toe black. Even his hair was midnight black. He just stood there. Nick didn't know his parent's neighbors but the way the man studied the home, he was clearly not taking an early morning stroll.

Backpedaling, Nick plodded downstairs and silently exited through the front door. Crossing halfway across the lawn, Nick looked up and down the quiet street. Dew sheathed the lawns and cars. But the entity that had been inspecting the home was no more.

⋐⋑⋐⋑

Nick might be in his forties, but since returning home, he felt himself slipping into the mindset of a child. The relationship with his father had never matured. Lloyd was the patriarch of the family, never to be questioned. His mother cooked his meals, cutting off the ends of the bread. He was still smitten with Brandi, still competing in a sibling rivalry.

As Nick boiled some water for instant coffee, his parents not awake, he decided to show up his brother. Last evening, prior to Gabe engaging in the private conversation with their father, his self-righteous younger brother had no problem assisting with Uncle Hank.

It was a silly game of one-upmanship. Juvenile. Shortly before the evening ended, his mom made a passing remark about Scrappy Four needing his shots. As always, Gabe offered to help. With his parents asleep, Nick decided he would steal some of his brother's thunder.

It took a few loud whispers before Four appeared. The little Westie sauntered slowly into the room. When the family pet saw Nick in the kitchen, close to the treats closet, his tail wagged feverishly.

At first, Nick was pleased that at least someone was happy to see him. Then, he realized it was only due to his proximity to the Milk Bones. "Okay, okay."

Nick removed a biscuit from the box. Like he had done with his own dog, the original Scrappy, he held the treat in his closed fist. Just like Scrappy One, Four lifted himself onto his back legs and danced in a circle three times. Nick couldn't help but chuckle. His father taught Four the same trick Nick taught One. "Good boy."

Not since leaving Avalon Hills had Nick owned a pet. He once dated a history teacher who had a cat named Napoleon. But to Nick, felines always seemed like a female pet for some reason. Dogs were *man's* best friend.

In spite of all the unconditional love dogs showered upon their owners, ultimately they always died. He remembered being away at college when getting the call from his mom. Scrappy had been *put to sleep*. The years of good times, walks, and tossing a ball always ended badly. Nick never handled death well.

Growing up, it was his parents who took care of Scrappy One. He never had to *care* for a pet. One veterinarian was just as good as the next.

Nick found the vet's name under a magnet on the fridge but they didn't open for three more hours. He decided to take Four to a vet down in Pittsburgh before his parents woke, before his self-righteous brother could score more brownie points.

"C'mon boy. Let's go for a ride."

Wearing blue-jeans, a nondescript button down shirt, Reeboks, and a Diamondbacks cap on his head, Nick was out of the house by six-thirty.

As if pulled by some unseen force from within, Nick detoured past Brandi's house on Hickory Circle, if, in fact, she still even lived there.

He didn't know what he expected to find. Upon arriving, everything was as it should be. Dark, quiet. The white pick-up sat parked in the driveway.

Over an hour later, with Four's mane disheveled from keeping his snout out the window, Nick arrived on the northern outskirts of Pittsburgh before business hours. With time to kill, he hit a McDonald's drive-thru. He checked his phone and found a highly rated local vet clinic.

After finishing only half of an Egg McMuffin, he turned to Four. "I remember these being better."

He purchased two hash browns on a second pass. Tearing

off tiny pieces, he daintily fed Four. "Don't tell anyone. This is our little secret."

Four yipped as if he understood.

એજ

With the leash wrapped around his wrist and Four limited to a three foot radius, Nick sat in the lobby of West View Animal Clinic, filling out the intake forms. With the exception of pet's name, breed, and address, Nick left much of the paperwork blank. He explained to the receptionist that he was unaware of the dog's shot history and age. The girl behind the counter disappeared into the back. When she returned minutes later, she advised Nick that it would not be a problem.

"I didn't know I'd have to do all this paperwork just to get a Parvi vaccination."

"Parvo."

"Right, Parvo."

The time spent in the lobby was far briefer than waiting for Dr. Rajagopal. After the dog was weighed and a tech dressed in purple scrubs asked some basic questions, she announced Dr. Shepherd would be in shortly.

Nick raised a questioning brow. "Dr. Shepherd? A veterinarian named *Shepherd*?"

"Gee, never heard that one before," the tech replied with a twinge of annoyance as she exited.

Seconds later, Dr. Shepherd entered. She was a diminutive redhead with a friendly nature and turquoise eyes that disappeared when she smiled. Nick thought she looked about sixteen years old. Or maybe he was just getting older. She gave him a passing nod before dropping to her haunches and bonding with Four.

After gaining the pooch's trust, she read the new client form. "You don't have a lot of information about Scrappy Four."

"I'm doing my parent's a favor. He's their dog but they're tied up and asked me to bring him in for his Parvo shot." Nick omitted the part about showing up his brother Gabe.

Shepherd curled her lip. Sadly, it was commonplace for

owners to pay inadequate attention to the medical needs of their pet. Nick scooped up the eager dog and placed him atop an exam table waist-high. He watched the veterinarian examine Four closely. She looked deeply into his ears, earned Four's trust to examine his teeth and the amount of decay on his gums. She pursed her lips, paying close attention. "How old did you say this little fella is?" aaa

"I'm not exactly sure. As I told the girl out front, he's my parent's dog. I think he's about seven or eight."

The vet eyed Nick skeptically and then returned to the oral exam with extra determination and an unsure countenance. She tenderly cupped Four's chin and spent an unusual amount of time looking into the dogs eyes as if she could see his soul. "I'd like to run some tests before we administer the vaccination."

"Pardon?"

She insinuated that the Parvo inoculation could be counterproductive if the animal had underlying health issues. She strongly suggested running a full blood panel, checking the dog for other possible health concerns.

"Do you think there's something wrong?"

She again peered deeply the canine's soulful eyes. "No. He seems healthy, active, and alert. But dogs are not like people. When they're hurting, they mask their pain. It shows a sign of weakness to others in the animal kingdom."

Nick's immature scheme to show up Gabe had backfired. Not only would Nick now have to fork over three hundred plus dollars, but the process would take several hours. He considered returning to Avalon Hills and bringing the dog to the usual vet. But that would be tantamount to admitting defeat. "Okay, let's do it."

❧❧

Nick needed to waste three more hours of his life. He scanned the immediate area and wandered into a nearby strip mall. Entering a small diner, he ordered a cup of decaf and some toast.

Hopefully, the sourdough would relieve the stomach discomfort brought on by either the breakfast sandwich or his plan going awry.

He nursed the food as long as possible. After an endless thirty minutes, he exited and walked the plaza. He made his way inside a Barnes and Noble. At least here he could sit and read a little, while killing more time.

At the sports section toward the rear, he came across a book about the team of his youth, the 1979 Pirates. Nick's heart skipped a beat as he recalled cherished memories when his beloved Bucs were a perennial powerhouse. Slipping the book from the shelf, he headed to a nearby table. And that's when he saw her.

The raven hair was unmistakable. The body language, the way she walked, moved. She'd gained a few pounds since high school but not much. She'd grown from a sexy alluring teenager to a strikingly beautiful woman.

What the hell is Brandi doing here?

Nick wavered a beat before accepting it was destiny. This was the moment. Back in Avalon Hills, he'd feel awkward knocking on her door out of the blue. He hadn't seen her in two decades, not since the birth of his niece. Nick hated himself for never keeping in touch with her. But now, running into her in a bookstore just outside of Pittsburgh…

It was fate.

The prophetic words of his sister-in-law came back full force. '*The lord has a way of leading us to our soul mate. You just need to put your faith in Him.*'

As she disappeared down an aisle, Nick's legs and heart led him closer to her. Butterflies in his stomach. His knees weakened. His mouth became as parched as the Arizona desert. Using his hand to smooth his shirt, he made himself as presentable as he could.

He turned the corner. Moved closer.

"Brandi?" Nick didn't know if he said it aloud or just in his mind.

She didn't react.

He whispered her name again and tenderly tapped her shoulder.

She spun, her face becoming momentarily concealed behind strands of hair whipping around. "Can I help you?"

Nick retreated. Flushed, embarrassment splayed across his reddening face. "I'm—sorry," he spluttered. "I thought you were someone else."

The woman rolled her eyes and continued flipping the pages of the latest Debbie Macomber paperback.

Nick shamefully departed and hurried to the exit at a frantic pace. Glancing around, he noticed plenty of other brunettes. All dark black hair, all with Brandi's build and body type.

He was seeing her everywhere.

Chapter 10

"Home sweet home," Nick bellyached cynically at just after two p.m. when he crossed over the Acheron River and approached the city limits of Avalon Hills. He'd wanted this to be a good day, hoping to at least temporarily knock his pompous brother off his pedestal. One giant leap for Nick-kind. But this too had backfired.

With Scrappy Four stretched out along the back seat of the rental car, Nick held his forehead against his fingertips. He'd been played for a fool.

The aptly named Dr. Shepherd advised him he needed to fork over three hundred for blood work before she felt safe administering the vaccine. However, after he signed the credit card slip, he learned it would take a few days to get the results. Yet, she gave Four the shot anyway.

Just when he thought his frustrating day couldn't worsen, he observed flashing lights filling his rear view mirror. A siren tore through the hillside.

Nick glanced at the speedometer, then turned on his directional, and eased the vehicle onto the gravelly shoulder.

Like a young boy being called into the principal's office, Nick found himself sitting up straighter. Not trying to appear suspicious, even though he was unsure what exactly a suspicious person looked like, Nick eyed the police cruiser.

The door opened and Nick observed an imposing authority figure dressed in a tan uniform, Smokey-the-bear hat and mirrored sunglasses approaching.

Shit.

"What the fuck do you think you're doing?"

Nick cocked his head at the imposing figure blocking out the sun. "Gabe?"

"Step out of the car."

Nick obeyed the order, not because Gabe was his brother but because he was sheriff.

"Mom called me frantic this morning. What'd you do?"

"I left a note on the counter next to the coffee maker so she'd see it first thing. I was up early, had trouble sleeping. I knew Four needed some shots and so I helped out. I brought him to a vet down in the 'burgh.'" As soon as Nick finished speaking, he grew angry with himself. Why the hell did he need to justify his actions to his brother?

Nick was startled when Gabe jammed his thumb into his chest. "It's not your place."

Nick was unsure if there was a hidden meaning. "Not my place?" *Does he mean to help with the dog or Avalon Hills?*

Gabe barked, "No, it's not. Mom and Dad have taken care of their dog for years."

"A vet is a vet. It was just a shot, Gabe. What's your problem anyway?"

"You're my problem, *brother*."

"You get that line from a movie or something?"

Gabe stepped closer to his older but slightly shorter brother.

Nick detected blueberry on his breath. For the first time since he was eleven and Gabe was eight, Nick expected them to come to blows. Unlike decades ago, Nick knew this time his physically fit brother, Sheriff Garrison, would come out the victor.

Gabe studied the perimeter. Nowadays pimply faced teenagers and anarchistic assholes loitered in the shadows, thirsting to record some incident of police brutality. Had Gabe not been in uniform he'd have no problem putting his snooping brother in his place. He backpedaled a couple feet, collected his thoughts. In a more civil tone, he asked, "What'd the vet say?"

"About what?"

"About the dog, Nick. What do you think?"

"I thought you were a sheriff, not a detective."

Gabe snarled, "Just answer me, for fuck's sake."

Nick shrugged. "She said nothing. It's just a damn shot. Jesus, Gabe."

Gabe was about to respond when a tinny voice emanated

from his collar-mounted walkie. He held up one finger. *Stay right here.*

Nick watched his brother walk out of earshot. First Gabe stiffened, became rigid. Then he ran his fingers through his full head of black hair. Pacing mindlessly at the rear of the police cruiser, he placed his palms on the trunk. Impatiently, Nick stood. More time passing for no reason.

Gabe advanced on him quickly. Halfway between the two cars, he called out, "We'll continue this another time." He made a gun with his hand, lowered his thumb like a hammer on a revolver.

Nick smirked at the melodrama. He watched Sheriff Garrison speed away. "Asshole!"

He lowered himself behind the wheel, glanced in the backseat. Four had coiled himself into a little ball. The dog had endured a hectic morning.

Curiosity got the better of Nick. Just as he felt pulled to drive by Brandi's home first thing this morning that same voice again spoke to him. There was no urgency to get home. His mom hadn't planned any big feast or invited anyone over. Four was conked out. Nick was amped up from the confrontation with Gabe.

He brought the automobile to life and followed his brother.

From about a quarter mile behind for ten minutes, Nick watched the police cruiser turn right, disappearing into the thicket. Nick came to a full stop on the desolate road as he came upon the same unmaintained trail his brother traversed. He was not far from the Jordan Turnout, the location where Nick met Wolfsie. Nick knew that beyond the trees and heavy woodlands lay the Acheron.

If he recalled, there were usually trails that meandered the copses about every third of a mile. Back in the day, the Acheron offered some of the best fishing holes in a seventy mile radius. *Way* back in the day, in another time.

Up the road a bit, Nick came upon another improvised trail. He turned off the main road and began bouncing-shaking-jumping his way along the long-forgotten conduit.

The herky-jerky movement woke Four. The dog put his snout out the window, occasionally biting at an insect.

With the clearing twenty yards ahead, Nick stopped. "You wait here. Be a good boy." He scratched behind Four's triangular ears, left the windows down enough so air could get in but no Westie could get out.

Nick exited and, hunching over, he stealthily advanced. Brushing aside low hanging boughs, stepping on fallen dried branches, Nick had a sense of déjà vu. The only difference between this moment and the one with Brandi over a quarter of a century ago when they witnessed a possible murder was that it was now mid-afternoon.

Brandi. It always came back to her.

Easing aside tree limbs, Nick caught site of his brother. Gabe and two others—deputies, Nick assumed—stood in a circle on the banks of the river. The waters broke delicately at their feet. The trio hovered over an object, their position preventing Nick from determining what the item was.

Gabe was the sheriff but seemed unsure what to do, confused. *Figures.* When his brother backpedaled to the police cruiser, the item they circled became visible. And from Nick's vantage point, it didn't seem to be moving.

The clothes on the lifeless form looked ratty, scruffy and the body was barefoot. Gabe returned from the trunk of his vehicle and draped a blanket over the corpse.

Once again, like almost thirty years ago, a dead body lay along the banks of the Acheron River.

Nick watched the scene for a while. As Sheriff Garrison and his minions wrapped things up, Nick furtively returned to his rental. He managed to turn the vehicle around in the narrow shrubbery and drive away.

Back in town, he drove through a car wash to clean the mud and grime from the Hyundai. And since it was only a short detour, he passed by Brandi's home again. Determining everything was as it should be, he returned home.

"We're back," Nick called out upon entering.

"Four!" Eve shrieked as she scuttled down the hallway. In spite of her age, she had no problem taking a knee. The animated dog rose to his hind legs and furiously licked her face. "Is he okay?" she asked Nick, not drawing her gaze away.

"He's fine, Mom. You saw my note, right?"

Finishing up with Four, Eve croaked and stood. "You didn't have to do that. I could've brought him in."

"It's fine. You're busy enough around here. It's the least I could do to help out."

"What'd the vet say?"

It was the same question his brother had asked. "She said he's fine. Healthy."

"He better be," she replied. "Want a treat?"

Four scurried over to the pantry.

As Nick walked deeper into the home, he peered right and stopped. His brother was pacing animatedly in the living room, apparently having a heated discussion with their father.

Lloyd shot a glance at Nick. Gabe abruptly stopped mid-sentence and eyeballed his brother.

"Gabe," Nick muttered by way of greeting.

Lloyd pulled himself from the sofa and lovingly draped his arm around his second born. "Let's continue discussing this out back."

Within seconds, Nick was alone, isolated, and feeling out of place. It had quickly become evident he didn't belong here. Nor was he wanted here.

⌘

With Eve upstairs catering to Hank's needs, Nick looked at the TV. Not watching, just looking. After an uncomfortable time, his father traipsed into the room. He stood motionless, staring at Nick but saying nothing. With hands shoved deep into his pockets rattling some change, Lloyd evaluated his son.

Nick depressed the mute button. "What is it, sir?"

Lloyd allowed the question to linger before answering. His tone was imperious. "Why did you take the dog to a vet?"

"I just—wanted to help out. You and Mom have been nice enough to let me stay here. She's been cooking non-stop. It's the least I can do."

"He's our dog, not yours."

"With all due respect, it was just a routine shot. I don't—never mind."

"What?"

"I don't see why you and Gabe are so up in arms about this. What's the big deal?"

"Gabe told me he talked to you on the road into town."

Nick snickered. "He pulled me over *then* talked to me."

Father and son glared deep into each other's eyes, each other's soul, searching. Nick lost and broke contact first but sensed his father's icy stare upon him.

Lloyd started to walk away when Nick spoke. "Have I done something to upset you?"

A bemused expression crossed Lloyd's stern face. He snickered. "*You?*"

"Yes, me." Nick asked the question but was shocked at the direct response.

"You most certainly have."

Nick gulped. In a small voice, he asked, "And what exactly have I done?"

Speaking as if he'd been waiting a lifetime to be asked this very question, Lloyd instantaneously shot back. "You've disappointed me greatly."

The jangling of coinage being shuffled in Lloyd's pockets was drowned out by the sound of Nick's heart being ripped apart. A lump in his throat materialized instantly. He hadn't been close to his father since he was ten, maybe eleven. He didn't know when exactly or what exactly caused the rift. He'd spent decades trying to pinpoint the exact moment, a specific incident, when their relationship died. But never discovered one.

Lloyd Garrison may have been home for dinner every evening at six sharp. But he was an absent father in Nick's life.

The distance between Pennsylvania and California first, then Arizona, had only soured a non-existent connection. Hearing the words firsthand, knowing that his father viewed him as a failure, was equivalent to his soul being shredded by a machete.

Nick's lips quivered but no words came out.

Chapter 11

The house was cemetery quiet. Palpable awkwardness hung in the air, strangling life from the Garrison home. Nick wondered if it was always like this at the dinner table or was made worse by his presence.

Eve made small talk, idle chitchat more suited for strangers in an elevator. But even his mom seemed…disturbed…about something. He suspected this wasn't in response to taking Four to a different vet.

Lloyd had only taken a few bites of roast when he pushed back from the table. "I'll be eating in the living room tonight," he broadcast and off he went.

Twirling his fork aimlessly in the mashed potatoes, Nick smirked at the irony. For years, he'd second guessed himself about leaving this town. Or, more appropriately, leaving Brandi. Now, he regretted returning.

The walls asphyxiated him. Not thinking logically, he threw out the idea of staying at Olive Tree Motel in town, but Eve hastily dismissed it. "Nonsense."

Still, Nick had to break free. At least for tonight.

$$\text{\textcurrency}\mathcal{3}\text{\textcurrency}\mathcal{3}$$

Compared to his enormous three-hundred-seventy-pound frame, it looked like a toy phone cradled against Norman's ear. Beads of sweat had been attached to his forehead for years, the armpits of his loud 1970s polyester shirt permanently stained. "Give it ten minutes and if it aint blowin' cold air, come up and I'll put yous in a different room." His slightly high-pitched voice conflicted with his appearance. He nodded mechanically as the hotel guest continued whining.

When the door opened and she entered the motel lobby, he instinctively straightened up and pulled in his gut. He was now down to a slender three-sixty-eight. He tersely ended the call, propped over the counter and presented an unattractive smile. "How may I help yous?"

"Frances Fitzgerald. I have a reservation."

Based on a name like that, he was expecting someone much older. "Oh?"

He flipped through the old-fashioned Rolodex, slipped out a small card. He studied her ID meticulously. Not concerned about fraud, he simply wanted to burn her pleasing smile, height, and weight into his memory.

He slid numerous forms across the counter. Of the five pages, only two were necessary. But it would keep the cute diminutive brunette occupied so he could gawk. Going over and above in the courtesy department, he advised Frannie of the endless array of features the shoddy motel provided. They offered a swimming pool, two—count 'em, *two*—vending machines, and even free HBO. The continental breakfast that consisted of prepackaged muffins delivered fresh every morning was served in their dining room.

Frannie followed his arm. The *dining room* was two dilapidated Formica tables squeezed into a corner under a plastic Ficus tree.

"There's also a restaurant just down the road a ways if yous haven't eaten dinner yet." He stopped, leaned closer and asked, "Have yous eaten yet?"

"Yes, I have. Thanks."

"They also offer the yummiest apple cobbla in three counties. Wouldja be interested in dessert?"

Frannie smiled at the pathetic flirtatious attempt of the giant more than three times her size. "I'm fine."

Yes, you sure is. "We serve breakfast from six until eight. Would you like me to wake yous?"

"Not necessary."

"We don't offer no bellhop services but I'd be more 'den happy ta bring your luggage ta ya room."

"I can manage."

Running out of options, Norman proudly proclaimed the

pool had just been cleaned this morning. "Didja bring a bathing suit?"

Frannie found herself thinking of her husband. The union of she and Davis was for show. However, she was grateful for being out of the dating scene. "I'm here on business. No time for pleasure."

"I always find time fa' pleasure. All work an' no play, right?" Norman laughed at the joke.

Unable to stall any longer, he gave Frannie her keycard. Rather than sliding it along the chipped countertop, he held it out for her and brushed her fingertips. *Warm. Soft.*

"If yous need anything, anything at all, I'm on until midnight."

"Thank you, Norman," Frannie responded with a well-mannered grin. She turned and departed the trifling lobby with Norman's eyes glued to her backside.

Half an hour later, Frannie had showered and changed into a pair of shorts and an oversized Bryce Harper jersey. She called home, touched base with her daughters, and was subjected to an endless barrage of questions from her husband. After checking in with her family, she powered up her laptop while sitting cross-legged on the twin. "Okay, Avalon Hills," she said to herself, "Let's see what your story is."

෮෨෮

Nick aimlessly drove around. The town was quiet, dark, and felt foreign. In spite of growing up here, in spite of the town's appearance not changing much since he fled, he felt no connection to the community. He was an outsider, a visitor in his birthplace.

Wandering, he found himself close to the Penn Turnpike. For a moment, he considered taking the entrance ramp, heading south to Pittsburgh and catching the next flight home. He had returned to Avalon Hills for one reason but there still had been no chance to deliver the news. By now, he just didn't care. His family would find out—eventually.

The only warmth in the chilly town stemmed from the memory of Brandi Conrad. But yet, in spite of the curiosity that wrenched his heart, Nick couldn't even bring himself to contact her.

Brandi was a sunny positive memory from his dark past. She'd always be perfect, beautiful, sweet. She'd always be that stimulating but vulnerable seventeen-year-old with the silent laugh and the slightly upturned nose. Nick preferred to remember her in that light. Since everything else in town had turned to shit, she would also probably disappoint him. Times changed. People changed. Nick didn't want to learn that Brandi changed, too.

He sat alongside the onramp of his escape route and weighed his options. After an internal debate, he headed back into town. He decided he had to quench that thirst, feed that hunger that burned. He had to contact Brandi.

Tonight.

His resolve was strong, determination high. He *needed* to find out. He *needed* to see her.

But by the time he turned onto Hickory Circle, the courage had evaporated. Succumbing to anxiety, he dimmed the headlights and sat across from the weather-beaten home. He wasn't even sure if she still lived there. But she once had and that was good enough. As much as he wanted to keep her precious memory untarnished, always remember her the way she was, he also wanted to imagine her still living in the same home. It was a futile attempt for Nick to believe that at least some things in life remained consistent. He lost track of time, staring at the ramshackle home. His eyes closed. His mind withdrew to a happier time. It was a moment when he had his entire life ahead of him, all his dreams intact. He was ready to take on the world. Exultant recollections when everything and anything was possible. Long before Nick—and everyone he knew—had been worn down by life.

He couldn't recall the restaurant he dined at with Gwen just a week ago. He needed his cell to remember her birthday. He never could recall the names of her bratty nieces. But with Brandi, although over a quarter of a century had passed, he remembered every detail.

Even back in the 80s, the living room furniture appeared antiquated, outdated, and mismatched. The green shag carpet, the fireplace that never worked with family photos atop the mantel, the console TV, the abundance of owl paraphernalia her mother jammed into every nook, the backyard swimming pool that smacked of too much chlorine.

What is Gwen's best friend's name? Megan? Morgan? Maggie?

He evoked the image of Brandi floating from the kitchen one night, moving in a rhythmic fluid motion as if she was one with the universe, a large bowl of vanilla ice cream drenched in chocolate syrup. She felt comfortable enough around Nick that she could eat what she wanted and not worry about her waistline in his presence. They sat cuddled against each other on the sofa, eyes glued to MTV, eagerly waiting for the next video. Brandi turned him on to Neil Young and April Wine. He got her into Def Leppard and Whitesnake.

They'd sit and watch *Family Ties*, *The A-Team* with that guy from *Rocky III* and *Dallas*.

"Did you hear that Bruce Willis from *Moonlighting* is going to make an action film?" she asked one night.

Nick shrieked. "Are you joking?"

"No, that's what I heard on *A Current Affair*."

The thought of David Addison Jr. transitioning to the silver screen and becoming another Stallone was downright laughable. "Yeah, right," Nick snarled. "And the guy from *Terminator* will become a politician."

He and Brandi smoked pot on occasion, once tried cocaine. While her parents were in town getting drunk at Texas Jack's, their make out sessions were intense, heated, passionate. They were two lovers wrestling in the darkness, unable to quell not just their raging hormones but their desire for each other, physically and emotionally.

She had purchased some cheap beer with her fake ID and invited Nick over to watch *9½ Weeks*. The erotic sexual thriller with Kim Basinger and Mickey Rourke was considered soft porn in its day. Several attempts were made, but he and Brandi never made it through the film, always double-timing it to her bedroom where they went at each other with unbridled passion. Though they never went *all the way.*

Nick now found his eyes tracking to the south portion of

the house, the window to Brandi's bedroom, or at least her former bedroom. What he saw snapped him back to reality. Peering through parted slats were dark eyes staring back at him.

Nick had been discovered. Snooping? Stalking? Trespassing?

The slats tightened, the face gone.

It had to be Brandi. It *had* to be. Now what? Drive away or go up to the front door? How long had she been watching him for? If he'd claim he was just driving by, she'd know he was lying had she been observing for more than five seconds.

The porch light came on, the worn door opened, and the homeowner stepped out. It was not Brandi.

He strode from the house with aggressive strides and approached the motionless yellow car situated in the center of the cul-de-sac.

Nick and the resident locked eyes for a prolonged few seconds.

Dressed in a black muscle tee, black cammo trousers, black sneakers, black spikey hair, and with piercings in his lips, nostrils, and one eyebrow, he shouted, "Hey!" His defiant tone matched his body language.

Nick tramped the gas pedal, squealed away as if fleeing a crime scene. Fishtailing slightly, he glanced over his shoulder to see the homeowner jog to the corner and gaze down the street.

Nick's heart pounded in his neck. He wasn't *really* doing anything wrong. There was no law against looking at a house, was there? It was a little after nine, too early for a potential burglar to be casing a home. But he sure didn't need the pierced homeowner calling the cops and, in turn, another confrontation with his brother the sheriff. Surely, there weren't many mustard-colored Hyundai's driving around Avalon Hills.

Whoever he was, the man not only had a combative demeanor but he looked somewhat familiar. Six feet tall, a few pounds overweight, late teens, maybe early twenties.

Where do I know him from? Nick was only a few blocks away when he heard the opening notes to Van Halen's "Panama."

He answered the cell phone, the number not immediately recognizable.

"Nick, that you?"

"Wolfsie?"

"Nick-fucking-Garrison. Where you at, man?"

"Just—you know, driving around."

"No shit? Hey, you anywhere near Texas Jack's?"

It clicked. That explained the background noise and the clear-cut slurring of his friend's words. "No, but I can be."

"Yeah, fuckin'-A. Why don't you get your sorry ass down here and meet your old buddy for a drink? I'm buying."

He knew firsthand Wolfsie was not a *happy drunk.* The thought of spending time with an intoxicated Ed Wolfe was less than appealing. But Nick had nowhere else to be. "Sure, okay. Give me about ten minutes."

"See you then, Nick fucking Garrison."

Nick returned the cell to his pocket. "Nick fucking Garrison. That's me."

Chapter 12

Texas Jack's was not a bar. It was a saloon. Styled after what most northerners envisioned the Lone Star State to be, the establishment was outfitted with mechanical bulls and barmaids in tight Wranglers and ten-gallon hats. The jukebox contained five genres: Traditional Country, Modern Country, Classic Country, Alternative Country, and Bluegrass.

Walking in, Nick was greeted by who he thought sounded like Johnny Cash. Traditional Country.

A pair of truck drivers was at the pool table, taking turns impressing a girl on a stool with too much leg showing. A pair of thirty-something's busied themselves at the dart board. Another patron slumped over the bar, either sleeping or about to pass out.

"Over here," shouted a visibly inebriated Wolfsie.

Nick sashayed over. Wolfsie struggled to his feet and fell against him. "My one true friend," he garbled while embracing Nick tightly.

"Okay, buddy, okay." Nick eased his wobbly friend back onto the barstool. From over the bar he was greeted by a look of concern. The bartender was a sweet academic-looking type. Curly blonde hair, crystal blue eyes, and wire-framed eyeglasses, she cocked her head as if saying, *Over here.* She looked too young to drink, much less work here. Nick wasn't getting older. Everyone around him was getting younger.

As Wolfsie drunkenly peeled the label from the bottle, Nick met the barmaid a few stools over.

"Your buddy's really sloshed. I tried to cut him off twenty minutes ago but he refused."

Nick though of Karri Wolfe and the lump in her breast. "He's got a lot going on right now."

"We all do," she replied. "But I can't serve him anymore and then have him go out an' kill someone. People round 'ere don't like this place anyway, and we don't need any more bad publicity. That's why I had 'em call ya'll."

Nick was flattered that, after all these years, Wolfsie thought of him first. He also wondered if the bartender really was from Texas. Her accent seemed pretty solid.

"I'll give ya one on the house but then I need you to take 'em home."

"I'll have whatever's on tap." Noticing her nameplate, he added, "Thanks, Jennifer."

By the time Nick slid alongside his friend, Wolfsie spoke. "Jennifer, my little Texas rose." He draped his arm over Nick's shoulder. "You know who this guy is?"

"Can't say I do," she replied evenly, dragging a rag across the countertop.

"This is Nick."

"Hi, Nick," she responded perfunctorily.

"Nick-fucking-Garrison."

Jennifer stopped and eyed Nick with a curious expression. "Garrison?"

Nick nodded embarrassedly. His surname was well-known.

"Any relation to Sheriff Garrison?"

"That's my brother, but we don't really talk."

Jennifer pursed her lips. "So, Mayor Garrison is your daddy?"

"We don't really talk either."

Jennifer's smile was now warm, almost over the top. She dabbed her hands on her jeans, extended her arm. "Pleased to meet you, Nick Garrison."

"You, also."

"Not just Nick Garrison," garbled Wolfsie. "Nick-*FUCKING*-Garrison."

Moments later, Nick steered/shoved Wolfsie to a booth in the far corner at Jennifer's request. She didn't want Wolfsie's drunken ass falling on the floor, sustaining a concussion, and then slapping her with a lawsuit.

As it was, a patron slipped on some hay strands a few years back and sued. The owner of Texas Jack's had to fork over big bucks and was ordered by the judge's ruling to alter the decor.

After some time in the restrictive booth, Wolfsie's eyes gained some clarity. "So, man, you thought about what we talked about?"

"About Karri?"

"Yeah."

Nick turned his palms up. "Nothing to think about. You guys are more than welcome to stay with me if she wants to get treatment in Phoenix. A second opinion never hurts." When Wolfsie answered with only a million-mile gaze, Nick added, "Or did you mean for me to talk to her?"

Wolfsie looked away, stared at the shapely legs by the pool table. The pretty blonde with a worn face smiled back.

"Over here," Nick said, snapping his fingers at his friend's nose. "If you want—"

"What I want is some help, damn it."

"Sure, anything for you. You know that."

Wolfsie scowled. "Yeah, sure."

Nick had met his friend twice since returning home and, again, he sensed his pal was holding something back. He knew, unfortunately all too well, some of what Wolfsie was feeling, was thinking. Nick was surprised when his friend wiped a tear from his eye.

Wolfsie abruptly blurted, "What do you think happens after we die?"

Alcohol. It leads to some interesting topics. "Hell, I don't know. I try not to think about it."

Wolfsie's boisterous laugh caused eyes to turn toward them. "You work in a cemetery, Nick. How can you not? Jesus, man. That's like a…I don't know…a surgeon who doesn't like the sight of blood or something."

Nick grinned. His friend had a valid point. "I don't know. Death is just a part of life, I guess."

"Not a good part."

"No, not a good part."

Wolfsie fisted his eyes, leaned back. "You know what the biggest irony of all is? It comes to all of us. You work at a cemetery. You see it. Even in death, the rich people get some huge mausoleum with marble fucking pillars like they're, I don't know, fucking royalty. And poor people get a marker in the ground and, if the family's poor, the weeds grow over and within a year you can't even see the person's name."

Nick nodded a confirmation.

"Rich, poor," continued Wolfsie philosophically. "CEO of a huge-ass company or some poor bastard garbage collector, we're all going the same way, man." He waved his arms around. "None of this shit really matters."

"I guess just make the most of the time we have." Nick hated to resort to such a platitude when his friend was looking for an answer to why his wife was being taken at a young age. But Wolfsie was drunk and Nick was not in the right frame of mind to discuss the meaning of life. Or death.

Nick's own words reverberated in his mind. Time was indeed short. It went too fast. He spat out, "Ever know what became of Brandi?"

Wolfsie's face morphed into a bizarre expression, one Nick couldn't identify. "Brandi?"

"Yeah, Brandi Conrad."

"Bedroom eyes, great ass, killer legs, sexy as hell Brandi Conrad?"

Nick felt slighted the way Wolfsie referred to her. "That's her."

"Oh, shit, man. I forgot you and her had a…what *did* you have exactly all those years back?"

Nick blurted out without a second thought. "A connection."

Wolfsie laughed as his mind travelled back to high school. "You lucky bastard, she was hotter than hot. I bet she was a freak in bed, huh?"

Nick grunted something between a yes, no, and I don't know.

"Yeah, I can tell she was by the way you're acting." Wolfsie leaned over, slapped Nick hard on the shoulder. "Good for you. That's why you're Nick-fucking-Garrison."

"Thanks, I think. So…Brandi, you know if she's still here in town?"

"I'm going to do you a favor." He moved his hands as if he had just washed them and there were no towel. "Jennifer, my Texas rose, be a doll and bring me something to write on."

Jennifer came from around the bar. She handed Wolfsie a piece of paper, a pen, and then eyed Nick while tapping her wristwatch. Wolfsie observed her shapely figure disappear behind the bar and then scribbled an address. "Here you go, my man. Don't say I never did anything for you."

Nick felt his pulse increase as he took the paper. It looked like an Avalon Hills address. "Is this…Brandi's address?"

"No, it's Brooke's."

Nick furrowed a brow. "Brooke Lauser, Mike's widow?"

"That's the one."

"Brooke knows how to get hold of Brandi?"

"You got questions? She's got answers."

Nick studied the address as if it could speak to him. He suddenly was unsure if he wanted an answer to the question about Brandi. Plus, even though he had liked Brooke, the little he knew of her, he'd feel strange around her. Her husband had just killed himself. Nick never was comfortable conducting himself around grieving individuals.

Nick propped his friend against a wall and opened the door of Texas Jack's. Wolfsie started to topple but Nick caught him in time. Guiding him to the street, Nick announced his plan. "I'll run you home. Then we can come back and get your car tomorrow."

"You're a good guy, man," slurred Wolfsie. "A true friend." He then pirouetted and shouted into the desolate street, "Ladies and gentleman, Nick-fucking-Garrison!"

Nick laughed. "Okay, buddy." He draped his arm over Wolfsie's shoulder and shepherded his inebriated friend toward the rental car.

"I think I'm gonna be—" Wolfsie pulled his arm across his gut, bent at the waist and doubled over. He dry heaved but didn't vomit. He stepped left and steadied his unstable body against a brick wall. Swallowing his dinner again, Wolfsie's perpetually sad eyes grew despondent. He stared at Nick, shoulders rising and sinking. "I—I don't wanna."

"Don't want to what?"

"Lose her. I can't. Karri's my life."

The combination of alcohol and his wife's breast cancer caused emotions to flow out of Wolfsie. Unable to contain the tears, he burst like a dam.

Nick moved closer and man-hugged his friend. "It'll be okay." He knew his words were unconvincing. Hopefully, Wolfsie was too buzzed to notice the hollow encouragement. "We'll take it one day at a time. See what happens. You never know."

The two longtime friends embraced, unaware of the approaching pedestrian. Nick was unexpectedly shoved from Wolfsie's grip. "What the fuck did you say?" screamed Wolfsie in a challenging tone.

The man turned. "I didn't say a word."

Nick hadn't heard a thing. But when he about-faced, his eyes opened wide. Piercings everywhere. It was the same guy who walked out of Brandi's old home. He was a bit paunchy but his dark clothes, heavily inked arms, and defiant posture left no doubt. This guy was trouble.

Wolfsie shouted. "I heard what you said. Say it again, you chicken shit bastard."

"Easy, Wolfsie." Nick slipped his arm across his friend's chest as a makeshift barrier.

The pierced badass turned to Nick. "You better keep your friend away from me." His voice was deep, threatening. Even his tongue was studded.

Nick attempted to ease Wolfsie back, surprised by his friend's rigidity. "Settle down." Over his shoulder, he added, "He's just been drinking."

"Come on, Hawkeye. Say it again. Say it again, motherfucker!"

The black clad man who stepped from Brandi's house again warned Nick. "Get him away from me." But he stepped closer, as if seeking a confrontation.

Nick had no idea what was going on. Had these men shared a history of some sort? And what were the odds that the same guy who exited Brandi's home just happened to be wandering down Main Street at this exact time? Had he come seeking an altercation?

Or had he followed Nick?

Nick didn't want to use too much force. His friend was livid but also unstable on his feet.

Before he realized it, Wolfsie slipped passed him and leapt at the man called Hawkeye.

He fired a long arcing roundhouse. Catching only air, not even coming close, he nearly lost his own balance. Hawkeye easily avoided the futile punch. He darted left and threw a blistering one-two combination into Wolfsie's gut.

"That's enough!" Nick yelled, stepping between the combatants. He pushed the pierced man aside, crouched next to Wolfsie.

Unable to hold down dinner this time, Wolfsie retched on the sidewalk. The other man walked away laughing.

After splattering the pavement, Wolfsie's staggered for a moment. He saw Nick's mustard mobile and upchucked again.

Nick asked the question for two reasons. "Who is that guy anyway?"

"Hawkeye. He's our town badass. Punk kid."

Nick looked north along the deserted street. He'd seemingly been swallowed by the night. "Hawkeye?"

"Yeah. You saw the way he looks. Even heard through the grapevine he's got a Prince Albert, you know. The tip of his dick pierced."

Nick instinctively winced. "Any guy who does that qualifies as a bad-ass in my book."

Realizing his stomach contents were fully redistributed on the street, Wolfsie explained. "Remember that show, *M.A.S.H*? Alan Alda. Hawkeye Pierce? People around town started calling him Hawkeye. Hawkeye Piercing."

Nick was now pleased he hadn't knocked on the front door of Brandi's old home and been confronted by its owner, a guy with metal poking through his genitalia.

"What else can you tell me about Hawkeye?"

"Best advice, my friend, is to stay away from him."

"You didn't," Nick pointed out unnecessarily.

"I'm drunk, that's why. But him?" Wolfsie pointed up to his temple. "He's not normal."

⌘

After depositing Wolfsie at home, Nick headed over to the Lauser residence. It was late and Mike's widow was most likely asleep but he took a shot. Brooke could supposedly provide answers. He was unsure why Wolfsie couldn't share the information himself. Perhaps Brooke and Brandi had become friends? Whatever the reason, Nick needed to fill the void in his heart and find out about Brandi.

He'd spent hours yesterday, searching online through various websites dedicated to locating old friends, former classmates, and lost loves. Brandi fell into all three categories. He accessed the website for Avalon High and located their alumnus section. Nothing.

It was as if Brandi never existed.

The Lauser home as expected, was dark. Nick was disappointed but also relieved. He always felt he came off as insincere when expressing remorse to grieving family members. He drove away.

Compelled by a tug deep within, as if it had become part of his daily regimen, he again found himself en route to Brandi's one-time home. A mile away, however, he stopped. He didn't want to encounter the town badass dubbed Hawkeye. Plus, it was obvious Brandi no longer lived there. Why bother?

He cruised around Avalon Hills a bit before returning home. The Garrison house was silent. For the first time since returning to Avalon Hills, Nick hesitated before entering. He had yet to feel welcome and, tonight, the feeling of being unwanted was overpowering. He again contemplated checking into the rundown Olive Tree.

Entering, Nick was immediately greeted by the jangling of a dog collar. "Hey, Four," he said as he squatted and massaged the Westie's ears. The cheerful dog yipped once, spun in a circle, and made his intentions clear. Nick took the dog's lead and ambled to the pantry closet. After rewarding Four with a Milk Bone, Nick trekked upstairs. He halted when hearing the disturbance.

Just like this morning, the conversation seemed muted, unintelligible. No lights were on in the house. *Outside*? Recalling the stealthy exchange between his father and brother, Nick went to the kitchen and gazed through the window facing the backyard. Empty.

Stone-like, he suppressed his breathing. After a moment of silence, he heard it again. Unclear. It was a conversation but words were unidentifiable. It was as if someone was talking in tongues.

He walked across the home and exited the front door. He half-heartedly expected to see the same man he noticed when he peered out from Uncle Hank's bedroom that morning.

His mind shifted into overdrive, his stomach tightened. As Nick recalled the spectral vision in the shadowy dusk, he started reflecting. The being was not well-defined, cloaked in the shadows of sunup. Nick had been unable to detect specific features but his frame and features were hauntingly familiar. *Hawkeye.*

And maybe, just maybe, it was the same image Nick glimpsed in the thicket along the Acheron River after meeting Wolfsie.

Is this guy following me?

Nick couldn't be sure. The coincidence would be uncanny. He now wondered how random the altercation outside Texas Jack's truly was.

Nick didn't know what to make of the irony. While he was busy spying on Brandi's old home, someone was spying on him.

Middle of a humid summer be damned, Nick felt chilled to his bone. He went back inside. Reaching the apex of the stairs, he again picked up the muttering. He realized the source of it was emanating from his uncle's room.

Standing in the doorway, the stench of urine seemed less pronounced. Or perhaps Nick, like his mom, was getting accustomed to the odor. At first everything seemed as it should be. Normal. *Animal Planet* was muted, a crocodile lying in shallow waters displayed. "Runaround Sue" played softly in the background. The only thing abnormal was Hank himself.

As always he sat flaccid in his chair. However, the rotary phone sat on his blanket-wrapped lap, the handset cradled against his ear.

"Uncle Hank, you okay?" Nick whispered, crossing the threshold. Catatonic, Hank didn't stir.

Overcome by sadness, Nick gulped, a futile attempt to push down the rising sadness.

Standing alongside his uncle, Nick eased the handset from Hank's surprisingly strong grip. As fingers unclenched, his uncle's head fell back, his neck seemingly unable to provide any support. A grunt tumbled from his crooked mouth. His dead eyes stared lifelessly up into an abyss of oblivion.

Nick noticed a folded blanket at the foot of the seldom used hospital bed. He folded it up as best he could, making it as small as possible, and sandwiched it in between the rear of his uncle's clammy neck and the wall. "There you go, all nice and comfy." His tone was overly joyful.

Full circle, Nick thought as he wretchedly regarded the shell the man had become. Grownups always conversed in an excessively happy, cheerfully irritating tone when conversing with a newborn. It was the same tone nurses and physicians used on people at the other end of the life spectrum as well. Full circle.

Nick found himself using the same inflection with what remained of Hank.

When Uncle Hank met his stare, Nick became paralyzed. A groan, an unidentifiable murmuring, was released from Hank. He sounded not like a man trapped in his own mind but like an animal dying a slow torturous death.

It was a flash, an instant. But for a fleeting second, Nick thought he saw a trace of alertness in those morose detached eyes. Recognition? Did Hank know his nephew? His lips quivered. His mouth opened and closed in a repetitive "O" shape. It was as if he was struggling to speak, to say something.

Nick watched in speechless wonder. Was his uncle coming to? Had he started regaining some mental acuity? Nick was about to call out to his mom but the moment already passed. Any hope for a miracle vanished in the blink of an eye. Hank's head lobbed back as if controlled by an invisible puppeteer. Nick wondered if he imagined the whole thing. Should he even mention this to his mom? Eve had spent three years caretaking her brother, bucking the odds, and hoping for a miracle that would never come. Would telling her what he saw—what he *thought* he saw—only make reality that much harder to accept? Physically Hank was present. But he'd never return from the journey his mind had taken.

Nick moved the antiquated rotary phone to the small table. Instinctively, he raised the handset. "Hello?"

Dead quiet. Then he noticed the phone wasn't even plugged into a jack. He didn't understand why the phone was here in the first place. Hank couldn't speak, could barely hold it. And now, Nick realized it was unplugged. Tomorrow, he'd ask his mom what exactly the point was.

Nick tenderly squeezed the skeletal shoulder. "Good night, Uncle Hank."

Looking back toward the casing that imprisoned his uncle, Nick departed the room. It *was* a good question: What exactly was the point?

Chapter 13

With sweat beading his brow, Gabe continued trying but it wasn't happening. His mind wandered in a million directions, thoughts clouding his focus.

"You want to take me from behind?"

He glanced down, hesitated for a moment, and withdrew from his wife.

"What's wrong, babe?"

Gabe said nothing as he swung his legs over the side of the bed. When he felt Yolanda turn and pat his back, he stood and walked away.

Yolanda rolled onto her back and stared at the ceiling. Gabe was distant, withdrawn. She watched him enter the bathroom and, behind a closed door, heard the water. After sex, Gabe always showered, cleansing his wife off him. It was one of the many things that had begun to irritate her.

The comment her brother-in-law made the other day had stuck in her craw. When Nick innocently asked how she was adjusting to being an empty nester, she hadn't considered it. Until now.

Their children were gone and, for the first time since the early days of their marriage, it was just she and Gabe. As they raised their children together, they grew apart. It was evident that during these last twenty-plus years, husband and wife became strangers.

Volunteering and occasional blogging were no longer rewarding. Yolanda knew Heavenly Father brought her and Gabe together. He had a master plan. But as she lay lonely in bed, she considered some time away would soothe her restlessness. Her oldest was in Washington. Perhaps she'd plan a visit, get away for a few days, and come home reborn.

Gabe exited the bathroom. In spite of his inability to perform sexually he exhibited confidence bordering on arrogance. Naked, he walked to his side of the bed. As he lowered himself next to his wife, he faced away.

"Is it me?" Yolanda asked sheepishly.

Gabe sneered. "Well, it sure as hell isn't me."

⌘

The curtain of sleep was drawn back and Nick found himself gazing at the ceiling. He'd been woken by the sound again. Shaking away the cobwebs, he realized this time it was different. The words *were* intelligible. Unlike the haphazard gurgling that emanated from Uncle Hank's room, he recognized this to be a coherent conversation.

After glancing through the window and not seeing Hawkeye reconnoitering the Garrison home, Nick glanced at the clock: almost 8 a.m. Determining he was not being watched, he tramped down the hallway and took the stairs. Approaching the first floor, the conversation became defined. The voices belonged to his brother and his father. *Why is Gabe here so early?* Whenever Nick approached, they hushed their conversation or took it outside. Therefore, he now crept to the bottom step, pressed his back against the wall, and eavesdropped.

"You sure it was Jonathan Decker?" he heard his father ask.

"Yes," Gabe sighed.

"What are you going to do about this?"

"Me? I thought this was *us*."

"Not any longer, son. I washed my hands a long time ago. It's yours now."

"You're the mayor."

Nick was surprised at the forceful tone his brother used when speaking to the Garrison patriarch.

"We both know it's only a title, son. Just like yours. Sheriff. The position doesn't amount to a hill of beans."

"But this is our town."

"And as sheriff of *our* town, it's your duty to protect us."

Nick heard his brother take a deep breath and exhale slowly. "And to do what's right?"

Lloyd prophesized. "Sometimes what's right and what's best do not go hand in hand."

A pause. "And on top of all of this, I've got that bitch from the Department of Commerce snooping around. She wants to, as she says, *talk*." Gabe sounded like he was weighing a heavy burden.

Bitch? Nick knew that Lloyd never allowed profanity. But in Gabe's case, he apparently made an exception. "You're my son. I know you can handle this."

Eve's body abruptly jerked. "Good heavens, Nick, you startled me."

So engrossed in listening in, he hadn't heard his mother's oncoming footsteps. He tried to play it off. "Mornin' Mom. I was just coming down for coffee." Nick revealed himself. "Good morning, sir. Gabe."

Father and brother stared at Nick then exchanged an uneasy glance between each other.

Gabe glared at his brother and commented to Lloyd, "I'll call you later, Dad."

"Please do."

Dad? Nick was expected to call his father sir.

Gabe paraded by his brother, the expression of repulsion spoke volumes. "Bye, Mom," he said as he kissed her cheek and departed.

With Gabe gone, parents and son stood awkwardly. Deafening silence as they each watched the other. It was the gunfight at the conclusion of *The Good, the Bad, and the Ugly*. Unlike Tuco, it was Eve who drew first. "I was just heading out to the store to pick up a few things."

Locked in a death stare, Nick and his father peered into each other's soul. Lloyd wondered how much his son had overheard. Nick wondered why he and his father had nothing between them.

Although they only stood fifteen feet away, they were worlds apart.

"I'll go, Mom."

"To the store?" Eve bellowed.

"Yes." Nick glared at his father a moment longer then added, "Please. I need to get the—get out of here."

Lloyd now spoke. "You can get out of here anytime you like."

∽∾∽

Struggling to decipher Eve's chicken-scratching on the shopping list, Nick's blood boiled. He ripped items from the shelves, flung them into the shopping cart, and grew more livid by the second.

Since returning to Avalon Hills—and what a mistake it was—Nick had been insulted and shunned. His father's condescending tone was more evident than ever, his remarks biting and hurtful. His brother's holier-than-thou brashness was beyond infuriating.

Nick blamed himself to a point. He'd never been close with either of them. Why should he now expect anything different?

With good reason, Wolfsie was distraught about his wife's health. Still, Nick was growing tired of his puzzling comments, statements that appeared laced with hidden meaning.

His other best friend from childhood, Mike Lauser, reached his breaking point and splattered his brains across the bedroom. And his wife didn't even have a proper burial, not allowing anyone to pay respects.

The whole thing sucked.

Picking up some frozen carrots, Nick decided he'd leave tomorrow. Screw it. He wouldn't even tell anyone why he'd come in the first place. No one was happy to see him, so they wouldn't miss him when he was gone.

The only thing that kept him sane these last few days was Brandi. But Nick decided to forego her as well. He preferred to remember the way she used to be: young, fun, beautiful, a slightly flawed angel. She'd always be frozen in time at seventeen. He chose to leave her memory untarnished. He couldn't deal with any more disappointment.

He wheeled the cart to his car, loaded the groceries with little care, and violently slammed the trunk. That's when he heard the voice.

"Nick?"

He spun, blinked repeatedly. He felt his heartbeat skyrocket. "Brandi?"

"It *is* you!"

Before Nick realized it, Brandi's body was against him. He was too surprised to return the sincere amorous hug. Then his hands finally made their way to her mid back and he pressed his heart against hers. He clutched her tightly, never wanting to let go.

The intensity of the long embrace left no doubt. This was more than two old friends running into each other. He felt Brandi's body ease back. But Nick didn't relent. He held her a bit longer.

At five-four, Brandi fit perfectly against Nick. Two pieces of a puzzle.

She stepped back. "Let me look at you." She held his hands, extended his arms. "You look great, Nicky."

Nicky. She was the only one who ever called him that. He hadn't heard it since he was a kid.

"I'm turning gray. But look at *you.*"

"Gray fits you. Very debonair."

For the first time since he could remember, he laughed. "If I had a dollar every time someone told me I looked debonair I'd have…well, a dollar."

Brandi laughed. The chuckle was the same as Nick remembered. A broad silent laugh with narrowing eyes as she threw her head back. She hadn't changed one iota.

Seeing the expression, the way she chortled without a sound, the smile that crossed her lips, Nick felt as if not one day has passed.

Wearing faded unflattering Khaki's, a three day beard, and an unbecoming green polo shirt, he said embarrassedly, "I look like crap."

The smile was still plastered on her face. "I'm wearing old sweatpants, an oversized orange shirt and you think *you* look like crap?" She stepped closer, whispered into his ear, "I'm not even wearing a bra." Then she laughed.

Same ol' Brandi, always keeping him on his toes. "I—didn't notice."

"You always used to gawk at my chest. You didn't switch teams on me, did you?"

"No."

"Good. That'd be a waste."

As quickly as the conversation erupted, it ground to a halt. Nick Garrison and Brandi Conrad stared into each other's longing yet empty eyes, relishing the moment. Once again, time stopped in Brandi's presence. Nick once heard somewhere that true love is being able to stare at each other in silence, not having to fill the quietness with pointless drivel. Just let the moment capture you and overwhelm your heart. Allow the magic in, revel in it, bask in the glow. He'd never bought into the mumbo-jumbo until this very moment.

Love-struck, he lost himself in Brandi's captivating brown-black eyes. Sexy but innocent, confident yet vulnerable. "You look…the same. Haven't aged at all."

Brandi threw her head back with a flourish. "It's called dye and having a talented girl do my hair."

"It's more than your hair stylist."

"I heard you were back in town, Nicky."

"Oh? From who?"

"Small town, people talk."

"Some things never change," Nick replied and then considered the Freudian comment. Brandi looked unblemished, radiant as ever. The butterflies in his nervous stomach and the liquefaction in his knees were proof. *Some things never change.*

Feigning hurt, she stuck out her bottom lip and asked pouty, "And why haven't you stopped by to see me, huh?"

Back on his heels, Nick stammered. "I just hadn't—I just didn't. I mean—I don't even know where—"

"Is knowing I'm braless making you nervous?" She winked.

"Same old you. Don't ever change."

"Me, change? Never." Brandi waited, and then repeated the question.

"You've always enjoyed making me blush, haven't you?" Nick claimed.

"It's easy. And so much fun."

Nick scratched his head because he didn't know what else

to do. His eyes dropped to her left hand. But the way she stood, he couldn't clearly see her ring finger.

As always, nothing slipped by her. Brandi extended her arm, bent her wrist and displayed her finger. "Is this what you want to know?"

"Umm…well, yeah. I guess."

"No, I'm not married."

Nick exhaled relief, wondered if she noticed. He didn't need to ask the natural follow-up. Brandi knew him better than anyone, seemingly able to read his mind and know his thoughts. "And no, I have no guy in my life."

Nick played her game. "*You* didn't join the other team, did you?"

"Tried it, wasn't my thing."

"Oh?" Nick's face reddened.

"You're blushing again."

"No I'm not," he insisted.

"Well, you are now." She chuckled. "You've seen the guys in this town. Can you blame me for trying?"

"I guess you have a point. I'm glad you're…you know."

"Glad I'm what, straight?"

Nick's head bobbed in a yes-no motion. "That, sure. And that you're you know—single."

"And what about you? Any special lady in your life?"

"Nope."

Brandi frowned. "Too bad."

Nick emitted a nervous laugh. "Why?"

"It'd be more fun to steal you away. More…forbidden. Competition is good for the soul."

Nick laughed. "Jesus, Brand."

"*What*?" she cried.

"You're great, always have been."

She smiled and stepped forward, unable to quell the urge. She again tightly wrapped herself around Nick. This time, he immediately reciprocated. He closed his eyes and allowed his mind to travel back through time. More than a quarter century had passed. But no time had passed. Nick was a teenager again. His life and dreams intact, the girl he'd never stopped thinking about held tightly against his heart. It felt…right. It felt like it was supposed to, like it was meant to be this way all along.

He breathed in, sniffing her hair. He liked her shampoo. He found his hands on the small of her back.

Brandi angled her head, looked into Nick's eyes, their lips inches apart. "Are you trying to grab my ass?"

Nick hesitated. "Well, no…I mean, I…well—"

"I told you I'm not wearing a bra. Now you want to know if I'm not wearing panties." She stepped back from him but never pulled her eyes away. "Nicky Garrison," she muttered and patted his cheek.

Dominant silence filled the parking lot. No shoppers, no cars, no passers-by. Looking at Brandi, nothing and no one else mattered.

"I wasn't even sure you still lived here," Nick spoke.

"You know what they say? Seeing is believing." She vacillated, added, "And tell me, Nicky, do you believe?"

"I do now."

She smiled. "How long will you be in town?"

Fifteen minutes earlier in the frozen food aisle, he'd made his decision. "I was thinking of leaving tomorrow."

"You can't."

"How come?"

"'Cause tomorrow, I'm taking you out."

Chapter 14

atience was a virtue Nick always lacked. And especially now, with the recent developments in his life, he had good reason. Life truly did go too fast.

He paced anxiously in the parking lot of *Kitty's Kustom Designs*. The merchant sold a wide array of seductive nightwear such as baby doll nighties and teddies. It was always Halloween at *Kitty's*. They maintained a wide array of nurse, French maid, and cheerleader outfits. The lot was around the corner and down a side street out of sight. It allowed the women of Avalon Hills to fulfill their fantasies and fetishes—or that of their lovers—without bearing the disapproving gaze of the judgmental citizenry.

Nick found it strange that Brandi requested picking up him up here. He understood her apprehension coming by his house. Why deal with Lloyd Garrison unless it was absolutely necessary? He was, however, bemused she would not give him her address. He doubted she still lived in her childhood home, the same one he saw the pierced Hawkeye emerge from.

Still, Nick pondered. Everything had been a disappointment since coming back. He had no reason not to trust her. She wasn't married, didn't have a boyfriend. On the other hand, her behavior was somewhat curious.

More time passed.

Nick waited.

This was a good impatience.

It was 6:02 when a car pulled up and Brandi waved through the open window of her Nissan. "Sorry I'm late."

Nick did a two-step, unsure if she'd get out and they'd hug. He took the safer route and got in.

She leaned over, slid her arm across Nick's shoulders, and

half-hugged him. *Less intense than yesterday morning.* Brandi may be unattached but that didn't mean she was ready for something.

"You're all dressed up," she remarked after eying him.

Free of stubble, wearing a conservative blue striped shirt, black Khaki's, and new dress shoes he'd purchased earlier today, he dismissed it.

"You look…stunning," he noted.

He couldn't help speaking from the heart. Her jet black hair was done up perfectly, similar to the way she wore it in the '80s. Just the right amount of lipstick and rouge. Teal eyeliner contrasted perfectly with her dark eyes. The snug black skirt that hung above her knees rode halfway up her curvaceous legs that were hidden by black stockings. Wearing a form fitting leopard print top, she'd gone from being braless yesterday to perhaps a push-up tonight. Nick wondered if she'd gotten a boob job. "You really look…wow, Brand."

She grinned, flattered Nick was pleased with her appearance. Brandi never saw herself the way others did. Confidence and self-esteem were not her strong point. Although she maintained her appearance throughout the years, she never put validity in the compliments that came her way. Guys—and some women—doled out the usual clichés like candy, but it was solely for the purpose of getting into her bed. With Nick, however, the sincerity in his words and the expression in his eyes left no doubt. He still was crazy about her. "Mind getting your tongue off the pavement so we can get going?"

Nick laughed.

"You're blushing."

Nick protested at first then relented. "I'm not…well, maybe just a little. Where are we off to?"

"It's a surprise."

"I hate surprises."

Brandi U-turned in the parking lot, grinned. "Trust me."

സസസ

Since running into her yesterday morning, Nick had been

less stressed. His father's insensitivity, his brother's arrogance, and Wolfsie's puzzling statements now slid off his back. As it had been all those years ago, life seemed less dark when Brandi lit the way.

After driving south for an hour, Nick wailed, "Pittsburgh?"

"No, Brandi."

Nick laughed. "No, I mean this better be a good restaurant to make it worth the drive."

"What do you care?" she replied. "You've been staring at my legs the whole time."

Rather than trying to deny it, Nick fessed up. "Guilty as charged."

Brandi chuckled, patted his left knee twice. "I just don't like hanging around Avalon Hills. You sure Mexican's okay?"

Nick suppressed his reluctance. Despite living in the southwest for many years, spicy food never sat well, especially as the years passed. But he was here for the company, not the food. "Mexican's fine."

The Juan and Only served Americanized Mexican food in an over-the top ambiance. Piñata's, multi-colored streamers, and ribbons hung from the rafters. Ceiling fans spun but did little to cool the place down. Bad paintings of bandoliers with big sombreros and bigger handlebar mustaches adorned the walls. The food servers had olive complexions as if they just arrived from the hills of Sinaloa.

The hostess guided them to a booth in a dimly lit romantic corner and stepped aside. Brandi sat in the center leaving Nick no room. He lowered himself opposite her.

When Brandi announced to the waiter that she would just have chips, Nick was relieved. He wanted tonight to be perfect and didn't want to deal with indigestion. The waiter shuffled away unhappily.

The two of them talked, laughed, and joked. The passing of twenty-five plus years meant nothing. Nick and Brandi picked up where they left off. The conversation was light. Nothing too serious would be discussed.

Brandi advised him she worked as a receptionist for a chiropractor in town. Although she had decided against higher education after high school, she'd always had a good head for business. To Nick, the petty work seemed beneath her. Then again, being a marble engineer, Nick had no room to talk.

"Ever think of getting out of town? You can get a better paying job somewhere else, use your brain a bit more."

"I can't leave."

"I did," Nick replied.

"And have you regretted leaving?"

Nick was again playing defense. People played too many games. He'd speak honestly. "It may have been a mistake."

Brandi explained she was mostly a homebody, preferring to spend the evening in the company of a good novel than a good man. On occasion, she'd go dancing but, for the most part, she preferred keeping to herself. She still liked Def Leppard, Van Halen, Poison, and the rest of the so-called hair bands along with some older stuff. "When exactly did it go from rock to *classic* rock?"

"You got me."

"Still listen to Neil Young?"

Brandi had gotten Nick turned on to Neil Young, but he rarely listened to him anymore. Too many memories. "All the time, sure."

Brandi's next question came out of nowhere. "Ever get married?"

"You suck at segues."

She leaned forward. For an instant, Nick thought she was going to reach for his hand. Instead, she removed a chip, dipped it into the hot sauce, and eased it between her lips, chewing slowly. "So?"

"No, never did. Came close once, a long time ago."

"What happened?"

Nick shrugged "Just didn't feel right."

"How come?"

"She wasn't the right one."

Brandi leaned back and mulled that over in silence.

"How about you? Ever try the whole marital bliss thing?"

"Nopers. I've never been a til-death-do-us-part kinda girl."

"That's a load of crap."

Brandi hiked her brows.

"It's me, Brand. I know you better than that."

"Oh, you do, huh?"

"Yes," Nick affirmed. "Deep down inside, no matter what you portray on the outside, no matter what clothes you wear, and no matter how you may act, I know you're an old-fashioned girl who believes in romance."

As Nick concluded his psychoanalysis, he wished he could recant his observation. He hadn't dated Brandi since senior year of high school, hadn't seen her since they met for breakfast twenty years ago. He had no right to come off omnipotent and all-knowing. He flinched at the realization he sounded like his father.

Brandi's eyes narrowed. "So, you think you know me, Nick Garrison?"

Nick quickly dropped a chip into his mouth to avoid answering.

She leaned forward, clasped her hands and rotated her thumbs. Her jaw tightened and she spoke in a hushed tone. "That night, overlooking the Acheron just after graduating? When I asked you to stay and you wanted me to come to California with you? Remember?"

Remember? I've never stopped thinking about it. "Of course I remember."

"I wanted you."

Nick simply nodded because he didn't know what to do.

She angled nearer and drew in her lips. "I wanted you to be my first."

"Your first what?" He paused. Then the proverbial light-bulb went off over his head. "Oh?"

"You seem surprised."

Nick attempted to stall by reaching for another chip. Brandi quickly slid the bowl away. "But...all those guys."

Brandi raised a brow while displaying a curious expression. "All those guys? What're you implying, Nick Garrison."

Nick threw his hands up. "I just mean—well, you were—popular."

Brandi tilted her head sideways. "They weren't you, Nicky." Before Nick could muster a response, not that he had any idea what to say, Brandi changed the subject. "So, why did you come back?"

"I just…needed to."

Brandi did her silent laugh. "Ironic, isn't it? You needed to come back. I need to stay."

Nick signaled for the waiter they'd like some more chips and refills on the water. Then, "So you never tied the knot?"

"Nope." She seemed proud. "I also came close once."

"Want to share?"

"We dated for a while. Respectable guy. He wasn't the best between the sheets. Had faults, like the rest of us."

"Why didn't you take the leap of faith?"

"We dated about seven months. Then one day he tells me he wants to go back to his wife."

"Ouch. You didn't know he was married?"

"I knew. He kept stringing me along, telling me he'd leave her. I was stupid and I and believed him."

"Sounds like a player."

Brandi laughed. "Sounds more like an asshole."

"Still, I'm sorry," said Nick. And he was. He leaned forward and moved his hand across the table toward hers.

She pulled back and signaled the waiter. "Check please."

❧❧❧

Starsky's was a combination bar/dance club. The dart boards and pool tables were unoccupied. People came for what went on downstairs.

The band, Every Night Fever, played cheesy 1970s pop tunes with some Disco thrown in. The lower level was packed tightly, the small dance floor was a jumbled cluster of sardines, the lighting was weak, the sound reverbed terribly, the watered down drinks were overpriced, and, in spite of the no-smoking policy, the place reeked.

Nick was having an unforgettable night.

With Brandi at his side, his troubles were pushed aside for one memorable evening. For the first time in recent memory, life was good.

When they entered and found a table at stage right, all eyes turned to Brandi. Nick's chest puffed out a bit. With his hand on the small of her back—*she's with me*—they lowered themselves to a table the size of a steering wheel. They people watched, talked over the music, huddled close, and reconnected.

The barmaid came by and Brandi ordered a St. Pauli's Girl. Nick was craving a Bud but said, "Make it two."

Although the tunes were distorted and coming in walls of muffled sound, Nick didn't mind. It gave him an excuse to slide his chair closer, to nudge her hair aside and bring his lips close to her ear when speaking. She did the same thing. When her sensuous lips tenderly brushed his ear, Nick's heart fluttered.

Every few songs, Brandi asked Nick to dance. Had there been less people, he would've accepted. Nick's moves on the dance floor more resembled spasmodic convulsions. In spite of Brandi's prodding, he held steadfast in his refusal. He'd do anything for her—except dance in public.

"*Seinfeld*, ever watch it?"

"Sure," Brandi replied.

"You know that episode with Elaine dancing?"

"Yup."

"Personally, I thought she danced pretty well."

Brandi laughed. "You're a nerd."

Within twenty minutes, in spite of their physical closeness, three different men had asked Brandi to dance. She politely declined.

Nick was confounded. They were obviously with each other. But yet some of these bar studs had no qualms asking her to join them on the dance floor. Was she so obviously out of his league?

"I have to pee," Brandi announced.

Most women would powder their nose, excuse themselves, or simply go to the ladies room. But not Brandi. Direct, honest. She had to pee. It was one of the numerous things that pulled Nick in. He watched as she glided across the club in a graceful fluency, shaking her head no to countless men who stopped her. One kissed her hand.

Upon returning, she sat and slid her chair close to Nick.

The band received polite golf claps after wrapping up Billy Joel's "Just the Way You Are." Wearing a white leisure suit, the lead singer who resembled one of the Bee Gees stepped to the microphone. Nick glanced at Brandi, checked his watch.

"Thank you," the singer proclaimed. "Remember, the more you drink the better we sound." He waited for laughter that never came. "Every Night Fever is going to take a short break but we'll be back in twenty. In the meantime, keep your boogie shoes on and get ready for our next set." As he glanced around the room, he saw Nick. Recollection crossed his face. "But first we want to do one more number before we go. By special request..."

A spotlight unexpectedly bathed Nick and Brandi in a white beam.

Nick stayed cool but the corners of his lips curled.

Brandi faced him, failing to suppress a smile. Flushed, she asked, "What—what did you do?"

The singer spoke. "From the early seventies, this is a song by a one hit wonder named Looking Glass. 'Brandy, You're a Fine Girl.'"

"Nicky! Oh my God!"

He patted her knee, a beaming prideful smile on his face. "Now who's blushing?"

"I can't believe you!"

Nick rose, genuflected and extended his arm. "May I have this dance?"

The spotlight followed them as they snaked between tables and made their way to the dance floor. They had it to themselves for a short time before others joined in.

They danced, smiled, and moved to the music. Beet red, Brandi couldn't help but shake her head. "I'm going to get you back, Nick Garrison" she said and flashed her charming silent laugh.

Nick returned the smile, his hands loosely clasping her hips as they swayed in unison to the song. When the chorus came, Nick mouthed the words in synch with the vocalist. "Brandy, you're a fine girl. What a good wife you would be."

Brandi's moves were far from prolific. But she looked sensual as hell, keeping the beat. And more memorable than the way she pirouetted to the music was her glowing cherished smile and affection-laced eyes.

Yes indeed, Nick thought to himself. *Life is, in fact, good.*

👁️‍🗨️

The night of dancing tired them both out. Brandi's eyes were half-mast. Like a little girl, she insisted she was wide awake but her expression and body language said otherwise.

Keeping in step with each other, they ambled to her car. Her body fell against Nick as he draped his arm across her shoulders.

"I still can't believe you did that. You hate dancing."

Nick beamed, pulled her closer.

"You're really not a bad dancer, Nicky."

"Thanks."

Reaching the car, Brandi handed over the keys. "I'm too tired. Would you mind?"

Two beers was not a lot. "Sure." After opening the door for her, he walked around to his side of the car. He struggled to get himself behind the wheel. "Okay if I move the seat back?"

"Are you implying I'm short?"

"No…"

She feigned anger. "You *are*! I can't help being short. Blame my parents!"

It felt good to laugh. It felt good to be alive.

"So what if I have little legs?"

"There's nothing wrong with your legs," he claimed.

"You should know. You've been staring at them since we left town."

"Busted!"

They met each other's stare. This was the moment. Nick wanted to lean over and kiss her. It felt like the right time.

Surprisingly, Brandi angled her seat in a slightly reclined position and closed her eyes. "Take me home, Nicky."

He brought the car to life and wondered what awaited him in Avalon Hills.

Chapter 15

The northwestern quadrant of Pennsylvania was cloaked in a foreboding, uncompromising blackness. It was as if Nick and Brandi were the last two people alive after some cataclysmic event.

Although the speed limit was seventy on the desolate gray ribbon, Nick never got the car over fifty. He wanted to stretch this evening out as long as possible. During the drive, he frequently glanced right. It wasn't just Brandi's appearance that exhilarated him but it was the seemingly unbreakable bond they shared. He thought about things, pondered the endless scenarios in his mind. What if…he had never left Avalon Hills all those years ago? What if…he had decided not to go after his dreams? Had he stayed, would a life with Brandi be enough of a dream? They were together now. Finally. After more than a quarter of a century, the fire still burned, the connection indestructible. Nick snickered at the irony. The lord works in mysterious ways his sister-in-law stated. How true it was.

True and paradoxical at the same time.

Nick crossed the Acheron and drove a few blocks down Main Street before pulling curbside. Brandi had nodded off with a smile coating her delicate features, her head angled toward him. With a gentle nudge, he woke her.

Her eyes lifted slowly, she gazed around, became rigid and tensed. To Nick, she appeared frightened. "Where are we?"

"The happenin' metropolis of Avalon Hills. I don't know where you live."

Brandi warily eyed the surroundings as if she'd never been here before. After a moment, she refocused. Unemotionally, she leaned forward and removed something from the glove box. "I'll take it from here. Put this on."

Nick arched an eyebrow then looked questioningly at her. "A blindfold?"

Brandi nodded while yawning.

"Do you have handcuffs in there, too?"

She didn't laugh. "Here."

"You're not joking?"

"No."

Puzzled, Nick said, "You're really not. You don't trust me with where you live? Wow!"

"I do trust you. But do you trust me?"

"Of course, but—"

She waved it in front of his face. "Just go with it. For me, for us."

Nick relented.

⌖⌖⌖

Frannie Fitzgerald was having a rough night. She was torn between her job as a federal employee—Stats Analyst III, thank you very much—and her job as a mother. Oh, and a wife, too.

Two days in Avalon Hills had harvested no results in solving the statistical anomaly. No answers to her burning questions had been uncovered. She'd had three conversations with Dennis Linebrink since arriving. She hated lying to her boss, telling him she was making headway. Each call he offered to fly out and assist her. Frannie knew his ulterior motives. Dennis would treat it not as a business trip but as a getaway.

Still, she knew she had to discover something. And quick. The clock was ticking. Her boss had been reluctant to let her go in the first place. The slack would not continue indefinitely.

Her repeated attempts to meet with Sheriff Gabe Garrison had failed. He was perpetually *out of the office* or *tied up in a meeting*. Tomorrow she'd give him one final chance and, if she reached yet another dead end, she'd go over his head and speak with the mayor, who also happened to be his father. She had managed to accost one of Garrison's deputies but he was sealed tighter than Fort Knox

Frannie was a public servant, a glorified paper pusher, not a detective. All she had was a strange collection of data. It was hard to find an answer when she wasn't even sure of the question.

Earlier, she ventured a few miles out of town and spoke with the older couple who were the proprietors at Berryhill Memorial Park. She learned a lot, but none of it beneficial.

Mrs. Berryhill's ancestors had owned the one-hundred-nineteen-acre farmland since before the Civil War. In the early twentieth century, they'd been bought out, their property converted to a cemetery. It appeared too large a plot of land for a small town. The family had agreed to sell with one stipulation and that was that the parcel stayed in the family. For over a century the Berryhill family had remained caretakers. The responsibility passed from parent to child like an heirloom. Frannie enjoyed the tea she was served by the elderly and lonely landowners. But, like everyone else she met, she came no closer to resolution.

She had peered through the wrought iron gate that surrounded where St. Agnes Hospital once stood. The infirmary had served the population of Avalon Hills and the neighboring communities that dotted the hills, starting in the 1800s. In 1980, the hospital was razed, touched only by the passage of time since then. Weeds had begun sprouting through fissures in the hospital's foundation.

A cemetery too big for a small town. A hospital now abandoned.

The one and only certainty was that something was not right in Avalon Hills.

Using chopsticks, she scooped the last of the Beef Lo Mein she picked up in town. Leaning back, Frannie interlaced her fingers behind her head. She looked around the room but didn't pay attention to any of the gaudy furnishings. She thought of her daughters. She'd raised them as best she could. Being a single parent many years and then marrying a man where love was assumed and not displayed, she had tried to do her best. She cultivated in her daughters to always do what was right, listen to your heart, not take shortcuts in life.

As Frannie weighed her own words, she realized she might have to wander into a gray area.

Her nephew lived out in Silicon Valley and did something or other with computers. Two summers ago, the Fitzgerald clan was visited by her nephew and his new wife. Frannie knew Matt always had a soft spot for his Aunt Frannie so she played it to her advantage. The bulk of that weekend had turned into a major cram session. Matt educated her on the fine skill of computer hacking.

She'd never had a need to do it, be it in her personal or professional life, but dabbled in it sporadically to keep her skills sharp. "It may come in handy one day," her nephew stated plainly at the time. That prophetic claim came to fruition tonight.

It took some time, but Frannie was in. She located the Avalon Hills High School website. A link took her to a site for old classmates looking to reconnect. She found Gabe Garrison's name. He'd been married a long time, had two grown children, worked as the sheriff and also listed an e-mail address.

Frannie hesitated, said a silent thank you to her nephew, and ten minutes later had successfully hacked into his personal e-mail account. *If Dennis finds out, I'm screwed.*

She perused numerous documents as well as those Gabe had saved in various files. The guy was meticulous. One file was marked *Dad.* Knowing the sheriff's father was also town mayor, she checked that first.

The correspondences were brief, two or three sentences. Gabe was not an e-mail type, nothing personal or damning. The notes consisted of generalities. Two recent ones from last week echoed concern about his brother coming to town. Gabe did not appear pleased.

Moments later, Frannie sat up ramrod straight and her pulse skyrocketed. Lloyd, Gabe's father, had written, "What did you end up doing with Jonathan Decker?" Gabe's response was equally curt. "It's taken care of."

Taken care of. A strange choice of words, ominous sounding.

Frannie opened more browsers. She accessed the Social Security mainframe, the IRS database, as well as the Mercer County website.

Thirty minutes later, her head was pounding. The Chinese

food had not been appetizing in the first place but she knew that was not the reason for her tossing stomach.

She made a triangle around her nose and closed her eyes, trying to seek a correlation of some sort. Just *yesterday* Sheriff Gabe Garrison and Mayor Lloyd Garrison were discussing Jonathan Decker. Why were they now concerned about a man who died four years ago?

∽∂∾

Gabe was sitting at his kitchen table, cleaning his revolver, when he heard the ping on his phone. He lowered the weapon, read the alert, and cursed.

His children were grown and living elsewhere so he left the loaded weapon on the table and double-timed it to his personal computer. Atop his inbox sat the most recent e-mail, a confirmation of the alert he received on his phone.

He chewed on his lip and tasted bile in the back of his throat. His computer—specifically his e-mail—had been hacked. Hacking e-mails was easy to accomplish. Preventing an alarm signifying said attack was not. Only an amateur would make this kind of fuckup.

It was obvious who the culprit was. Tomorrow, he'd meet that nosey bitch from Washington and have the situation *taken care of.*

Chapter 16

"Ta-dah!"

Blindfold removed, Nick blinked and eyed his surroundings. Standing in the threshold of the front door, he was immediately struck with the similarity to Brandi's childhood home. The furnishings were modern but the layout was identical. The carpeting was thin, no padding. He sensed cold coming through the slab.

Brandi took his hand and chuckled. "C'mon, I'll give you the grand tour."

The kitchen was beyond the living room. A badly scarred old wooden dinette set was positioned in an alcove. Off the living room, two short flights of stairs lay next to each other. One led down, presumably to a basement and/or garage, the other to the second level of the home. The steps creaked as Nick and Brandi walked upstairs. The second level consisted of a short hallway, fifteen feet max. The master bedroom was the prevalent room in the home. A large California king was situated in the center, surrounded by traditional furniture: two nightstands, bureau, dresser, mirror. The blackout curtains kept the room dark.

"Trust me, nothing ever happens in here," Brandi joked.

The second bedroom housed an antique looking roll top.

"I remember that desk," Nick commented.

"That's been in our family forever."

"Only two bedrooms?"

Brandi nodded. "It's small but it's only me. It works."

"It's…quaint," Nick said. "Homey."

"Quaint and homey? Who am I, June Cleaver?"

Back in the living room, Nick pursed his lips and nodded as he took it in.

"I'm serious, Brand. This is nice." *I could've gotten used to this.*

She squeezed his hand tighter, said "Thanks," and rested her head against his bicep.

After a moment she guided him across the room. "Why don't you put some music on? My CD's are here." She pointed to an armoire then showed him how to turn on the stereo. "And I'll be right back."

A stereo, not an iPod. He loved this girl.

As Nick browsed her collection, Brandi busied herself out of sight in the kitchen. "I still can't believe you did that!" she called out

"Did what?"

"Got them to play that song. And danced, too?"

Nick beamed, glad she valued the act and his attempt to dance.

Brandi returned a few moments later. She held two beers and a bowl of potato chips.

"You sure it's not too late? You were zonked out in the car."

She feigned umbrage. "I sure was. And you didn't even try cop a feel. What's up with that?"

"That's not me. You know that." Nick inched closer.

They peered into each other's eyes. The moment seemed right. Again. Nick leaned into her.

Brandi glided aside and lowered the chips and drinks onto a coffee table. "I'll be right back." She winked and went up the stairs.

Nick may have not been *like that* but he found his eyes roaming to her backside in that black skirt.

He fell onto the worn sofa and waited, wondering what she was doing. Was she in her bedroom waiting for him to come up? Was she slipping into something revealing, provocative? Maybe she'd fallen asleep. Nick was about to investigate when she cheerily bounded down the stairs hiding something behind her back. Her form-fitting leopard top and slit black skirt was replaced with a baggy shirt and older blue sweatpants. Her hair seemed flatter and she'd washed off some of her makeup. Even dressed down, Brandi looked angelic.

"Hope you don't mind that I changed."

"N—no, m—make yourself comfortable," Nick stuttered.

"Thanks, considering it's *my* home."

Nick cocked his head. "What ya got there?"

"Oh, this?" She grinned devilishly. "Let's see how good your memory is."

"When it comes to you…" His words trailed off.

Standing by the sofa now, she displayed the VHS tape. "Remember?"

Nick burst out in laughter. *9 ½ weeks*. The same erotic thriller they watched numerous times as teenagers but never were able to get through. "Think we'll finish it?"

Brandi spoke with fawn-like eyes. "You never know."

By the time the counter passed the fifteen minute mark, Nick didn't give a damn about the lame film.

Brandi lay curled on the sofa, her head on the opposite arm. Wearing white socks, she occasionally pressed her feet against his crotch. Nick was unsure how to act, what to do. But as his blood grew warm and his manhood rose, the gentle pressing became more frequent and more intense. He glanced toward her. Her eyes were looking at the TV vacantly, a thin smile etched on her face.

"Something wrong?" she breathed.

"Not a thing. Everything is…perfect."

"Good."

Nick felt his senses heighten. Blood coursed through his veins. He was filled with passion, arousal, fire. Decades ago, he'd craved Brandi, wanted her. The feelings, both physical and emotional, had not soured at all. If anything, they had grown and matured.

This was no longer a high school crush. He was not some seventeen-year-old kid with raging hormones, looking to nail the hot chick. The sexual attraction he felt for her still burned. But now, in his late forties, it was deeper. It had meaning.

Staring at the screen, Nick found his hand on Brandi's calf atop her sweats. Tone, lean. He tenderly slinked his hand along her leg, closer to her hip. His hand moved up and back inches at a time. She didn't object.

Reaching her defined rounded hip, he thought he saw her

smile widen. He cupped her hip, caressed it. In return, she straightened her right leg and pressed it more firmly against the bulge in his trousers.

Nick emitted a slight outbreath.

Brandi purred. "Nice knowing I still have that effect on you."

Nick was too caught up in the rising passion to come up with any type of witty retort. He caressed her hip with more hunger. She continued ironing his bulge with her foot.

It felt right. It felt perfect. Heavenly. He had never stopped thinking of her, wanting her to be part of his life. That became more evident, indicated by the time spent with each other this evening.

The long drive, the conversation, the dancing, the unbreakable bond they shared, the connection they felt left no doubt. Brandi was *the one*. Always had been, always would be.

Nick realized he made a life changing colossal mistake years ago. Leaving Avalon Hills may have not been an error. But leaving Brandi definitely was.

Under normal circumstances, things could develop. Sure, they were both older. The first half of their lives had been apart. Perhaps the second half they would share a common path, intertwine their lives, their existence. And move through life together.

But these were not normal circumstances that brought Nick home to Avalon Hills. Nick felt cheated. "Brand," he whispered.

"Mm hmm?"

"We need to talk."

His voice was soft, words barely audible over the movie. Brandi leaned over, muted the film. Her smile faded, her face tentative. "What is it, Nicky?"

"Earlier you asked why I came back here."

Brandi paused the movie and sat up.

"I wanted my parents to be the first to know. But...I want to tell you." He swallowed hard.

The sadness on his face and the distant look in his eyes warned this would not be good. She titled her head, lovingly cupped Nick's face in her hand.

He leaned his face into her soft palm. Then turned and kissed her fingers. "I won't…won't be here much longer."

Brandi furrowed her brows as if to say *that's it?* "I didn't expect you to move back here."

Nick released a nervous laugh. "I don't mean that. I mean I'm—"

"No!" she cried out and placed her fingers along his lips, silencing him.

"Brandi, look—"

"No, I said! Damn it. Not now, not *tonight.*"

"I'm not going to lead you on like that other guy," Nick claimed. "I'm not going to string you along."

"You're *nothing* like him. Trust me."

"This was a mistake. I never should've…I won't hurt you again. It wasn't fair back then. It's not fair now."

"I'll decide what's fair and what's not, thank you very much."

Brandi Conrad, tough as always. It was one of the infinite reasons, Nick realized, he'd never gotten over her. It was the feelings he had for her that prevented him from ever engaging in a real relationship with someone else.

"I need to come clean with you," he insisted. "This is just so…crazy. You, me, us, the fact that I still feel it. Don't you?"

Brandi's eyes confirmed it. Her mouth tightened, she nodded once and bit her lip.

Nick said, "You being here with me. Now. It just doesn't seem fair. It's not—damn it, it's not fair."

"I'm here now," she said and kissed his forehead.

"I know but—"

"But nothing!" Brandi stated. "Tonight. You and me together. Don't try to figure things out. Don't overanalyze. Just go with it."

ɛ⅊ɛ⅊

Upon waking, Nick was immediately struck by the searing dull ache. As his eyes refocused to consciousness, he fretted. It was the first time since returning to Avalon Hills that he awoke to a pounding headache.

He quickly determined the origin was his neck, not his head. It was brought on by the twisted position he'd fallen asleep in, having dozed off on Brandi's sofa.

Brandi was still out. Her head rested on his hip. They were completely dressed. He grinned as he heard her gently snoring. "Brand," he muttered.

She didn't move.

A hint of morning light was permeating through a slit in the thick curtains. He nudged her again, repeated her name. Brandi stirred, mumbled something, and repositioned herself.

Nick wanted to stay here. With Brandi. Forever, if he could. Sadly, forever was not eternal.

Confounded, he wasn't sure what to do. She slept peacefully, looked extremely restful. It felt as it should. He did not want to wake her. On the other hand, having her wake to an empty home was tacky.

After two more failed attempts to rouse her, Nick twisted and reached for a throw pillow. Contorting himself, he rose while replacing his hip with the cushion. He watched as Brandi, still asleep, rubbed her eyes and shifted herself, facing the rear of the couch.

Nick realized he could not leave. They'd arrived in Brandi's car. He had no way to get home. He'd have to stay here until she woke.

He stood in the living room and watched her sleep. Nothing sexual had happened. In high school they had made out plenty. But they'd never consummated their relationship.

Part of Nick was disappointed it hadn't happened last night. More than ever, based on the events of the evening and the synched emotions they still shared, it seemed the next natural progression.

In spite of Nick's dissatisfaction that they hadn't taken their intimacy further, he accepted it. He wouldn't be like those other guys who used her and then took off. It would happen when *she* was ready. He'd wait until the end of time—if only he could.

Readjusting his disheveled shirt, Nick tiptoed to the front door. He had no transportation, but if he located the towers atop Aliquippa Mountain, he could get his bearings. Maybe he was within walking distance to Main Street and could pick up breakfast for them.

Nick quietly unlatched the deadbolt, pulled back on the knob and eased the door open.

The shrill thunderous explosion rocked the house to its foundation. *"Jesus!"*

Brandi—now awake, probably along with the entire city—flew off the sofa. "What'd you do?" she shouted over the shrieking wail.

"Nothing," he yelled back. "I just was going to get some air."

Brandi shoved him out of the way, frantically opened the coat closet door, reached in.

Nick stepped back and watched as she entered a code on a keypad. The earsplitting alarm stopped, but Nick could still hear it in his head. "What the hell?"

"It's a security system."

"Security system?"

Brandi closed the closet and matter-of-factly claimed, "A lot has changed around here since you left."

"I guess so."

Brandi looked around and rubbed her hands together. "I should probably take you back to your car."

Nick was shocked, both by her obvious eagerness to get him out and by the tremble in her voice. Something was wrong. Brandi was…different.

As he watched her stroll to the kitchen table, a dreadful possibility entered his mind. Was someone on their way over? Did Brandi have a boyfriend? Why had she panicked? "Something wrong?"

Brandi shook her head, displayed a generic smile. It was not *that* kind of smile. She raised her arms. In one hand she held car keys, the other one a blindfold. "Turn around, Nicky."

Nick protested slightly. They still had the connection. The flame still burned. Yet, for some reason, Brandi did not want her residence revealed to Nick.

Bizarre.

Chapter 17

I *t's strange how the mind works.*
Shortly after losing her husband, Frannie decided a cross-country road trip would be therapeutic for the family, back when her daughters were young and gas was cheap. Somewhere in the Midwest, Kansas, she thought, they'd spent an enjoyable afternoon in a mock western town. Saloons, blacksmiths, a boarding house, a makeshift graveyard, and a theatre lined the dusty streets.

Now standing at the counter in the Avalon Hills police station, she recalled the smell of the jail in the western town. Old, musty, stale air.

The deputy, a thirty-something rotund woman with big hair and too much makeup, sauntered to the opposite side. "Sorry, Miss Fitzgerald, he's not in."

Frannie had been playing this game for days. It was tiresome. She looked across the small expanse. Two desks sat cattycorner, one for each deputy. Eying the closed door of Sheriff Garrison's office, she spotted light through drawn blinds of his door. "Are you sure about that?"

The deputy leered. "Maybe you'll have better luck tomorrow."

"We both know I won't."

"Sheriff Garrison is a busy man."

"He must be." Frannie thanked her anyway and walked out.

She felt the deputy's watchful eyes follow her. Upon exiting, Frannie calculated her next move. It seemed as if pedestrians along Main Street were casting a vigilant gaze upon her. Back in her rental car, she entered the coordinates into her navigation system and drove away. Ten minutes later, Frannie found herself traipsing across a weedy lawn. A tricycle lay on its side. The older run-down home, like the yard, was unkempt. After knocking on the door, she slid her hands over her shirt making herself presentable and professional.

"Finish your fuckin' oatmeal!" she heard as the door was yanked open. The woman standing before her had probably been attractive at one time. Blonde hair, light blue eyes, and a decent figure. However, she wore unflattering yellow shorts and a washed out white top with faded yellow stripes. A coffee mug in one hand, a cigarette dangling from her mouth, she barked, "And who the hell are you?" Her eyes were bloodshot.

Frannie was overcome with alcohol that spewed from the woman's pores. It was obvious she wouldn't be invited in for tea and crumpets. She forced a smile. "I'm looking for Elizabeth Decker."

"You found her. Who are you?"

"My name is Frances Fitzgerald and I'd like a few minutes of your time." Frannie extended her hand. It was not taken.

"Who the hell is Frances Fitzgerald?" she snapped, ash falling from the cigarette.

"It's about your husband, Jonathan."

Elizabeth squinted, eyed her visitor, and took a step forward. Frannie envisioned the woman smacking her. "I told the sheriff everything I know. And that ain't nothin'."

"I'm not here on behalf of Sheriff Garrison. I'm here on my own." Frannie offered her warmest smile. It accomplished nil. "I work in Washington and have a few—"

"*Washington?*"

"Yes, ma'am."

"DC?"

"Yeah, ma'am."

"Don't you people got better things to do with my taxes than sendin' folks all the way out here?"

"I'm here at my own expense."

A child's voice protested about breakfast. Elizabeth screamed over her shoulder. "Eat the fuckin' thing before I whoop your ass."

Knowing she didn't have much time, Frannie took the direct approach. "I'm wondering if you could tell me how h died."

"Look, lady, he's dead. It don't matter."

"It matters to me."

The haggard woman took a prolonged puff then flicked the butt airborne where it landed on the dead lawn. "Cardiac arrest four years ago. Happy?"

Frannie offered condolences. "I'm sorry. He was a young man."

"Woulda turned forty last Tuesday." She took a drawn out sigh. "Jonny never took care a' himself. Ate like shit, worked too hard, smoked three packs a day, got too fat. It was too much strain on the ol' ticker." Elizabeth slipped her fingers between her ample bosom and withdrew a fresh pack of cigarettes. She slipped one out, lit up. "These things'll kill ya."

"I quit six month ago," Frannie lied, seeking a way into Elizabeth's good graces—if she had any. "You mentioned Sheriff Garrison. Has he spoken to you recently?"

"Garrison," snarled Elizabeth. "Now there's a pompous ass if I ever seen one. Yeah, he came by. Three times in two days asking about Jonny."

"Do you mind if I ask what was discussed?"

"Actually, yeah, I do."

Frannie regrouped and after a beat, commented, "It just seems odd he'd speak with you about your husband so frequently four years after he passed away."

"He didn't pass away, lady. He fuckin' died. And left me with nothin'. Didn't even think to get no life insurance policy."

"I'm sure it's tough," Frannie offered, trying to locate the woman's heart.

"You want to know what Garrison discussed with me, why not ask him yourself?"

"I've been trying to a few days now but he's always busy. Lots of work for a small town sheriff."

"Probably up at the Tri-Delta Plant outside a' town."

During her research while compiling reports for her boss, Frannie came across information about the factory north of the city that had been closed by the EPA. "Would you happen to know exactly where Tri-Delta is located?"

Elizabeth shook her head disgustedly. She could tell this worthless bureaucrat would not stop pestering her until she gave in. She also didn't need her neighbors seeing her talking to a stranger. "Hang on," she said and slammed the door.

Frannie took a deep breath, widened her eyes, and thought of her first husband. When she lost Tom, she grieved much differently than Elizabeth. She was starting to think the woman had forgotten about her when the door was again jerked open. The woman handed her a scrap of paper with directions. "Here ya go."

Frannie thanked her, again expressed condolences over her loss, and handed the woman her card. "I've jotted down my cell on the back if you'd like to talk."

The woman frowned as if saying *Talk about what?* She took the card and slipped it into her sweaty cleavage next to her Marlboro's.

∽✺∼

Thirty minutes later, with Avalon Hills now miles behind her, Frannie was northbound on a one lane road that twisted through the thick terrain. Every once in a while, the trees parted and she was presented a peek of the Acheron River.

She slowed as she came upon a narrow bridge that traversed a dry creek. Elizabeth Decker had told her the turnout was a quarter mile beyond. The lady reeked from beer and cigarettes, but she definitely knew her directions. Exactly a quarter mile farther, Frannie saw the cutoff and turned left.

After a pockmarked mile, the narrow path opened up on the vacant Tri-Delta factory. She stopped along an abandoned guard shack, the arm of the security gate long since gone. A faded weather-beaten placard dangled crookedly. *Tri-Delta: Dreams of Tomorrow, Here Today* the forsaken sign proclaimed.

The four brick smokestacks were dormant but reached to heaven. The combination red bricks, gray tiles and windswept paneling made Frannie feel as if she just travelled back in time to the industrial revolution. A wrought iron security gate wrapped around the plant as far as the eye could see.

Frannie saw a police cruiser parked in front of a torn open space in the fence. Weeds grew everywhere. The factory and its landscaping appeared untouched for decades. A relic left over from a previous time. Her eyes followed a makeshift trail that fed to the factory itself. She noticed Sheriff Garrison squat down and disappear inside through a gaping hole.

Frannie inhaled slowly, exhaled, and with suddenly unreliable legs, advanced on the factory. As she approached the sinister structure, she thought of her daughters.

It hadn't rained since arriving but the ground beneath her feet was wet and muddy. Her flip-flops sank into the sludge as she slogged closer to the derelict building.

Although Frannie was only a few miles outside of town, the area seemed gloomy, overcast. It was as if the plumes of pollution that had been belched into the sky permanently sheathed the area in an iron pall. A breeze blew from the west. Papers and Styrofoam cups danced across the property. Sheets of metal and plastic swayed in the blustery draft. Coming closer, Frannie detected a strange odor. Ammonia combined with something else she couldn't identify.

She lowered herself through the hole in the wall and entered.

Massive openings, where windows had once been, did little to provide light. The expansive interior was blanketed in gray-black shadows. Unhinged pipes teetered precariously from the ceiling high above like gray icicles. The malodourous air hung heavy. Flights of stairs led nowhere. Neglected apparatuses and contraptions remained inactive like sleeping dinosaurs from a forgotten time, rust eating away. Coiled copper wires were strewn about the floor. Barrels and large drums lay discarded in a random chaotic fashion. Rhythmic plick-plick-plick of water dripping from somewhere echoed through the hollow chamber.

Frannie paced slowly, taking it all in. A wood panel cracked beneath her feet. She gasped, sprang back. As she looked around, she saw numerous cavernous holes dotting the floor like a lunar landscape. She'd always been pleased with her petite appearance but now was grateful that her one-hundred-nineteen-pound frame would not put an extra burden on the unpredictability beneath her feet. As if tip-toeing would reduce her weight, she went to the lip of a deep hollow chasm and peered down. The blackened abyss stretched beyond the foundation and seemingly into the bowels of hell.

As her heartbeat accelerated, she wondered what she was doing here. *I'm a Statistical Analyst III, not Indiana Jones.*

"Mrs. Fitzgerald!"

The beaming voice thundered across the ruins as if shouted from God Himself.

The unexpected shout caused Frannie to momentarily leap back, coming within inches of plummeting into another cavernous hole. Hand over her pounding chest, she looked in the direction of the sound. The authoritative tone and confident stride left no doubt.

Sheriff Gabe Garrison entered through a breach on the opposite side that bordered the Acheron. He was forty yards away but rather than taking a direct route toward her, he zigged and zagged. Without looking down, having no trouble manipulating the rebar that protruded through the floor, it was obvious he knew this place like the back of his hand.

He was just a few feet away from her now. Frannie scrutinized the sheriff. He was a handsome man, firm jaw and deep-set eyes. She'd always been partial to men with a hint of swagger but his was too extreme for her taste. "I've been trying to speak with you." She resented the nervousness that tinged her words.

"So I've heard. How can I help you?"

She quickly looked around and decided on an indirect approach. "I find it curious there's no graffiti anywhere. Building long since forgotten, you'd think kids would come up here to have a little fun, drink, make out, smoke some weed, and express some creativity."

"I'm the sheriff of Avalon Hills," he boasted smugly, "and when I declare a structure off limits, the community listens. We may appear backwoods to you, Ms. Fitzgerald, but people here still respect authority. What I say, goes."

"Law of the land," she remarked.

"Indeed." Although the area was dimly lit, Gabe could not help but notice her diminutive appearance. She wore a teal top, baggy jeans, and no makeup. Her breasts were small but perky. She exuded an innocent sexuality about her. "Technically you're trespassing. I can have you arrested." The idea of frisking her caused a stirring.

"I was hoping to have a few minutes of your time."

"And you just happened to wander up here hoping to find me?"

Frannie nodded.

"And who suggested I'd be here?"

"People in town."

Gabe created a short list of possibilities that he quickly narrowed down to one obvious big mouth. "Elizabeth Decker is a drunk. An embittered widow who thinks if she downs enough whiskey her husband will come back."

Frannie's lack of denial proved him right. "Speaking of Jonathan Decker, I'm wondering what you can tell me about him."

Gabe moved closer.

Frannie retreated after glancing over her shoulder, making sure no holes in the earth would swallow her.

"Jonathan Decker died four years ago. But you knew that already. Why don't you ask what you really want to?"

Frannie gulped, backpedaled. "Heart attack at thirty six?"

He corrected her. "Cardiac arrest." He inched nearer.

"Do you think there was more to it than that?"

Gabe snorted. "What I think is that it was simply Mr. Decker's time." He rubbed his chin and took a prolonged glance at her small frame. *Frisking would be fun.* "People meet their demise at all times in strange ways. Now, why don't you ask *the* question?"

Many may have found his exemplary smile charming. Frannie found it unsettling. "I'm just a bit confused as to why you would be concerned now, four years later."

Gabe played his trump card. "And why I'd be communicating with my father about it?"

Frannie did a poor job of hiding confusion. "What do you mean?"

Gabe stuck up his hand, quieting her. "I am the sheriff of Avalon Hills. My father is the town's mayor. What we discuss in e-mail is no one's business." He paused, stepped closer. "I think I've been very patient with you."

Frannie was growing panicky but tried to quash it. "Patient? I've wanted us to talk for several days now, Sheriff. You've been avoiding me."

"True."

"Why?" Backing up against a cold slab she couldn't retreat anymore.

Gabe drew in his lips, searching for the correct words. "You feds are all the same. This isn't Ruby Ridge. This isn't Waco. What goes on here is of no concern to Washington."

Attempting to distant herself from her employer, Frannie joked. "Hey, I'm no fan of Washington either."

"May I be blunt?"

Frannie nodded.

"I suggest you turn around, get your sweet little ass back to Pittsburgh, and catch the next flight home."

"Is that a threat?"

"We may be a small hick town, Ms. Fitzgerald. This isn't New York or Chicago. But we do have crime here. The roads out of town get very slick. I would just hate to see something unexpected happen to you like it did to Jameson Parker."

Who?

Gabe continued. "You seem like a nice person, a smart person. Don't get mixed up in something that's way over your pay grade. Arlington National Cemetery is filled with heroes who acted on behalf of their country."

Frannie's skin crawled. The hairs on the nape of her neck stood up. Perhaps she should have had her boss come with her, after all. Perhaps she should have ignored the findings and not presented the report in the first place. *What the hell did I stumble upon?*

As her throat closed, the sheriff pawed her shoulder. He guided her toward the gap in the wall. Gabe Garrison was pompous, arrogant, and self-righteous. No doubt about it. However, he spoke the truth. All in all, Frances Fitzgerald was in way over her head. Her career was important but not worth risking her life.

The outside air felt refreshing, crisp. Trudging through the muck, she ran-walked to her car. She glanced back to see the sheriff intently watching her depart. Frannie felt herself getting choked up, fear getting the best of her. She wiped a few tears from her eyes. Her fingers trembled.

As she approached her car, she started wondering how quickly she could leave. Waiting at the airport for the next flight would give her time to concoct a story for her boss. Dennis would be upset her time away had yielded no results.

He could kiss her ass. At this moment, she was too terrified to care.

She fumbled for the keys, beeped the car unlocked, and sat down. Bringing the engine to life, she peered across the field. Gabe's eyes cut through her like lasers. She shuddered.

Frannie was halfway back to the main road when she noticed it flapping beneath the windshield wiper. A note. Someone had been following *her*.

Out of sight from prying eyes, Frannie stopped the car and retrieved the item. The note displayed several series of random unrecognizable numbers in no discernible pattern. It was signed BD.

Like the mention of Jameson Parker, the name Gabe mentioned, Frannie had no idea who BD was.

∽∾∽

The music of one's youth always held a special place in their heart. No matter what styles come and go, nothing was ever as good as what you grew up listening to. For Nick's grandparents it was Glenn Miller and artists of the Big Band era. His parents grew up during The British Invasion. Nick came of age with the hair bands of the '80s. And today's kids listened to…whatever crap they listened to.

Still, being woken to Van Halen's *Panama* was jolting. Nick sprang up in bed, free of head pain. He reached out to his nightstand, scooped up his cell. "Hello?" he grumbled scratchily.

"Good morning. I'm looking for Nick Garrison." The voice was vaguely familiar.

"This is Nick."

"Mr. Garrison, hi. This is Dr. Shepherd at West View Animal Clinic."

Pittsburgh. Scrappy Four. "Yes, hi, good morning."

As the veterinarian spoke, her voice took on an unsure tone. "I got the lab results and blood work back on your dog." She paused.

Nick filled the emptiness. "Is something wrong?"

"No, nothing's wrong. Your pet is healthy, very healthy."

Nick sighed in relief. Had something been wrong after taking the dog to a different vet, his parents—mainly his father—would blame him. "Is there a problem?"

"That's just it. There is no problem whatsoever."

"So everything's good?"

"Everything *is* good. Too good."

Haltingly, Nick asked, "Am I missing something?"

He heard shuffling papers. "How old did you say Scrappy Four is?"

"Six, maybe seven years old. I'm not sure exactly. Why?"

"Veterinarians don't use any style of carbon dating to determine age like for elements. We don't count rings on a tree to ascertain its age. There's really no way to precisely predict a canine's exact age. After looking at Four's gums and teeth decay, I was hoping for clarification. And that's why I sent out the results."

"You've lost me, Dr. Shepherd."

"Four is healthy, very healthy, too healthy."

"And why's that bad?" questioned Nick.

"He has no teeth decay at all. You've claimed he's six or seven. Yet, he seems to still be a puppy. He doesn't seem to be aging."

Chapter 18

Despite the fact that he hated clichés, one Nick found himself thinking was *The more things change, the more they stay the same.*

Much of Avalon Hills had remained unaffected by the indefatigable hand of time. The same stores and businesses of his youth still operated today. His father was still condescending, his brother was still an asshole, and Brandi was still in his heart.

On the other hand, much had changed. Childhood friend Mike Lauser had killed himself. Ed Wolfe was dealing with his wife's breast cancer by speaking in double meanings and drowning his despair in alcohol. The Acheron, the river of his youth, had been soiled with poisonous chemicals.

For the first time, in probably a decade, a horn was honked in town. Brought back to reality, Nick glanced in his rear view, waved an apology to the motorist behind him, and drove on.

He had put this morning's strange call from Dr. Shepherd out of his mind. She was probably some crackpot vet, looking to make a few extra bucks. He said nothing to his parents about the conversation.

Nick was determined to drive by Brandi's former home or perhaps her current home. Despite the fact he spent the night with her, its exact location remained a mystery. Nick ruminated why she acted so strangely after returning from Pittsburgh.

He was fairly confident she no longer lived on Hickory Circle. He'd seen the pierced Hawkeye come out one morning and the interior of Brandi's home showed no sign of a male resident. His mind continued trekking that path. He also didn't notice a computer or laptop. A hi-fi stereo and CD's, not an iPod. He hadn't noticed Brandi in possession of a cell phone.

And the movie was on VHS, not a DVD or Blu-Ray. Nick always felt as if time stood still around Brandi. *Hmm...*

Nick stopped, looked down the short cul-de-sac but did not drive it. From the side street, he studied the house. He scooped up his phone. No missed calls, voice-mail, or texts from Brandi. Disappointed, he drove away for his rendezvous.

Moments later, he parked his rented yellow Hyundai and approached Wolfsie's house. Nick was apprehensive about seeing Karri. Cancer wasn't exactly fun. Then again, based on Uncle Hank's vegetative state, a massive stroke was no picnic either.

Wearing a rust colored polo and blue khaki's, Wolfsie bounded through the front door enthusiastically. "Nick fucking Garrison!" He acknowledged Nick's Guns-n-Roses T-shirt with his chin. "Still trapped in the '80s I see."

"If I'm going to be trapped somewhere, can't think of a better place."

The men fist-bumped. Wolfsie was in unusually good spirits, showing no indication of his wife's medical condition. To add to the atypical behavior, he handed Nick a bottle: Water, not beer. "Karri's resting. Is it okay if we hang outside?"

"Yeah, sure." The chilled refreshing beverage was perfect for a muggy day. "How is she?"

"She's doing well."

Nick nodded. "You seem to be doing well also."

"I'm trying."

"And succeeding."

Wolfsie took a large gulp. "It is what it is, Nick. I guess we should be lucky we found the lump early. At least we have a chance to beat this thing."

"There's always hope," Nick stated, then wondered if that qualified as a cliché. Based on his friend's outlook, it appeared Wolfsie had *made peace* with whatever Karri's fate might be. *Making peace? Another damn platitude.* "Anyway, what's so urgent that you wanted me to stop by?"

Wolfsie draped his arm around his friend's shoulder and steered him to a craggy bench off to the side of the front yard. He sat, patted the spot next to him. The bench was small, creaky. As Nick felt awkward sharing a bench with another guy, he slid over a few inches, wondering if the decaying seat would support their combined weight. "I just wanted to thank you."

Nick said, "Thank me for what?"

"For offering to talk to Karri. And offering your place to us."

"The offer's still on the table."

Wolfsie nodded his gratitude. It was the third time Nick had met with his old chum and Wolfsie had already smiled more in five minutes than the previous two times combined.

Nick and Wolfsie chatted a bit. It felt nice to gab. They were two guys catching up. Nick decided to move the dialogue in a different direction. "You'll never guess who I saw last night."

"Who?"

"Brandi."

Wolfsie's face scrunched like he'd just downed a hot pepper. "Brandi?"

"Brandi Conrad."

"*Brandi Conrad*?" Wolfsie yelped.

Somewhere between irony and pride, Nick laughed. "Yeah, can you believe it?"

"No. I can't."

"I know, right?" Nick beamed. "We ran into each other outside the market the day before yesterday. Talked a bit. Then we went out last night."

Disbelievingly, Wolfsie repeated, "You went out *last night*?"

"Way out. Went down to the 'burgh, ate a little, danced a little, and then came back."

"*Came back*? Where?"

Wolfsie repeating his statements caused Nick to laugh. "To here. Well, not *here*. But to her home here in Avalon." Nick paused. "And don't get the wrong idea but we spent the night together."

Wolfsie had just sipped and nearly choked. "Spent the *night together*?"

"Nothing happened. Well, not really."

Nick grinned sheepishly. The recollection of Brandi's feet and calves rubbing his crotch caused him to blush.

"You spent the night with Brandi?"

"Yup"

"Brandi Conrad?"

"Yep."

Wolfsie waggled his head and stared at an imaginary spot on the ground. "I can't believe it."

"Me neither."

Wolfsie faced his friend. Their eyes locked. "No, Nick. I mean that *can't* be."

"It *can* be." Nick laughed. "It happened." Hearkening back to a recent conversation he had with his sister-in-law and resorting to yet another cliché, Nick announced, "The Lord works in mysterious ways."

"He may work in mysterious ways. But it can-not-be."

"And why not?"

"Because Brandi Conrad is dead."

Chapter 19

The irremovable smile from last evenings recollections was still plastered on Nick's face as he stated, "That's not funny, Ed."

Surprised Nick used his given name, Wolfsie replied, "It's not meant to be funny."

"Don't screw with me."

"I'm not screwing with you, bro."

Nick cocked his head and gave his lifelong pal a million mile stare. "If you're joking, I'll kick your ass!"

"Nick, I'm not joking."

"I—saw her last night. That's imp—I saw her. Just last night. We went out. We danced—"

Wolfsie put his hand on Nick's shoulder, his perpetually sad eyes taking on a more sorrowful expression. "I know I always mess with you. But I also know Brandi always had a special place in your heart. Even *I* wouldn't make a joke about this."

Had. Past tense. Nick found himself up and pacing. "That can't be, it can't. I saw her last damn night."

Wolfsie waited a beat. "Just over two years ago, traffic accident just outside of town."

Nick searched his friend's face. Wolfsie had always been a practical joker. But even he couldn't take a joke this far without finally breaking. "If you're screwing with me, Wolfsie, I…I don't know what."

"I'm not. I swear to you I'm not."

"It's impossible. How?" Nick continued, wearing out the lawn.

Last night was no dream. It couldn't be. There was tangible physical proof. They touched. They danced. Skin against skin. They laughed. He saw her home. Sure, okay, he may not know exactly where she lived. But he was in *her* home, on *her* sofa, watching *her* TV.

"It's not fair."

Wolfsie shot a glance toward his home where his ailing wife was battling cancer. "*You're* talking to *me* about what's fair? Life isn't fair."

"Life isn't fair," Nick mocked. He'd had it up to his eyeballs with clichés. He wanted to prove the claim was ludicrous, laughable. He'd drive Wolfsie straight over to Brandi's home right now—if only he knew where she lived. He'd call her, have Wolfsie talk to her on the phone—if only he had her number. "Traffic accident, huh?"

Wolfsie nodded.

Brandi always drove recklessly. As a teenager it was almost expected. You were invincible and would live forever. But even last night as they drove south, she exceeded the speed limit. "Was she drunk?" Nick didn't know where that came from.

"I heard she *did* have some alcohol in her blood, yes. But well under the legal limit, not enough to impair her. She was coming back from the 'burgh. Word around town was she fell asleep."

Nick swallowed hard. Last night Brandi handed Nick her keys and asked him to drive because she was tired.

Two years ago?

For the first time since returning home, his head pounded something fierce, rattling his skull. He scanned the neighborhood as if other houses could provide an answer. In the distance, he caught sight of the TV towers atop Aliquippa Mountain. Daytime. But the two lights alternated. One blink, one second. Time passing by, second by second. Life elapsing one flickering moment at a time. Back to Wolfsie, "How?"

"Told ya, man, car accident."

"No, I mean, how could I have seen her last night?"

"Maybe it wasn't her."

Nick snickered at the absurdity.

Wolfsie stood and moved closer to his friend. "The mind is a strange thing. People always imagine things, use images to fill a void. It's like those people who lose a loved one and then swear they saw the departed soul that evening. Just a couple days ago Karri self-examined and swore the lump was gone. Wishful thinking. People claim to see things simply cause they *wish* to see them."

"I felt it, too."

"Seeing, feeling? Same difference."

Nick grunted and resumed pacing. "You're saying I don't know Brandi? You're saying I wouldn't know it was someone pretending to be her?" Nick heard himself talking louder, defiantly. His anger was directed at Wolfsie as if *he* caused Brandi's supposed accident. "And why? Why would someone pretend to be her? Just to mess with me? Christ, Wolfsie. I would know Brandi! I would recognize her! I never stopped loving her!"

Wolfsie bowed his head. "I know you never stopped."

Nick skulked away. "I never should've left. I never should have fucking left. Damn it, what was I thinking? How stupid could I have been? I went to the other end of the country, looking for something when everything I ever wanted was right here." Nick slammed his hand against his head. "I was so smug back then."

"Smugness *does* run in the Garrison men."

Nick stopped mid-stride. "Point taken," he conceded.

Wolfsie said, "I can't explain what you saw or what you think happened last night—"

"I *know* what happened. I felt it." Nick pointed to his own chest. "In here. First time in more than twenty five years I felt it."

"What I know are facts. And facts don't lie. Brandi's gone, man."

"Bullshit!"

Wolfsie shot his friend a pitiful look. "Come, I'll show you."

ⅭⳄⳄ

Nick couldn't move. Just south of where the corroded bridge spanned the Acheron River and led away from Avalon Hills Wolfsie parked on the shoulder. Nick leaned against the passenger's door and watched from a distance.

Wolfsie traversed a small hill, forty or so yards off the road. He went to the tree line and specified a piece of sheared off bark. The deep-rooted elm was one of hundreds that stood bold and proud. Nick had driven past this very spot numerous times since returning.

"She apparently veered, overcorrected," Wolfsie explained. "Word was the car flipped twice and hit the tree right here head-on." He squatted and pointed.

Nick refused to encroach on the hallowed ground. In spite of it being mid-afternoon and both the temperature and humidity at eighty, Nick felt clammy and chilled. For no reason other than to prove Wolfsie wrong, Nick clipped, "What was she driving?"

"Nissan something."

Nissan? Same car she drove last night. Paranoid, Nick asked, "And where's the car now?"

Wolfsie grinned somberly. His friend was refusing to accept the loss. "It was totaled."

"Let's go to the junkyard," Nick insisted. "Prove me wrong!"

"It's two years ago, man. It's been torn apart and scrapped."

"It's Brandi's car. I want to see it, okay?"

Wolfsie ignored Nick's challenge. "They say it was quick. Pretty much instantly."

Wolfsie knew the details. The engine block tore through the dashboard, severing her legs, nearly splitting Brandi in half. Her upper torso hurled like a rag doll through the windshield. Her face shredded by glass, her neck broken. He kept the specifics to himself.

Nick got back in the car and with Herculean strength slammed the door. "Let's go."

"Where?"

"The junkyard. I want to see her car. Ya know, the one she *supposedly* died in."

Avalon Hills Scrapyard was located seven miles west of town around the far side of Aliquippa Mountain. As Wolfsie drove the twisty road, Nick refused to even give the blinking lights a courtesy glance. Frames, hubcaps, tires, and engine parts littered the landscape in frenzied chaos. The office, inside a trailer, was saturated with the stench of engine grease and cigarette smoke. The owner, Ziggy, as indicated by an oval patch sewn onto his blue overalls, had pronounced jowls and a worn-down demeanor. Deep creases in his forehead brought to mind the grill of a 73 Plymouth Duster. When Wolfsie asked to see Brandi's car, the man guffawed.

"It's important. For my friend," Wolfsie said.

Ziggy went through the motions. He retrieved files from a tall green metal cabinet and rifled through them. He then verified his findings on an old fashioned Apple computer. "Like I told ya, nothin'. It's standard we keep 'em intact ninety days, just in case Sheriff Garrison needs to conduct an investigation. But, nah, this one's long gone."

Wolfsie thanked the man and turned. Nick had already departed.

Once outside, Nick declared, "Still no proof."

Wolfsie pursed his lips. Denial was a powerful emotion. His friend could not wrap his mind around the fact that Brandi had died. It would be difficult under normal circumstances. The fact that Nick claimed to have spent time with her last night made accepting reality that much more challenging.

"C'mon," Wolfsie mumbled.

The drive back into town was silent. Nick stared out the window, blind to the verdant hills rolling by.

Wolfsie felt sad for his friend, but he'd been there himself. Learning his wife was battling cancer was impossible to accept. But just like he had come to terms with Karri's fate, Nick would need to accept Brandi's.

The Avalon Hills Public Library was situated in the so-called cultural district. Built in 1924, it was constructed to resemble the famous New York Public Library. That was where the similarities ended.

Nick had an idea why they were here. His fast steps only surpassed by the rapid beating of his heart. He couldn't wait to shoot down more fabricated evidence his friend would provide.

Wolfsie was a stranger in a strange land, unable to recall the last time he'd been enveloped by a sea of books. The endless rows and shelves were intimidating. With Nick in tow, he approached a grandmotherly type at the reference desk. She was probably an original employee from 1924.

"May I help you?" Her voice was frail, her demeanor sweet.

Recalling library etiquette, Wolfsie spoke in a hushed tone. "I'm looking for old newspapers from just over two years ago. Both Pittsburgh and our local paper."

"My word, we don't keep newspapers in stock that long. If they're from that long ago, I suggest their websites."

Old library, old smell, old librarian. But they had joined the twenty first century.

The librarian lifted a pencil that she probably swiped from a miniature golf course and jotted something down. "We offer two computers," she pointed "that have access to the World Wide Web. This is the password to unlock it. If you wouldn't mind, please limit it to fifteen minutes."

Wolfsie thanked the woman, turned to Nick. "Let's go."

"Yes, let's go," Nick clipped. As he abruptly spun, he collided with a woman. "Sorry," he grumbled and stormed away, oblivious to the fact he knocked three books from her hand.

As the woman squatted down, Wolfsie also did and helped her gather her books. "My friend's having a bad day," he offered.

"I'd say." She smiled at the fetching blue-eyed man and his chivalrous act. They stood in unison. "Thank you," she said.

Wolfsie eyed the books. "*Divine Comedy* by Dante and books on Greek mythology?"

The woman shot him a hopeful glance. "Are you familiar with Greek mythology?"

"I've watched *Clash of the Titans* if that counts."

The woman smiled.

Wolfsie rolled his eyes toward Nick. "Again, I apologize for my friend, ma'am."

The woman chuckled. "Ma'am? Thanks for making me feel old."

Wolfsie offered a hand. "I'm Ed."

She cupped the books in the crook of her left arm, extended her right. "Nice meeting you, Ed. I'm Frannie."

⤦⤥⤦

Wolfsie keyed the password, accessed the internet, and opened four separate browsers. Alongside, Nick leaned back, showing more irritation than interest. Arms folded defiantly across his chest, breathing fire, foot tapping impatiently, Nick exulted, "Could their system be any slower? God, I hate this town. Always have."

Wolfsie ignored Nick's remark and kept working, while Nick busied himself by shooting daggers at everyone around them. A moment later, Wolfsie tapped the monitor. "Have a look for yourself."

Nick whined and angled closer. Wolfsie had pulled up the obituaries dated June 3 two years earlier for the *Pittsburgh Post-Gazette*, the *Butler County Eagle*, and the *McKeesport Daily News*. He'd also accessed the archived section of the weekly local paper.

Wolfsie slid aside, allowing Nick a clear view.

The obits were nearly identical. They listed Brandi's dates of birth and death, the fact she was survived by one older brother living down south. No funeral or services were planned.

Only the article in the *Avalon Hills Bugle* made reference to the single car rollover. Wolfsie's peripheral vision was on Nick. He watched his friend read the epitaphs. Nick was void of emotion, detached.

After finishing, Nick smirked. "Let's switch seats. Give me five minutes and I'll show you an alien meeting with the president and Elvis pumping gas in Jersey."

Wolfsie frowned.

"You really believe everything you read on the Internet?"

"Jesus! Nick, come on."

Wolfsie considered his friend. An impenetrable wall surrounded Nick, a wall that no facts or hard data could breach. Wolfsie took a deep breath, exhaled slowly and stood. He had only one option remaining.

⤦⤥⤦

Half an hour later, Nick glowered through the window of Wolfsie's car. "Why are we here?" he asked in a small voice.

"You have to see for yourself," Wolfsie said, exiting.

Nick remained in the tomblike silence of the car. He tightened his jaw, peered around angrily. *This is all such bullshit!* "Fine!" he wailed to no one and aggressively heaved himself from the vehicle.

Wolfsie stood twenty yards away in the shadow of an elm, head lowered, looking somberly at the ground. Nick huffed and puffed his way over. Sidestepping headstones and grave markers, his legs began to liquefy as he came nearer. His breathing became labored. He didn't want to see this. Didn't need to see this. But something within his soul pulled him onward.

Nick stood to Wolfsie's left but he refused to look down. Standing at-ease, he scanned the horizon. He probed the bushes, admired the way the grounds were maintained. He looked over his shoulder and verified the car was still there. He regarded everywhere—except what was at his feet.

Wolfsie stood in reverence.

Nick didn't know how long it took. Seconds? Minutes? Time always stopped when it came to Brandi. He shut his eyes tightly, willing himself to be somewhere else. Anywhere else. His lids lifted, his eyes lowered.

Brandi Jane Conrad was engraved on the granite headstone. Date of birth. Date of death. Nothing else.

Cold.

The only sound of life was a flock of birds slicing through the air. After a moment of silence, Nick spoke without drawing his gaze away. "Jane. She always hated her middle name."

"I'll be back in the car," Wolfsie said gently. "Take as much time as you need."

"I'm ready when you are."

Wolfsie frowned. Nick worked in a cemetery so perhaps Brandi's name on a plaque didn't carry significance. Still, he was surprised his friend wanted no time for reflection. "You sure?"

Staring at the slab, but speaking to Wolfsie, Nick asserted, "This doesn't prove anything either."

Wolfsie moaned. He was out of options. Repudiation was one thing, but Nick was well beyond that. Sarcastically, Wolfsie asked, "What, you want to dig her up?"

The glare Nick shot back indicated he was already considering it.

"Christ, Nick. Let the girl rest in peace. Please, you need to—"

"I need to what?" he shouted. "Accept it? Accept she's gone? She's not. She can't be. I just saw her last night!"

Wolfsie slowly shook his head. "Nick," he whispered with a note of caution.

"Don't 'Nick' me." Nick moved closer to his friend, nostrils flaring. "Then tell me how last night could have happened. Explain that to me."

"People see things they want to see all the time. It's not that uncommon."

Nick bit his lip hard, threw his hands against his hips. They'd been friends since high school but now that didn't matter. "Fuck you!" he shouted. He turned to the grave. "And fuck that!"

Wolfsie placed his hands on Nick's shoulders in a calming manner. The next thing he saw was Nick wiggling away, drawing his arm back. The blinding right cross caused Wolfsie to crumble.

Down on one knee, dazed and stunned, Wolfsie patted away a trace of blood from his lip. "Shit, Nick."

❧❧

A volcano could lay dormant for hundreds of thousands of years. It appeared as a quiet peaceful cone-shaped mountain. However, beneath the surface, it was simmering and festering. Pressure built until the power was too forceful to contain and it erupted with an earth quaking explosion.

And then the energy and pressure was again at rest.

As Nick looked at his fallen friend, he realized he too had erupted. "I'm sorry, Wolfsie." Reality had set in. He knelt alongside and assisted Wolfsie upright.

Wolfsie dismissed the apology, stunned by Nick's unexpected explosion.

Nick pursed his lips as he pivoted to study the headstone. His knees weakened. He swallowed hard and his brows arched. Like a volcano lying asleep for too long, Nick's emotions gushed. Her name became unclear through the tears that blurred his vision. His shoulders rose and lowered. His breathing grew heavier, deeper. He felt a massive emptiness in his chest. It was now Nick who was down on his knees. Sobbing uncontrollably, he lovingly tousled the stony slab, muttering softly, "Brandi."

๛

Nick had no answers. He couldn't explain the events of last night. The warm familiar feelings, the sweet sensations or the magic that rose in his heart *were* real.

But yet, he had undeniable proof. He saw the physical location of the accident, four different obits, and her final resting place. The fact that Brandi was…gone…could not be disputed. There was no great conspiracy at work here. And even if there was, why? What for? There was no logical reason. Was there some master plan to have Nick driven insane? Was the entire town of Avalon Hills out to get him?

Brandi had died, but she'd live on in his memory. Now he had to figure out why someone was trying to convince him otherwise.

Nick regarded the whole matter as a dream. Even the most realistic dreams lacked specifics. Smells, emotions, sights and touch became vivid in a realistic dream state. But details were left out, details such as an address. He didn't know specifically where Brandi lived. He couldn't recall much of the conversation they shared driving south to Pittsburgh. At dinner, they shared chips. Plain, simple. They listened to Every Night Fever but he could only recall them performing one specific song, the song he requested.

Am I going nuts?

The Acheron River, the body of water that circumvented the city, had been filled with chemicals and toxins for decades.

Was something in the water causing Nick to lose touch with reality? Was he going insane?

Was this what ultimately caused Mike Lauser to blow his brains out? And if Mike had been mentally compromised, if Mike had lost touch with reality, was Nick beginning to unravel in the same fashion? Would he eventually crack like his friend and take his own life?

Fear of losing his grip on reality scared the shit out of him.

He'd come home for one reason and one reason only. Although he hadn't found the time to have *the discussion* with his parents, he knew he'd have to make time, time that was ticking away second by second.

☙☙☙

Eve raced down the hallway. "Nick, what happened? Where were you all day?"

He bent over, kissed her cheek. "Just out, Mom."

"I was worried sick."

"I'm fine."

Striding closer, Lloyd exclaimed, "Your mother asked you a question. Where were you?"

"And I answered," Nick countered, leaving out *sir* this time.

"*Out* is not an answer," Lloyd spat.

Nick observed Scrappy Four on his hind legs, scratching feverishly on his father's shin. Lloyd reached down, rubbed the dog's ears, and then sauntered to the pantry where the dog treats were stored. Four rose onto his back legs and spun in a clockwise circle, the same trick Scrappy One performed when Nick was a boy. Recalling this morning's call from the veterinarian, Nick asked, "How old is Scrappy, mom?"

"He's almost seven, why?"

"Shut your mouth, woman!" Lloyd snarled. "If he refuses to answer a question, why should you?"

"Jesus Christ! Give me—"

Lloyd was in his son's face in seconds flat. "I will not have the Lord's name taken in vane in my home!"

"I'm an adult. I can say what I want."

"Not in my home you can't. And as long as you are under my roof, you will abide by my rules."

"What am I, sixteen again?"

Lloyd moved closer to Nick. Eve positioned herself between her first born and her husband. "Lloyd! Nick! Stop this, right now!"

Oblivious to Eve, father and son glowered at each other, searching each other's soul. Nostrils flaring, Lloyd declared, "Perhaps it's best you stay somewhere else."

"Fine!"

He stormed upstairs, angrily walked down the hall, and slammed the door as if his father wouldn't hand over the car keys. He *was* sixteen again.

Nick lowered himself onto his bed, fury coursing through his blood like a raging fire. He didn't want to check into the derelict Olive Tree Motel. On the other hand, he couldn't stay here. The cauldron of tension that had been simmering like a volcano between father and son for decades was about to blow.

Head in his hand, elbows on his knees, Nick rocked gently. So deep in thought, he did not hear the engine outside. Had he looked through the window he would have noticed the white Ford pick-up from Hickory Circle. And he would have seen the mysterious Hawkeye behind the wheel.

Chapter 20

Frannie had accompanied her stoic husband to more galas and social events around Washington DC than she could count. As Davis displayed his younger wife for all to see, she'd dutifully played her role. She mingled with numerous power brokers and the elite of the political landscape. Diplomats, foreign dignitaries, committee chairmen, even the First Lady conversed with her on one occasion. When Frannie informed people she was a statistical analyst III over at Commerce, she was always met with a pitiful gaze. Working with numbers, studying figures, and performing comparative data analyses never appealed to anyone.

And really, Frannie herself was never thrilled with it either. It was boring mundane work. But she had fallen into a tolerable career and a decent paycheck.

Yesterday, her background proved beneficial.

After the unsettling confrontation at the abandoned Tri-Delta factory with Sheriff Garrison she was unwavering to leave town as quick as possible, return home, and erase Avalon Hills from the ledger of her mind. The note slipped beneath her windshield changed her intentions.

To a novice, it appeared a series of random figures in no special sequence, a string of arbitrary unsystematic digits. Back at the hotel that evening, it took Frannie ninety minutes to decipher the coded chain.

One series were coordinates. She linked them to the Avalon Hills Public Library. Other numbers related to an antiquated card catalog system. Nowadays, most libraries used OPAC, or Online Public Access Catalog, but Frannie grasped what the outdated numbers were.

She took a circuitous route to the Cultural District, fearing the town sheriff was following her. Keeping her cautious eyes on her rear view mirror the entire drive, she parked three blocks away on a tree-lined side street. Wearing her hair tucked beneath a Washington Nationals baseball cap, a neophyte attempt to remain concealed, Frannie clandestinely entered.

She traced down the books the note guided her to. Two were about Greek Mythology, one was *The Divine Comedy* by Dante Alighieri.

The latter was widely regarded as one of the greatest pieces of literature ever written. It was divided into three separate sections: *Inferno, Purgatorio*, and *Paradiso*. In college, Frannie appreciated many classics by Stevenson, Longfellow, Steinbeck, and Hemingway. She now regretted not being required to read works by Dante. She was older now, her mind not as sharp as it had been during her academic days.

Dante's masterpiece described the author's supposed journey through Hell, Purgatory, and Heaven. Reading between the lines, the hidden meaning was somewhat deeper, more thought provoking. It related to the voyage, or quest, of one soul to find God. Much of Dante's work and interpretation of an afterlife was pulled from theories originally put forth by the ancient Greeks.

Lying on her side, her diminutive frame curled into a fetal position on the bed, Frannie felt herself drawn in. The TV that played low as well as sounds outside her room, went unheard.

She read about Charon who, according to Greek Mythology, was a ferryman that transported the souls of the departed into the underworld. One had to pay to be taken across the river. "Sort of like the death tax," the federal employee thought. Charon was also the one who decided who was worthy of gaining passage based on them receiving what he deemed proper burial rites. Those who did not hand over the fee or were judged undeserving would be left behind where they wandered the banks of a river for one hundred years.

Frannie felt a chill slither up her spine and end with the skin crawling on the back of her neck. In both Greek mythology and Dante's classic, the body of water Charon crossed with deceased spirits was named the Acheron River.

Losing track of time, Frannie continued reading/studying the three books. She walked to the vanity to throw some water on her face when she noticed something slipped under her motel room door.

She hugged herself nervously in response to the chill that cut through to her marrow. Frannie crossed the room, walked over, unfolded the paper, and peered out from the drapes that fronted the parking lot.

This note, like the previous one, had numbers scribbled but it included instructions as well. More clues. The same individual who had followed her to Tri-Delta had resurfaced. This note was also signed *BD*.

☙ ❧ ☙

"I'm here to see Sheriff Garrison," Nick declared.

The deputy with too much makeup met him on the opposite side of the counter. "Do you have an appointment?"

"No."

"And you are?"

"His brother." The baffled look on her face resulted in Nick adding, "It's mutual. Neither of us admits we have a sibling."

Somewhat flustered she said, "Let me see if he's available."

Nick watched her traipse across the room, wrap her knuckles on the closed office door, and stick her head in. Moments later, Nick was allowed passage to meet with the great and powerful sheriff.

Gabe's office was small. A book shelf on the right consisted of everything except books: small figurines, framed photos of the sheriff with some of the city's business owners, trophies he received for excelling at target practice. It was hard to find but there was a family picture of Gabe's clan. Alex and Chelsea were kids. Gabe and Yolanda still looked happy. The opposite wall was adorned with yet more photographs, awards, and commendations. Nick wondered if his egotistical brother had printed them up himself or if he really was *that* gifted at his job.

Gabe was terse. "I heard from Mom you and Dad got into it last night."

"What else is new?" Nick shook his head. "The tension in that house, you can cut it with a knife."

"Only since you came back."

Nick let it go.

"Still staying there or you need a place to crash?" As expected, Gabe didn't offer his own home but mentioned he could get Nick a ten dollar discount at the Olive Tree.

"I am for now. Mom smoothed things over. Dad and I pretty much ignored each other this morning."

Gabe breathed deep. "Funny, isn't it?"

"What is?"

"It's usually the first born who's the favorite. Not in this case."

Nick let that go as well.

"Anyway, what do you want?"

Nick had swallowed his pride by coming here. He hated seeking an informational handout, especially from his self-important brother. It would only fan the flames of Gabe's narcissism. But Nick was desperate and wanted—no, needed—to find an answer. "What can you tell me about Brandi Conrad?"

Gabe met his brother's eyes with an unflinching stare. "What about her? She's dead, two years now."

Brandi. Dead. Those two words sounded awkward together. "I know."

"Then why are you here?"

"You were sheriff two years ago. What can you tell me about the accident?"

"It's ancient history, brother. Why do you care?" Gabe leaned back, his swivel chair creaked slightly. He rubbed his chin, the look of bewilderment twisting into one of recollection. "Oh, that's right. You had a thing for her. I remember now."

"That's why I'm curious."

Gabe weighed his decision. "Early June, if I remember. She came home late one night after partying and drinking down in Pittsburgh. It had rained, road was slick. That, combined with alcohol, resulted in her losing control and T-boning a tree just outside the city limits."

"Was she over the legal limit?" Nick had been told by

Wolfsie she wasn't. He just wanted to test Gabe's honesty.

"No, she wasn't. But the combination of the long drive, *some* alcohol, and the road conditions came together in a perfect storm. And that was that."

Gabe was not pleased with Nick's presence, less so being on the receiving end of an interrogation. He'd been upset when his brother returned to town a few days ago. Now, Nick had the audacity to come in and question something that happened years ago. And without making an appointment? He blatantly looked at his watch. "Anything else?"

"Got somewhere to be?" Nick snapped.

"If I do, it's not your concern. I don't report to you. I don't report to anyone. You may be my brother, but you're a guest in my town and an uninvited visitor in my office."

Nick sneered. "Sounds like you're challenging me to a gunfight on Main Street at high noon."

"Listen to me, Nick." Moving only his eyes, Gabe peered around his office as if the proper words floated in the air, waiting to be grabbed. "This is no great revelation. You and I have never gotten along. Not as kids, not as adults. We've had no communication in twenty-five years. And that suits me fine. You were the one who should have stayed here, not me. But you left. You went out, chasing some bullshit dream, and I was forced to stay behind. You were the first born, but I—I had dreams, too."

Nick's brows knitted. He realized that, although Gabe had always focused on good health and eating right, concerned more with his physical appearance than most men, his brother looked worn as if carrying a heavy burden upon his shoulders. "You're upset 'cause I'm older? That's absurd."

"You got other questions?"

"Did she…was it quick?"

Gabe ran his fingers through his hair. "You want the truth or should I tell you what you wanna hear?"

Even without responding directly, Nick had gotten his answer. "How quick?"

Gabe scoffed. "I'm the sheriff, not the coroner. By the time I got out there, she was pretty much a goner."

Nick shut his eyes securely.

"Probably better off," Gabe continued. "She wouldn't have wanted to live through it anyway."

Air was sucked from the room like a vacuum. Nick slouched as if someone deflated his lungs. When he opened his eyes, Gabe was standing at a tan filing cabinet. He watched his brother thumb through some files.

Yesterday Nick had been taken on *The Brandi Farewell Tour* courtesy of Wolfsie. Seeing Brandi Jane Conrad on a marble slab cemented the deal. He still had doubts, unable to explain how he could have spent the night with her. Or who—as paranoid as it sounded—was behind this outlandish conspiracy to convince him Brandi was still alive. And more importantly, why?

Nick reasoned it could only be one of two things: either some powerful forces were at work behind some crazy machination, or he was going insane. Neither possibility was comforting.

"Here," Gabe claimed. One by one he started tossing photos onto his desk for Nick to peruse.

Classic black and white crime scene photos. Details were hard to pinpoint based on the poor lighting. The first one showed a person lying cockeyed through an obliterated windshield, face down, strewn partially across the hood of a car. The raven black hair was in disarray, shards of glass embedded in arms and hands.

A second photo revealed the image of a woman slumped back in the driver's seat, her body mangled peculiarly in an unnatural angle, head turned away, face hidden by matted blood-soaked hair. The steering wheel was askew and part of the engine block lay strewn across the front seat and her lap. Nick nearly threw up.

"We eased her back through the windshield hoping to get a pulse. That's why the two angles." Gabe tossed a third photo, a fourth, a fifth.

Nick couldn't look.

"Damn shame," Gabe noted as he scooped up the photos and returned them to the file. "She was smokin' hot."

Nick let that comment slide as well.

But Gabe wasn't done. "When she died, Avalon Hills lost

the best piece of ass to come through these parts in a *long* time."

Nick did not let that go. He sprang from his chair, sending it crashing to the floor.

Gabe swiftly backpedaled, hand at his sidearm. "Go ahead, brother, go ahead. You know what you get for assaulting a police officer?"

The hairs on Nick's neck straightened, his hands fisted. "Then what time are you off-duty?"

"Threatening a police officer is also a punishable offense."

The two brothers bore into each other's eyes, spewing fire, waiting for the other to make the first move.

Gabe broke the silence and shot his brother with a remark more painful than anything a bullet could do. "Ever think had you not left to chase some bogus dream Brandi would still be alive? Tell me, what's it like to have the blood of the only woman you ever loved on your hands?"

It took everything Nick had to stand down. This chat with his prick brother had accomplished nothing other than displaying what an arrogant son of a bitch Gabe was, something Nick had known for decades.

On the other hand, sheriff or not, Gabe Garrison shouldn't be allowed to utter such hurtful things without fear of repercussions. Nick knew he'd come out on the losing end of an altercation. But if he just could get in one good blow…

Attacking a police officer carried serious jail time. And Nick doubted his father, the mayor, would pull strings for him. Still, it might be worth it. Nick didn't give a shit anymore.

Hard as it was to not send his brother across the room, Nick backed down.

The look of rage morphed into a deplorable grin. "How do you sleep at night, Gabe?"

"I sleep fine," Gabe answered. "I sleep with a woman who loves me and not with the realization of what I pissed away."

Nick waggled his head.

"Now," Gabe said, using his drawn revolver as a pointer. "Get out of my office."

Nick flung open the door forcefully and filed out.

Gabe followed him to the doorway. The big-haired deputy

was on her way in and presented her boss a folder. "This is the Jonathan Decker file, sheriff."

"Thanks, Beth. And if *he* sets foot in here, consider it trespassing."

Nick stormed out of the station and furiously strode to his car. What was Gabe's problem? Never getting along was one thing. But his brother was acting certifiable. Nick wondered if he would have really shot him. Or arrested him? He speculated if his brother had purposely tried to provoke him into a confrontation just so he'd have an excuse to lock him up.

Nick accepted the time to leave Avalon Hills was now at hand. He'd return to Arizona and meet his fate. He just hated departing now. It would, in Gabe's mind, send a signal that *he* had won. Gabe threatened, Nick took off. On the other hand, Nick had no reason to stay, especially since Brandi was…

Turning over the engine, Nick backed out of the tight parking spot. His second over-the-shoulder glance resulted in him frowning.

He watched the pedestrian stridently plod up the steps and enter the police station. *"Why is Wolfsie talking to my brother?"* Nick wondered.

Chapter 21

Pushing through the heavy tension and unmerciful conflict that strangled the life from the Garrison home, Nick sidled alongside his mother. Entering the living room, Eve announced, "Lloyd, Nick wants to talk to us."

Sitting in his chair, eyes glued to the TV, the family patriarch nary shot a glance at his wife and refused to acknowledge his son.

Eve reached for the remote which he switched to his left hand, beyond her grasp. "*After* the show."

"He says it's important."

Lloyd spat. "It's *always* important with *him*."

"You don't have to talk as if I'm not here."

Lloyd's mouth opened but he said nothing, choosing to give his undivided attention to *TVLand*.

"Did you want something to drink, Nick? Chips, perhaps? I have those little candies you used to like."

Unable to recall which candies she was referring to, Nick declined. "No thanks, Mom."

"Do you mind?" snapped Lloyd. "I'm trying to watch." He arrowed up the volume and drowned out the conversation.

Restlessly Nick sat.

And waited.

He felt like a kid again, about to justify to his parents why he committed some teenage hijinks. On TV, Dr. Huxtable and wife Clair were sitting at their kitchen table talking to their oldest son. A girl Theo had a crush on since fourth grade rejected his continuous requests to go to a high school dance with him. The entire family dilemma was resolved in a matter of twenty-one minutes—with commercials. *If only real life problems could be resolved that easily.*

Lloyd sat but never once laughed or even slightly grinned. Nick found *that* laughable. The Garrisons were totally dysfunctional. Yet, Lloyd enjoyed watching a sitcom where everyone was cheerful and got along.

Cliff and Clair danced in the kitchen as the screen faded. Lloyd did not turn off the show until the credits finished rolling. Perhaps, just for spite, he waited even longer, watching the opening scene of *King of Queens*. Finally, he decreased the volume to where it was background chatter. "Yes?" he said, looking at Kevin James instead of his family.

"Lloyd, why don't you turn it off?"

"It's low."

Eve sighed. "Nick wants to speak with us."

Rather than shutting the TV, Lloyd pressed mute. "Happy?"

Eve leaned forward, hands clasped in her lap, and attentively faced her son. "Okay, you have the floor."

Nick had played out this very conversation hundreds of times since first getting the news. The entire cross country flight he rehearsed his speech, deciding on the correct lines, proper body language and degree of inflection. He journeyed from Arizona to Pennsylvania for this one moment. But now the moment arrived and Nick could think of no way to ease into it other than just blurting it out. "I'm dying."

"You're done? Done with what?"

"Not done, Mom, dying. I'm dying."

Eve's expression didn't alter. "Dying? That's hogwash."

"No. No, Mom, it's not hogwash."

The expression on Eve's face transformed slightly. "No one's dying. You're just being overly dramatic. How? I mean, you're still a young man. Dying? Good Lord, you're silly."

"No, I'm not silly and yes, I really am."

Eve put on a face Nick had never seen her wear before. She studied her son, examining him, wondering if this was a childish prank of some sort. Perhaps it was his juvenile attempt to get closer to his father. "Dying? Please! That's ridic—that can't be."

Nick drew in his lips. The exchange was not playing out as expected. Equally surprising was the fact that he didn't seem to care anymore. The earthshattering news that had devastated him seemed distant. He announced his own death sentence matter-of-factly. *I'm dying. And would you please pass the potatoes.*

"Dying?" Eve cackled. "What a cockamamie story. Lloyd, do you believe this?"

With his son and wife looking at him, Lloyd responded plainly, "Everyone's dying. One day at a time."

Eve turned back to her son. "Okay, you're dying. And how are you supposedly dying?" She made quotes in the air when saying *dying*.

"*Supposedly* a brain tumor. It's called an astrocytoma. I have glioblastoma, the highest grade and fastest growing type."

Realization edged across Eve's face. "And what does your doctor say?"

"Dr. Rajagopal referred me to an oncologist and—"

"Dr. *who*?" Eve yelped. "What kind of name is that?"

"He's Indian, Mom."

Eve squinted. She put her palm at the back of her head and extended her fingers simulating feathers and a headdress. "Indian doctor? You mean like a woo-woo-woo?"

"No, Eve," interrupted Lloyd. He pressed his index finger between his brows. "One with those with red dots like Gandhi."

"Couldn't you find an American doctor?" Eve asked.

"The oncologist was named Dr. Greenberg."

"A Jew? That's better. What did he say?"

Nick inhaled, slowly emptying his lungs. "He said they can make me comfortable."

"That's it? That's all they can do? Make you comfortable? This is just...foolish. I've never heard such malarkey." Eve sprang from the chair with sudden movement not displayed in decades. "Have you had any symptoms?"

"Yeah, but I didn't think anything of it."

"What symptoms?" Eve drew her eyes away from her first born child and searched her husband for...help.

Lloyd stared back, void of emotion.

"Headaches," Nick began. "Really bad headaches when I'd

first wake up but I thought it was sinus pressure. Had trouble focusing at work. I'd be in the middle of doing something and then I'd forget what I was doing. Couldn't concentrate on things. I even fell down a couple times."

"Fell down? Did you hurt yourself?"

Nick laughed. Here he was dying of an advanced astrocytoma and his mom was concerned about an *owie* on his knee. "No, I didn't. They did some tests and determined I had two seizures as well."

Eve cupped her mouth. "Seizures? Why didn't you tell me?"

Me, not us. "I didn't realize it. They were minor. I felt this bad pain come over me like my skull was shredded with a fork but I thought they were just…pains. Who'd think seizures?"

"Why didn't you call me?"

"And tell you what, Mom? I'm two thousand miles away. I should call you and let you know I have a headache?"

"Yes, you should!" Eve shouted.

Nick shook his head.

She continued. "I'm your mother. I have a right to know."

"I'm a grown man in case you forgot."

"You don't have kids of your own so you don't understand."

"Ouch."

Eve pressed on. "I don't give a rat's behind how old you are. You always will be my son."

Nick stayed silent.

Eve asked, "And when did you start getting these alleged symptoms?" Quotes in the air again.

"Six months ago," Nick lied. It was closer to nine.

"Six months and you did *nothing*?" Eve squealed, aghast. "How could you do nothing for six months? My heavens. And how come you've said nothing since you've been here?"

"I haven't had any symptoms since I got here."

Eve held her thoughts, mulled that over, then muttered, "Still, six months?"

"I guess I'm stupid," Nick replied, playing the role of admonished child.

Eve walked over, sat alongside. She rubbed the back of his

neck. "You're not stupid. But how did you let this go on for so long? I don't understand."

"I didn't think anything of it."

Nick met his mom's helpless eyes. When he'd first learned of it, he was sure it was a mistake. Someone in some lab somewhere must've screwed up somehow. Surely, they mixed up his test results with some other poor slob who *really* was dying. Cancer only affected old people. Grandmothers who knit, grandfathers who smoke. Not a forty-something Nick Garrison.

Or a forty-something Karri Wolfe.

Hearing he had cancer was surreal. This wasn't tongue cancer or lip cancer. This was *brain* cancer. Or more specifically the very macabre glioblastoma—which sounded even more fatalistic. Hearing from Dr. Greenberg and another oncologist he received a second opinion from that it was too late and untreatable made it final, permanent. Nick was a relatively young man but the curtain was being lowered in the second act of what he assumed would be a three act play.

Nick Garrison, like everyone he knew, fell into complacency. A routine of normalcy where he'd wake every morning, go to work, put in his eight hours, come home, and lose himself in TV or a ballgame. Day after day, week after week, month after month. His life passing by one heartbeat at a time. Blinking like those taunting lights atop Aliquippa Mountain.

Until now when he had no time left.

Eve continued massaging her son's neck and shoulders. She glanced at Lloyd, but only briefly. "We can beat this. We can fight this. As a family, we—"

Nick cocked his head. "No, Mom, we can't."

"You'll see a doctor here. We have good hospitals in Pittsburgh."

"There's a great cancer center in Phoenix where I live. If they can't help, no one can."

Eve glared at her son. She belligerently rose to her feet and jammed her hands against her hips. "No. You will fight this. *We* will fight this. And we will win. As a family. I didn't raise a quitter. Isn't that right, Lloyd?"

Lloyd said nothing. Nick looked at his father. For the first time in two days his father acknowledged his existence.

Nick rose and took his mother's papery hands in his. "There's nothing we can do. It's out of our hands."

"Oh, horseshit!" she screamed and pulled away.

"Eve!"

"What, *Lloyd*?" she yelled. "This is my house, too. And if I want to say horseshit I will say horseshit!" Eve screeched it louder and louder until her voice started breaking and she resembled a raving mad woman. The cracking voice and defiant tone began to weaken, replaced by tears. It became more of a plea. "Horseshit. Just—horseshit."

Nick draped his arm around her frail upper body. She felt small, puny, vulnerable. "Mom, it's okay. I had a hard time accepting it at first also, but—"

"I'm accepting nothing. You may want to give up, but I'm not. I'm your mother and no son of mine is going down without a fight."

Nick knew there were steps one had to go through when dealing with grief. *Supposed steps.* He'd already accepted his fate. His mom, on the other hand, had a long road ahead of her. As he embraced her, her sobbing face pressed against his chest, Nick looked at his father.

Lloyd sat stoically, devoid of emotion as if he was an innocent observer. This was not his son and wife but rather two performers on a stage in a bad high school play. Finally, he stood, hiked his pants, and headed for the door.

"Sir?"

"Where are you going, Lloyd?" Eve cried.

"Out."

Chapter 22

Obeying the instructions of the note slid under her door, Frannie exited the highway and drove into the rest area located midway between Avalon Hills and Pittsburgh. The sprawling grounds were well maintained. A sprinkler system turned on behind her. A handful of cars, two semi-trucks, and a luxurious motor home sat in the parking lot. As she'd been instructed, Frannie sat at the second picnic table on the north side of the rest rooms. She studied her surroundings, glanced at the time on her phone and waited to meet her contact, the elusive and shadowy *BD*.

It was late morning and weary motorists lumbered around. A young family sat nearby, saying grace before the mom divvied up sandwiches and bottled water. A small boy joyously tossed a tennis ball to a bouncy black Lab twice his size while his parents studied a road map. An older man stood impatiently outside the ladies restroom of the A-frame structure, grumbling at his wristwatch.

He caught Frannie looking at him, shook his head, and mouthed *"Women."*

Frannie smiled courteously and continued sitting at the weather-beaten table. The person she was meeting was late. Frannie wondered if she'd been played. She angled forward and glanced north, fearing a set-up by Sheriff Garrison.

"Pard' me," said the man who'd been waiting for his wife, "Mind if I plant myself here?"

"Not at all."

Wearing a plaid pullover tucked into army green trousers pulled too high, the man creaked as he sat. "Much obliged." Sitting sideways, he stared longingly at the rest rooms. "What is it that takes you women so long?"

"Takes time to lower the seat after men always leave it up."

The man chuckled a throaty laugh. "Touché." Spotting Frannie's ring finger, he commented, "Waiting for your husband?"

She wavered and then lied. "Yep."

The man flashed a cursory grin and returned his willful gaze to the restroom exit. Elbows on his knees, he wrung his hands as if cold and began humming a tune.

Frannie continued perusing the landscape, then she eyed the elderly man. The melody sounded familiar.

His humming transformed into gently mumbled but terribly off-key lyrics. "All these places have their moments…with lovers and friends I still can recall. Some are dead and some are living—" He brusquely stopped and expressed embarrassment. "I'm not much of a crooner."

"It sounds familiar but I can't quite place it."

"My wife, huge Beatles' fan."

"'In My Life,'" Frannie cried out. "I recognize it now. I've always believed that somehow newborns come out of the womb already familiar with Lennon and McCartney songs, 'Yellow Submarine,' 'Ob-La-Di, Ob-La-Da.'"

"'With a Little Help From my Friends,'" the man added.

Frannie laughed. "Yes, that one also."

"How rude of me." Turning to face her, he extended his arm. "I'm Burt."

She took the gentleman's hand. "Frannie."

"Burt Dyer."

Clasping the man's hand, she froze. Burt Dyer. *BD.*

"Come, we should talk," he said.

Moments later, Frannie was in the lavish motor home. It was massive inside, offering all the creature comforts one needed. It literally was a home with a motor. Aptly named. "This is very nice."

"Thank you." Burt removed two bottles of ginger ale from a small fridge, poured one for his guest and himself, and sat across from her in the kitchenette.

"I'm guessing you were not really waiting for your wife."

"Correct." He took a brief sip. "My wife passed eleven years ago. Complications from surgery."

"Sorry to hear."

Burt shrugged. "We divorced a *long* time ago. Summer of 1970. First, I thought she was just distraught after The Beatles split up. Kept waiting for her to get over it and come back to me. Never happened. Can't say I blame her for staying away. I was young and too self-centered to think about anyone else." He lowered his head.

"Any children?"

"Two daughters—somewhere."

Frannie faltered. "I'm sorry."

"Took a trip down to Dallas a few years back to see my oldest. Wouldn't even let me in the door. Five grandkids, never met any of them." Burt did a poor job of hiding his sadness.

Frannie conjured images of her daughters and said a silent prayer her family would never suffer this same doom. "So it's just you and this motor home?"

"Yes, ma'am."

The idea of a frail looking man who topped out at one-sixty driving a seven-ton vehicle along the highways and byways of America by himself bemused her. "So you live in this full time?"

"Yes, ma'am. I don't drive around too much anymore. My eyes aren't what they used to be and gosh darn Chevron thinks money grows on trees. I park it, stay in one location for a few weeks, maybe more. Then move on." Burt halted before adding, "I'm not much for staying in one place."

A lull ensued and Frannie took the opportunity to bring the conversation around to the purpose of her being here. She admitted she enjoyed deciphering his coded messages. "Just wondering, how did you manage to get such a large vehicle down that road at the Tri-Delta Plant to leave me that note?"

"I left this monster at the RV Park and asked if I could borrow a car from someone camped a few spaces over. Their son actually drove me. Truth be told, I'd been keeping tabs on you for a while."

Frannie shuddered. "On me? Why?"

"Scratch that. Actually on Sheriff Garrison. I noticed you'd made several attempts to converse with him, meetings he clearly avoided. Your persistence in trying to talk with him made it plain as the nose on my face you had something important you wanted to discuss."

Frannie sipped her beverage. "You can say that."

"I learned your name from the front desk clerk at the motel, researched your background. You work for the Census Bureau under the umbrella of the Commerce Dept."

Feeling infringed upon, Frannie shifted in her seat. She started to ask how Burt uncovered her background but answered her own question. Seven months ago, when suffering a bout of insomnia, Frannie created a few online profiles on social media that detailed her work history and background. She'd never even gone back to update the data.

Burt said, "The fact that someone with your knowledge and proficiency is in Avalon Hills piqued my interest."

Frannie threw her thumb north in the general direction of the Garrison's stronghold. "Do you spend a lot of time there?"

"I come back once in a while. Not too often anymore. I'll stay maybe four five days or until Sheriff Garrison gives me the heave-ho."

Come back? "So you're originally from Avalon Hills, Mr. Dyer?"

"Burt, please. Would you like some more?"

Frannie had never been a fan of ginger ale, but she was a gracious guest and her lips were dry. "If you wouldn't mind, thanks."

As Burt lumbered to the fridge, Frannie remarked, "He appears to run that town with an iron first as if he's a megalomaniacal land owner from feudal times."

"The mayor or the sheriff?"

Good point. "I was referring to the sheriff."

"Thank goodness for that," Burt replied evenly.

"Why do you come back—Burt?"

"To see where it all started. And, for me personally, where it all ended."

"Ended?"

"You're an intelligent young woman who has overcome many personal tragedies. I'm sorry for your loss as well. Raising two children from a young age after the loss of your first husband is not easy to conquer. I applaud your strength."

Infringed upon now became violated. Learning about her work history was one thing. Exposing the death of Tom hit too close to home. Frannie could only manage a generic, "Uh huh."

Determined to redirect the spotlight away from her past, she rifled through her oversized purse and retrieved the report, the same one she presented to her boss Dennis when announcing her plans to investigate northwest Pennsylvania. Along with some extra figures she'd compiled since arriving, she slid the documents across the Formica table.

Burt cast an eye at Frannie, somewhere between amusement and pride. He spent only a minute or two, barely glancing at her discovery. What Frannie had found so baffling and inexplicable had little impact on her host.

He handed the pages back to her. "I won't insult your aptitude. We both know full well things are not on the up and up in Avalon Hills. Your narrative backs up what I've witnessed firsthand."

Frannie frowned. "Good. Then maybe you can explain it to me because I'm not sure *what* I exposed."

He leaned back and bore his eyes into Frannie's soul. He waged an internal battle, deciding how much he could trust her, how far he could go. He was in the two minute warning of life and the clock was ticking down. If he ever intended to share his awareness of what was transpiring up there, he needed to do it soon. Now. The game was almost over. He declared firmly, yet matter-of-factly, "People don't die in Avalon Hills."

Frannie waited for more. Her expression did not flinch. It took a few seconds to comprehend what she'd just heard and when she spoke all she could come up with was a less than brilliant "Huh?"

"Let me word it differently. People die, but they don't leave."

Frannie raised one eyebrow, thoroughly puzzled. She started mentally kicking herself. She'd convinced her boss to let her fly out here. She uncovered some strange data. She put herself in jeopardy by following Sheriff Garrison to the long forgotten Tri-Delta Plant and had her life threatened. She'd followed the trail of clues laid out for her by *BD*. And now, after jumping through all these hoops, *this* was the result? *I'm a fool*. "Please tell me you're kidding, Mr. Dyer."

The stoic unchanged look on his weathered face indicated he was not.

Frannie fell against the back of the bench seat. A faraway grin became a pitiful laugh. She was disappointed with him but furious at her own naiveté. Sarcastically, she claimed, "You're saying Avalon Hills is a ghost town—with real live ghosts." She waggled her head. "My God, I've wandered into a Dean Koontz novel."

Understanding her skepticism, Burt said, "Not ghosts, Frannie. Displaced souls."

"Oh, that's much better."

Burt smiled and allowed her a moment.

She worked with numbers, undisputable figures, and numerical probabilities her entire life. Facts didn't lie. Two plus two always equaled four—except this time.

He raised and lowered her own report. "You proved it yourself."

"I uncovered an anomaly, something that doesn't add—" She cut herself off and thought of her deceased first husband. "Now you're telling me departed spirits are walking the streets of Avalon Hills. Do they stop at Starbucks in the morning, too? Maybe take a dip in the community pool?" Frannie dropped her head, snorted, and mocked a famous movie line. "I see dead people." She began returning her reports to the manila folder.

Burt took her wrist, stopped her, and shook his head no. "As you yourself discovered, in spite of what the Social Security Administration and other agencies show, you see the truth. Thirty one seventeen. The population of Avalon Hills hasn't changed at all in decades."

"Thank you for your time, Mr. Dyer. But I really should be getting home." Frannie resented sounding abrasive to the older man, but she couldn't help it. This was just…nuts. "I don't mean to take it out on you. I'm just angry with myself."

Speaking with a great eloquence, Burt began his tale. "The ninth of February 1964 was a Sunday. Adjusting for population growth more Americans tuned into Ed Sullivan that night to watch the Beatles than watch the Super Bowl today. But not me. I was working transport at St. Agnes."

"Transport?" Frannie asked, then kicking herself for allowing Burt a reason to continue.

"We transported bodies to the morgue, located in the basement."

Frannie chilled at the image of an entire basement filled with corpses. "Why'd the hospital close?"

"It was a—" Burt made quotation marks in the air "—business decision. The suits in their ivory tower in Chicago decided St. Agnes was not profitable enough." He smirked. "I always assumed hospitals were to help sick people get better, not to turn a profit. How naïve. They shut it in '80 or '81. I'm getting older so dates run together."

Frannie said nothing. If Burt couldn't remember dates, it was very likely he couldn't remember facts either. But she listened anyway.

"Anywho, I remember the time. It was eight-eleven that Sunday night when the call came down. A young kid in his early twenties expired. Bad car accident. The surgeons couldn't save him. He died in the OR. We transported the corpse."

"We?"

"My associate Harlan Miley and myself. We secured the cadaver and brought him down to the basement so county could pick him up at the cracka' dawn Monday—" Burt cut himself off, began picking at a cut on the table. "It happened in the elevator."

"What happened?" Frannie asked, once again sipping the ginger ale.

"He sat up."

"Who did?"

"The decedent."

Frannie raised one eyebrow. "The guy who died? The dead guy sat up?" The derision was strong and undeniable.

"Yes, ma'am. Harlan and I were in the elevator. I was drinking some coffee. Harlan accidentally knocked the cup. I dumped some on the cadaver and, seconds later, he sprang up. Scared the bajeebers out of us."

Frannie knew *something* was amiss in Avalon Hills. But *this*? This was absurd, ludicrous, and downright insane. It took everything she had not to laugh in the face of this senile old coot. She found herself longing to be in the terminal at Pittsburgh International. "Doctors make mistakes all the time," she pointed out bitterly.

"Pardon?"

"You always hear about surgeons proclaiming people dead and then, voila, they come back. Misdiagnosis. Or even those people who die during an operation and see the bright light at the end of the tunnel. They died and come back."

Burt understood Frannie's hesitance and incredulity. The unbelieving mien on her face—somewhere between pity and suspicion—had been on his wife's face for years leading up to their divorce. "This man had been dead for twenty-seven minutes. His heart stopped. No brain activity. Nothing. Dead." Burt slid his leveled hand across his neck in an *off-with-their* head fashion for emphasis.

"Twenty-seven minutes?"

"Twenty-seven minutes," he confirmed.

"And the other transport tech, Harlan Miley? He's the only one who can corroborate this claim?"

Burt nodded. "Yes. And, at first, he did. But he recanted his story after they got to him. It became his word against mine."

"Who got to him?"

"The powers-that-be I guess you could say. The guardians of the secret."

I wonder if they'll serve a meal or just snacks on the flight. "Did you two ever discuss what happened in the elevator?"

"Lord, yes. But a week later, his child was murdered. His daughter Peggy was taking a bath and *somehow* an electrical appliance *accidentally* fell into the tub. Harlan immediately changed his story."

"And you're saying it was no accident?"

Burt feigned a smile. "With all due respect, Ms. Fitzgerald, you spend too much time behind a desk. In your world of numbers everything adds up. But out here in the real world, things don't always balance. No offense."

"None taken."

"These people are very powerful and will stop at nothing, even resorting to murder if need be."

Frannie massaged her throbbing temples. Her skull pounded. "But the man in the elevator died. If you're saying people don't die—"

"People *do* die. But they come back." He threw his chin at the manila folder. "You see the figures. You see the stats. You compiled the reports yourself. Do you have another explanation?"

Frannie snickered. "No. No, I don't. But eternal life is not a possibility that ever crossed my mind. I mean, if—if there's something there that prevents people from dying, or staying dead—my God, listen to me. If people die and come back, then why isn't this shared with the world?"

"I can't answer that," Burt replied. "But if you had secret, a very important secret, would *you*?"

"Something of this magnitude, I most certainly would."

Burt waggled his finger. "Let me amend my question. Let's say, for the sake of argument, you created a concoction that cured the common cold. You mixed numerous ingredients, threw in a pinch of this and a dollop of that. However, you only had a very limited quantity and could not recreate your remedy. Now, would you tell the world of your very limited and rare concoction or would you keep it under wraps for your own immediate family?"

Burt had a point. "I'd try to replicate the antidote, the serum," Frannie responded.

"And if it was completely impossible? Would you share it with the world or keep it locked away in your kitchen pantry?" Burt let that linger in the air before adding, "And I'm talking a common cold. What goes on up in Avalon Hills is a remedy for death, something that comes to every living creature to ever walk the earth. Not exactly a stuffy nose."

Frannie asked a follow-up, realizing immediately it was silly. "How come no one ever sued for malpractice?"

"People sue when a loved one dies, not when they are brought back."

Frannie downed the second glass of ginger ale though she craved something stronger. After gathering her thoughts, she reiterated, "Harlan Miley never backed you up?"

Burt shook his head. "My word against his. But no one wanted to listen to me."

"And no one else came to your defense?" Frannie didn't want to come off accusatory and skeptical, but she couldn't help it.

"Who?"

"The doctors, the surgeons, nurses? Somebody?"

"Why would they?"

Frannie breathed deep and slowly exhaled. "I have to admit, Burt, I find this quite far-fetched." Then, added with a smile, "No offense."

Burt returned the smile. "None taken. I wouldn't believe it either if I was sitting where you are. But I know what I saw. That man was stone cold dead. Twenty seven minutes."

"Do you have any theories on how or why that could have happened?"

"I do but nothing substantial. I have no proof, of course."

"And what is it?"

Burt hesitated. "I've already told you enough."

"With all due respect, you haven't *told* me anything. You've just added more questions."

Burt stared into the distance, into a memory. "I wasn't always an old man. I was young, proud, and had a lilt in my step. Now I'm watching the sun set on my life. I've done what I could—which was not much. I started looking for an answer and searching for the truth. And the only thing I got out of it was gray hair and more wrinkles. You're still young. To quote JFK, the torch has been passed to a new generation. Think of this as my death-bed confession."

Frannie pursed her lips. "You're telling me I should pick up where you're leaving off?"

"Actually, Ms. Fitzgerald, I'm just telling you what I know. What you do with the information is your choice. But personally, my unsolicited opinion, is for you to forget about this place. You'll spend your remaining days looking into a black hole, trying to find a light where one does not exist. Trust me, I know what it's like to waste a life."

Frannie smirked. "Then why did you even drag me into this?"

Burt contorted his body, whimpered from his decrepit bones stiffening. "Let me ask you this. If you could go back in time and change one moment in your life, what would it be?"

Without hesitation, Frannie declared, "I'd stop my first husband from going out drinking that night. That changed my life. Several lives."

"Me? I'd have called in sick the night of February 9, 1964. That one single event I witnessed in the elevator altered *my* life. I know what I saw, Ms. Fitzgerald. And I refuse to amend my statement. That changed—no, ruined—my life. My wife left me. I lost touch with my children. I have grandkids I'll never know. I don't blame them though. Who wants to associate with the town crackpot?"

"What'd you end up doing?"

"I stayed in town doing menial labor. Tried my hand at landscaping for a bit. After some years, I was hired by the city as a street sweeper."

"But you did finally leave," Frannie pointed out.

"Yes, in '84. I was pretty much ordered to."

"By?"

"Lloyd Garrison, the then and current mayor of Avalon Hills. He didn't want his precious little piece of heaven soiled by me any longer."

"Sheriff Gabriel Garrison's father?"

Burt nodded.

"Lloyd Garrison's still alive?" Frannie asked, then laughed. "I guess that's a funny question, all things considered."

"Yes, alive and well."

Frannie leaned back, studied the homey feeling of the Winnebago. Something in her mind clicked. Fearing the answer, she posed the question anyway. "The man in the elevator that night, the one who returned from the great beyond after twenty-seven minutes?"

"Yes?"

"What ever happened to him? Did he remember anything?"

"Ironically, he was the one who kicked me out of town."

Frannie scrunched her face momentarily before reality set in. "You're saying—"

"Yes, the boy in the elevator in 1964 was Lloyd Garrison."

Chapter 23

Lloyd rounded the counter and was halfway across the office when he howled, "Is he in?"

The big-haired deputy sprang to her feet and positioned herself between him and her boss's door. "Mayor Garrison, he asked not to be disturbed."

Lloyd glared at her. His *don't-fuck-with-me* expression resulted in her backing away. Opening the door with a flurry, Lloyd peered at his son. Gabe was stooped over his desk in defeated posture, working his pulsating temples. The slamming office door thundered as if the gates of Hell had just broken open.

Gabe's eyes were bloodshot, partially closed. He appeared to be a defeated man.

"Hung over?"

"No," Gabe grumbled. He took a deep breath and leaned back. "What's up?"

"I'm here about your brother."

Gabe snickered. "Nick, always Nick. I guess he went running to Daddy 'cause I threatened him?"

Lloyd frowned.

"He came in and started busting my balls about Brandi Conrad." Gabe went on and explained how the argument almost became physical.

Now sitting across from his son, Lloyd said, "That's not why I'm here." Lloyd was old-fashioned, a man's man. He was the type who never revealed emotions or feelings, be it to his children or his wife. Love was understood, not shown. However, he was still a father and his son's crushed stature did not go unnoticed. "What's wrong?"

Gabe glared at his father, glanced at the window that was

behind drawn verticals that prevented the sun from entering the darkness of his office. "What's wrong," he repeated mockingly. "Everything, Dad. Every-fucking-thing. It's all turning to shit."

"What is?"

"All of it," shouted Gabe. He then lowered his voice and resumed a civil tone. "I checked the tanks at Tri-Delta. They're nearly dry."

"We knew this day would come eventually," Lloyd prophesized.

"It all started with Jonathan Decker washing up on the banks of the Acheron after trying to escape."

"And I assume you talked to his wife?"

"Several times. Elizabeth claims she knew nothing about it. But she's sloshed twenty-three hours a day so she probably wouldn't have remembered anyway."

Lloyd pulled on his chin. Although he didn't display it, he did genuinely feel sorry for the burden bequeathed upon his son. "The writing's been on the wall for some time now. We knew we'd reach this point."

"And, of course, it happens on my watch. How convenient. You put me in charge, dump all this, this…responsibility on me. We both know it should be Nick. He was first born. This should be his problem to deal with, but no. He runs away and this shit falls entirely on me."

In a fatherly tone, Lloyd stated, "You need to get over the resentment you have toward your brother. Nick left decades ago. Now man up and deal with it."

Gabe leaned forward and angrily jammed his finger into his desk. "I didn't ask for this."

"And you think *I did*?" Lloyd shouted with greater fury. "I didn't want it either but I dealt with it. And now, as my son, it's your duty to deal with it. So, deal with it."

"Whatever."

"Is there something else?" Lloyd asked after a pause.

"Plenty."

"Tell me."

"I'm not even sure where to start, Dad. It's just all falling apart."

Lloyd snickered. "Why don't you start at the fucking beginning?" He refused to allow profanity to be uttered in his Christian home. Outside of the residence, however, he became some character from a Tarantino film.

"Nick's been asking about Brandi."

"I assume you quashed that?"

Gabe rolled his eyes. "Yes, *Dad.* I quashed it. I don't like what I'm doing but I'm not incompetent either."

"How did you take care of it?"

"It's taken care of."

Unconcerned with the deputy hearing him beyond the closed door, Lloyd impatiently shouted, "Don't mince words with me, boy. Not now. We don't have the time."

Gabe retrieved a staple remover from the center drawer of his desk and began fiddling with it. At this moment, he hated his father. But more accurately he hated his brother. Gabe's dreams had been forfeited because his brother followed his. And since Nick fled all those years ago, Gabe's life had turned into one of blind servitude, honoring his obligations. "I spoke to Ed Wolfe. Wolfsie. We made a deal."

"Do you feel confident Ed threw Nick off course?"

"I'm hoping."

"I didn't ask that," Lloyd said. "I asked if you feel confident that he got his point across."

"Yes, I do."

"Good. What else?"

"Yolanda is going to Washington to spend some time with Alex."

Lloyd scowled. "And why is your wife spending time with your son cause for concern?"

"I don't think she'll be coming back."

"Have you been having problems in your marriage?"

"Yes," Gabe answered embarrassedly.

"How long?"

Gabe emitted a laugh. "Six or seven years."

"Have you tried talking to her? Have you told her she can't go?"

"Yes, we talked. A lot. I even offered to go to a marriage counselor if it would help. I suggested we head up to the Catskills or maybe over to Niagara Falls for a weekend. Told her a few days out of this town would be good for us."

"She didn't buy it?"

"Didn't even give it a second thought. You know how stubborn she can be."

Lloyd rose, stood, and opened the verticals to allow some light in. After a beat, he spoke in a resigned, even-keeled voice. "Then you know what needs to be done. Anything else I should know?"

"I had one of my deputies follow Frances Fitzgerald. I wanted to make sure she was leaving town after I talked with her up at the plant. But halfway to Pittsburgh she met Burt Dyer in a rest area. They talked in his motor home for almost one hour." Gabe withdrew a file from his desk and slid out photos the deputy had snapped from across the interstate.

Lloyd gave the pictures a quick once over. "Burt Dyer. Can't believe that old codger is still alive and kicking. Should've resolved that situation in 'eighty four."

"The man saved your life. You owed him."

Lloyd considered his son's observation. "He didn't save my life. A greater force did. Still, had I fixed the Burt Dyer situation back then, he wouldn't matter now." He shuffled the rest area photos strewn across Gabe's desk. "I'm guessing Frances Fitzgerald did not go home."

"She's back in town."

"Foolish young woman she is." Lloyd paced and began formulating a plan. It didn't take long. He was not happy about the proposition but he had no choice. He also was greatly displeased his son was clearly not up to acting alone and keeping the secret veiled. No one helped Lloyd when he'd been bestowed with this. It became evident that Nick, not Gabe, deserved to be entrusted with this rite of passage. He was better suited for it.

Verifying the office door was completely closed by patting it, he stood to the left of his son. "You do know what's next?"

Gabe dropped his head, kicked at an imaginary spot on the floor.

"Do you?"

"Yes, Father."

Lloyd showed no sign of his age. Seventy two years old or not, his sharp mind was only exceeded by his unyielding fortitude when devising a plan. "You want Yolanda or Frances?"

Gabe mumbled something. When his father instructed him to speak clearer, he repeated his statement. "I said I'll handle Yolanda. She's my wife. I should be the one."

Lloyd heard uncertainty. "Are you sure?"

"Yes."

"I wish I heard more confidence in your voice," Lloyd chided.

"I said *yes!*"

"Then I'll take care of the Fitzgerald woman," Lloyd confirmed with a nod. He started making his way to the door. "We'll clean this up. Then tomorrow we talk to Nick."

Lloyd's hand had just managed to reach the doorknob when Gabe wailed. "Talk to Nick?"

He turned. "Your brother is dying, Gabriel."

"So?" Gabe shot back, unaffected, unmoved. "That's not my concern."

Lloyd stepped toward his son. "It most certainly is your concern."

"Nick—Nick's a loser. He's the one who bolted and left me behind, left me to deal with all this. Now, I'm supposed to help him? I don't think so."

"Nick is your brother."

"I don't give a shit if he's Mother fucking Teresa. No."

Lloyd was in his son's face in seconds flat. "No?"

"No! He doesn't deserve it. He hasn't earned the right. He's the one who ran away. I'll be damned if he should now benefit."

Lloyd compressed his lips. "We most likely will all be damned, son."

Gabe lowered himself behind his desk and resumed toying with the staple remover. "You put me in charge. I make the decisions now. And I say no." He nervously peered at his father then added reasoning to his words. "You taught me we need to have rules, order to all of this. There are procedures regulating how it works. Now you're saying the rules don't apply to the great Nick Garrison?"

"He's *your* brother. He's *my* son. So, no, they don't."

"I'm not happy about this." Gabe flung the object across the room where it smashed against one of his awards and exploded into a million pieces. "Not happy about any of this."

"I'm not happy about a lot of things, Gabriel. I'll pick you up tomorrow night."

Chapter 24

Replaying how the conversation went down, Nick wasn't surprised by his mother's reaction. Her refusal to admit her child would precede her in death was followed by determination to defeat a disease dating back to Biblical times.

His father, as expected, walked away.

After Lloyd left, Eve insisted they have lunch. She wanted to know all the details. As they picked at the food, they were having two separate conversations.

Nick advised his mom he didn't want a big funeral. Actually, the more he thought about it, he didn't want *any* funeral. Other than a few casual acquaintances, there was no one to invite. His parents were getting up in years and a cross-country flight would be taxing. Gabe wouldn't care and Nick knew his sister-in-law Yolanda would undoubtedly not come without her husband. And Gwen, his girlfriend back home, had split with him just before he left. Knowing all too well how headstones and grave markers were maintained Nick requested to be cremated. He didn't care what was done with his ashes.

Eve would have none of it. Every time Nick brought up what to do *after,* she focused on avoiding the *after.*

"I've got a life insurance policy worth two hundred thousand. Half goes to Gabe's kids, the other half to you and dad."

For the first time in her life, Eve screamed at her son, "Stop it, Nick! Just stop!" Nick attempted to cup his mother's hand but she yanked free. "I won't listen to this kind of talk." She stood, furiously heaving her silverware and slamming it into the sink. A drinking glass shattered. She fled to another part of the home.

After cleaning up the obliterated tableware and depositing

the splintered shards in the garbage, Nick ventured upstairs. He lay on the bed in his old room and stared at the ceiling for a bit. Second guessing himself, he wondered if even coming clean to his parents and travelling to Avalon Hills to say good-bye was the right decision. Perhaps he should have stayed in Arizona. He lived most of his life alone. Why not die alone? Eventually someone would be concerned that he hadn't shown up for work, once they noticed unpolished headstones. Police would kick down the door and Nick's rotting smelling corpse would be discovered. Then his parents would get the call. The end.

He turned sideways and was greeted by the lights at the summit of Aliquippa Mountain. As he thought about his life— or lack thereof—the towers blinked hundreds of times. Eight or nine minutes passed just like that. Eight or nine minutes closer—

Nick turned away, averting his eyes from the stark remind-er of mortality. He had just dozed off on his way to a restful sleep when he felt something wet against his chin. Nick's eyes slit partially. "Scrappy," he said because it came naturally.

Not Scrappy Four. Not Four. Scrappy.

Nick readjusted himself onto his back. The happy dog stretched himself out on Nick's chest and continued licking with fervor. Nick peered into the dog's deep expressive brown orbs. The more he scratched behind his ears, the faster the licks came. He talked in gibberish, silly tones, and strange sounds reserved only for cute pets and small children. Or for Uncle Hank.

Nick eased the Westie away and gently sandwiched the pooch's head. "Tell me, Scrappy. How old are you really?"

The dog tried to wiggle free.

"Scrappy? Scrappy Four? Four? C'mon boy, give me a sign."

The dog continued squirming, his pink tongue stretching as far as it could, desperately attempting to reach Nick's chin.

As Nick sat up and swung his legs over, the dog hopped off the bed and yipped once. Nick lowered his hand to pet the ca-nine again. Although he had no treat in his hand, the dog ea-gerly rose onto his hind legs and pirouetted in a clockwise circle exactly three times. The same trick his childhood dog performed. Supposedly, the same trick his father had taught Four.

Nick dropped to his knees, now eye level. "Scrappy? Scrappy, is that really you?"

The dog rose and again did the same trick. His tail wagged enthusiastically. It was as if the dog was seeing a long lost friend for the first time. Nick had the same feeling.

With the dog following close behind, Nick made his way down the hallway. He stood in the threshold and peered in. "Hey, Uncle Hank."

Nick used the same joyous inflection he just used for his pet. Perhaps if he sounded jovial enough, Hank would magically be roused from his inert captive state.

As always, Hank sat in the chair, oblivious to the world around him. Eve had recently washed his hair and shaven his face. She missed a few spots. His lids were mostly closed but his red-rimmed eyes stared impassively toward the floor. His mouth drooped, spittle again hanging from the corner of his lip. Nick walked in, removed a tissue from a Kleenex pack, and dabbed away his uncle's dribble.

Moving across the room to the sounds of Danny and the Juniors singing "At The Hop," Nick eased aside the curtains and allowed the early afternoon light to penetrate the murky chamber. He squatted beside his uncle and looked at *Animal Planet*. Lumberjacks and mountain men with scraggly unkempt beards were talking about a large hairy creature that they once saw sitting on a log.

"How 'bout it, Uncle Hank, think they'll ever find Bigfoot?"

As anticipated Hank did not react, did not flinch, did not budge. Nick's eyes wandered to his blanket-covered chest to determine if he was breathing.

In spite of his mother's tireless efforts, being in close proximity to his uncle for more than a few seconds, Nick couldn't help but realize the stench that wreathed the man's feeble body. The man was a prisoner of his own mind. Unable to move, talk, think, react. Trapped in his own skin. Hank's tongue edged forward and now dropped between severely cracked lips.

Nick deliberated his uncle. And thought of his own fate. In some ways, perhaps being dead was better than being alive.

Nick walked out and found Eve sitting at the computer. He knocked on the doorframe. "Mom?"

She didn't hear him at first. Her head was tilted up, looking down her nose through her bifocals. She was reading something online about brain tumors.

"Mom, I'm going out for a bit."

"Okay. I'll have dinner at six," she announced without turning around.

"Sounds good, thanks."

She turned to face him. "And, son?"

"Yeah?"

"I love you."

ↄ๑ↄ

He contemplated calling Wolfsie but ultimately chose not to. His friend had come to terms with his wife's breast cancer. The last time they met, when he chauffeured Nick around on the Brandi Conrad Farewell Tour that ended at her grave, his friend had been in good spirits. He'd accepted his wife's fate—whatever the hell that meant exactly. He didn't want to bring Wolfsie down by sharing his own medical problems.

The more he debated, the more he realized he didn't want anyone to know. Announcing his own impending death would only bring out the phony looks of sorrow and artificial concern.

The instant Nick lowered himself onto a stool in Texas Jack's and ordered a beer, the barmaid smiled. "I guess your friend's doin' better."

At first he frowned, then glanced at the name badge. She was the girl who called Nick when Wolfsie was getting drunk. "Hey, Jennifer, how are you? Yes, he's better. Thanks."

"Haven't seen him around these parts so I figured whatever he was dealing with has passed."

"Not really," Nick said, "but he's coping."

"That's all any of us can do. And how are you, son of Mayor Garrison and brother of Sheriff Garrison?"

Nick forced a smile. "Peachy."

He swigged one beer quickly, nursed a second one, and followed that up with several ice waters and a strong coffee. It was a slow afternoon at the bar and he enjoyed bantering with the affable Jennifer. It was refreshing to shoot the breeze and, as Billy Joel once sang, forget about life for a while. The two hours passed quickly.

"You're easy to chat with," remarked Nick. "I guess that's part of your job."

Wiping down a nearby counter, Jennifer smiled over her shoulder. "And looking great in Wrangler's also helps."

Nick smiled. "How long have you been here for?"

"Since noon."

Nick laughed. "No, I mean working here."

Facing Nick, she tilted forward and displayed some cleavage in a simple way. "Almost four years now. Though it doesn't seem like a day over seven."

"So you know a lot of people?"

"Sure do." Jennifer looked around the establishment. There was only one other patron and he was in the corner pecking away at his phone. She considered coming out from behind her bar and pulling up a stool. Nick was kind of a cute guy. But, more importantly, he was a Garrison.

Nick broached the subject. "Do you know someone named Brandi Conrad?" *Do, not did. Present tense.*

Jennifer answered without hesitation. "Brandi, sure." Her pleasant smile broadened, apparently recalling happy memories. "She was quite the girl."

Was. Past tense. "How well?"

"Somewhat. I wouldn't say we were BFFs. She'd come in from time to time. Very pretty girl. Spent time fightin' off the guys. And some girls, too. I think her looks intimidated a lot of people. And if that wasn't enough to scare 'em away, she could drink most guys twice her size under the table."

"Did she drink a lot?"

"Not to excess. She'd stop in on a Friday night now and then and throw back a few. She didn't get drunk but just buzzed enough to cut loose. She knew her limit."

Nick contemplated the statement. Brandi liked drinking but

knew when to cut herself off. Yet, she died driving drunk. Curious.

Jennifer turned the tables. "And how well did *you* know her?"

Nick hesitated. "We dated in high school a bit."

Jennifer knew her clientele. Working in a bar afforded her a better look into the human psyche than any sociology degree ever could. Nick's words, eyes, and body language left no doubt he was suppressing his true feelings. "Sure," she said coyly. Jennifer turned and pulled a log book out from a drawer near the register.

"Do you remember anything about the night she—the accident?"

Jennifer finished whatever she was doing, turned around. Maybe Nick was mistaken but it seemed like another button on her blouse had been undone. She wore a somber expression but her story confirmed what Nick had heard. "It was a nice funeral. Small, but nice."

Nick didn't know what to say to that. Working as a marble engineer, a funeral was a funeral. "I should be going." He stood, thanked Jennifer for the drinks and, more so, the conversation.

"Don't be a stranger."

Stepping into the late afternoon, Nick put on his sunglasses and looked for his car. He turned right, left. Then right again. His eyes widened as he surveyed the sidewalk. He'd recognize that jet black hair anywhere. "Brandi?"

The figure continued walking away and then disappeared around the corner.

Nick took off in pursuit. "Brandi!"

When he reached the corner, she was twenty yards away. She wasn't running but she was not out for a casual stroll either.

Nick sprinted up the sidewalk, reached out, and placed his hand on her shoulder. "Hey."

Her startled expression speedily transformed into a welcoming smile. "Nicky!"

Nicky. "I was calling your name."

"Sorry, I didn't hear. How've you been?"

Her amorous eyes, alluring smile, perfect features. She was flawless in Nick's eyes. He couldn't utter a sound.

Brandi laughed. "Cat got your tongue?"

Nick stared at her, cautiously joyful. He wanted to hug her, hold her, pull her close, and never let her get away. He'd made that mistake once. And it ended up bad for both.

He studied her, examined his surroundings. The street was fairly quiet but he noticed small children playing in a yard half way up on the other side. A truck's engine belched on Main Street. Boughs blew gently in the late afternoon breeze. Specifics. Details. This was no dream.

An inquisitive expression on her face, she cupped Nick's left cheek. "You okay? You look like you've seen a ghost."

"I—I—" Nick stammered. His mind shifted into overdrive, incoherent thoughts colliding against one another. Questions, possibilities, confusion. *How can this be*? He placed his hand over hers, sandwiching her warm fingers against his face. He closed his eyes. Touch. Feeling. Sensation. This was real. Tangible.

Yet it couldn't be.

Brandi eased his head downward so their eyes would meet. "Nicky, what's wrong?"

"I—I don't know what to say."

She giggled. "I have that effect on people."

Nick's thoughts were too disarrayed to share in the laughter. "I heard—I heard things. About you."

"You know how small towns are. Trust me. Probably only half of them are true."

He slipped his face free from her caring touch and held her hands. "I'm serious, Brand. Wolfsie, my brother." He threw his thumb over his shoulder. "Jennifer at the bar."

She seemed interested. "I hate rumors. What did you hear?"

It was so outlandish, so downright silly, he couldn't even bring himself to speak such ridiculous words. But Brandi pulled a loose string and Nick unraveled. "They said you were dead."

Brandi arched a brow. "Dead?" She threw her head back and did her silent laugh. The same laugh she displayed in high school, the same laugh that never changed.

"Yeah, I know. Crazy. But that's what they told me."

She placed her left fingertips against the inside of her right wrist and, after a moment, announced, "I've got a pulse. If I'm dead, no one told me."

Feeling lightheaded, Nick placed his hand on her shoulder, both to steady himself from the world that was spinning as well as verifying she was real. "I—saw it."

"What did you see?"

"The tree. The articles online."

She cocked her head. "You believe everything you see on the Internet?"

Nick held her gaze and then grinned "That's exactly what *I* said." He stared into her eyes. "I also saw your—you know."

"Saw my what? Hey, were you peeking through my window when I showered?"

The situation was tense, perplexing, and confounding. However, as always, Brandi made things less dire.

"Your grave, your headstone."

"My headstone!" Brandi screeched. She was amused, clearly enjoying this absurdity. "Does my headstone at least say something nice about me?"

Trying to draw a connection in his mind, Nick mumbled, "This makes no sense. How can you be here?"

Brandi extended her arms, turned her palms up toward the sky in a *here I am* gesture. "Seeing is believing."

"Why would they tell me—How could—"

"Nicky, look at me." She again forced him to behold her. "Do I look dead to you?"

"Well, no."

She put her hand over his as it clutched her shoulder and squeezed. "Do I feel dead to you?"

"No."

Brandi stepped closer, her body against Nick's chest. On her tiptoes, she moved closer. The initial contact of her lips caused Nick to recoil. His head jolted but he was quickly flooded with emotions at the recognizable kiss, the tender passion, the familiar warmth. He felt his lips parted by her tongue.

Brandi cupped the nape of his neck with one hand while resting her elbow on his shoulder, pulling him deeper into her mouth. It was the way she kissed, the way she always kissed. Passionate, fiery, and hot-blooded.

Nick closed his eyes. When they opened, her chestnut eyes stared back at him. There was a familiarity in them. Love and lust, longing and loss.

She winked at Nick. "Not a bad kisser, you know, for a dead girl, huh?"

"But—"

"But nothing, Nicky. I'm here, you're here. Just—just go with it and don't question everything. Like I said, seeing is believing."

"I don't get it."

Brandi shrugged. "Someone's messing with you. Someone's playing with you."

"But why would they want me to think you're, you know…"

"No idea. People do crazy things all the time."

Nick countered, "What's gained by it?"

Brandi angled her head, a sympathetic expression on her face. She scrutinized Nick. His face seemed aged, growing older by the second before her eyes, due to the confusion that tore at his spirit. "Nicky, do you believe I'm here?"

"Of course."

Brandi sighed. "If you believe in me, if you believe I'm here, then I'm here."

"Seeing is believing, right?"

Brandi shook her head. "No. In this case *believing* is seeing. If you believe I'm here, then I'm here."

Nick's bewilderment was slipping away, being replaced by joy. He'd lost Brandi over a quarter of a century ago. Yesterday, he learned he'd lost her again. And this time forever.

But now, now she was here. In the flesh. He would not lose her again, not ever again. "It's good seeing you. I mean, *really good.*"

"It's good seeing you, Nicky." She raised her hands and patted away tears that developed at the corners of his eyes, tears he was unaware of.

"Someone must be chopping onions somewhere."

"Of course. That's what it must be, Mr. Manly."

"Damn onions," he bemoaned and chuckled. "What do we do now?"

Brandi peered around, glanced at her watch. She appeared to be at a decisional crossroads. "Let's talk more about this. Dinner at my place?"

"Yeah, sure, yes. I'd love to."

"First you have to do me a favor."

"Anything," Nick said, heart filled with a sense of rebirth. None of it made sense. But, as Brandi insisted he was just going to *go with it*.

"Show me where I'm buried."

Nick couldn't help but laugh. "I bet you're the first person to ever say those words."

"C'mon."

Nick was guided along the street to Brandi's car. Her arm around his lower back, his hand draped over her shoulder. They walked in stride, side by side. It felt good, the way it was always meant to be.

Nick downplayed everything he'd been told. Sheared off tree bark? That could be a result of bitter Pennsylvania winters. The articles online? Nick didn't really pay attention to how Wolfsie got to the websites. The articles and obits just appeared. Brandi's name on a headstone? Well…perhaps that was a simple mistake.

Nick recalled hearing a few years ago how Arlington National Cemetery had mixed up burial plots.

But why? What was the reason they—whoever *they* were— would want to convince him Brandi was gone.

"Here," she announced as they reached her car. Nissan. The same make she drove the night she allegedly died. The hairs rose on the back of his neck. He stopped, stared at the death car. He looked for signs it'd been repaired. "Something wrong?"

Nick visually analyzed the automobile and then smiled broadly at Brandi. "Not a thing. Everything is as it should be." Looking deep into her eyes, he moved closer. Wrapping his arms around her in a protective fashion, he gently kissed her lips.

"Down boy." Brandi tittered. A moment later, she opened

the passenger's side door, leaned in. "Are you looking at my butt?" she cried out from the interior.

"Perhaps."

Brandi reversed from the car and presented the blindfold.

Nick raised a brow. "Brandi, jeez."

"What?"

"I've been to your home before. You invited me for dinner. What's the big deal?"

She didn't answer immediately. Instead, she eyed Nick with a strange expression. It was sorrow mixed with a trace of uncertainty. "I'm sorry," she claimed but waved it closer. "For me."

Nick found himself laughing. "You and those damn puppy dog eyes." He turned around.

From behind, Brandi wrapped the covering, knotting it tightly. "No peeking," she joked. "Wait. Don't move."

Nick heard rushed footsteps. He heard a door open. He heard an engine turn over. He gabbled her name questioningly and struggled with the complicated knot. When he finally yanked the blindfold off, he stood helpless as Brandi sped away, swallowed up by Avalon Hills.

Chapter 25

"Hey, Nick!"

Karri Wolfe sashayed onto the front patio and embraced her husband's friend. She and Nick exchanged a formal peck on the cheek. As she backed away, she smiled. "Ed said you were back in town. It's nice to see you."

Karri's face looked drawn, gaunt. Her eyes tired. She'd lost some weight but then again Nick hadn't seen her in years. "Nice seeing you, too. How're you holding up?"

Karri feigned a smile. "I'm doing well, considering."

Looking at her, Nick realized they were brought together by a common bond. Both were fighting cancer, but battling it in different ways. Nick was burying his head in the sand like an ostrich. This approach was made easier since his pain had subsided—no, completely ceased—since returning. Plus, he was focusing on Brandi. Karri, on the other hand, had come to terms, accepted her fate, accepting her mortality or whatever other pacifying clichés people came up with. "I'm sorry."

"It is what it is. A positive attitude goes a long way."

Psychobabble bullshit. "It sure does." Nick grinned. "Is he around?"

"Ed? Sure, I'll get him."

Nick was surprised he was left standing in the doorway and not invited in. Through the closed door, he heard Karri calling her husband. A minute later, Wolfsie appeared.

Before he could utter a greeting, Nick clipped, "What the *hell* is going on?"

"I'm happy to see you, too." He joined Nick on the front landing and closed the door behind him so his wife wouldn't hear. "What're you talking about?"

"I just saw Brandi Conrad." Nick wasn't sure why he felt it necessary to use her full name. "Why'd you lie to me?"

Wolfsie's brows creased. "Brandi Conrad?"

"Yes, Brandi Conrad. I want to know—"

"That's not possible."

"Oh, it's not?" Nick's emotions were all over the map. He was puzzled by seeing his dead former sweetheart in the flesh. He was furious with his friend.

"Where'd you see her?"

"Outside Texas Jacks," Nick snapped. "I went to have a drink, walked out, and saw her. On the street. On the damn street!"

"You went to Texas Jack's without inviting me?"

"Dammit, Wolfsie, that's not the point. I want to know why you lied to me. *You.*"

A pathetic look crossed Wolfsie's face. "You need to calm down."

"I am calm," screamed an un-calm Nick. He stepped closer to his friend. "I want to know what's happening. I want to know why you lied to me!"

Wolfsie puckered his lips. "Then let's go."

"Go where?"

"Let's go see her. I know she's dead. You say she's alive. Take me to her. Prove me wrong."

Nostrils flaring, Nick stammered. "I—wish I could. I don't know where she lives. But that's irrelevant. The point is *I* saw her."

"Uh huh." Skeptical, not believing, doubting Ed.

Nick paced in a circle. The anger in his voice became a cry for help. "Don't do this to me, Wolfsie. Please. I'm asking you as a friend."

"Asking me what?"

"We've known each other since we were kids," Nick pleaded. "Doesn't that mean anything?"

Wolfsie's body language said *What do you want me to tell you?* "I'll make up something if that's what you want to hear, if it'll make you feel better. But Brandi's gone, man. For good. She ain't coming back. I'm sorry, bro. I showed you the accident site. You read her obits. I took you to her grave."

An irate Nick violated his friend's personal space. "Then help me dig her up."

Wolfsie released a drawn-out pitiful sigh and pathetically muttered Nick's name.

"You want me to prove Brandi's alive. Then you should prove to me Brandi's dead!"

"Nick, you need some rest," Wolfsie said by way of an answer. He attempted to soothe his friend by placing his hand on his shoulder but Nick slinked away.

"I'll do it myself then."

Wolfsie chose his words methodically. "I know you loved Brandi. You did back in school and you do now. It's obvious. But if you truly love her, let the poor girl rest in peace."

"I'm going. With or without you."

"You're going to desecrate her memory just to try and prove me wrong? That's not cool at all."

"With or without you."

"Now you're Bono?" Nick didn't laugh. Determining Nick was beyond the point of reason, Wolfsie upped the ante. "That cemetery is public land. You go digging around and I'll call the police."

Wolfsie opened a door, Nick kicked it down. "Speaking of the police, tell me, my *friend*. Why'd you meet my brother yesterday?"

"Huh?" Wolfsie was a lot of things. A good liar was not one of them.

"I saw you walk into the police station. I just got through talking to him and as I was leaving I saw you walk in." Nick paused but not long enough for his friend to fabricate a reason. He shouted, "What the hell is going on around here?"

Wolfsie was back on his heels with nowhere to go. Rather than addressing the accusation, he surrendered. "Fine, let's do it. You wanna dig her up. Let's dig her up."

Nick stood there, Wolfsie having called his bluff. Proposing such a ghoulish act was easy; carrying it through bordered on sacrilege.

"I've got tools and shovels in here," Wolfsie cried over his shoulder while shuffling across the yard and rolling up the garage door.

Nick hesitated, weighed his decision that now seemed outright ghastly and fell in line behind his friend.

The Chevy Traverse sat centered in the two-car garage. The remainder was used for storage.

Nick entered and observed Wolfsie crouching in a far corner. He jerked slightly as a loud whirring sound thundered overhead. Chains clanked and the garage door lowered encasing both men inside.

When Nick turned back around, his eyes widened, his stomach dropped. But in a roundabout way his suspicions were confirmed. Unable to pull his eyes away from the threatening black revolver his friend aimed at his gut, Nick could only mumble, "Wolfsie?"

"Go home, Nick. *Please.* Go back to Arizona and forget about this place." Wolfsie had the power of death in his hands but his voice conveyed weakness, lack of confidence.

"Wolfsie, tell me what's going on around here. As a friend—"

The clinking of a bullet being chambered stopped him.

"Go. Forget about this. Forget about Avalon Hills, forget about our friendship, forget about Brandi."

Nick centered on the gun. It was the first time he'd ever been staring down the barrel of a firearm. It unnerved him knowing his life hung in the balance. Although Wolfsie was one of those whose eyebrows arched in a way that conveyed a perpetual sadness on his face he now appeared on the brink of tears. He undoubtedly hated himself for doing this. "Why?"

"I don't have a choice."

"We're friends. You owe me at least this much."

"I owe Karri more than you. And yes, we are friends. That's why, as your friend, I'm begging you to leave."

Nick curled his lips, dropped his head, and walked to roll up the garage door, his back on the weapon.

"You won't make it out alive, Nick. If you keep pushing, you'll die."

"I'm dying anyway," Nick mumbled.

Chapter 26

It was Stephen King's masterpiece *Cujo* that hooked Brandi. Despite being a child of the '80s—the MTV generation—she, unlike other Gen X-ers, preferred books to movies. Hollywood never delivered details provided by the written word.

Although she immensely enjoyed King's style, he was not *this* good. She'd read the same paragraph four times and had no idea what the best-selling author was talking about. Her mind was elsewhere.

She stretched her legs, resting her feet atop the coffee table. She glanced at her worn couch, the same couch Nick sat on days earlier.

Nick.

It all came back to Nick. She'd been kicking herself all evening about ditching him the way she did, abandoning him on the sidewalk like some horrible parent discarding an unwanted child in a shopping mall.

Brandi had only made a sandwich for dinner but couldn't even finish that. She channel surfed a while but the pointless drivel on the idiot box was more mind-numbing than usual. And now, even her saving grace, the newest King novel, was doing nothing to assuage her restlessness. And guilt.

She cherished Nick. Always had, always would. Brandi Conrad was a realist, not a romantic at heart. She'd never bought into the whole soul-mate stuff. However, if one did exist, hers was Nick Garrison.

She'd fallen for him in high school. Her heart fluttered when they were together and felt empty when they weren't. The weeks became months, months years. Cold harsh winters relented to the rebirth of spring only to again morph into shorter days and darker frostier nights. And she waited, waited for Nick to come back for her. She filled her hollowness with pseudo-Nicks but the void in her soul never was satisfied.

There was Nick. And then there was everyone else.

But now, after a lifetime, Nick returned home. Finally. The moment she dreamt of was now a reality. Yet, she couldn't ride off into the sunset with him.

It was obvious that, in spite of the passage of time, his feelings hadn't wavered either. She heard it in his words, could feel it in his heart, and saw the love in his eyes. Unlike the novel, she had no problems reading Nick.

And that's what made this all so hard. So damned hard. So damned unjust.

Brandi stiffened and tensed in response to the rustling outside her front door. Hopefully, somehow, maybe Nick found her. By the time the door opened, she was on her feet with hope. It was not Nick. It was his brother.

"Brandi," Gabe announced swaggering like he owned the place.

In a way, he somewhat did. He opened the closet door, reset the alarm.

Wearing a jeans skirt that hung to her knees and a light pink top with three of the four buttons undone, Brandi suddenly felt chilled. She attempted to slyly clasp the remaining three.

Gabe shook his head no.

Hugging herself, she asked, "What do you want?"

Dressed in his sheriff uniform—handcuffs, baton, gun—he motioned with his hands for her to drop her arms so he could observe her. When she pretended to not understand, he vocalized the request.

Arms at her side, Brandi stood like an inanimate object, a piece of meat to be gawked. She felt dirty, violated, as Gabe eye-raped her with his penetrating heartless stare.

As if he was the homeowner and not a guest, Gabe sauntered to the kitchen. He returned with a chair, placed it in the center of the living room and patted the seat. "Here, sit." The piece of meat now reduced to an obedient dog minding its master.

Without a choice, Brandi obeyed the command. She

stepped around the table and lowered herself into the chair as instructed. Gabe stepped back and ogled. "Sit up straighter. I want your tits sticking out."

"What do you want, Gabe?"

"Ooh, someone's a bit feisty tonight." He snickered. "That must be the effect my brother has on you."

"Nick has nothing to do with this." Brandi was surprised at the potency in her voice.

"Nick has *everything* to do with this."

Brandi became rigid. She was anxious, nervous, even terrified. Cherishing the control, Gabe skulked around the chair with measured steps. His breathing deepened. The fact she had no idea what would happen next titillated him. He slid his handcuffs from his belt, lowered them onto the table in plain sight and from behind, he tousled her raven black hair.

Reflexively, she angled forward, freeing herself from his touch. "Get your hands off me."

Methodically, he came around and dropped to his haunches just in front of her. Elbows on knees, he wrung his hands while examining her. He shot only a passing glance at her face. Most of his attention was directed on her chest and legs. "What do you think I'm here for?"

She pursed her lips and stared into nothingness, unable to meet his soulless gaze.

"Jonathan Decker died," Gabe announced. "For real this time."

"I heard."

"Poor bastard thought he could make it across the river. That your doing?"

"No."

"You sure about that? I know you can be quite the little hell raiser."

"I had nothing to do with Decker's death."

"Sure," he replied with dripping sarcasm. "Tell me about Nick."

"What about him?"

"You accosted him twice. You know direct contact is prohibited."

Brandi sneered. "Accosted?"

"What would you call it?"

"I ran into him once at the market. This afternoon, *he* saw *me*. I didn't go seeking him out."

Gabe smirked. "Of course not. Then why is he asking about you? Why is he digging up ghosts buried in the past? Pun intended."

"Why don't you ask him?" Brandi snapped.

"I'm the sheriff of Avalon Hills. Weren't you raised to respect authority?"

"I certainly was. And when I see someone deserving it, I'll let you know."

Gabe laughed. "Once a bitch, always a bitch."

Brandi said nothing.

Gabe redistributed his weight on his bent knees. His infringing glare caused Brandi to shudder and gooseflesh to coat her arms. The touch that followed caused her to cringe.

He placed one hand on each of her bare knees, savoring the panic he triggered. He glanced up, noticed Brandi staring into space, cowering in her distant happy place. "Look at me."

She lowered her head but her eyes closed.

"I said look at me!"

Regrettably, she minded the directive. Gabe tenderly worked his fingers higher along her shapely legs. He gently eased aside her skirt with his knuckles. He repositioned himself again, this time due to the developing hardness in the tan trousers of his sheriff uniform. "So hot," he breathed. "So damn hot."

Unlike with his wife, Gabe never had trouble getting and maintaining arousal with Brandi. She exuded sexuality as much now as back in high school when she dated his older brother. Brandi had been Nick's girl back then. And in a way, still was. It gave Gabe one more reason to despise his sibling. Not only did Nick vacate Avalon Hills in order to chase his dreams but he'd also been with Brandi. Gabe loathed that lucky bastard brother almost as much as he despised his father. Nick was lucky in that he avoided having to deal with the daily regimen of serving the greater good of Avalon Hills like Gabe did. However, Gabe having Brandi in his control was yet another twisted way of exacting revenge on Nick.

With her skirt pushed above mid-thigh Brandi's eyes closed. She was again ordered to open them. The unwanted fingertips that erotically inched higher up her inner legs and sensitive thighs caused her to faintly gasp.

With labored breathing, Gabe cupped her legs and eased them apart. The muscles in her legs tightened, resisted.

Gabe scowled. "I thought open legs was second nature to you." He laughed at his own joke as his fingers unhurriedly snaked higher. He could feel her warming and her breathing became heavier. No matter what game she played and protested, he *knew* it was an act. Brandi—and all women like her—enjoyed playing the good girl. They acted one way but yearned to be taken. Classy during the day, whores at night. "Black panties? Nice."

As if acting independently, Brandi's legs clamped shut, sandwiching Gabe's intrusive hands.

He wallowed in the control. Having Brandi give herself voluntarily was thrilling. But *taking* her was downright electrifying. He violently heaved her legs apart with such force her skirt ripped slightly and rose to her hips in one aggressive motion. Sitting in a chair in the middle of her own living, skirt to her hips, completely vulnerable, she muttered, "I hate you."

"Yes, but you love what I do to you. And for you." He moved his touch higher, sensed the heat that teemed from her body. "If it helps, you can call me Nick. After all, you fucked him plenty."

Brandi never had consummated anything with Nick. But letting Gabe think she did was a minor victory for her.

Gabe's mind fired on all cylinders. Thoughts like machine gun fire bulleted through his brain. How should he take Brandi? What would be the best way of hurting his brother by using her?

Gabe moved his fingers higher still. He was pleased with himself, amusingly surprised at how stiff and stirred he'd become. Definitely different with Brandi than his wife.

Yolanda, his wife, his wife who needed to be taken care of, his wife who wouldn't listen and as such would suffer the consequences.

He wondered how he'd do it. Would he be able to? She was

his spouse, after all, the mother of their children. And what about the kids? How would Alex and Chelsea handle her death? Gabe realized no one in town would question the demise of the sheriff's wife, especially when your last name was Garrison.

But his children would want details. Eliminating his wife was a sad necessity, collateral damage. He felt confident he'd carry through. However, lying to his children about it would be challenging. He needed to make sure they'd suspect nothing. Maybe he could convince her to leave and never come back. Would his father find out? Maybe, just maybe, Gabe could lie to his father about killing her and the old man would be none the wiser.

Shit.

Gabe had become so sidetracked with thoughts of Yolanda's pending murder Brandi became a non-entity. The result was flaccidity. He couldn't let this opportunity go to waste.

Moving quickly, before it was too late, Gabe sprang to his feet. His unexpected movement startled her.

Gabe stood and straddled her, using his strong legs like a vise around hers. With his crotch inches from her face, he frantically began undoing his belt, his pants, his zipper. By the time he completed fiddling with all the obstacles in his way, it was too late.

"Damnit!"

Brandi stared at his crotch, at his boxers where no protrusion appeared. She looked up at Gabe, raised one eyebrow. "Oops."

She heard him call her a name. She felt a blow sledgehammer across her cheek. The room spun. Her face burned. A second blow sent her and the chair crashing to the floor. Darkness crept in from her periphery. Nausea washed over her.

The last thing she saw, before slipping into unconsciousness, was Gabe standing over her.

<h1 style="text-align:center">Chapter 27</h1>

Nick returned home. The strange encounter with Brandi—only to be discarded on a sidewalk—left him with more questions than before. As if that wasn't enough for one day, his longtime friend threatened him at gunpoint.

On the flipside, Eve seemed content. She prepared pork chops for dinner along with au gratin potatoes and a healthy salad. He couldn't recall his mom ever serving a salad. Apparently, she was fighting astrocytoma with ranch dressing.

As Nick picked at the food, his mom displayed a hearty appetite. Her actions were almost as confounding as Wolfsie's. This morning Eve was adamant about fighting the cancer, refusing to accept her son's mortality. Tonight it was as if the conversation never happened. She seemed in good spirits, almost upbeat, showing no indication her first born was on borrowed time. During dessert, a lemon meringue pie, she advised Nick, "Your father is busy tonight. That's why he couldn't join us."

"If I said good, would that be inappropriate?"

"Your father's a hard man to understand. But you should cut him some slack, Nick. He *is* your father, after all."

"I've cut him slack my entire life, Mom. I'll never be good enough in his eyes. If he hasn't accepted me in all these years, he never will. He's still angry 'cause I went to school in California."

Eve smiled. "I've known him longer and I'm not sure I understand him either. But I will tell you that on that score, I agree with him."

Nick was stunned. "You don't think I should've gone either?"

"I know that's not what you want to hear, but no, I don't."

"What's wrong with going after my dreams? You and Dad, okay, mostly you, raised us to never settle. Fine, it didn't work out in the long run, but at least I tried. I took a shot." Nick paused, surprised his mom didn't have his back on this one. "I'd rather fall short of my dreams than settle for factory work."

"Not everyone in Avalon Hills ends up in a factory. Your father and brother didn't."

Nick shook his head disbelievingly.

"I'm just saying you never know what would've happened had you stayed. Maybe you would've wound up with Gabe's job. Maybe you would have ended up marrying that pretty girl from high school. Brandi, right?"

"Yes, Brandi." Nick bowed his head, sipped his coffee, and moved the focus away from him and back onto his father. "I wish Dad would at least give me credit for trying. There's nothing wrong with wanting something better."

"Your father's had a difficult life. He's dealt with things you and I will never understand."

Nick clipped, "At least he's had a life. His wasn't cut off sooner than expected." He then shamefacedly added, "Sorry for raising my voice."

"You needn't apologize. Have you suffered any more pains in your head?"

Nick joked. "No pains without Dad around."

Eve grinned. She rose, walked to the carafe, and started refilling their mugs. "More coffee?"

"No thanks."

Eve either ignored her son or pretended not to hear. As she topped off his mug, she said, "TS Eliot once said, 'I've measured out my life with coffee spoons.'"

"Um, okay." He paused and, when his mom returned, Nick dejectedly added, "I'm just tired of trying, tired of trying to understand and figure things out."

"The Lord works in mysterious ways," Eve claimed.

"You been hanging out with Yolanda?"

Eve patted her son's hand and shifted the conversation to town gossip, issues less confounding than a son's relationship with his father.

Moments later, she began clearing the table and loading the dishwasher.

"I'll do it, Mom."

"I have a better idea," Eve announced after a pregnant pause. "Why don't we look at old pictures?"

"Really?" Nick's lack of enthusiasm was evident.

"Sure, I think it'd be nice. I haven't looked through those photos in years. Tonight seems like a good night."

Nick relented. "Where are they?"

Without drawing her eyes away from rinsing the plates, Eve advised, "Back right corner on the floor of your father's closet. They're in boxes marked old photos."

Old photos. Makes sense. Nick shuffled off.

With Nick out of earshot, Eve took a deep breath, exhaled slowly, and spoke to no one as if seeking absolution. "Lloyd, forgive me."

ဢဢဢ

Air hung heavy and stale in his parent's bedroom. Nick couldn't recall the last time he'd seen this furniture. The bedroom set was as old as him but was holding up better.

Nick felt like he was snooping, going into the closet without his father's permission. He pulled the cord dangling from the fixture and illuminated the large walk-in. His father's suit jackets and sports coats had a fine coat of dust layered across the shoulders from not being worn in ages. Only a few looked fresh, the ones his father apparently wore when his duty as mayor required formality. Dress shirts were crammed alongside slacks and trousers. The clothes were all jam-packed tightly, wrinkles imbedding into the fabric. Nick wondered how the clothing rack supported the abundance of clothes. The shelves were filled with boxes and stacks of folded shirts that his father wore more frequently. Easier to get to.

Back right corner on the floor.

Nick pushed eased aside a shoe tree. The dim lighting made it difficult to read the box. He tilted his head. Three cardboard boxes, one stacked on top of the other, were labeled *old photos* in black marker.

Bending at the waist, Nick put one hand on each side of the top box and wiggled it free. The years of not being moved resulted in one side sticking to the rear wall. Nick heaved it free, backpedaled out of the closet, and lowered it on the bedroom floor. He returned for the second box. As he started removing this one, something caught his eye. He did a double take, halted for a beat, then carried the second box out as well. When he removed the third one, the hidden object came into view.

The vivid long-forgotten memory exploded his brain. Thoughts tore across his mind that suddenly trembled and pulsated in his skull. He pulled the item from the concealed obscurity. Mesmerized, he retreated from the closet and held it up. Studying, analyzing…

Nick attempted to bring forth the faded remembrance of a lifetime ago. He closed his eyes, this time not to recall but to try and make sense of this widening madness. The boxes of photos were now unimportant.

He didn't recall leaving the bedroom, walking down the hallway, or traipsing down the stairs. At the lip of the kitchen, clutching the object with trembling fingers, Nick breathed, "Mom?"

Eve exhibited relief and regret, sadness and satisfaction. "Good. You found them."

It was clear he'd been purposely sent on this scavenger hunt to uncover the item. The request to look at old photos clearly was a ruse, a cover story. In this way, Eve could find her inner peace of staying loyal to Lloyd and not directly betraying him. If Nick just happened to stumble upon something else—so be it.

Eve dried her hands on a dishrag and hypnotically walked to her son. She took the item, walked unsteadily into the living room, and lowered the object in question onto the floor between the sofa and a chair, the focal point of their discussion. "We need to talk, Nick. You need to be told."

Nick's legs couldn't move. His eyes could not pull away from the haunting memory that came crashing back and now appeared a generation later as if being yanked from the recesses of his memory. Over a quarter century had passed but it was yesterday once again.

He and Brandi kissed in the hills overlooking the Acheron River. He made a half-hearted attempt to have her come with him to California. Their conversation was interrupted by a rustling sound. Peering through the thicket, they observed a murder. A man struggled for his life, splashing in the breaking waters. There'd been two flashes of light. Two popping sounds. And just like that a man had been executed.

The individual who pulled the trigger wore a peculiar style of olive green snakeskin boots. Footwear Nick had never seen before or since.

That is, until he noticed them hidden in a dark corner of his father's closet. Nick gulped and somewhere between a question and a statement, mumbled, "Dad's a murderer."

Chapter 28

Like a predator stalking its prey, Lloyd Garrison sat outside his home and calculated his next move. He waited an hour after the house became dark before entering.

With the exception of the tick-tick-tick of a clock that marked the passage of time, the home was tomblike silent. Amber shadows cast by moonlight and vaporous streetlights illuminated the first floor in an apropos gray-white pall.

Stealthily, Lloyd sauntered up the stairs. The door to Nick's room was closed. He made his way to see his wife's brother. Staring at Hank, Lloyd couldn't help but pity the poor bastard. A small desk lamp and flashes from TV provided the only light.

Lloyd skulked in, unable to recall the last time he ventured into Hank's domain. The room became blacker, more foreboding when Lloyd entered and switched off *Animal Planet*. He silenced the doo-wop music, upbeat tunes from a simpler bygone era.

As he stood in front of the trapped spirit, Lloyd reached down to remove the unhooked rotary phone from Hank's lap. He thought the man was sleeping but when Lloyd attempted to move it, Hank grunted an unintelligible sound like some pathetic thing in its final death throes.

Peering down at the poor excuse of a life that sagged forward, Lloyd became slightly amused as a string of sputum dripped from the corner of Hank's mouth before dropping to his threadbare shirt. Eying the feeble soul, Lloyd felt blessed. The two men were only a year apart but different paths in life kept the distance greater.

"You don't need the phone, Hank," Lloyd claimed as he yanked it from his lap. Hank's grip was stronger than Lloyd

,anticipated. "Martha's not calling you. Your wife's long gone. Dead. And in a much better place than you." Lloyd exited, leaving Hank imprisoned in the unforgiving obscurity.

In his bedroom, his steps became lighter. Eve was sleeping in a curled position facing away. He studied her for a moment and synchronized his steps with her gentle snoring. He opened the closet door, pulled the cord. Everything seemed undisturbed. Soundlessly, he removed the clothes he needed and departed.

Back in the kitchen, he scribbled a note for his wife, advising her he'd be gone most of tomorrow due to things he needed to take care of. He signed the note with a large *L*.

Lloyd slept on the sofa that evening. By the time his family woke he was gone.

☙❧

Just as it had been since the beginning of time Mae's Muffins and More—or 3 M's as locals called it—opened at six a.m. sharp. Lloyd Garrison was their first customer today. He sat in the last booth of the first row, allowing himself a clear sight line out onto Main Street.

The retro diner was decorated in a 1950s motif. Mini jukeboxes were attached to each individual booth. Humphrey Bogart, John Wayne, Marilyn Monroe, James Dean, and others watched from hanging photos. The older residents of Avalon Hills much preferred the home cooking of Mae's to the other mom-and-pop places that relied on prepackaged food and microwaves. Lloyd pulled the menu from the metal prongs and opened it.

"Whatcha want?"

He gave a passing glance to the human tattoo that doubled as a waitress. Although she wore a pink poodle skirt and blonde hair in pigtails, she looked nothing like the generation she theoretically characterized. He noticed the badge clipped to her collar. *Jayne*. The owner's granddaughter, maybe great granddaughter. Nodding at her name, Lloyd asked, "Like Mansfield?"

When Jayne scrunched her face, her eyes disappeared. "Huh?"

"Never mind. How's Mae doing these days?"

She clucked her gum twice, blew a bubble. "She's fine. Whatcha want?"

"Not a morning person, Jayne?"

"It's six a.m.," Jayne croaked. "I got a hangover and last night when I told my man I was three weeks late, he told me it aint his problem. So, no, I aint no morning person. Whatcha want?"

Lloyd ordered two eggs over easy, sour dough, hash browns, and strong black coffee. "Sorry about your boy-friend."

"I'm not. He's an ass turd."

Ass turd? Lloyd watched as she huffed her way behind the counter to place the order. A large eyeball with long eyelashes was tattooed on each of her calves. Her legs were watching him while she walked away.

He considered politely telling Jayne she needed an attitude adjustment, but decided to keep that to himself. There were three kinds of people you never wanted to get on the bad side of; people working on your car, people serving you food, and anyone named Garrison.

Lloyd finished his breakfast and left before the morning rush. His request for a coffee-to-go was met with a much-expected protest. "Hope things work out for you, Jayne."

"Yeah, whatever."

He was out of Avalon Hills before the sleepy town woke and dressed for their Sunday ritual of taking the sacrament. Although he only went to church for Christmas and Easter—the celebration of the birth of Christ and then his returning from the dead—he felt a desire to go today. He knew when this day ended he'd need to cleansed of breaking the sixth commandment. It was the first time in years Lloyd had been forced to act in this brazen manner. He was confident when passing down the duty to Gabe that his hands would never again become soiled.

Hindsight was 20/20. Lloyd should have known his young-est didn't have the grit and prudence to handle the responsibility. It was Nick who seemed the obvious clear-cut choice to fill his father's shoes. Unfortunately, however, Nick left behind his hometown, his friends, and his girl. The result fell into Gabe's less-than-capable hands.

Lloyd needed to have his heart and mind in the right place for the task at hand. As was his custom, he made his way deep into the Allegheny National Forrest. He parked and traversed into the thicket of The Heart's Content Scenic Area situated several miles east of town. It was an ironic name. Lloyd's heart was anything but content.

In his younger days, he'd frequently walk the nature trails that snaked amongst the aged white pines, picnic tables, and campgrounds. Today he was back for the first time in years.

He'd never been much for scenery but it somehow seemed to mollify his restless soul. He felt one with nature, closer to God.

Ambling through the peaceful woodlands with only his thoughts, Lloyd hoped an alternate option would come to him. He yearned to see the light and find a way out of the act he needed to commit. When no revelation came to him, Lloyd realized he had no way out.

Worn physically from the hike and drained mentally from thinking, Lloyd got back in his car, mumbled a silent prayer, and returned to Avalon Hills.

ഗെന

Sleep didn't come to Nick until almost three a.m. He thought he heard his father shuffling about within the darkness and considered challenging him about the boots but decided to wait until morning. By the time he woke, however, he learned he'd have to hold off until this evening. Once again he was *waiting*. More time passing by.

Since his arrival from Arizona, the Garrison residence was, as expected, chockfull of tension. His father was out for the day—*taking care of things*—but the air was stifling and suffocating.

For the first time, Nick was now questioning his mother's actions. Since getting off the plane, Nick realized nothing was as it seemed. Not only were old adversaries, such as his father and brother, still his enemy but regrettably he accepted childhood friends could not be counted on. Mike Lauser put a bullet in his own head and Ed Wolfe threatened to put a bullet in Nick's gut. The one person left who he could still count on was his mother. But she, too, seemed standoffish and secretive.

Last evening, she used the guise of sending Nick to find old photos. The fact he *accidentally* came across his father's snakeskin boots, the same boots worn years ago when he took a life and broke a Commandment, was not mere coincidence.

After he presented his discovery to his mom, she seemed ready and willing to shine some light on this gloomy picture. Much to Nick's surprise, she provided nothing to go on.

She was playing it close to the vest, not revealing a thing. Nick viewed her actions like a magician. She spread a deck of cards across a table but, instead of giving the ol' *pick a card, any card, don't tell me what it is* shtick, she sat in silence. Nick not only had to pick the card, he had to master the trick without knowing the secret.

Eve realized her son was frustrated but remained tight-lipped. During breakfast, she engaged Nick in idle banter before traipsing off to her bedroom. Later, she announced she'd be meeting her daughter-in-law for lunch.

Yolanda? Perhaps she could help unravel this mystery. They always connected well. When Eve claimed, "She wants to talk woman to woman," Nick's plan was effectively squashed.

Shortly after Eve left for her lunch date, Nick felt a need to break free from the confining residence. The walls of the home, the walls of the entire city, were tightening like a noose, choking him and stripping away his sanity. Plus, as unfeeling as it sounded, he didn't want to be alone with Uncle Hank.

Nick spent the day seeking resolution. He spent some time parked outside Brandi's childhood home where the man nicknamed Hawkeye now lived. He contemplated knocking on the door, but what could he say? *I loved a girl who once lived here and now people tell me she's dead. Can you help?* Even to him it sounded crazy. Plus, the perforated and inked Hawkeye had a quick temper. Nick had witnessed his short fuse for himself when he effectively kicked Wolfsie's ass outside Texas Jack's several nights ago.

Nick did, however, knock on the door of one possible ally. Karri opened but did not unlatch the chain. "Wolfsie's not in," she said. To Nick, she sounded curt.

"You know where he is? It's important."

"Sorry, Nick. I don't."

He stalled, asked if he could talk to her for a few minutes.

"I was just on my way out," was her reply.

Nick didn't push. He did, however, cross them off his list of possible helpers.

After another drive by Brandi's old home proved meaningless Nick headed out of town and traveled the two-lane that shadowed the Acheron River. He off-roaded the jarring terrain at the Jordan Turnout. It was the same location he met Wolfsie when first coming home, when he learned of Karri's cancer. Perhaps he'd run into him again.

No such luck.

Restless, passing time until this evening when he was determined to pump his father for answers, Nick ventured back into town. Entering the self-proclaimed cultural district, he entered the library. He signed a form and was granted computer access from a high school aged girl who didn't remove buds from her ears.

Nick lowered himself into an obscure corner station, away from potentially prying eyes. Glancing around, waiting for the computer to come to life, was when he saw her. She was seated three cubicles left, intently reading something online. Her jet black hair was unmistakable.

He rose, surprised at the lack of strength in his wobbly legs. Brandi had left him stranded on a sidewalk. Nick was upset about that, puzzled by her actions, baffled by the rumors of her death.

But he couldn't stop thinking about her. Despite the years and the twenty-seven-hundred miles, he couldn't stop thinking about her. As he moved closer to her, he had no idea what to say.

"Can I help you?" the stranger clipped, bothered by the intrusion.

"I thought you were someone else. Sorry." Nick sheepishly returned to his corner cubicle.

Searching the recesses of his mind, Nick attempted to recall the exact date almost thirty years ago he and Brandi witnessed the murder. He was unable to even remember what day of the week much less the specific date. He located a 1987 calendar online. He knew it was late June, shortly after graduation. Somewhere between the twenty-fifth and twenty-eighth of the month.

Nick accessed archived editions of several newspapers. Only the *Pittsburgh Post-Gazette* and the local weekly *Avalon Hills Bugle* offered online articles and obits from that long ago. He browsed the in memoriam section for every day from June twenty-fifth through July third. Nothing caught his eye. Over that same timespan, he saw no mention of a murder in Avalon Hills.

His thoughts and emotions were jumbled. On one hand, he was relieved. It was early in his father's mayoral tenure. He probably pulled whatever strings necessary to cover it up. Nevertheless, his father had gotten away with a homicide.

My father, the killer. He wasn't sure if he should laugh or cry.

He sat for a few moments, gauging his next move. When the fog lifted, he checked the community bulletin board pages of the *Avalon Hills Bugle* starting in late June through mid-July. The periodical listed the activities and petty crimes that would never get space in a big city newspaper. A resident was bitten by a dog, an intoxicated man was arrested for public urination, an unnamed juvenile was caught spraying graffiti on the rear wall of a furniture store, someone checked out of *The Olive Tree* without paying his bill, and an elderly woman had her Buick taken for a joyride. *Life in the big city.*

Nick pulled on his chin. He realized he hadn't shaved in a few days as he scratched stubble. He made the natural progression. If no murder was reported, perhaps the victim was never found. Nick started surfing the Internet for persons who'd gone missing around that time.

It was more time consuming than he expected. Twice the librarian came over and advised him in no uncertain terms he'd exceeded his allotted time. There were only three patrons in the entire library and four unoccupied computers.

"This is important," Nick said pleasantly.

The girl hesitated and, after advising him rules were put in place for a reason, she granted Nick another session. However, he'd need to fill out the same form again.

Nick thanked her for her generosity and resumed his research.

During the months of June and July in 1987, five individuals went missing in northwestern Pennsylvania. One was a man named David L. Roth which resulted in a fleeting smile. He suffered from Alzheimer's and wandered away from a nursing home. He was found four days later. A second was seventeen-year-old Judy Morales. Nick paused. The name sounded familiar. She apparently went to Avalon High. He thought they may have had a class together. She ran away from home but showed up over the state line in Akron. The third missing person was Henry Desmond, age sixty-six. *Too old.* The man Nick saw murdered that night was younger, twenties or thirties.

The fourth missing person was Owen Jefferson, twenty-nine. He fit the age range. Upon further research, Nick came across a photo of Jefferson. He was African-American. This victim was Caucasian.

The fifth person was a thirty-four-year-old male named Jameson Parker. Nick shifted in his chair and raked his hair, staring at the monitor as if it would clarify. "Jameson Parker," he murmured to himself. "Where have I heard that name?"

Nick opened a second browser and again accessed the community bulletin board for the *Bugle.* Jameson Parker was the man wanted for not paying his hotel bill.

Nick clucked his tongue and leaned back, interlacing his fingers behind his head. He repeated the name softly. He continued playing cyber-sleuth and Googled the name.

"Sir, we're closing in five minutes," the librarian warned, materializing over Nick's shoulder.

He stuck up his hand and continued searching. "Just a second, please."

Jameson Parker was married with three children. He was

listed as having green eyes, light brown hair. His height and weight of five eleven and one seventy eight fit that of the body type Nick observed that fateful evening on the banks of the Acheron. Nick felt confident he'd found the victim.

What confounded the situation was Parker's place of residence. Fairfax, Virginia, several hundred miles away but just outside of Washington DC. Equally troubling was learning Jameson Parker was a federal employee working for the Census Bureau under the umbrella of the Commerce Department.

Chapter 29

Frannie had been on tenterhooks since the altercation with Sheriff Garrison up at the Tri-Delta Plant. Her subsequent encounter with Burt Dyer, where she gathered some secrets about Avalon Hills and the city's long time mayor, only fanned the flames of her edginess. Now, when she heard someone rapping on her motel room door after dark, she nearly gave herself a heart attack.

She held her breath in check, debated answering. With papers and reports strewn across her bed, Frannie uncoiled from her cross-legged position and stole over. She felt isolated, far away from home, and vulnerable. Peeking through the eyehole, she saw the oblong face of an older man with white hair. She thought she knew her visitor but asked anyway. "Who's there?"

"Ms. Fitzgerald, it's Mayor Garrison. May I have a few minutes of your time?"

Frannie vacillated before nervously blurting, "I just stepped out of the shower. I'll be just a minute." Unsure where that came from, she stroked her face and considered her choices. She had none. After all, it's not every day you get visited by someone back from the dead. *Twenty-seven minutes.*

After stalling as long as possible, and with no valid excuse, she kept the door chained but peered through the narrow gape. "Yes?" She realized she should have at least thrown some water on her hair.

"May I come in?"

"Now's not really a good time," she feebly claimed. "I—I was just on my way out."

He presented the same amiable grin worn during countless re-elections. Of course, no one was ever foolish enough to campaign against Lloyd Garrison. "It's rather important. I'd like to give you some answers that would be beneficial."

Frannie needed *something* to bring back to Dennis. Her boss would waste no time criticizing her for a wild goose chase. Plus, Mayor Garrison was old and harmless. She unlatched the chain and allowed him passage.

Once inside, he thanked her, eyeing the surroundings as well as the reports scattered across the bed. Wearing navy blue Khaki's and a pristine white shirt, Lloyd commented, "Working hard or hardly working?"

"Working hard," she replied with a cursory smile. Frannie's skin grew clammy. *Twenty-seven minutes.* "How can I—what can I do for you?"

Lloyd stared off toward the bathroom and adjacent vanity. No steam billowing, no mist over the mirror. His grin indicated he knew she lied about showering. "First off, Frances—may I call you Frances?"

"Yes."

Lloyd took a prolonged gaze at her. Based on her name, he expected her to be older. Crow's feet spread from her eyes, a few strands of gray were noticeable but, overall, she appeared younger than she was and far more youthful than her name implied. "First off, let me apologize on behalf of my son. He informed me what transpired at that old factory north of town. Gabriel tends to be a bit, oh, hot-headed at times but it's a requirement of being sheriff."

Frannie waved it away.

"I'm hoping he didn't alarm you too much," Lloyd offered.

She shrugged in a yes-no fashion. "He's just doing his job."

"As am I. And as are you. That's why I wish to talk to you. Your job." Lloyd paused, attempting to overcome the increasing uneasiness in his heart. He noticed the diamond ring and hoped she didn't have children. "You seem like an intelligent woman, hard-working, dedicated."

"Just a public servant trying to earn a living, Mayor Garrison."

"Please, Lloyd. We're just a small town out here in the middle of nowhere. A small island in a very large sea. But the residents of my fine city like it that way. We all know each other, look out for each other. And yes, protect each other."

"Like Mayberry?"

Lloyd leered, unsure how he felt about Avalon Hills being compared to the backdrop for *The Andy Griffith Show*. "Perhaps. As my son pointed out, albeit too forcefully, we tend to be less than welcoming to visitors." He threw in an overt smile for affect. He hadn't campaigned in a while but the pleasing demeanor and reassuring charm still worked.

Frannie regarded her guest. He was a grandfatherly type, stern but sensitive. Trustworthy. Like her, he also was a public servant. She took a deep breath and decided to come clean. Hopefully the mayor could help. The sooner she got answers, the sooner she could see her daughters. Scooping some papers from the bed she sidled alongside Lloyd. "I'm hoping you can possibly help with—this."

"I'll surely try," he offered.

When his eyes came upon the information, it solidified his next action. It was unavoidable. Frannie spoke but he didn't bother listening. He already knew what the reports proved.

"These are the written transcripts of conversations I accessed through the local cell provider in town after obtaining a subpoena," she lied. Frannie chose not to mention she hacked into the company's database. The skills taught by her nephew had benefitted her yet again. She owed that kid a steak dinner. "I'm perplexed about…well, I'm not sure how Elizabeth Decker can have several conversations over the last ten days with her husband Jonathan when he died four years ago."

"They most likely reissued his number," Lloyd implied apathetically.

Frannie disagreed. "They reissue that same number to a person his wife has extended conversations with? That's not very likely, Mayor."

Rather than addressing her concern, Lloyd steered the discussion down the road he wanted to travel. "I believe my son mentioned to you the name of Jameson Parker."

"Yes. Yes, he did." Frannie's face showed eagerness. "I didn't know the name."

"Have a seat," Lloyd insisted as he slid out a chair from a badly chipped octagonal table. He displayed a manila folder, his intentions clear. *If you want to know what's in here and want answers, you'll need to sit.*

Resolution. Finally! She could get answers, get home soon, and save face with her boss. Taking a deep breath in preparation of her quest coming to an end, Frannie lowered herself.

Standing behind her, Lloyd reached around and positioned the folder on the table but kept his fingers on top of the binder as if about to unveil a dearth of knowledge and wisdom. He said, "Jameson Parker, like you, was a federal employee. He, like yourself, was hardworking, devoted to his job. He, like you, came upon something that…well, let me say…that he should not have uncovered. " Lloyd let the moment linger. "I hope you have a strong stomach." He drew back his hand.

Frannie stared at the dossier, tried to see *through* it without touching it, opening it. She took several deep breaths, her heart rate quickened. Timidly, she unwound the cord that sealed the file.

The first clasped page was set up in a resume format with bullet points detailing Jameson Parker's work history and personal information. The next page was an eight-and-one-half-inch-by-eleven-inch, black-and-white photo of the man. It appeared to have been blown up from his employee badge. When she flipped to the third page, Frannie stifled a scream and covered her mouth.

The man's face was obliterated. His skin color was ashen and pale, his hair matted, wet, as if he just came out of a shower. Or a river. His nose was flattened. His mouth was frozen open as if screaming for help in the midst of an excruciating death. His left eye socket was hollow. Frannie's dinner rose in her throat. "What—what—"

"He was interfering, Ms. Fitzgerald. Just like you."

Frannie felt a cold piercing wire cutting into her throat with incredible force. Startled, her legs instinctively flailed, kicking at nothing. Her hands went to her neck, her fingers desperately clutching at the cable choking her life away, slicing through her supple neck. In her mind, she heard herself begging for mercy. But all that came out was an animal-like grunt.

More for himself than his victim, Lloyd whispered, "Forgive me" and twisted the garrote tighter around her tender neck. With his fingers through a coiled loop at each end, he yanked harder. Once, twice, again. A green-yellow projectile of phlegm was expelled from her mouth followed by a large clump of blood.

Frannie toppled backward. The chair fell, but she did not. Dropping to one knee, she felt herself getting wrenched and manipulated like a limp ragdoll. She frantically dug her nails into her own neck, trying to get any purchase against the instrument of her death.

The old mayor was not harmless, after all.

Just as when she entered the Tri-Delta Plant, her mind wandered to her children. "Mommy loves you. Mommy always will love you." She only heard her voice in her head. She continued to gurgle and choke. In her mind, she saw her daughters smiling faces. Then the stabbing pain lessened and darkness wrapped around her.

∽∾∽

Brandi was most likely the reason. The recollection of last night was vivid, stark, and powerful. The way she looked, the way she felt, her scent, what he did to her. It was a pleasing combination of the physical and emotional along with the control he exhibited over his brother's girl.

Eyes closed, sweat dropping from his brow, he saw Brandi in his mind and continued aggressively thrusting into his wife.

"Gabe—oh—Gabe."

As if being awoken from a dream, Gabe opened his eyes and stared down at his wife. He momentarily wondered how she got beneath him.

Wide-eyed and startled by his passion and lust, Yolanda wondered what caused the change in her husband. He hadn't been this stimulated in a long time. She had an idea but at this moment, she didn't care. She wanted it to continue.

Moaning rhythmically, Gabe angled his shoulders behind the back of her knees. With Yolanda bent in half, he hammered her harder than ever before. This was not about sex and passion; it was about control and power.

Yolanda's cries of passion were in synch with each aggressive lunge. "Oh—my—Gabe—"

Gabe concluded with a series of overpowering stabs as he erupted.

He stayed motionless and allowed his panting to subside.

Yolanda grinned in amazement. Winded, she cupped his sweaty face. "What got into you?" She laughed like a giddy schoolgirl. "Or better yet, what got into me?"

He couldn't help but be pleased with his performance. The satisfaction and exhaustion on his wife's face was secondary. He owed it all to Brandi. Still inside of Yolanda, Gabe claimed, "Ya know, if you stay you can get this every night."

Yolanda smiled. "I may have to rethink it."

Gabe flashed a hopeful expression. Perhaps he wouldn't have to follow through with the pact he made with his father. Gabe knew he'd never be able to perform like this every night. Unless, of course, he stopped over at Brandi's first.

He understood, however, it was the passion of the moment speaking. Yolanda was stubborn. Once she made a decision to do something there was no stopping her. If she didn't leave tomorrow, it'd be the next day. Or the day after. "Maybe you should rethink it." He resumed moving his hips.

"Ohhh—shit—Gabe—you're gonna—kill me."

The seemingly innocuous comment snapped him back to reality. He slowed his hips, choosing to end things on a good note.

Yolanda pouted. "No more?"

Gabe shook his head. "You want it again? You need to stay."

Her face was both fulfilled and sad. "You know I can't. I just need to get away for a few days. It'll do us some good. Just a few days."

"Yup." He got out of bed and headed, as always, to the bathroom to cleanse off his wife.

Gabe's obsession to shower immediately after sex had bothered her for quite some time. But after his performance tonight, it didn't seem such a big deal.

Tonight was the most exhilarating sexual experience they'd had in some time. Yolanda was sapped, but craved more. Her husband might be too worn out for an encore in bed, but perhaps in the shower…

Yolanda laughed devilishly. Her legs were rubbery as she made her way toward the bathroom. Beaming from ear to ear, she reached out for the knob. However, the door opened and Gabe exited. He seemed shocked to see her up and about.

Yolanda was confused as to why he was not wet, then more surprised when she observed the gun in his hand. "Gabe?" was all she could manage.

"I want you to know I'm sorry."

Yolanda backpedaled. Confused but still smiling from the multiple orgasms, she wondered if this was something kinky. "Gabe, what—is this?"

"It's called a sacrifice for the greater good."

The three pops from the Smith and Wesson sounded like one.

Yolanda saw quick bursts of light from the .45 caliber. She frowned. She heard the sounds, saw the flashes but felt nothing. She instinctively looked down at her nakedness. Reflexively, her hands cupped the crimson opening in her belly where smoke rose from a widening red patch. Upon seeing it, she now felt the burning splitting pain. Her extremities grew cold. "Gabe?"

He raised his arm.

Yolanda had no time to react. It happened too quickly. She felt the barrel of cold steel pressed into the center of her forehead. Then she heard one more explosion.

ဆဝဆ

It was a little after nine-thirty when Lloyd drove to the rear of the sparsely illuminated police station. He killed the headlights upon entering the lot and noticed Gabe exit his cruiser. The sheriff used the key fob to release the trunk but stayed by the driver's side. He didn't want to look in.

Lloyd reversed so both vehicles were back-to-back. He acknowledged his son with an unassuming nod and scrutinized the trunk where the bullet riddled corpse of his naked daughter-in-law lay. He considered scolding his son for not having the decency to at least blanket the dead woman but chose not to. Time was short.

Matter-of-factly, Lloyd opened the trunk of his own vehicle manually. As if he was unloading groceries, he hoisted the body of Frances Fitzgerald and indiscriminately chucked his victim alongside his son's victim. When her lifeless arm not yet succumbing to rigamortis bobbed out he emotionlessly threw it back in and slammed the trunk. "Let's go."

The conversation during the drive was clipped and direct. "Any issues I should know about?" Lloyd asked.

"None."

"No way she would've stayed?"

"None."

"She was a good girl, that Yolanda, but she brought this on herself. We couldn't risk her leaving town and telling the world our secret."

"Uh huh."

"You did what you had to, Gabriel."

"Sure."

Upon arriving at the derelict Tri-Delta factory, Lloyd proclaimed, "I'll wait in the car." His intentions were clear. This was Gabe's mess. Gabe would clean it up. Lloyd had dirtied his hands for the last time.

It took twenty-five minutes to dispose of the corpses. Gabe hoisted Frannie out of the trunk first. He threw a blanket over his shoulder and draped her cold lifeless form over the coverlet. He lumbered through the opening in the security fence that wreathed the perimeter, and trudged across the marshland. He exited only after a minute, maybe two. Back at the rear of the cruiser, he used greater care with his wife's corpse than he'd used on Frannie. This time he remained inside longer.

Lloyd knew Gabe was saying goodbye. *But fifteen minutes?* He impatiently drummed his fingers on his knee and waited. When Gabe emerged and lowered himself behind the wheel, he appeared worn. "You okay?"

"Wonderful, Dad, just wonderful."

"Got rid of them?"

Gabe nodded, glanced his father with contempt. It was obvious he wanted details. "I dropped them into one of the pits in the factory floor. No one will ever find them." He added with a smirk, "Don't worry. You're free and clear."

"You check the tanks while you were there?"

"Yes, Father."

"And?"

"They're minimal." Gabe shrugged. "Two weeks, two months, two years? No idea how much we have left."

Lloyd took a deep breath. Gabe's inability to calculate an approximate timeframe only reaffirmed his belief that Nick never should have left. "Let's go talk to your brother."

Gabe turned the ignition but voiced his concern before driving away. "I'm not happy about telling Nick."

"I haven't been happy in thirty years," Lloyd countered.

"I don't feel comfortable with letting him in. He doesn't deserve it. He left. I stayed. It's not the way it's meant to be."

"We already talked about this. I'm not having this same discussion."

Gabe pressed. "When you handed this over to me, you said it was my call. *Mine.*" He threw his thumb into his chest. "I was the one with the power. But yet, you're still involved, still pulling the strings. I don't appreciate you changing the rules in the middle of the game."

"There are no rules when family's involved. Now, drive."

Gabe jerked the car into gear. "If you weren't here, I'd let Nick die."

"I am still here, Gabriel. And as long as I am, you will listen to me. Now, let's go save Nick."

☙☙

In spite of their popularity, none of those TV programs appealed to Nick.

They were identical—the body would be discovered in an alley, the grizzled wise-cracking detective and the neophyte he was partnered with always bucked the odds and managed to find the murderer from a microscopic trace of DNA found on a hair follicle that was entwined in a comb buried in the bottom of a dumpster in the back of a body shop. And, luckily, justice was served in time for the local news.

Unlike Nick, who felt he was missing *something* with the lure of these programs, his mother was glued to them. With everything going on, he envied her ability to detach herself. "Which one is this anyway?"

"CSI," Eve replied, unable to draw her eyes away. "No, wait. It's SUV…I think."

"SVU." Nick chuckled, then added, "These shows are all alike."

"It's SUV 'cause it's got that Ice Tray fellow."

"Ice T."

Eve glanced at her son. "What did I say?"

"You said Ice Tray."

"I did?" Eve turned back. "It's SVU, I'm pretty sure."

Nick sang, "CSI, SVU, M-o-u-s-e."

Whichever show it was ended. The local news out of Pittsburgh just began when headlights swept the living room. Nick and Eve exchanged a glance. "Your father's home."

They rose and walked to the front door. After returning home, Nick quickly began realizing things weren't on the up and up. Mike Lauser's suicide, Wolfsie's strange behavior, his father's boots hidden in a closet, the murder years ago of Jameson Parker. And of course, Brandi. Tonight, Nick would at long last, get answers. From his father.

With Eve standing a few feet behind in the anteroom, Nick stepped onto the patio. He was relieved to see his father, less than enthused to see his brother.

Lloyd lifted himself from the passenger's side of Gabe's police cruiser appearing overcome. His shoulders sagged as if the burdens of a lifetime were finally weighing him down.

Nick impulsively flinched when hearing what he assumed were firecrackers left over from the Fourth of July. The three pops came in rapid succession and ripped apart the tranquil residential street. Loud enough to wake the dead.

Nick saw a figure emerge from the shadows. The silhouette boldly crossed the lawn.

Closer to the house.

Closer to Lloyd.

Arms extended out, an object that appeared to be a gun gripped tightly.

Another pair of popping sounds and Lloyd Garrison collapsed face first onto the driveway of his home.

It was as if Nick was watching a movie. An observer. He heard a scream from behind. It sounded like his mom. The shape moved closer to Lloyd's body and took aim.

Another explosion of rapid gunfire. This one louder. So close together, Nick couldn't count. The being who stood over Lloyd was swiftly pitched like a marionette controlled by a puppet master.

"You bitch!" Gabe shouted.

He boldly moved around the front of the car, stepped over his father's convulsing body, and continued squeezing off rounds until clicking on an empty chamber.

Hypnotically, Nick felt his legs pull him forward, both to his father and the shooter. Two bodies lay on the front lawn of the Garrison home. Neighbor's porch lights turned on.

Nick skulked closer to the assassin, to the…gun*man*? For some unknown reason, he approached guardedly. The person was obviously dead. The amount of blood was stomach-turning. The long brown hair shielded her features. It was a woman.

"Who…" Nick muttered.

Eve crept alongside Nick and clutched his arm. "Brooke Lauser."

Nick's distorted face asked *why*? Why would Mike Lauser's widow assassinate his father?

Eve hearkened back to the last time she saw Brooke. The distraught woman stopped by. She was frantic, hysterical. Her husband had just shot himself and Brooke came by begging Lloyd to help. He refused. "You should have helped her," Eve whispered to the night.

"Mom, what the hell is going on?"

Eve ignored her firstborn's question. She turned to her second born who was kneeling, sobbing over Lloyd's lifeless form. As far back as Nick could remember, his old-fashioned mom was the dutiful wife. She cooked, she cleaned, she raised the kids, and was borderline subservient to her husband. So when she now displayed a forceful tone, it was shocking.

He'd never heard his mother speak with this level of sternness and authority. "Gabe! Gabe, listen to me."

No response.

"Gabe." Firmer now. "You know what you have to do."

Nick inched closer. A distant siren began piercing the night.

Gabe peered at his mother with a thousand-mile stare. His welled-up eyes glistened dimly like a fading star at the end of the universe. He was brought back to reality by a swift slap across his face.

"I need you to focus, Gabriel. Are you focused?"

He nodded silently.

"Don't look at him, look at me. Are you focused?"

"Yeah—Yes."

Eve didn't have much time to spare. She peered into Gabe's eyes. "Bring my husband back."

Chapter 30

For the second time in as many days, Nick was looking down the barrel of a gun. First it was his friend, now it was his brother.

As Gabe situated their father's lifeless form into the front seat of the cruiser, Nick insisted on tagging along to…wherever they were going. Gabe answered by drawing his weapon.

Nick watched helplessly as his brother sped from the driveway and raced into the darkness. "It's okay," Eve called out to her nosy neighbors. "Everything's all right." She and Nick stood in such a way as to prevent Brooke's body from being observed. Their position did not completely conceal the corpse that lay bent on the lawn, but it was all for show. Residents of Avalon Hills knew better than to ever question a Garrison.

Seconds later, a cruiser approached. Out stepped the big-haired deputy. "Everyone back inside," she called out and advanced on Nick, Eve, and the cadaver behind them. "Brooke Lauser, two kids, damn shame."

The screaming of Gabe's sirens diminished in the distance. Nick didn't want to lose him. "I'll be back later." Disregarding his mother's insistence that he stay put, Nick hustled around his car, threw himself behind the wheel, and took off in pursuit of his brother.

಄಄಄

Rocketing north, Nick's rented Hyundai could not keep pace with the souped-up police car. He relied on following the sound of the wailing siren and minding the flashing strobe lights dancing against the tree lines. He lost the tail twice but was able to pick up the sirens' distinctive pitch.

Why hadn't Gabe called for an ambulance? A medical chopper could've arrived faster and ferried Lloyd to a hospital quicker than Gabe could drive him. And why was his brother heading *north*? If he was going to try and race to a hospital, Pittsburgh was south. Unless—

No.

Nick promptly eradicated that possibility from his thoughts. His father could not already be dead. Not his own father.

His dad had not been moving, chest down, face pressed against the concrete driveway. Nick observed three or four bullet holes in his father's back. There was a bullet wound in his upper left shoulder but most of the damage centered near his spinal cord. Paralyzed? Punctured lungs? But surely not dead.

Through the thicket, Nick caught a glimpse of a sapphire ray appearing and disappearing; the refraction of the cruiser's lights. It seemed as if Gabe was heading to the Acheron.

Nick smirked at the irony. Things were coming full circle. Once again, he found himself negotiating the trail of the Jordan Turnout.

☙❧

Gabe was on his knees in the shallow waters of the Acheron. His father's body was fully submerged beneath the surface, except for his head and shoulders that rested motionless in Gabe's makeshift lap.

Using his hands like a scoop, he gingerly dabbed his father's face. A baptism in Holy Waters.

"C'mon, Dad. Please." Gabe's voice was small, pleading, conquered. His words cracked as he appealed to a higher power. He whispered soft prayers while continuing to let droplets slide from his curled palm onto Lloyd's ashen face.

Eyes closed, his father cold.

"Please, Lord, I beg of you. One more second chance."

The image of Yolanda entered his mind. His wife was the religious one in their home. Now, just hours after he murdered her, he could feel her eyes looking down from heaven and laughing. *Karma's a bitch.*

Gabe peeked at his watch and estimated the time since that Lauser woman pumped led into his father. *Thirty-two minutes, give or take.*

Gabe continued stroking his father's unresponsive face. He was fighting a losing battle. It was as if all the forces of the universe were aligning against him, mocking this mere mortal who was trying to alter destiny yet again, this mortal who was playing God.

The pseudo baptism continued. Gabe looked up to the sky. He drew his eyes back and peered through the murky zigzagging path of the Acheron in the direction of the Tri-Delta Plant. He continued begging. *Thirty-six minutes.*

So immersed in his attempt to resurrect his father he was oblivious to splashing water brought on by approaching footsteps.

"Is he…" Nick couldn't finish.

Methodically Gabe continued the futile attempt while glaring scornfully at his brother. Nick observed from ten feet away, reluctant to come closer. Although Gabe was weeping and his voice reticent, his tone was undeniably combative. "This is your fault, brother, all your fault."

Nick met his brother's eyes for only a moment. He continued gazing at his father's submerged body. He—they—had just lost their father and he was in no mood to engage in bullshit sibling rivalry at this point. "What're you doing?"

Gabe initially ignored the question. When Nick repeated it, he snapped. "What the hell does it *look* like I'm doing?"

The words fell from Nick although they were illogical. "It looks like you're trying to bring him back to life."

Satirically, Gabe roared, "Ta-dah. We have a winner!"

Nick emitted mirthless laughter. He strode forward, the Acheron undulating around his ankles, his shoes sinking into the sludge. "Gabe, you have to tell me what's going on. I'm your brother. Dad—Dad would want me to know."

"Oh really?" screamed Gabe, his voice echoing against the forest wall. "Is that so?" He looked at his watch again. *Thirty-eight minutes.*

Gabe sprang to his feet with a swiftness and agility that startled Nick. In less than reverent fashion, he gripped Lloyd's armpits and pulled-yanked him to the shore.

"Jesus, Gabe." Nick moved forward to help. His father should at least be carried, not dragged like a sack of potatoes.

"Get the hell back!" Gabe blocked Nick with his shoulder. Upon reaching the shore he lowered his father, slid the back of his hand across his nose. "What am I supposed to tell Mom?" he asked of no one. He couldn't help but laugh pathetically. All these years of doing what was right, what was expected, what he was supposed to. And now, he was powerless. The very forces he'd battled all these years had ultimately prevailed. He muttered, "This ends tonight."

Nick sought clarification. "What did Mom mean by 'bring my husband back'?"

Instead of responding, Gabe again imputed his brother but Nick had grown tired of the riddles, the mysteries, and the endless array of secrecy. Stridently, he insisted, "I want to know what happened tonight."

"Go to hell."

"What is going on here? This whole town? Tell me, Gabe, dammit."

"Go to hell!"

"Why would Mike's widow kill our father?"

Louder and with venomous hatred spewing from him, Gabe screamed, "Get the hell away from me!"

It started coming together. Nick just wasn't sure what the *it* was. The Acheron had been poisoned with chemicals from the upriver Tri-Delta Plant. The adjacent plot of land on the opposite side was quarantined. His mother's comment to *bring my husband back.* Wolfsie's threat of violence after coming to terms with his wife's unavoidable death. The name of Jonathan Decker being tossed around four years after his death like it happened yesterday.

The discovery of his father's snakeskin boots hidden away in a remote corner of a closet, the same footwear he wore the night he murdered Jameson Parker in cold blood nearly thirty years ago.

Indignantly, Nick leapt forward, grabbed his brother by the

collar of his sheriff's uniform, and viciously jerked him to his feet. "Where's Brandi?"

Gabe slapped his hands away. "Don't you ever—*ever*— touch me."

"Where is she, Gabe!?"

"Go home, *Nick*. Go home to your nice little life in Arizona, whatever you have left of it. Run away again. Just like you did before. Just like you always do."

Nick refused to back down. Not this time. "Tell me where she is. "

"Fuck you!"

Nick's hands clenched. It took everything he had to restrain himself. So filled with rage, anger, and fury, he was ready to tear his brother from limb from limb. "I'll find her." He glimpsed Lloyd's body. He knew he should feel a sense of loss but it was difficult. He'd never been *Dad.* They'd never been close. Father and son were strangers. Nick's only grief was directed toward his mom. His eyes met his brother's taciturn stare and again he affirmed his goal. "I'm going to find Brandi," he avowed. He turned his back on Gabe.

Nick had barely taken a step when the sound behind caused him to halt. Regrettably, it was a sound he was becoming familiar with—the clunk of a hammer being cocked. He turned around, looked at the firearm in his brother's hand. "You going to shoot me?"

"Get the hell out of town and forget Brandi. I'll handle this. Just like I always have. You just run away. That's what you're good at. Running."

With determination, Nick stepped closer to the weapon. "I'm gonna find her, Gabe. You want to stop me? Then you'll have to kill me."

Click. Nick recoiled. *Click. Click. Click. Click.*

Gabe continued squeezing the trigger. He'd called Nick's bluff. But he hadn't reloaded since emptying his firearm into Brooke Lauser.

Nick's heart beat in his neck. The fact that Gabe was ready—willing—to kill him, indicated nothing remained between the Garrison siblings other than contempt. Nick walked away, determined to never again turn his back on his brother.

Chapter 31

His shoulders were squared aggressively. His hands were fisted. He spoke in a *don't-lie-to-me* tone. "Where is she?"

Eyes half mast, Wolfsie opened the door partway. His right arm was out of view, probably clutching a baseball bat or something that could be used on an intruder. "Jesus, Nick. What time is it?"

"Tell me where she is, Ed. No more jerking me around."

"It's like three in the morning." Wolfsie yawned. "She's sleeping."

"Not Karri, Brandi."

Wolfsie rolled his tired eyes. "Keep your voice down. I don't want to wake the whole neighborhood."

Shouting, Nick obviously didn't give a damn about the whole neighborhood. "No more bullshit, Wolfsie. Tell me where Brandi is."

"Christ, Nick. We've been over this before." Wolfsie paused. His demeanor changed from drowsiness to uncertainty. *Maybe nervous?* "Did you dig her up?"

Wolfsie's comment indicated the first chink in the armor of deception. The fact he seemed troubled by the possibility that Nick really did exhume Brandi's casket was the first layer being peeled back. Nick bluffed. "The grave's empty."

Wolfsie shut his eyes tightly and dropped his head. His lack of a response confirmed it. Brandi's grave *was* empty.

"Who is it, baby?"

"Just Nick," Wolfsie called over his shoulder. "It's okay. Go back to sleep."

"Hi, Nick," Karri mumbled with a half-hearted wave from the shadowy hallway.

"Karri," Nick responded evenly.

As Wolfsie's wife shuffled away, Nick considered his next play. The history he shared with Wolfsie extended back decades. However, turnabout was fair play. Since Wolfsie fired the first volley of falsehoods, Nick would now even the score. Although he loathed himself for dragging Karri into this, she'd be the perfect bait. "The deal's off."

"Deal, what deal?"

Nick had the upper hand. He was pumped up, adrenalin coursing through his blood like a narcotic. On the other hand, Wolfsie had not completely woken, was not thinking clearly. Recalling seeing Wolfsie walk into the police station to meet with Gabe, Nick took a stab in the dark. "The deal you made with my brother."

"I don't know what you're talkin' about. Nick, it's the middle of—"

"I saw you walk into the police station. Then, all of a sudden, the next day, you're totally okay with your wife dying?"

"I don't know what to tell you, my friend." Wolfsie's counterclaim was weak.

Nick was getting somewhere. Like a fabric unwinding to reveal a mystery, Nick pulled the loose string and kept the ploy going. He just wasn't sure what to say. He repeated his previous statement, this time with more grit. "The deal's off."

Wolfsie was back on his heels, literally and figuratively. He collected his thoughts. "How? Why? Sheriff Garrison gave me his word. Why would he change his mind?"

Nick sustained the charade. "You know as well as anyone that Gabe and I don't get along. When push comes to shove, he always looks out for himself. All of Avalon Hills knows that. But while you and he may have reached some agreement, *I'm* his brother. *I'm* blood."

Wolfsie stared wistfully into his friend's eyes searching for weakness, for any sign of deception. Nick held steadfast and appeared to be truthful. Suddenly, Wolfsie's face turned beet red. He wiped a tear from the corner of his eye. "He promised. Your brother promised me."

Nick maintained the charade. "I know he did."

Wolfsie thought out loud. "I don't get it. He told me that if

I threw you off track, if I steered you away from Brandi, he'd save Karri. He gave me his word."

Nick stifled his shock. *Save Karri?* It was evident now that Wolfsie had lied to him, double-crossed him. His friend had been blackmailed by his brother. Nick repeated his opening statement. "Where's Brandi?"

Wolfsie ran his trembling fingers through his hair, absorbing it all, and glanced over his shoulder. Trying to accept Sheriff Garrison betrayal, he breathed, "He's—going to let Karri die?"

Unsure how to respond, Nick let that comment linger.

As if emerging from a catacomb of deep thought, Wolfsie opened the door and, this time, welcomed Nick to his home. "We should talk."

❧❦❧

It was a new day in Avalon Hills. The carroty antennae of sunrise snaked through open slats of the kitchen blinds, bathing the room in a beam of warmth and light. There were no clouds anywhere. Yet, in spite of the fact that it was a picturesque morning, Nick felt shrouded in a dreary gloom.

He'd been up twenty hours but the combination of adrenalin and caffeine rushing through his blood kept away the pull of drowsiness.

Wolfsie was also wide awake as he put up yet another pot of coffee, their third in three hours.

Nick's head throbbed something fierce. When he came banging on his friend's door, he was adamant on getting answers. Now that he had many, he was unsure what to make of them, how to feel, what it meant.

It had taken Wolfsie a good forty minutes to open up. Once he did, however, he burst like a dam. To Nick, his friend appeared almost thankful to release the mysteries as if he was cleansing his soul.

The Tri-Delta Plant opened its doors in the 1920s and became one of the largest steel producers in the rust belt. Shortly after the country found itself embroiled in World War II, Tri-Delta joined the war effort. They ratcheted up their machinery and began building tanks and aircraft parts. The plant was operating twenty-four-seven, unemployment in western Pennsylvania was below two percent, and people were working sixteen-hour shifts. Times were good. People were happy. Everyone made a buck.

While Tri-Delta operated in the east, the US government was going full-throttle to develop the atomic bomb before Nazi Germany. The bulk of testing and research occurred in the New Mexico desert at Los Alamos National Laboratories. The copious experiments resulted in the creation of much nuclear waste and poisonous materials. The feds were so focused on Fat Man and Little Boy they had neither the time nor the wherewithal to contemplate waste removal. The United States had to develop the bomb first at any human or financial cost.

Wolfsie explained, "Even though the nation was unified to defeat the Nazis and crush the Japanese empire, good ol' capitalism remained front and center. Defeating an enemy is one thing. But if it could also improve the bottom line and look good for the shareholders, it would be that much sweeter.

"Harvey Ducharme, the owner of Tri-Delta, saw a golden opportunity. He wanted his company's fingerprints on the weapon that would win the war. He was a despotic type who pulled out all stops. Ducharme claimed—backed up by reports logged by *experts* he handsomely paid off—the atomic weapon, once built, would be more effective if fired from a tank than dropped from an aircraft. The government scoffed at his outlandish claims. However, they awarded him the funding needed for research and development. The main objective was to win the war. It didn't matter which American company grabbed the brass ring."

Wolfsie continued. "Germany surrendered first and, since Japan's an island, there was no way to get this so-called super tank onto the mainland. So the project proved fruitless. But, hey, Ducharme and his stockholders didn't care."

Nick continued listening intently. "How do you know all of this?"

"A lot of it is hearsay. Much is conjecture and second hand. I'm not sure how much of this is true, Nick. However, it all does come together in the end. Want some more coffee?"

"No, thanks."

Wolfsie refilled his own mug and picked up where he left off. "By 1943, Germany had begun to realize the war effort was lost. Hitler's Thousand-Year Reich was falling almost a thousand years short. So, out of panic and desperation, they began delving into something else. Immortality."

Nick was no historian but he knew the atrocities, horrors, and torturous experiments the Nazis perpetrated. Nevertheless, this sounded extreme, even by their standards. "Immortality?"

"Wars end when the losses become too great, be it in blood or money. Seeing the writing of their demise on the wall, out of despair, they began experimenting with resurrecting soldiers killed on the battlefield. A limitless army that can't be killed would be invincible."

Nick snorted at the absurdity. "A zombie army? Please."

"The world was different back then. Flight was still in its infancy. Jet engines hadn't replaced propellers. Only a small percentage of Americans owned an automobile. Very few homes had TV's or telephones. Scientists were so nervous when creating the atom bomb they thought the force could potentially knock the planet from its axis and send us all hurtling through space. So bringing soldiers back was not that much of a stretch. The entire world was testing new limits and possibilities."

"Seems crazy," Nick commented.

"What's even crazier is our government also dabbled in it."

Nick cocked his head like a dog hearing a high pitch.

Wolfsie nodded. "You've heard of penis envy? This was country envy. If the Nazis built a tank, we had to have a bigger one. If they were going to create a bomb that could destroy cities, we had to have a bigger bomb. If the Japanese built a slick aircraft like the Zero, we had to build a slicker one."

"I see—I think."

"It still goes on today. Toyota builds a car that gets forty miles to the gallon so Chevy has to build one that gets forty-one. The Russians were determined to get to the moon. We had to get their first. So, if Hitler and his minions were going to create an army of immortal soldiers...well, we had to do it

first. Hence, Tri-Delta and the reemergence of Harvey Ducharme."

Nick met his friends gaze with a skeptical grimace. "You're
telling me that here, just outside of Avalon Hills, Pennsylvania, the place we grew up, they tried to…to, I don't know.
Cheat death? Sorry, man, but that's insane."

Wolfsie's expression indicated he accepted his friend's
misgiving. "They tried but obviously never succeeded."

Nick snickered. "Obviously."

Wolfsie brought it closer to home. "As soon as World War
II ended, the Cold War started. And so the experiments of attempting to create un-killable soldiers continued. The Nazis
were definitely *out there* in their thinking. On the flip side,
however, much of what they initiated, we perfected. Hey, it's
well-known that a lot of Nazi scientists were ushered out of
Berlin and worked for us. A battalion of American military
who couldn't be killed would go far, if and when, we fought
the Soviets."

"And these experiments went on at Tri-Delta?"

"Yes, until the mid-eighties when Washington pulled their
funding and closed the plant. After forty years, they accepted
they could not play God. That, and the fact the president realized if we ever did face off against the Russians, it would be
nuclear, not boots on the ground. The money used for Tri-
Delta was eventually allocated for Star Wars, the Stealth, and
other projects in the war machine. Tri-Delta was abandoned,
dismissed, and left to rot in the sun—the innards ripped out
and destroyed. Well, most of them anyway. They left behind
some tanks, cisterns, vats, and other crap."

Nick held his thoughts for a moment. He recalled meeting
Wolfsie at the Jordan Turnout shortly after he arrived back in
town. "Was there really a chemical spill or not? You told me
there had been."

"There most certainly was. And still is. The tanks are located on a deck overhanging a bend in the Acheron. Time has
caused them to corrode and decay. Its contents drip into the
river and in turn, the water supply."

"I don't understand why people who worked there never
said anything," Nick wondered aloud.

"Sworn to secrecy. You know how many people worked on the Manhattan Project? How many have worked at Area 51 or Los Alamos? No one talks."

"Point taken." Nick leaned back, clucked his tongue, and interlocked his fingers behind his pounding skull. "I still don't see how this relates to…everything going on now."

"In February '64 a man was involved in a car accident. He died on the table at St Agnes. As he was being transported down to the morgue, one of the techs dumped coffee on the body."

Nick snorted at the ineptitude. "Things like that are probably why they closed the hospital."

"He'd been dead for twenty-seven minutes. But he came back."

"Came back?"

"Back to life," Wolfsie said. "Back from the dead. After twenty-seven minutes."

Wolfsie had always been a practical joker. The serious expression on his face, however, indicated this was no laughing matter. He was…dead serious. Nick chortled, "You're saying coffee brought this fella back to life?"

"Not the coffee, the water *in* the coffee. St. Agnes got their water supply from the Acheron. And upriver is the Tri-Delta Plant, the plant where for nearly half a century experiments were performed on eternal life."

Nick asked, "But if Tri-Delta operated since the forties and was not shut down until the eighties, how did this guy get brought back in 'sixty-four?"

"Unbeknownst to anyone at the time, the tanks had been leaking into the river surreptitiously. No one can say for sure if Lloyd was the first one to be rewarded with a second chance."

Nick stared at Wolfsie wide-eyed.

Wolfsie turned white as a ghost. *Shit.*

"Did you say Lloyd?"

Wolfsie exhaled slowly. "Yes, the man who died that night at St Agnes, years before you were born, was your father."

Nick could feel his heart thumping in his neck. The plea he heard from his brother over his father's corpse now made sense: *Please, just one more second chance.*

One more second chance.

Rather than waiting for the barrage of questions, Wolfsie explained what he knew in detail. "Every day people who have near-death experiences make the most of their opportunity. Their second chance. They follow their dreams and now do what they always had wanted to, once realizing time is short and life is precious. Maybe they visit Australia, climb Mt. Kilimanjaro, buy that fancy red sports car, become an artist, find religion, or devote their life to helping others. Lloyd Garrison, your father, saw an opportunity. And took it."

Wolfsie sipped his coffee and continued. "He met Eve, they married. They had you, they had Gabe. Then your father runs for mayor and won hands down. Politicians on any level enjoy not only the prestige but also the power. And what power is greater than life, deciding who dies and who is permitted a second chance."

Nick accepted this as the reason why his father had run largely unopposed all those elections. *Eventually* everyone would need his help. You didn't want to wind up on the bad side of the man who had your life in his hands.

"You're saying my father is playing God?"

Wolfsie confirmed with a nod. "As Lloyd got older, however, he grew tired of dealing with the responsibility and the obligation. The duty of deciding who is worthy and who is not wreaks havoc on one's spirit. And so he handed the reigns over to his son—his second born son. It was now Gabe who was, for all intents and purposes, a plain God."

That's why Dad never forgave me for leaving. This responsibility should have been mine.

It also explained why the Garrison family was well respected and, to a point, feared by the townspeople. Similar to the way many people went to church just to score brownie points with the man upstairs, the residents of Avalon Hills treated the Garrisons like deities.

Attempting to sum up, Nick remarked, "So the Acheron is like a fountain of youth?"

Wolfsie considered that for a beat. "No, not really. A fountain of youth gives you everlasting life, eternal youth. The

Acheron doesn't give you endless life. Rather it takes away death."

Nick scoffed. "So someone has to die, has to be dead? *Then* they get brought back?"

"Yes. Not really saved *before* but revived *after*."

Nick contorted his face like a small boy trying to figure out a difficult math problem. "But if you said Tri-Delta never succeeded in their attempt to bring people back, then how—how can people be brought back?"

Wolfsie shrugged. "I don't claim to understand the science of it all. Maybe the chemicals amalgamated together from all their experiments and the waste from Los Alamos. Maybe all the protons and ions and all that stuff fused some chemical cell bond that miraculously heals. I don't know. Or there is one other possibility."

"And that is?"

"Maybe they really did accomplish their goal. Eternal life."

Nick raised a cynical brow.

Wolfsie pursed his lips. "Penicillin, Small Pox vaccine, and even Viagra were discovered by accident."

The two friends sat introspectively for a moment. Nick studied his friend. Yesterday, when Wolfsie threatened to shoot him, Nick was angered. Now, he understood his friend's brazen act. "That's why you made the pact with Gabe. Because of Karri."

Solemnly, Wolfsie responded, "Believe me, Nick, I am sorry. You have no idea. But Gabe said that if I threw you off Brandi's trail, convinced you she was dead, then he'd save Karri when her time comes. How could I refuse? I love you like a brother. But Karri's my wife, the mother to my children."

"I understand. I do."

Wolfsie's guilt was not eased by his friend's acceptance.

"So, Brandi's grave?"

"Empty."

Nick leaned forward. "Then tell me where she is."

"That I don't know."

Nick held Wolfsie's gaze. His friend explained everything. All the questions Nick had had been answered, the riddles solved. Wolfsie holding back one final piece of the puzzle seemed unlikely. It was apparent he truly didn't know Brandi's whereabouts. "Where do they go?"

"Who?" Wolfsie asked.

"People come back to life only if my plain God brother deems them worthy. Then where are they all? I mean, there's a funeral home in town, a cemetery. Why bother?"

"For show. Avalon Hills has to put on the image of being a regular town."

Nick laughed boisterously at that remark. The most poignant lesson of this overnight cram session was that Avalon Hills was anything *but* a regular town.

Nick recalled Jameson Parker, the federal employee who come to Avalon Hills decades ago and promptly disappeared. "So as far as the Fed knows our population has remained unchanged?"

"Yep."

"And you truly have no idea about Brandi?"

"If I knew where she was," Wolfsie confessed, "I'd tell you." He organized his thoughts before moving forward. "The worst part about losing someone you love is saying goodbye. And yes, knowing you'll never see them again. But with this, at least you know they're alive—somewhere."

"But just like in real death, you never get to see them again." Nick then mocked himself at the ridiculous statement. "Real death."

"Real love, Nick, is caring more about the other person than yourself. If your father and now your brother set up the rules that we can't see our loved ones after they're resurrected, then so be it. You have to go on faith. You don't question it. Just like…well, God. You don't question Him. You go on faith." Wolfsie smirked. "What can I say? The Lloyd works in mysterious ways."

Chapter 32

It felt like Nine/Eleven all over again. After terrorists at-
tacked New York and Washington and a plane came down
a little south of Avalon Hills, the entire nation was fearful.
In the span of an hour, everything we knew had shifted. America's sense of security and invincibility was now replaced with
panic, vulnerability, and doubt about a gloomy future.

Word of Lloyd Garrison's assassination travelled quickly
throughout town. And the residents of the small hamlet now
were also filled with fear, vulnerability, and uncertainty about
their own unclear destiny.

Lloyd Garrison had turned over the reins to his son a while
ago. But everyone knew Gabe lacked the discretion, concern,
and empathy of his father. Whereas Lloyd displayed a kind
and just heart, Gabe remained unpredictable and brash. Lloyd
viewed his responsibility as an honor. Gabe saw it as an en-
cumbrance.

Gabe and Eve decided to have Lloyd cremated. His ashes
would be scattered from the summit of Aliquippa Mountain
and gently waft over the lands he protected and served. Burial
at Avalon Hills Memorial Park was never considered. The
Garrisons did not covet a shrine, a destination for those making a pilgrimage.

While Eve busied herself by planning the details, Gabe did
a poor job of suppressing his anger. He had emptied his gun
into Brooke Lauser's body but it still was not enough. Gabe
knew Brooke's parents lived down in Florida somewhere. He
couldn't wait for them to come up here and get the Lauser kids
the hell out of town. He even considered pulling some strings
and refusing to allow Brooke's burial alongside her husband.
Hell, maybe he'd even have Mike's body exhumed and

moved. He didn't want their rotting flesh desecrating his domain.

He'd look into that later.

He also had to eventually make the arrangements for his wife's funeral. The death of Lloyd Garrison was well known, the murder of Yolanda was not. Gabe chilled when he envisioned making that call to his children, *their* children.

He had other issues to resolve first.

Gabe returned home to get some shuteye. It didn't happen. The bedroom showed traces of his wife's blood splattered across the walls. There was a prominent crimson stain on the floor. He decided it'd be easier to replace the furniture and carpet than to clean it. His attempt to sleep on the sofa also proved pointless. She was dead but he could still feel her presence. He hated when death hung in the air. Maybe he'd just burn the whole place down.

Burn the whole place down? Interesting idea.

He entered the Avalon Hills Police Station. After waving away the condolences from his two deputies, he instructed them to take some time off. After they departed, he wrote a note: *Office Closed for Personal Reasons.* He included his deputies' home and cell numbers, taped the sign to the front door of the station and locked himself in.

He made his way to one of the two seldom used cells, curled up in a fetal position on the cold backbreaking slab, and drifted away.

He slept for two hours but it felt like eight. Rested, Gabe locked up the station behind him and drove to Stan's Tool and Housewares.

As soon as Sheriff Garrison entered the store, Stan came around the counter and warmly shook his hand. "I'm so sorry for your loss, Sheriff. Your father was a kind man, very kind. Good heart. I always considered him a friend. But he's in a better place now. I am very, very sorry. For both you and your mother. Eve's a wonderful woman." He bowed his head as if in prayer. "Is there anything I can help you find?"

"No," Gabe snapped and yanked free of the geezer's unwelcome grip.

Stan was over the top in his condolences. Gabe eyed the

timeworn business owner and made a mental note. When Stan's time came, he decided the answer would be a swift and decisive *no.*

He expeditiously located what he needed: pick-ax, sledge-hammer, bolt cutters, two spades, industrial strength slip-jaw pliers, an electric saw, and thick woolen gloves. "What do I owe ya?"

"It's on the house," Stan claimed with an overly wide smile. "And please give my sympathies to your mother. Fine woman she is."

Gabe nodded his appreciation to the sniveling little kiss-ass. *Definitely a no.*

Back in his car, but before driving away, he made a call from his cell.

"Captain Ford, Munitions."

"Russ, Gabe Garrison."

A prolonged pause. "Gabe, hello. I heard the news about Lloyd. Your father was a good man."

"Yes, he was," replied Gabe. Never much for small talk, it seemed overwhelming now. He played the game for a moment. "How are things over at Fort Brick?"

"All quiet on the Pennsylvania-Ohio front. How's your mom holding up?"

"As well as can be expected. Listen, Russ. I need a favor."

Tenseness in his voice. "Sure, anything for a Garrison."

Damn straight. And don't you forget it. "I need three propane tanks and one flamethrower."

Captain Ford snorted. "With all due respect, that's asking a lot. We recently put in a new inventory system. Everything is meticulously logged, triple checked, and has to be signed off by two people."

Gabe wasted no time pulling rank on the army captain. "How's Harriet's diabetes? Outlook still grim?"

The intent was clear. Still, Ford resisted, albeit for show. "Gabe. I don't know if I can. This system we installed is a real ballbuster."

"Find a way. I'll be there in an hour."

❧❧❧

Approaching the rusting gate that enfolded the forsaken Tri-Delta Plant, Gabe tramped the pedal hard. The powerful police cruiser lunged forward and mowed down the shoddy fence. "Tonight," he said to himself. "This all ends tonight."

He steered hard left, fishtailed slightly. The rear of the vehicle stopped just feet from the gap that fed into the factory floor. Like a man on a mission, he managed to empty the vehicle's contents in two hurried trips and distribute everything inside. He was sweating, fuming, pissed off, and out of control. "Tonight," he vowed again.

He bypassed cavernous holes in the floor that resembled a lunar landscape. He sidestepped rebar that protruded from the ground. In the distance, he heard the mild plink-plink of water dripping into a puddle.

Gabe stopped for a moment, lowered his tools, and stared into one of the black foreboding abysses that reached down to hell. He took a knee and gazed into his wife's final resting place, the chasm where he'd tossed her body just last night.

Maybe, eventually, he'd pine for her, but not now.

Gabe was unsure how to feel. Murdering Yolanda was easier than expected. She was a sacrifice. He knew that if he allowed her to leave, she'd never return. And with the knowledge she had, she could destroy everything he and his father had worked on for nearly half a century. He couldn't take that chance.

The irony, however, was caustic. He dared not risk the chance of Yolanda blowing the lid off this. However, in a matter of minutes, *this* would all cease to exist. The secrets of Avalon Hills would be no more. He'd slaughtered his wife for nothing.

After spending a few moments at the lip of the bottomless pit that served as her grave, Gabe made his way to what his father had once called the reservoir of life everlasting.

Slipping on the recently purchased woolen gloves, Gabe first chose the industrial strength pliers. He knelt down by the leftmost of three oval tanks that stood fifteen feet tall. The steel arm had fastened the tanks in place since World War II. Mold, rust, and oxidation only served to make the unforgiving grip even tighter.

Gabe released a primeval scream, an attempt to summon deeper strength as he struggled to relax the bolts. Sweat beaded on his brow and began falling from the tip of his nose.

He thought of his father and everything Lloyd had given up for the greater good. He thought of his mom who was now a widow, due to that Lauser bitch. He saw Nick in his minds-eye. Yes, Nick, who was preordained to have this responsibility simply because he was first born.

The fury and uncontrolled rage roused primordial instincts buried within. He screamed again, his own voice coming back at him in echoes reverbing off the dank factory walls.

The rivets began to give. Gabe was making progress.

It *was* going to culminate tonight once and for all.

Forty minutes later, Gabe was shirtless and winded. The physical exertion took a toll on him. His black hair was saturated with sweat. Rivulets of perspiration teemed from his well-chiseled upper body. The tan slacks of his sheriff uniform were soiled and grimy. He hadn't noticed the tear in the left knee of his trousers until now.

He backpedaled a few feet, hoisted himself onto a ledge, and studied his handiwork. The trio of tanks was effectively destroyed, having suffered the wrath of Gabe's unbridled anger. They lay cockeyed, toppled sideways, after Gabe unsecured them from their moorings. He took the pick ax and shattered the thin protective sheath that enclosed the tanks. The fluid dripped from the destroyed vats, trickling along the factory floor, the reservoir of eternal life completely drained.

Over.

Finally.

Amen.

Breathing heavily, Gabe bundled his supplies, threw his shirt over his shoulder, and marched across the Tri-Delta yard to his cruiser. The physical exertion caused him to smell his own stench. He needed to get home, shower. Then he'd stop by his parent's—correction, his mom's—to sort out details and peruse some paperwork in Lloyd's name. He hoped Nick wouldn't be there.

He was in no mood to deal with his brother, Nick Garrison, the root of all evil in Gabe's life.

Nick.

Brandi.

Yes, of course, Brandi.

Before reaching his police cruiser, Gabe raked over his shoulder and looked at destruction he caused. What better way to celebrate than one night with Brandi? One final night.

As he promised himself, tonight everything would end. And that everything included Brandi Conrad.

⌀⌀⌀

At a touch past eight in the morning Nick pulled curbside. He beheld his childhood home. It was where he and his brother were raised. It was the only home his parents had ever owned. It was the home where his father had met his maker.

Mentally drained, emotionally spent, and physically sapped, he stared gravely at the very spot his father was murdered less than twelve hours earlier. The failed resurrection he observed in the Acheron River and then knowledge he gleamed from Wolfsie until sunup left Nick utterly bushed.

He sauntered in and heard a cry from the kitchen. His mom feigned a smile, did a double take at her fatigued son. "Would you like breakfast?"

Routine. Everyone liked normalcy at times like this. The kitchen table was covered with the clutter of photographs, legal documents, and a sea of balled up tissues. Another fresh box of Kleenex at the ready.

Nick waved away breakfast and pulled up a chair next to his grief-stricken mom. "I want to help you with this stuff."

"You'll be no good to me half asleep. Go, rest. And then you can be sharper."

Nick eventually caved. He kissed his mom, then hugged her tighter than he had in decades. "Love ya, Mom."

"Love you, too," she whispered into his chest as they embraced. "And even though he didn't show it, your father loved you also."

Nick sniffled and made his way upstairs. Before walking to his bedroom, he peeked in on his uncle. As expected, Hank was hunched in his chair, draped under a blanket, and oblivious to the world around him. "My Girl" by the Temptations wafted gently across the room and Hank's stooped head and dead eyes stared listlessly into a void. For a fleeting second Nick envied his uncle's detached state.

Who could've ever imagined that his uncle who'd fought health problems his entire life would outlive Nick's father. Nick trundled off to his bedroom, collapsed onto his bed. The last thing he saw before succumbing to sleep were the intermittent lights at the summit of Aliquippa Mountain.

One second at a time blinking away…

∽∾∽

Nick rose at noon feeling revitalized. A shower, fresh clothes, and he made his way downstairs ready for whatever the new day threw at him. That is, until he was greeted by a hostile scowl, courtesy of Gabe. Sensing the tension between her sons, Eve warned, "Boys."

Nick poured himself some coffee and sat down opposite his mother and brother. He attempted to permeate their conversation, put in his two cents. But it immediately was apparent his input was unwanted. He marginally hoped that perhaps tension in the Garrison home might dissipate with his father gone. That was not the case. Nick was a fifth wheel.

He was assigned busy work. "Nick," his mom began. "Would you be a dear and run to the store? There's a list on that counter. I just need a few things for dinner."

The little boy being sent on an errand so the grownups could take care of things. "Sure."

Gabe advised he wouldn't be around this evening, due to other commitments. Eve was disappointed but understood her son's obligations. The image of Brandi flitted across his mind as he turned to Nick who stood uneasily in the middle of the room. "Think you can handle the shopping list without screwing that up, too?"

Nick's eyes flared but he held back.

Exiting the home and getting into his car, Nick pursed his lips. His mustard mobile was grimy from various off-roading excursions. He decided to wash the car in a weak attempt to conceal any damage he may have caused. Funny how the mind worked.

After washing the vehicle at a self-service bay, Nick was again pulled by something in his heart to cruise past Brandi's childhood home. He drove by rather than stopping. Killing more time, hoping his brother would be gone by the time he returned home, Nick then drove to the Jordan Turnout. Since he just washed the vehicle, he simply stared down the foreboding trail from the main road. He considered walking the mile and a half to the Acheron, but elected not to. It was pointless.

Back in town, Nick wound up sitting at Texas Jacks. "Are you always here, Jennifer?"

The sweet, bespectacled blonde smiled. "How would you know, unless you're always here? What can I get y'all?"

Nick ordered a Bud. She returned with both the beer and her condolences. "Sorry to hear about your father."

Nick thanked her with a head nod and a huge swig.

Jennifer was good at reading her clientele. It quickly became obvious Lloyd's oldest didn't want to dwell on the past. She promptly engaged Nick in idle banter, chatting him up about nothing and everything.

Nick appreciated the diversion. A cute barmaid with a pleasing disposition, charming smile, and outgoing personality. At least there was one normal thing about Avalon Hills.

The ninety minutes passed quickly. He thanked her for the beer as well as the conversation. Jennifer scribbled seven numbers on a napkin, hesitated. "Are you planning on staying in town now?"

"No. I'll be heading home to Arizona soon."

Jennifer folded the napkin, stalled, and seemed perplexed. Arizona's hot summers? Pennsylvania's frigid winters? With Lloyd Garrison gone and now his son Gabe in charge, there was less reason to stay. She flashed her most cutesy smile and stared at Nick with bedroom eyes while handing the note over. "Don't be a stranger."

Nick felt his ears warm as he took her phone number. Jennifer seemed like a good person; Talkative, delightful, attractive in a Plain Jane sort of way.

"I'll keep this." He slipped her number into his pocket. If

things were different, then maybe. But Nick knew there was only one girl he was fated to be with.

He just had to find her.

He walked out of the neon lighted bar and instinctively hiked his shoulders. The weather had unexpectedly turned nasty. Bright sunshine replaced by thunder clouds rolling in from the west. The heavy air was encumbered of humidity. Papers and debris somersaulted down Main Street in the blustery wind. There was a storm coming.

Traipsing down the side street to his car, he retrieved Jennifer's number from his pocket. He smiled, discovered a bounce in his step. He was only a few feet from his car.

By the time he sensed someone approaching behind, Nick pivoted but it was too late.

He saw a long looping arm come at him. An object of some sort blocked all view of the oncoming storm. He managed to glimpse a face chockfull of piercings before everything went black.

Chapter 33

Weightlessness.

Nick was flying. No, floating. But it was as if only his torso was. His extremities felt insubstantial.

No, he wasn't suspended in air but rather bobbing in water. But how since his arms and legs were useless? And now he was beginning to slip beneath the surface. Drowning. He struggled to cry out for help but his brother and father ignored his plea. Gabe was on his haunches in the Acheron yards away, their father's head was cradled in his lap.

Nick began to slip below the surface. Water began surging into his nostrils, his lungs started to fill. He was coughing, choking. He couldn't scream. His arms were still inoperable. His feet angled down in hope of finding purchase below the black-as-death waters.

He was about to go under when he heard someone call his name. He located the origin. Brandi.

She stood on the shoreline, wearing the same leopard print top and black skirt as the evening they drove to Pittsburgh. The only difference in her ensemble was her footwear; she was wearing Lloyd's olive-colored snakeskin boots.

He shouted. His words never leaving his throat.

She smiled and waved hello.

No, she was waving goodbye.

Water swathed his face, his head. And he slipped below.

The stasis of his restricted arms and legs was painful. Water was not enveloping him but rather splashing *onto* him.

"Wake up," a voice urged.

The soreness in his bound wrists and ankles was severe but nothing compared to the aching in his brain. His head had been replaced by a block of cement attached to his neck.

Nick blinked once, twice, and gazed into foreboding blackness. He ascertained he was bound to a hard metal chair bolted onto a concrete slab, his wrists secured behind his lower back, his ankles tied together and hooked over one another.

Unaware if he was suffering some sort of brain injury or temporary blindness, he could see and focus on nothing.

The voice emanated through the darkness. "Finally awake?"

Nick heard himself respond with a grunt reminiscent of his debilitated Uncle Hank. In spite of being roused with water splashing his face, his lips were parched, his throat as dry as the Arizona desert. He managed a timid, "Yes."

Nick heard a chain pulled. He cocked his head and shut his lids at the brightness that bathed the area. When he managed to slit his eyes, he was met by a perplexing vision.

Sitting just a few feet in front of him was the town badass, the one who kicked Wolfsie's butt, the individual who'd been following Nick, the guy Wolfsie had warned him to stay away from.

Late teens, maybe early twenties, he was chubby cheeked with an olive complexion. He had a studded lip, piercings up and down both ears, one through his left eyebrow and another through his right nostril. The man had more studs than Chippendales. His hair was short, dark, and had a pronounced four inch spike near the front of his dome that looked like a greasy black Washington Monument attached to his skull.

Leaning forward, Hawkeye studied his hostage and wrung his hands together in a *What-should-I-do-with-you?* fashion. "Nick Garrison." Unsure if it was a statement or question, Nick remained silent. "The one and only Nick Garrison."

Not knowing how to reply, Nick took in his surroundings. Walls were not painted. There was wooden shelving on two of three sides. A trace of exhaust fumes hung in the air. Nick was in an empty one-car garage.

The man rubbed his chin and analyzed Nick before extending his right hand, forgetting his prisoner was tied. "Luke."

Trying to get on the good side of the man who knocked him out, he went for humor. "As in Skywalker?"

"As in the Bible."

Nick confessed he wasn't up on it.

"Luke the Evangelist was the patron saint of artists, physicians, and surgeons."

Physicians and surgeons, two things unnecessary in Avalon Hills. "I see," was Nick's generic response.

Luke continued. "He was a disciple of Paul. Luke was the only one who remained alongside his friend when Paul was painfully crucified upside down. Luke was a trusted ally who would go to the end for someone he cared about."

"No offense, but you don't strike me as a theologian."

Luke grinned. "I'm really not much on all the biblical crap either. My birth name is Lucas, but I like telling people that story 'cause it's cool." He paused. "Luke, not Hawkeye."

Nick gestured in a way that said *I don't know anything about that.*

"It's a small town. I hear what people say." Luke acknowledged a TV tray with a pair of water bottles. "Thirsty?"

"Very," Nick answered licking his lips.

He'd seen this scenario played out in enough movies to know what would happen next. Luke would give him the water *only* if Nick talked, spilled the beans about something. Therefore, when Luke rose, unknotted the cord before retying his left hand, and handed him the bottle with a smile, it surprised him.

Luke even went as far as suggesting, "Drink it slow."

Nick tried to but his throat seared and his mouth was filled with cotton. After he downed two thirds of the bottle, he thanked Luke.

"You're welcome."

Like everything else he'd learned recently, this, too, puzzled him. Luke had metal poking out of his face. He had tattoos up and down his beefy arms and hair pointing magnetic north.

He'd also displayed a short temper and a powerful right hook when clobbering Wolfsie several days ago. And yet, even though he slammed something into Nick's skull and abducted him, the little hellion seemed affable.

Trying to keep the mood light, Nick remarked, "Must be hell getting through a metal detector at the airport."

"You should see the look on their face when they search me and find my Hafada."

"Hafada?"

Luke proudly announced, "That's the one in my scrotum."

Nick found himself drawing his legs together. "I'll take your word on that."

Luke smiled. The two men—hostage and captor—scrutinized each other a moment. When Nick asked how long he'd been out for, the only response was "a while."

"I was supposed to have dinner with my mom tonight," Nick offered.

Luke glanced at his watch. "Missed it. Don't worry. I sent her a text from your phone saying you made other plans."

"Thanks," Nick heard himself say.

"You're welcome." Since this entire scenario was not playing out as Nick envisioned, he decided to push the envelope. "Any chance you can untie me?" As Luke considered it, Nick added, "My feet are numb and my legs feel dead."

"Promise you won't run?"

"Can't even if I wanted to."

Another unforeseen turn of events. Luke grinned and promptly freed Nick. Upon finishing, Luke pointed out, "Most of these body piercings I did myself. So if you try to escape, I'll ram a Hafada through your balls."

"You have my word. Trust me on that." Unrestrained, Nick struggled to stand. His legs burned and his equilibrium was off kilter. As the room spun, he reflexively reached out at nothing for leverage.

"Here, here," Luke said and eased his prisoner against the wall. "You probably have a slight concussion. I am sorry for that."

"An abductor with manners? That's a new one."

Luke's face conveyed remorse. "I didn't know how else to bring you here."

"Where is *here* anyway?"

"Forty-Eight Hickory."

Nick nodded, then his eyes widened. "Hickory *Circle*?"

"Yep."

It shouldn't have been a surprise but it was. He'd driven by

Brandi's old home countless times and had seen Hawkeye/Luke peering through an upstairs window. "I once dated a girl who lived here. Long time ago."

Luke nodded.

"I loved her," Nick shot back, stunned at his proclamation to a stranger. "Still do."

"Aww, isn't that romantic?"

Sarcasm was a refined talent, one that Luke had yet to master. He rubbed his chin while scrutinizing Nick who was feverishly massaging his wrists, trying to get sensation back. Luke hoped Nick would not try to overpower him when sensation returned. He did a quick calculation and concluded he could get to the hidden revolver in three seconds tops.

"Conrad, the woman who used to live her," Luke stated flatly.

"That's correct. Brandi Conrad." Nick shouldn't have been stunned by that either but he was. Avalon Hills was a small town. New homes were never built, older ones were recycled with new tenants. And, true, in a tightknit community everyone knows everyone. But his gut told him there was more. "Can you tell me anything about her?"

"What's to tell? She used to live here. Now she's somewhere else."

Somewhere else. Not dead, not alive. Somewhere else. Nick didn't know what to make of that.

Before Nick could ask a follow-up, Luke took control. "Heard about your dad. Sorry, dude. That sucks."

"We all have to go sometime."

Luke waggled his head in a yes-no fashion.

"Your father still alive?"

Luke smirked. "Dead. To me anyway. Mom hoped we'd have a father-son relationship. Never happened."

Nick curled his lips. Perhaps he and Luke were more alike than he realized.

"Besides," Luke added, "dude's a grade A prick."

"Brothers, sisters?"

"Just me," Luke replied. "You?"

"One younger brother." Nick laughed. "Guess you could say he's a grade A prick, too."

Luke didn't laugh, choosing instead to meet Nick's eyes with an indescribable stare.

"So what now? I'm sure you didn't knock me out just so we could chitchat."

Luke readjusted his position, now putting most weight on his left leg as he leaned against the opposite wall six or eight feet away. Arms folded across his chest, he remarked plainly, "I'm not sure."

Nick felt himself tense at that comment. For the first time he pondered a potential altercation with Luke. Nick had a couple inches on him and the guy was slightly chunky. Not fat, but not muscle bound either. That being said, Luke had a good twenty years at least on him. And really, any guy who pierced his nuts was probably not someone to be messed with.

"I hear you're dying."

Nick frowned. He moved his lips but no words immediately came out. The only people who knew about his brain tumor were his parents, his brother, and Wolfsie. "How do you know that?"

Luke shrugged. "Small town, people talk."

"Yeah, but still—"

"Are you?" Luke asked with determination in his voice.

Nick was not ready to confirm it yet. "Everyone's dying," he responded noncommittally.

"That's not what I asked."

"I'm really not sure anymore."

"Explain."

Nick expounded after a long drawn breath. "A short time ago I was diagnosed with grade IV glioblastoma. That's a high grade astrocytoma with little chance for success. High mortality." Not wanting to overwhelm the kid with medical terminology, Nick added, "Serious shit."

Luke rotated his wrist in a circular motion. *Keep going.*

"I went for a second opinion, third opinion. Even looked into faith healers and thought about going down to Mexico to try some experimental treatments like Steve McQueen did." Nick noticed the blank expression on Luke's face. "Ya know, Steve McQueen, The King of Cool?"

A blank stare. Nick continued. "I'm in my late forties. I

know that seems old to you but it's not. I was mad at God. I blamed everyone and everything. But ultimately I realized I was accomplishing nothing. I could go out pissed or go out gracefully. That's why I came back here. To say good bye to friends, my parents, and even my brother. How old are you anyway, Luke?"

"I ain't as old as you."

It was a strange situation. The freak with piercings and tattoos had beat the tar out of Wolfsie, slammed something into Nick's skull, kidnapped him, tied him up, and brought him unwillingly to a garage. But yet Nick—normally reserved—found himself opening up to this stranger. There seemed to be a silent connection, almost assumed. "Here's where it gets odd. I'd been having symptoms for a while. I'd lose focus, be doing something and half way through forget what I was doing. I was tired a lot. I woke up with bad headaches every morning."

"I dated this chick for five months once," Luke interjected. "That was like waking up with a bad headache every morning."

Nick smiled. "But since I've come back to Avalon Hills? Well, the headaches have stopped. No lethargic feelings, no trouble focusing. It's…bizarre."

Luke pursed his lips, dissected his hostage's response. His prolonged pause indicated to Nick that had been a critical question.

Nick ended the extended silence. "So, am I dying? Well, yeah, I guess we all are. Do I *feel* like I'm dying? No, no I really don't. I haven't felt this good in a long time. Well, other than the pounding in my head, thanks to you."

Luke apologized again. Chin in hand, he stared at Nick as if trying to solve a riddle, evaluating him.

The concentrated glare caused Nick to murmur, "What?"

Luke remained hushed. He started chewing his lip. Nick wondered if he'd accidentally bite down on the stud.

The glare softened. When Luke came off the wall, Nick involuntarily flinched. Luke headed off to an adjacent wall. He pressed a button and the garage door grumbled loudly. As the chains thundered and clanked, another light came on from the overhead motor.

Nick looked right as the opening door revealed the white Ford F-350 with the Steelers pennant parked in the driveway. Luke started across the garage toward the pick-up.

Perhaps it was Luke's proximity. Perhaps it was the somewhat familiar grin. Maybe it was the bright light that now inundated the garage. The skin pigmentation. The eyes. The jet black hair. Luke had similar features to—

Nick hadn't realized it until this very instant. Before he could put together a coherent sentence Luke confirmed it. "I'm taking you to see my mom."

Chapter 34

The Bradshaw Inn was located twenty miles south of Avalon Hills, almost halfway to Pittsburgh. The owner was a shrewd businessman, not the former quarterback, but no one would ever know. The lobby of the mid-level roadside motel was decked out in football memorabilia, stirring images and other various mementos to the heyday of the Steelers teams from the past. Nick recalled seeing it from the highway when he and Brandi drove to the city.

It was just before noon when he followed Luke into the lobby. "It's too early to check in."

Luke winked. "I got it covered."

The petite young blonde with her hair in pony tails, eye black, and dressed in a makeshift cheerleader outfit, glanced up from behind the counter, then did a double-take. "Lucas Conrad!" she cried out, blushing sheepishly.

"Hey, Dawn." His smile displayed the magnetism he inherited from his mom.

Nick stood behind Luke's shoulder and watched the kid work his magic. It was three hours before check-in time, but that didn't matter. These two visibly had a history.

Dawn eyed Nick suspiciously, leaned over, and whispered, "You're not changing teams on me, are you Lucas?"

"After you, I'd have to be insane." Luke beamed and created a cover story. "This dude's my uncle. He's here in town a couple days but you know the hotels up in Avalon suck. And he's a football fan so figured why not here?"

Okay with his story, Dawn rose to her tippy toes and leaned closer to Luke, making sure he could take a gander at her cleavage. "I got that mint flavored lube you like so much."

"And you *don't* like it?"

She pouted and feigned hurt. "What kind of girl do you think I am, Lucas Conrad?"

The two bantered back and forth in double-entendre before she handed Luke a keycard. "Twenty three, around back by the laundry room. You're not getting nineteen. That's *our* room."

The room had two double beds in a generic setting. Nick was a bit perturbed. Luke was Brandi's son. That much was clear. Brandi was alive. Finally, he'd get to see her, to be with her, to take her away. Once and for all everything would be right in the universe, the way it should be, the way it was *meant* to be. Written in the stars, soul mates, kismet, fate, destiny or whatever other platitude you'd want to call it. Nick and Brandi. Brandi and Nick. Together forever. The wrongs of the past would be righted.

But Nick was restless. He was so close. He wanted to get her. Now. And never look back.

However, for some reason Luke insisted they wait. When he pushed for a reason, he heard the same cliché he'd been told by Brandi: *Just go with it.* Without Luke's assistance, Nick would be nowhere, so he held his concern in check.

Since leaving 48 Hickory Circle—Brandi's old home, her son's current home—Luke remained tightlipped. Nick learned nothing new. His questions went unanswered. He didn't want to know the *how's* and *whys*. What happened in the past was dead and buried. He wanted to know about Brandi today: what movies did she like, what made her laugh, what foods did she enjoy, had she ever really fallen in love?

Luke seemed a trustworthy ally. He was Brandi's son, after all. That being said, Nick found himself unable to discard the apprehension in his heart. Everything he thought he knew about his childhood home was a sham, an untruth. His father lied to him for his entire life. His mother, by covering for Lloyd, was guilty by association. Gabe was…well, Gabe was Gabe. And his best friend, Wolfsie, although he had reason to, had also been less than honest. It was natural for Nick to think that perhaps Luke also was part of this conspiracy.

But he was left with no option but to put blind trust in the hands of a man who bludgeoned and then kidnapped him.

Based on the two beds, Nick expected they'd share the

room but when Luke advised him he'd back at four a.m. to-morrow and walked out Nick was bewildered. He figured they'd make some sort of plan, talk things through. But there was none of that.

"Where are you going?" Nick asked, sounding a like a lost little boy.

Luke clucked his tongue and shot a glance toward the motel lobby. "I got a thing for cheerleaders."

Nick grinned and just before Luke exited, he called out, "Hey!"

"Yeah?"

Nick extended his hand. "Thank you, Luke. Very much."

Luke pumped his hand. "Thank me after you get my mom away from here so she has a life again."

Nick found himself alone in the stony quietness. He checked his wristwatch, verified the time on the nightstand alarm. *Four a.m.,* fourteen long hours away. Once again, Nick found himself waiting. He was waiting, thinking, and, as always, alone with only his thoughts of Brandi.

For the first time he could recall, he wanted time to pass quickly.

Chapter 35

Except for a dreamlike fog that twisted through the streets, Avalon Hills was cloaked in lifelessness. It was 4:35 and night had not surrendered its grip to the dawn. Low on the eastern horizon tentacles of azure blue snaked their way into the darkened sky. Nick had attempted to engage Luke in conversation but Brandi's son remained mute. Doubt slithered into Nick's gut once again. Since leaving the motel, Luke remained reticent. Perhaps, introspective?

Nick wondered if he was having second thoughts. He again thanked Luke.

Luke ignored him.

"So Bran—your mom has lived here all along?"

Luke was deep in thought, studying traffic patterns that didn't exist. He remained silent.

This is wrong. This is all wrong.

Nick's worry heightened as they turned off Main Street. The sleepy town was quiet and still. "A big white truck like this really draws attention to us."

Quiet.

Nick was about to suggest they should've taken his rental but held that thought. A white truck was enough of an attention getter. An ostentatious yellow mustard-mobile would be tantamount to the cavalry charging in with bugles trumpeting their arrival.

Nick's fear of being double-crossed intensified when Luke killed the headlights and turned onto Hickory Circle.

"Why are we here?"

Luke spoke for the first time since leaving the motel. "I'll be right back." He depressed the garage remote clipped to the visor. As the door clanked open, he exited the Ford and traipsed across the lawn. Nick watched curiously as Luke shuffled some boxes around before returning to the vehicle. He got back in, pressed the button to close the garage, and handled Nick the item he retrieved.

Nick resisted.

"Take it," Luke insisted.

"You really think we'll need a gun?"

"With your father gone and your brother now in charge, what do you think?"

"But—"

Luke snapped. "This is serious shit we're putting down this morning. We're in danger. You. Me. My mom. Lives are at stake, dude. Are you blind?"

Nick had gone from mistrust and paranoia to naiveté.

Luke eyed Nick skeptically. There was obvious doubt in his expression. As much as Nick hadn't trusted Luke, it was evident Luke harbored the same reservations. "Dude, you sure you got what it takes?"

Nick drew his eyes from Luke's unrelenting glare to the cold steel in his hands. He lifted his head and studied the home Brandi was raised in. Like a distant memory from his innocent childhood, the house called to him. After a lifetime, the moment was now at hand to right all wrongs. "Let's get her."

∽∾∽

Neither of them conversed for a while. They were both getting their minds right, putting on their game face, psyching themselves up. Maybe all the clichés were crap. But there was no need for idle banter, patronizing banalities, or platitudes. They'd be risking their lives and moving heaven and hell to get Brandi.

Proceeding north, it appeared to Nick they'd ironically be taking the Jordan Turnout. However, Luke turned left a mile before.

Nick frowned but said nothing. He had to follow Luke's lead.

The unmaintained trail was rutted, and cratered with deep cavities and rapid drops. Nick held the dash with one hand, his other clutching the seat. His actions were futile as he and Luke bobbed around in the cab like on an amusement park ride geared for small children.

Its narrow width indicated the path had probably been designed for foot traffic, not a large F-350. Branches and twigs snapped off. Boughs of low hanging trees scratched and clawed the vehicle on all sides like gnawing teeth guarding the gates of hell.

The tires ate up and spit out the road beneath the rubber. As if it was a living breathing thing, the automobile seemed to revel in being used for the exact reason it was built for.

Bounding behind the wheel Luke called out, "You sure?"

Nick was determined like never before. Adrenalin raced through his veins. His heart pounded in his neck. He was so close to Brandi he could sense her. "Damn right I'm ready."

Pleased with Nick's resolve, Luke and he exchanged a fist bump. "Fuckin' A!" Luke tramped down on the pedal. The engine roared louder through the foreboding woods.

They were through the clearing. The grating and scraping ceased. Suddenly, all grew quiet around them. The road beneath them was now paved, asphalt having replaced the rocky trail. Luke depressed the pedal even more.

Nick felt the front of the Ford lift as they rocketed up a steep well-paved thirty degree incline. An entrance ramp of some sort. Nick readjusted his backside when seeing a large wrought iron gate stretching across the apex of the rise. Their vehicle was big. The security fence seemed bigger.

"I take it you don't have a key."

"I do," Luke replied, "but this'll be more fun." Pedal to the floor.

"Ohhhhh," Nick bellowed. He wasn't certain but it felt like the vehicle became airborne. The front of the vehicle mowed down the barbed-wire barrier with ease. Bulleting across the narrow bridge, he looked right. They were crossing the Acheron River and zooming to the other side.

A mile and a half upriver, he could make out the shoreline at the Jordan Turnout. He recalled meeting with Wolfsie just after returning to town. It was when Nick first learned about Karri's lump and when Wolfsie informed Nick about the chemical spill from Tri-Delta. Nick recalled seeing a narrow bridge crossing the Acheron. The bridge spanned the river to a parcel of land that had been quarantined, secured by electrified fences and an abundance of no trespassing signs. Nick recalled thinking it was a foreboding and impenetrable barricade.

And now they were heading directly into that same foreboding area.

Brandi had been here all along, on the other bank of the Acheron, imprisoned opposite the Jordan Turnout. He'd been so close so many times.

The earsplitting shrieking was followed by a peculiar orange glow that suddenly swathed the bridge. Nick hadn't noticed before but, along the viaduct, large lights and strobes had been situated every fifteen or so yards. "What the hell is that?"

"Their alarm system."

"Alarm system?" Nick shrieked. "Whose?"

"They. Them. Your brother's."

It shouldn't have come as a surprise. But hearing the Garrison family's direct link to this was disconcerting.

"They'll be here soon," Luke claimed. "We'll need to move quickly."

The vehicle abruptly lurched right. For a fleeting instant it appeared Luke would drive off the bridge and take them into the river. He then realized they were back over land.

Nick was almost flung across the cab as the kid maneuvered the switchback with precision. He clearly knew exactly where he was going. Nick wondered how many times Luke had visited his mom here.

The F-350 fishtailed slightly, the two right side tires came off the ground for a beat. After a few seconds heading back toward the Acheron, Luke yanked the wheel hard left. Again the road was eroded and pitted, but not as bad as on the Avalon Hills side of the river.

With fire in his eyes and fortitude in his heart, Luke pulled right and skidded to a stop. "We're here." He yanked the keys from the ignition and disappeared out the door.

Nick almost fell out of the vehicle, so engrossed he'd forgotten to unlatch the seat belt. Once free, he double-timed, trying to catch up to Luke. Then, he stopped. His heart thumped in his chest. His legs almost giving out beneath him. Realization sledgehammered his gut. He'd done it. *They'd* done it.

It was difficult to see at first. The small bungalow—more like an A-frame cabin that seemed better suited for a ski lodge high in the mountains—was hidden in plain sight. It was cherry wood and absorbed into the woodlands that enclosed the cottage. Cold looking. Yet, Nick chuckled. In what was probably the kitchen, he observed what his mom would call *homey* curtains hanging in the window. Even in the midst of all this chaos, Brandi wanted to create a feeling of normalcy.

Luke was at the front door, inserting the key. Nick turned around and regarded his precise location. With the warning sirens slightly muted by the thick shrubbery, he shot glances back and forth between Brandi's prison/home and the sinuous waters of the Acheron fifteen yards beyond the thicket. He was directly opposite the Jordan Turnout. Had he seen her residence before? Looked right at it? Nick then realized he had been here once. After their date in Pittsburgh, Brandi had blindfolded him and brought him to this location. He just didn't know where *here* was. He'd known the home from the inside but hadn't seen it from the outside. Until now.

That didn't matter. What happened before—be it a few days or a lifetime ago—was irrelevant. He sprinted to Brandi's front door. *Finally.*

Luke struggled with the lock for an interminable twenty seconds. When the tumblers clicked and the door opened, another warning siren erupted. Unfettered, Luke trounced in, opened a closet door and disengaged the alarm.

Nick followed, found a lamp, and turned it on, the only light in the house.

"I'll go get her," Luke announced.

"I'll—"

Upon hearing the commotion, Brandi hurried down the stairs and now stood at the entrance to the living room, hugging herself, trembling. With bed hair and wearing shorts and a frayed T-shirt, she claimed, "Nick? *Luke?* What—oh my God, what are you both doing here?" Her voice was shallow, her skin pale. She was shuddering like a sheet draped from a clothesline on a windy day.

"We've come to get you, Mom."

"Get me?" she cried, exchanging glances between her son and the only man she ever loved. "What—what is going on? I can't leave. You know that."

"Yes, you can, Mom. All of us. Together."

That comment staggered Nick, though, after some quick introspection, it shouldn't have. Once freeing Brandi from her captivity in Avalon Hills, Luke would be targeted. He couldn't stay behind. Nick thought of his sister-in-law: *The Lord works in mysterious ways.* He'd broken up with Gwen. He'd been alone. And now, suddenly he not only had the girl he was destined to be with but her son as well. Instant family.

Brandi extended her arms and backpedaled in a *stay-away* pose. She was unmistakably horrified as evidenced by the gooseflesh on her arms, the dread in her eyes, and the quivering in her words. "No, I—can't. Luke, just go back. Go home. I can't endanger you. If something was to happen to you, Luke—" Pleadingly, she turned to Nick. "Please, take my son home."

Nick moved closer.

"I'll gather some of your things," Luke barked as he leapfrogged the stairs and ran to the bedroom.

"Luke, no!" Brandi reached for her son's shoulder but he'd already passed her. She faced Nick. "Do you love me? I mean, really love me?"

"I never stopped."

"Then if you love me, go. Leave. Right now. Take Luke back to town. You go home to Phoenix. For me. This never happened. "

"No can do, Brand."

Luke reappeared with a box, lowered it by the front door, and scampered back again to the second level of the cottage.

"Luke, Stop!"

"Can't, Mom." He vanished out of sight again.

Brandi was out of breath, her throat restricting, her eyes welling. "If you want me to beg, Nicky, I will."

Nick placed his hand on her quivering shoulder, turning her gently into the beam of light. He observed a contusion under her left eye. Someone hit her. His resolve and determination to free her was now secondary to the age old desire for revenge. "Who did that?'

She ignored the question, pushing away Gabe's assault from her memory. Tugging on his shirt, almost kneeling, she shot a horrified glance at her front door as if expecting someone to enter any second. "Nick?"

He shook his head. "We can talk about this on the plane."

The slap across his face stung him. As she brought her arm down, Brandi looked at her hand as if it had acted independently. "I'm sorry. But please. I don't know what else to say. If you love me—"

Nick raised his right arm, tenderly cupped her face in his hand. He felt a lump in his throat. "My God," he whispered, "you really are stunning."

"Nick—"

He raised his other hand, tenderly sandwiching her soft face and delicate features. "Tell me we're not meant for each other. Tell me you don't feel it, Brandi. You want me to leave? Look me in the eye, look in your heart, and tell me this is not *right*."

She closed her eyes tightly as tears rolled down her flushed cheeks. She placed her hands over Nick's, pressed them against her own face. The touch was warm, tender, loving. And truthful. Her tone was weak but she still resisted. "Just leave me."

"I made that mistake once. I'm not doing it again."

"Mom, anything else?"

Sweating from the exertion and everything he and Nick had endured, Luke slid the back of his arm across his perspiring forehead.

Brandi and Nick stood as one, peering into each other's soul.

Louder this time. "Mom, you need anything else?"

"No," she breathed, unable to draw her gaze away from Nick. "I've got everything I need."

Nick smiled. "Good, let's go."

Pumped up, Nick kissed Brandi's forehead and strode across the room. He squatted and, with a heave-ho, lifted three of the four boxes.

"Luke," Brandi called out. "I didn't raise you to stand

around. Give your Uncle Nick a hand with those."

Air was sucked from the room. The only sound the muted piercing of the distant alarm system penetrating the early morning. Nick vacantly lowered the boxes. The trio exchanged glances. Nick was wide-eyed, Luke pursed his lips and stared down at nothing and Brandi had a *What did I say?* expression on her face.

"I'll get these to the truck," Luke mumbled and quickly heaved all four boxes in one powerful hoist.

Nick knitted his brows, his eyes softened. He moved closer to Brandi. "Uncle Nick?"

Brandi's countenance hastily changed from *What did I say?* to *I thought you knew.* "I—just figured since you two, you know, planned this, that you talked and he—told you."

"Gabe is Luke's father?" Nick's mind flitted back to checking in at The Bradshaw. When Luke fabricated the cover story about Nick being his uncle, he assumed it was just that; a cover story. He now realized it was not.

Brandi said, "Remember when we had dinner in Pittsburgh? I told you about that guy I dated, the asshole who strung me along before going back to his wife?"

"Gabe?"

"Gabe." Brandi's crying had begun to lessen but tears now reappeared. "It was a long time ago. I'm sorry."

"Sorry for what?"

"You weren't here, Nicky. You left and…well, I know this sounds like I'm seventeen again but your brother was the closest thing to you I could get." She fell against Nick.

"It's okay, it's okay." He comforted her, patting her upper back in a reassuring manner.

"I didn't mean for it to happen."

"Brand, it's okay," Nick lied. His heart was simultaneously filled with love recaptured and anger, happiness, and rage. His piece-of-shit brother had ended up sleeping with the only girl Nick ever truly cared for. And most likely for spite. Nick and Brandi had never made love, never consummated their relationship. Yet, it was that self-righteous Gabe who had shared her bed. Another casualty of Nick fleeing Avalon Hills all those years ago.

Part of him wanted to speed back to town, confront his brother, and, once and for all, release a lifetime worth of frustration on that son-of-a-bitch. Tempting. Nick loathed clichés but one jumped into his mind. Gabe may have won the battle but Nick would win the war. Brandi Conrad was leaving. For good. With him.

Brandi slinked away from Nick and dabbed at her eyes with the bottom of her shirt. "Luke's a good kid. I know he doesn't look it, but he's got a good heart."

"He got that from you."

Brandi sniffled. "I can't believe you came back for me."

From the entryway, Luke clapped his hands. "Okay, lovebirds. Let's hit the road."

Brandi rose to her toes, kissed Nick on the lips. It wasn't *that* kind of a kiss. Instead, it was a peck of gratitude. "Thank you, Nicky." She took one final look at her bungalow before departing for good. "Take me away."

ℰℬℰℬ

Luke verified his mom's entire life—four boxes worth—were secure in the bed of the truck. He started making his way around when Nick swiped the keys from him. "Hey! My truck, man."

Nick glanced at Brandi who stood at the passenger's door. "Yeah, but that's my girl."

"Dude!"

"Get in." Nick brought the engine to life. Brandi sat between her two men, unable to draw her eyes away from her savior. She'd never been a romantic at heart, never put much stock in fairy-tale endings. But if there was such a thing as a knight in shining armor, his name was Nick Garrison.

Nick peeled away from the home, retracing the path Luke took. The sirens clamored through the forest.

As they came closer to the switchback and approached the narrow bridge spanning the Acheron, Nick eased down the visor. Dawn was breaking. A new day was upon them. "Brand?"

"Yeah, Nicky?"

"Remember what I told you on that hillside before I left?"

Brandi curled her lips. "I remember everything, but I'm not sure what you're referring to exactly."

Nick looked forward, his face bathed in the warm glow of morning. "I promised we'd ride off into the sunset together."

Brandi chuckled. "Yeah, but this is a sun*rise*."

Nick laughed. "I'm trying to be romantic."

"Romantic? You come barging into my home at five in the morning and what, no flowers even? That's romantic?"

He laughed. Unsure if he said it to himself or aloud, he heard, "I love this woman."

Nick turned the wheel hard left. Detecting blacktop beneath the tires, he mashed the gas pedal. The engine roared and the powerful V-8 engine lunged forward.

They had just gotten onto the bridge, before them an asphalt ribbon leading over the Acheron and, ultimately, their life together.

That's when Brandi, looking ahead, mumbled dreadfully, "There goes our Hollywood ending."

Chapter 36

Two police cruisers were parked nose-to-nose. A third one, an SUV, was also present. The escape route effectively blocked.

Anxious quiet filled the cab of the F-350. Nick considered flooring it, effectively transforming the vehicle into a battering ram. But successfully bashing three vehicles out of their way was dubious.

Nick assessed the scene. Two deputies crouched behind their cars, rifles propped across the hoods, the trespassers in their crosshairs. Gabe appeared from between the vehicles and strode arrogantly toward them.

"There another way out of here?" Nick asked.

"No," Luke shot back.

Brandi shook her head. "I told you. Just forget about me."

Nick raised his hand in a *shushing* gesture.

"Take me back," Brandi pleaded. "We'll tell him it was a mistake. Tell him it was my fault."

"Brand, you know I love you. But please, hush!"

Brandi stared at her hero, unsure if she wanted to laugh, kiss him, or smack him.

Gabe signaled to his deputies and, a moment later, the deafening alarms stopped sounding. He lifted the bullhorn to his lips. "Nick Garrison. Get out of the car now and no one gets hurt."

"Why'd he use your full name?" Brandi asked.

"To show we're not brothers right now. He's the sheriff, I'm the law-breaker." Nick eased his foot off the brake. The Ford coasted forward.

"Nick Garrison. You have encroached onto private property." Gabe's altered voice sounded tinny through the bullhorn.

"Exit your vehicle immediately or you'll leave us with no choice but to use force."

"Nicky, please."

"Can we mow 'em down?"

Nick ignored both Luke and Brandi. He inched the pick-up forward. Then, he stopped when he heard Brandi ask, "What the hell is that?" looking at her chest.

Nick glanced at her. A red dot appeared directly over her heart.

Brandi looked at Nick. He had one between his eyes.

"Laser guided weapons. They have you in their sights," Luke commented in a defeated tone.

"This is your last warning," the sheriff commanded.

The trio exchanged unsure glances before Luke asked, "What's that on his back?"

Nick squinted through the windshield. Gabe had the bullhorn in his left hand but his right hand gripped a strange looking device. Nick observed the apparatus feeding into a bulky backpack that clutched a propane tank. Nick remarked flatly, "It's a flamethrower." He took a deep breath then cried, "I'm coming out."

"Nicky. No—"

He winked at Brandi. "I never stopped loving you. Don't ever forget that." Nick hoisted himself from the pick-up. He made sure his movements were slow and deliberate. Arms raised high above his head, the red dot following him, he advanced closer to his brother.

Gabe leered triumphantly, victory on his face. He lowered the bullhorn and, with a smug gait, walked closer.

The two brothers stood facing each other on the center of the bridge over the Acheron River.

"You trespassed," the sheriff said and rattled off a county ordinance.

"What're you doing, Gabe?"

"Doing what needs to be done, what's always needed to be done. What *you* should be doing, had you not left all those years back."

"Let us go, Gabe."

Gabe shook his head. "You broke the law, *brother.* And

people who don't follow the rules must be punished to the fullest extent."

"You won, okay?" You wanted me to leave. I'm leaving. But let me take them with me."

"I don't think so. You leave, Brandi stays, and Luke will be taken care of."

"Luke, your son?"

Unaffected that his brother knew the truth, Gabe scanned the Ford's cab twenty yards away. "You know what's funny, Nick? She's not even good in bed. All this trouble that bitch caused, this strife between you and me, due to some skank whore who's not even a good fuck."

Nick swallowed his anger. "Then let us leave."

Gabe continued baiting. "She does have her good points. Nice tits, great ass, and quite a talented mouth if you get my meaning. But that's about it."

Nick stood, silently doing a slow burn.

"Then again, you wouldn't know that. She admitted she never did spread her legs for you, huh? Trust me, you're not missing anything."

"There's a difference between love and sex."

"Not with her there's not. You may think so but she doesn't."

The look of contempt on Gabe's face resulted in Nick putting the pieces together. He recalled the bruise on Brandi's cheek. "*You* hit her?"

Gabe grinned. "Bitch needed to be put in her place. She deserved it."

Nick chose to look forward, not back. He'd get nowhere with his brother. "You can do whatever you want here as sheriff. But as my brother I'm asking for a favor. Let us go."

"That's not how it's supposed to be." Gabe paused and then spoke in a louder tone. "You think you can just waltz in here and decide who stays and who goes? That's not the way it works, Nick. Who gave you the right to play with the laws of the universe? Who gave you the right to play God? Tell me, *who*?"

"Who gave *you* that right?" Nick yelled, stepping nearer. "Who gave *Dad* the right?"

"Don't you dare talk about our father in that tone! My entire life's been fucked up 'cause you left. You got to go after your dreams. I couldn't. I had to stay behind and deal with all this…all this bullshit! And I saw the disappointment in our father's eyes. The old man never approved of me. It was meant to be you."

Nick sneered at the irony. He'd always viewed Gabe as the favorite. Apparently his brother felt Nick was the chosen one. "That's what this is all about? Revenge? Sibling rivalry bullshit? You want to be the better man, fine, you're the better man. I don't give a rat's ass. You're pissed about what happened years ago, fine. You're the one with the firepower, Gabe. You're the one with the authority. I'm here, now, asking *your* permission. If that doesn't prove who's in charge, I don't know what else could."

Gabe glowered at his brother contemptuously. Hatred spewed from him, anger and rage that had festered over a lifetime. He drew back his arm and cold-cocked Nick. "That's for fucking up my life." He landed a powerful jab into Nick's abdomen, causing him to double over. The red laser followed him. "And that's from our father who you disappointed by leaving." Gabe stepped right and kicked Nick in the side of his head. Seeing stars and white hot pain searing across his skull, Nick collapsed into a fetal position onto the asphalt. "And that's for thinking you're better than me."

Nick was dazed, struggling to breathe. He tasted blood in his mouth. He thought he heard Brandi scream somewhere in the distance.

A fierce thunderous kick in the ribs caused Nick to whimper and roll over. "And that's because she never looks at me the way she looks at you."

Nick glared up at his brother. He struggled to crane his neck and took in the Ford where Brandi was trying to get out to help but was held by her son.

Gabe drew the .45 Smith and Wesson from his holster, cocked the hammer. "And this is because I'm the sheriff."

A crack.

A scream.

A cry of pain.

Nick looked at his chest expecting to see a hole.

"My leg! My fucking leg. I've been shot!"

Nick and Gabe simultaneously looked across the bridge. The big-haired deputy was roiling on the ground clutching her knee.

"Deputy Bernabe!" Gabe screamed

Nick looked to the Ford. He recalled Luke retrieving a gun. Through the windshield, he noticed Luke shrug. It wasn't him.

Another explosion rattled the shores of the Acheron. The second deputy crumbled to his knees, screeching, gripping his right shoulder with his left hand.

"Deputy Williams!" Gabe shrieked.

With his back to Nick, he began sprinting to his seconds-in-command. He couldn't call for back-up because the entire three-person force of Avalon Hills was already on site. He only covered half the distance to his wounded comrades before he abruptly stopped and lowered his head. It was now he who had a red laser dot pointed at his heart.

Both deputies rolled around in agony, whimpering and cursing, when a rifle appeared across the hood of one the cruisers. Gabe couldn't make out the figure that had gotten hold of Bernabe's weapon.

His mind spinning, pain cutting through his torso, Nick managed to get to his feet and, despite the injuries, he sidled next to Gabe.

"Turn around, Sheriff Garrison, and walk to me backward," the unseen operative directed. Gabe did as instructed. The red speck was now pointed at the propane tank on his back. "One false move and they'll be scooping up your body parts for three miles. Now come to me."

Traipsing cautiously, Gabe backpedaled to the man who'd taken control.

Nick kept pace with his brother. He saw the top of a head emerge from behind the cruiser. He squinted, he frowned. "Wolfsie," he murmured.

Moments later, the three men stood in a triangular pattern fifteen feet apart. Wolfsie still held the weapon pointed at Gabe's propane tank. "You shot two officers, Wolfe. You just signed your own death warrant."

"They're just flesh wounds," Wolfsie replied to Gabe's back, then faced Nick. "You gonna be okay?"

Grateful and humbled at his friend's heroism, Nick swallowed and nodded. In the end, Wolfsie came through for him. "I owe you everything."

"You owe me nothing. It's called friendship."

Gabe was the one whose life now hung in the balance. In spite of Wolfsie holding a rifle aimed at the propane tank, he debated calling the bluff. If he made a move, would Wolfsie really squeeze the trigger? The explosion would not only kill Gabe but also himself and Nick. Still, Gabe decided not to take that chance. He didn't care about his brother or anyone else for that matter. But he didn't want to die.

Gabe realized they were unaware he'd destroyed the tanks at Tri-Delta and bargained with leverage he didn't have. "You let me go and I'll make sure your wife lives."

"Somehow, Sheriff Garrison, I don't believe you. You double-crossed me once. And if I lower this weapon, you'll do it again."

Gabe snickered. "Then consider Karri dead. You want to live without her, so be it."

"Karri *is* dying. I'll have to live without her anyway. But I still have to live with myself." Wolfsie looked beyond Nick's shoulder to the Ford. Disbelieving, he shrieked, "Is that Hawkeye?"

Nick hiked his brows. "His name's Luke, Luke—Conrad."

"That's—wait, Hawkeye is *Brandi's* kid?"

Nick chuckled. "I didn't see that one coming either."

Wolfsie studied the cab of the Ford. The jet black hair was unmistakable. "You got her?"

"I got her."

Wolfsie laughed loudly. "And that, ladies and gentleman, is why you are—Nick fucking Garrison."

"And you are Wolfsie—fucking—Wolfe."

"Sorry about, you know, lying to you before."

Nick cocked his head. "I think you've more than made up for it. So now what?"

"Now, my friend, take your girl and ride off into the sunset."

With Gabe in Wolfsie's sights, Nick sprinted back to the Ford. He ignored his brother completely. Getting behind the wheel, he drove forward. He didn't use the F-350 like a battering ram. Instead, he gently nudged one of the cruisers out of their way. He looked through the open window. "Thanks again, Wolfsie."

Wolfsie ignored the gratitude. "You going to be okay, Nick?"

Nick draped his arm over Brandi's shoulder and pulled her against him. "I am now."

∓

Nick and Brandi waited outside while Luke went into the lobby of The Bradshaw. It was not even 10 a.m.—long before check-in. Nick reacted to her questioning expression. "He's working his magic."

Brandi leered. "Like the magic I work on you?"

"The apple doesn't fall far from the tree." Nick leaned over and kissed her. Nothing special, nothing romantic, nothing that made hearts leap and stomachs sink. Just a regular smacking of lips as if they'd been together forever.

"Dawn's off today but Cindy's working. I still managed to get us rooms," Luke claimed as he got in.

"Dawn? Cindy? Who exactly are Dawn and Cindy?" Brandi asked in her mom-voice.

"Just a couple girls I know."

"A *couple* girls? You never mentioned a Dawn or a Cindy to me. And—why do you know girls who work in a motel?"

"Jeez, Mom."

Nick interjected. "Brandi, you've been dead for two years. You and Luke have some major catching up to do."

Normally, she'd retort with a typical Brandi quip. However, when she lost herself in Nick's eyes, all she could say was, "Actually I've never felt more alive."

∓

The trio entered the motel room. Brandi sat on the bed.

"Comfy." As she laid back and stretched out, uncle and nephew used Luke's phone to book a flight to Sky Harbor International in Phoenix. The first departure was on *United* but not until 11:50 tomorrow morning. There were two seats on a flight that left later today and one on a red eye that Brandi was opting for but Nick discounted that idea. "We're a family. We travel together."

With their seats reserved, Luke walked to the door. "I'll let you two get reacquainted with each other while I'll be next door getting reacquainted with Cindy."

"Lucas Garrison!"

"*What*!"

Brandi waggled her head and chortled. "My son, the gigolo. Just don't forget—you know—I'm too young to be a grandma."

"Cindy's pretty klutzy so if you hear any screaming she probably just stubbed her toe." He winked and bounded out of the room grinning, leaving Nick and Brandi alone.

Stretched across the bed, she moved to one side and patted the mattress. "C'mere."

She was still wearing blue shorts beneath a large white sleep shirt that hung to her knees. In spite of what she'd been through this morning, she looked radiant as ever. Gorgeous. Full of life.

Nick removed his shoes and crawled up alongside the girl of his dreams. Their bodies intertwined, fitting together like puzzle pieces, as if they just *knew* where arms and legs would be placed. Within seconds, they drifted away into a land of dreams.

It was the most magical fulfilling moment Nick ever experienced sleeping with a woman. Sleeping.

⌘

It was late afternoon when they were awoken by a knock on the door. Luke, grinning from ear to ear and with his hair mussed, decided they should order some Chinese food.

"Your mom doesn't like Chinese." He turned to Brandi. "Right?"

"I do now. Lots you need to learn about me."

"I'm looking forward to it."

Nick ordered Sweet and Sour Pork, Brandi went with Mongolian Beef, and Luke settled on Kung Pao Scallops. Then they all shared. Nick chose to let the conversation unfold on its own. It quickly did and Brandi explained how her imprisonment worked.

Weekly, either Gabe or one of his deputies would bring Brandi food, books, or movies. She was forbidden from entering Avalon Hills. It was *forbidden*. Luke was Gabe's son and, therefore, the only one permitted to visit someone who *died*: Once a week for five minutes and always supervised by Gabe.

When Nick asked how she knew he was back in town, Brandi nodded to Luke. "During one visit Gabe used the bathroom. Luke mentioned about a mysterious guy who had parked outside my old house on Hickory as if he was casing the place. Upon hearing the physical description, I immediately knew you were back in town." Brandi paused, swallowed some beef, and used one of the chopsticks to make a point. "I broke one of the commandments and went into town."

"You put yourself in jeopardy?"

"Yes."

"So, running into me at the store was not mere happenstance?"

"I wanted to see you, Nicky."

All the time Nick had spent searching for Brandi and she was searching for him.

Brandi said, "I'd been following you. I couldn't walk up to you in the middle of a crowded store so I waited for you to be alone. The parking lot outside the grocery store was perfect. Same reason I picked you up on the side street before we went to the 'burgh. No prying eyes."

"What about the time I saw you just before you ditched me on the sidewalk?"

"That time I snuck into town for another reason. Running into you was not planned."

"And the Nissan?"

Brandi explained. "Gabe always left the car on this side of the river hidden in the trees. Sometimes he'd let me drive around. He came with me, of course. Sounds silly but driving with the windows down and some Neil Young or April Wine blasting was something I missed."

Nick didn't want to know what sort of *deal* Brandi had to make to be allowed access to a car. He still had a lot to learn but there was no hurry. They had their whole lives. Changing the subject, he asked, "That wasn't the same car the night you…you know?"

"Same make and model but not the same car."

Brandi continued talking about daily life across the river, what a routine day consisted of. Nick sat and listened. He realized she was for all intents and purposes a prisoner in her home, under house arrest. Her cottage was her cell.

As she spoke, Nick found himself paying less attention to her words. He realized how much he missed her, how much he never stopped loving her. The way her lips moved, inflection in her words, the way she occasionally ended her sentences in a higher pitch, the way she animatedly spoke with her hands when excited, the way she met his eyes when speaking, the way in which she tucked strands of hair behind her ear, the way she stared lovingly and proudly at her son, her silent laugh. He missed it all so much.

"Nicky, you okay?"

"Never better."

They finished off the food. Nick asked, "Do you remember what it was like?"

Brandi curled her lips. "The accident? No, just flashes really. I remember driving home that night. I saw the bridge leading to Main Street. Then, I guess I fell asleep. All I remember was hearing a deafening crash and my body lunging forward."

Nick gulped. "I mean—" He rolled his eyes toward heaven. "—anything about…it?"

"Death?"

The word brought a tomblike stillness to the room. "Yeah."

"You mean did I see the white light and relatives who passed on before me and all that?"

"I guess."

Brandi waggled her head. "I didn't *see* a thing. But I did *feel*…something. Departed loved ones? God, maybe? I don't know. I felt...I guess I'd say I felt a peacefulness come over me."

"I see."

"I thought you were going to address the elephant in the room."

"What do you mean?"

"The obvious question," Brandi said with a half-hearted smile. "Why me?"

It was valid. "Okay, why you?"

"'Cause of you, Nicky."

"Me?"

"I was your girl, you were my guy. Your father decided, based on our connection, I be gifted a second chance. Of course, that changed when your dad stepped aside and handed the reins over to Gabe."

"How so?" Nick asked timidly.

"Your father did what he felt in his heart. But your brother? Well, Gabe could never measure up to you. He always battled jealousy and envied you. The fact that he...could have me whenever he wanted was his little demented way of exacting revenge on you. Sure, he could never be Nick Garrison but he could be with Nick Garrison's girl. Whereas your father did what was right—or tried to anyway—your brother used it as a power trip."

Nick shifted about in the chair, feeling soiled and stained knowing that he and Gabe had the same blood in their veins. Gabe had forced himself onto Brandi, non-consensual sex for...years. What choice did she have? Nick pointed to Brandi's face. "The bruise on your cheek?"

"A present from Gabe."

"Prick." Nick mulled that over, then asked, "Did he do that often?"

"When he, you know, forced himself on me, he insisted I call him Nick, especially when he was...well, not too gentlemanly. He wanted to be rough and have me use your name while he did. I refused. And this is the result."

Nick was furious with his brother. He now regretted Wolfsie not squeezing the trigger and incinerating the bastard. That's when a question entered his mind. *Propane? Why?* It didn't make sense. The alarms had sounded when Nick and Luke breached security. Gabe and his cohorts showed up quickly. *Too quickly*?

And why with flamethrowers? Gabe surely would have no qualms about spilling Nick's blood. Or Brandi's. Or even Luke's. But even for a man hell-bent on revenge, flamethrowers seemed extreme.

Unless Gabe had already been en route.

Luke stood, stretched his muscles, and looked at his watch. "I should get going," he announced. "Dawn will be here soon."

Brandi rolled her eyes. "What about Cindy?"

Luke winked. "What about her?"

Nick couldn't help but laugh. Maybe there was something to be said about a face full of metal. "Can I talk to you a second?"

"Course."

"I mean outside."

Brandi arched a brow.

"It's guy talk," Nick stated. He kissed Brandi on her lips. Then kissed her a second time.

Brandi reached for the remote mounted to the nightstand, aimed it at the TV, and began channel surfing.

Five minutes passed and the door opened again.

"Where's Nick?" Brandi asked confused.

Luke was pale.

Brandi swung her legs over the side. "Luke? Where's Nick?"

"He said—he said he's going back."

Brandi shut her eyes tightly. *Damn.* "He's going after his brother for revenge. I should've kept my mouth shut and not told him about Gabe."

"That's what I thought, too. But he said he's not going back for Gabe."

"Then why?"

Chapter 37

Long before Arizona was a state—two thousand years before—a massive volcano erupted just north of what would ultimately become Flagstaff. Nick had visited Sunset Crater seven or eight years ago. He found his mind now flashing back to that journey. The landscape around the cinder cone for miles in all directions was black, dead and void of life. If one envisioned the topography of Hell it would be similar to Sunset Crater.

Or to where Nick was now.

Unlike the National Monument, however, the damage here was not two thousand years old; it was not even a day old. This was manmade, not a result of nature.

Nick stood amidst the charred remnants of where Brandi had been confined for two-plus years. The pungent aroma of burned and singed materials hung in the air. Soot everywhere. The air thick.

Charcoal black stretched as far as the eye could see. The ground beneath his feet was burned and consisted of a damp sludgy texture. Elms and pines that kept Brandi's home hidden and obscured now were thinned, burned, and lifeless. The boughs bare. The once veiled community now out in the open.

The propane tanks.

Gabe and his deputies had not come to the Acheron in response to the security breach. Rather, they were already en route. Nick knew he saved Brandi. He just hadn't realized until now he was cutting it so close. He saved her with minutes to spare.

Gabe enacted his own scorched earth policy, eradicating the area from the landscape and leaving no traces behind.

Nick still didn't understand why his brother acted so rash.

With their father out of the way, the secrets of Avalon Hills, Tri-Delta, and the furtive land across the Acheron where people lived eternally was under Gabe's rule. The younger brother would no longer be held in check by their father.

But burning everything seemed overkill.

A few hot spots remained but for the most part the hillside lay dormant and seared. Gabe apparently called firefighters from neighboring counties to suppress the *forest fire*. Smoke hung in the air. There'd be another hour of sunlight but the area was swathed in an ominous black-gray cover.

As he had listened to Brandi recount what her life became, Nick started pondering the propane tanks. His mind kept asking more questions, eventually taking the next natural step. That was when he spoke to Luke in private and gave him the best description he could remember.

It seemed obvious now that Brandi was not the only one. Granted, she was bequeathed a second chance due to her connection with Nick. But why just her?

As Nick walked amongst the rubble that had been Brandi's living room, he gazed over the burned terrain. With the trees thinned and the entire area out in the open, he looked at the plethora of burned out cottages and cement slabs. Nick estimated about six dozen where others, like Brandi, had been imprisoned.

The dwellings had been built randomly, no discernible logic to their location. This was definitely no master planned community. Instead, it was a hodgepodge of huts and bungalows scattered haphazardly about the hillside.

The structures, based on the size of the foundation and burned out plywood, were all similar. Some bigger, most smaller. But all those who died in Avalon Hills and then received a second chance were relocated here, to what now resembled the landscape of Hell. Everything was burned, ruined, blackened by fire, and covered in ash. Furniture and TV's had melted from extreme heat.

A few items lay scattered about, random objects that someway avoided the inferno; a headboard, a pair of woman's shoes, a photo album, what looked like a dog crate. Searching house to house—or frame to frame—Nick traipsed through the wreckage and rubble. Bodies were burned, many beyond recognition. Corpses lay twisted. Their faces, or what was left of them, forever locked in the throes of painful death. Mouths ajar, jaws dropped, screaming out from the agony as their flesh blistered and burned away. Others had been unable to escape their prison and died from smoke inhalation.

Gabe was a mass murderer.

Nick wasn't sure what to make of the irony. These people had been allowed a second chance to have more time, brought back from beyond because Lloyd or Gabe said so. But ultimately, they died anyway. Or more accurately were killed.

Burned to death, more painful than their original demise.

Nick had his father's genes. Now he tried to put himself in his father's shoes. Brandi had *died* just over two years ago. Fairly recent. Her home was lower on the hillside. Therefore, Nick assumed the ones who'd been relocated longer ago would be higher along the banks where the thicket had been deeper and residents more camouflaged.

Baked rubble cracked beneath his feet as Nick ambled to higher ground. It was the fourth or fifth shell he entered near the ridge when he heard a soft gentle moan.

He stopped, suppressed his breathing and listened. To his right.

Nick scooted over. He first noticed two unmoving legs protruding from beneath cauterized slats of wood. One shoe was missing. Nick bent over the motionless form and gently eased aside the rubble. The person was dazed, perplexed. But seemed uninjured.

Nick slid his hand below her shoulders. "You okay?"

"Wh—what happened? Was it a meteor?"

"No," Nick replied, though it was a fitting observation based upon the surrounding carnage. "Fire. Can you sit up?"

The woman winced, took in her surroundings. "I think so."

Nick helped her to an upright position. She took a deep breath, emitted a deep hacking cough and blinked hard several times.

As her mind struggled with the enormity of the situation, Nick studied the injured woman. She was in her mid-thirties, several years younger than he. It was who he came back looking for. As his throat constricted and he wondered how this could be, he stammered, "Anything broken?"

The woman shook her head and murmured, "I don't…think so. Would you mind helping me up?"

"Not at all." Nick offered his arm for leverage. Once standing, she felt woozy. Her left knee buckled but after a moment she insisted she was okay.

Nick pulled his arm back. "Sure?"

She confirmed she was and stared at the blackened hillside, trying to comprehend. Relying on Nick for support, she allowed herself to be guided from what had been her prison. Finally she took a gander at the man who pulled her from the debris. "Thank you."

Nick nodded his response.

The woman's face altered into a disbelieving expression, her eyebrows knitted. She placed her hand on Nick's biceps and angled him so she could get a better look at his face through the small drops of remaining sunlight. Her mouth opened.

"Nick? Nick Garrison?"

"Yes."

"I don't understand," she said easing her level palm against her hip. "You were only this tall."

"I'll explain on the way."

೧೨೧೨

Eve switched on the porch light and swung open the door. Her face was flushed, her eyes red and puffy. She'd obviously been grieving. Her face indicated happiness when seeing her son. "Nick," she said softly and hugged him tightly.

"Hi, Mom."

Ending the embrace, she looked to the woman alongside. Playing the role of gracious host, she displayed a welcoming smile. "I'm Eve and who—" She was unable to finish the sentence. The blood drained from her face.

The visitor's expression exhibited equal puzzlement. The two women stared at the other as if looking across the endless ripples of time, independently wondering *How this could be.*

Nick made the *reintroductions*. "Mom, I'm sure you remember Aunt Martha."

The women raked at each other, then at Nick.

"Eve? Eve, oh my God." Martha stepped closer and bear hugged her sister-in-law who she hadn't seen in thirty plus years. Not since Nick was a boy.

Martha had died decades ago. But here she was again, standing on the front porch as if not a day had passed. She hadn't aged.

Eve took the embrace questioningly, too flummoxed and choked up to return it with equal fervor. When the two women uncoiled, they continued beholding each other. Eve's lips quivered but no intelligible sounds came out.

It was Martha who spoke lucidly. "My husband's here?"

"Yes, Hank's upstairs."

"I'd like to see him," Martha said with a smile. "It's been a while."

Wide-eyed and disbelieving, Eve stepped back and welcomed her long since departed sister-in-law into her home. "He's not doing well, Marti. He's had some health problems. Couple strokes."

Sadness flashed across Martha's face. "It's okay. I still want to see him."

Eve breathed, "I understand."

Mechanically, she traipsed with a cautious step through the foyer. She repeatedly glanced back at Martha, making sure this was no dream. She knew what Lloyd did. But to witness it firsthand, to see with her own eyes a relative who died thirty some years ago and not having aged a day trekking through her home was…surreal.

Reaching the bottom of the stairs, Eve again warned Martha. "He's almost comatose. He's totally unaware of what's going on. Hasn't spoken in years."

"He's my husband," Martha stated. "'Til death do us part."

The two women took the stairs, Nick following several feet behind.

The lifeless thing Hank had become slouched in the orange chair. His shoulders drooped, his legs contorted at an angle. A pea-green blanket was draped over his feeble weak body, a body that his mind deserted some time ago. Martha inhaled deeply, blew it out slowly. And shot a questioning look at the TV.

"He likes *Animal Planet*," Eve explained. "And Doo-Wop music." Interestingly the 1954 hit "Earth Angel" wafted across the room.

Sensing a presence—several presences—Uncle Hank succeeded in raising his head. His mouth opened, his lips quivered, his eyes were blank, oblivious to everything and everyone around him.

Martha made her way across the room. Somewhere between falling and lowering herself, she was on her knees, devotedly stroking her husband's clammy hands and papery skin. The years had been unkind to Hank. His continuous health problems had not aged him well. But none of that mattered. Hank and Martha were together again. Thanks to their nephew Nick. Tears of happiness flowed as she mumbled his name repeatedly.

Hank's eyes rolled over and he began taking in this young woman who was caressing his hand. Ever so slightly, his face wrinkled. His eyelids fluttered, slowly at first, then quickly as if trying to differentiate between reality and a vision from his youth.

The woman looked familiar. A distant memory, an image from a lifetime ago. She looked like his wife, felt like his wife. The touch was recognizable, similar to the way his Martha had held him. But it couldn't be. Too much time had passed. His wife had died decades earlier. *How?*

For all intents and purposes, his cognitive reasoning ceased years ago, his mind trapped in his skull like a dead organ. Still, through the fog and haze and images and flashes of his life, Hank was mindful enough to identify the familiar yet distant sensation of her skin on his, and although he knew it could not be he decided to *just go with it.*

His lips trembled. His eyes took on the sadness of a life missed. "Mmm—mmm—mah—mah—Martha?"

"Yes. Yes, honey, it's me. It's really me."

೧೩೩

Eve tapped her son on the shoulder and motioned for Nick to follow. "They should be alone."

Back downstairs, both Nick and his mom conveyed different types of expressions as they gazed up toward Hank's room. Eve's was one of confusion, Nick's was one of pride. He not only achieved his goal of liberating Brandi. He also reunited his aunt and uncle.

Internally, Nick chuckled at the causticness. His father and then his brother had given countless people eternal life. But it was Nick who gave them happiness.

"I don't get it."

"I don't either, Mom."

Eve stroked her neck, her face. "She—Marti hasn't aged at all. Not one day."

"Yet another mystery of Avalon Hills, I guess." Nick shrugged. After a beat, Nick asked, "How old was Aunt Martha when she died?"

Eve pulled at the corners of her mouth and thought. "Thirty-eight."

Nick said, "I guess Aunt Martha will always be thirty-eight. Frozen in time."

Eve spoke thoughtfully. "I knew what your father did. But—not to this detail. This is—seeing it—God in heaven, this is astonishing."

The sounds of gentle sobbing wafted from upstairs. Nick guided his mom to the front porch. The night was dark, moonless. The smell of a distant fire bathed the town.

Nick updated his mom. He advised her he'd liberated Brandi with the help of her son. He felt some remorse at keeping the identity of Luke's father to himself. After all, Luke was Eve's grandson. But she had two already. The revelation that Gabe had fathered a child out of wedlock with Brandi wasn't something she needed to find out about. He also kept to himself the destruction Gabe caused, killing scores of innocent helpless people in a fiery inferno. Nick no longer needed to engage in sibling rivalry.

After seeing his brother in action, Nick knew he was the better man. What Lloyd had worked on and worked for his entire life, Gabe effectively wiped out in a single afternoon. It was Gabe's doing. Let him eventually explain it to their mother.

Every once in a while, Eve kept glancing into the house, shaking her head. She couldn't accept the fact that Martha had not aged in three decades.

Nick's mind wandered back to an evening years ago on the banks of the Acheron. He now said the same words to his mom he had said to Brandi. "Come with me."

Eve didn't answer.

Nick repeated the suggestion.

"Come with you where?"

"To Phoenix, with me, with Brandi and her son."

"Ohh, Nick," Eve said with a smile.

"Why not? You'd get away from the winters."

Eve arched a brow. "And deal with those summers? No thanks."

"You get used to the heat," Nick lied. He paused before adding, "Besides, no offense, but what do you have here? You've got Gabe. But your grandkids have moved away and —well, dad's gone also."

"I appreciate it, son. But I've also got a life's worth of memories here. I was born in Avalon Hills. I'll die in Avalon Hills."

Nick rebuffed but his argument was weak. "But you're all alone now."

"I've got my sister-in-law back to keep me company. Marti and I have plenty of catching up to do." She angled her head, placed her frail fingers against his left cheek and kissed him on his right. "Besides…"

"Besides what?"

"You've got Brandi. After all these years, you've got the girl you were supposed to be with. Go live your life with her."

Nick swallowed down the rising lump. "Will you come visit?"

"I'll be there for Thanksgiving."

"Sounds perfect." Nick embraced her tightly, kissed her on the cheek, and retreated to his car. He opened the door, waved goodbye, and started to get in.

Through the doorway, he noticed something scamper by

her feet. It was moving fast, an eager white blur with a rapidly wagging tail.

"Scrappy!" Nick smiled as the Westie hopped into the car and readied himself for a ride in the passenger's seat. Nick looked at his mom.

"Take him," she called out. "He's your dog anyway. Always has been."

Nick blew a kiss to her, brought the engine to life, and drove away with his childhood dog at his side.

⃣⃣⃣

Nick used his keycard, opened the motel room door, and stepped in. "Honey, I'm home," he chuckled. Scrappy scampered by and excitedly put his nose to work. There were plenty of new smells to discover.

"Brandi?" Nick tensed. The room was silent. *"Brand?"* Louder this time, more urgent.

The door to the bathroom opened and she materialized. Wearing navy blue sweatpants, a faded *Penguins* T-shirt, and her hair pulled back tightly, she looked ravishing. But as Nick moved toward her, he realized she also looked pissed.

"Where the hell were you?" she demanded, hands on her hips, foot tapping the floor.

"I had to take care of one final thing." He moved closer and enveloped her but she wormed free.

"Dammit, Nick."

"You're so cute when you're pissed." He offered a small smile.

"I'm not joking." Her rigid form and stern demeanor indicated she definitely was not.

"What is it, Brand?"

"You don't get it, do you?"

Nick put his hands up in a *hold-on-a-sec* posture. "Whatever it is I apologize. But you have to tell me so I won't do it again."

"Luke told me you went back, back *there.*" She extended her arm. Nick realized she was pointing south, not north to Avalon Hills. He knew better than to correct her.

"I did."

Her stern expression weakened, slightly at first. Within seconds, she was beet red and sobbing.

Nick moved toward her. "What's wrong? Is it Luke?"

"You can't leave me," she said through a veil of tears. "You left me once. I can't lose you. Not again."

He took her into his arms and wrapped her trembling body in his. He caressed her back, held her close to his heart, and apologized.

After a moment, she spoke in short gasps. "Promise— you—won't—leave?"

"I made that mistake before. Ain't happening again."

Brandi giggled as she felt wetness of a twitching nose against her hand. Looking down, she laughed as the canine's tail wagged. She crouched down and allowed the dog to slobber her face. Thinking back to her high school days, *their* high school days, she smiled at Nick. "Is this who I think it is?"

"Yep. Scrappy, the one and only."

A moment later Scrappy scooted away and resumed sniffing duties. Standing, she found her face sandwiched tenderly in Nick's loving caress. They stared into each other's eyes, each other's hearts and allowed the magnitude of what they accomplished to slip into their soul.

"I—I can't believe you're really here with me," Nick whispered.

"Like I told you the other day, seeing is believing." She cupped the nape of Nick's neck and brought his lips to hers. They kissed passionately and deeply. Their bodies fell against each other, coming together in perfect harmony and synchronicity.

Although she didn't need to, she asked anyway. "Promise you'll never leave me again, Nick Garrison?"

"You're not getting rid of me, Brandi Conrad."

She flashed her alluring grin tinged with a devilish look in her eyes. She put her hands over his and moved them inside her shirt. As she guided them to her firm supple breasts they simultaneously emitted a pleasurable moan.

Craving each other, thirsting for one another, blood turning into a raging river of passion and desire, Nick and Brandi kissed with the hunger of teenagers. When he stopped unexpectedly and craned his neck, she frowned.

"What is it?" she asked.

"Your eyes were open."

"I'm with you now, not your brother. I don't have to close them anymore when making love."

Nick tousled her hair. "There's so much I want to tell you. So much I need to tell you."

Brandi pressed a finger against Nick's lips. "Not now, not tonight. We have our entire lives for that."

The message was clear. Tonight would not be one for conversation.

Nick scooped Brandi into his arms. She laughed as he carried her a few feet away and gently lowered her onto the bed.

After all these years they made love as if they'd never been with anyone else.

⁓∽⁓

The swaying tentacles of a new day slithered through the gap in the drapes. Nick lay on his back, staring up at the ceiling, smiling. He glanced at the nightstand clock. Just after seven. They had ninety minutes before needing to drive south to the airport and begin their life journey as one.

The amount of light that slipped into their room indicated it would be a bright sunny day. Beautiful. Perfect. As would all the days be from this point forward. The union of Nick and Brandi, their life together was underway. Day one as a team.

Nick turned over, coiled up behind her curvaceous body. He eased aside her jet black hair and affectionately nuzzled her neck. After a few gentle pecks, he moved higher and started nibbling on her ear. "I love you, Brand," he breathed.

He knew she was a heavy sleeper and after their shared passion last night—all night—it didn't surprise him. Nick grinned to himself in a *I-still-got-it* expression.

"Brandi, honey. We have about an hour and a half to kill."

No reaction.

"Brandi?"

He angled his head so he could get a clear view of her face.

Touching her shoulder, he now realized she felt icy, clammy. A crimson stain was on her pillow, dried blood and froth on her lips.

Chapter 38

Not even twelve hours earlier Nick never imagined he'd never return. But here he was, back in Avalon Hills, close to the Jordan Turnout, across from where Brandi, Aunt Martha, and the others were banished, down river from Tri-Delta, in the waters of the Acheron.

Just like he witnessed his brother doing with their father, Nick was performing the same ritual. On his knees, Brandi's body was below the surface, her head cradled in his lap as he scooped water and dispensed it onto her ashen face. Unlike last night when they kissed, her eyes were now closed.

A heartbreaking thought shredded Nick's heart. Lloyd had died once, back in 1964. He only had *one* second chance. Perhaps that's why Gabe's attempt at resurrecting him was unsuccessful. Now, Nick was here with Brandi. She had died two years ago. Would she also be denied another chance? He pushed that thought away.

"Please, Brand. Come back to me," he sobbed. Helpless, he continued begging, appealing to a greater power. "I promised I'd never leave you. You can't leave me either, okay? Okay? Come back, Brandi. Come back to me."

Nick glanced right. The disfigured hillside was wholly exposed. Scorched trees stood ominous and foreboding like sentries at the gates of hell. He could see Brandi's prison/cabin—or what was left of it.

"C'mon, Brand. C'mon. If not for me, for Luke."

It was difficult to see through the curtain of tears blurring his vision as he glimpsed Luke standing on the shore, leaning against the front of the white Ford. His head hung. He only occasionally looked toward the river. He appeared accepting of the fact his mom would not return.

Nick, on the other hand, wasn't giving up. With each passing second, each minute, the powerful hands of destiny clawed away Nick's hope. It'd been about forty minutes he guessed but he wasn't sure. As always, when it came to Brandi, time stood still. The insurmountable odds of a miracle waned.

Nick refused to give up. "I promised you. I came back for you. Now you come back for me. You're a fighter, Brandi. Always have been. They can't take that away. Fight it. Please, fight it. You're not a quitter. Don't quit now. Don't—don't leave me here alone."

So immersed in trying to alter fate Nick did not hear encroaching footsteps sloshing through the waters, nor did he initially hear his name called.

"Nick."

It took three times until he reacted. When he peered up, his face was flushed, his eyes nearly shut. "Gabe, please," he beseeched, "I beg of you." He extended one hand over Brandi as if presenting her to a superior being seeking a miracle. "It's Brandi."

"I know who it is."

"As my brother, Gabe. As the sheriff, as the one who's in charge of all of this, please—please. It's Brandi. See? It's Brandi." Hs voice broke.

Gabe shook his head pitifully. He wasn't angry. He wasn't vengeful. He was just aloof and uncaring. "It's too late."

Keeping Brandi's head in the crook of his arm, Nick reached out, groping for his brother's pant leg. "It's not too late," Nick supplicated. "I'll give you everything I've got. I'll give you whatever you want, Gabe. Please, I have things I needed to tell her."

Gabe took a step back, beyond his brother's outstretched hand. He glowered at his brother with a pathetic expression. "The healing powers are gone, finished. It's over, Nick. Over and done."

Nick refused to accept that. "No, it's not. Don't say that." Nick held Brandi's upper body and reached to Gabe. Down on his knees, he continued groveling. "You can do it. Dad used to. Now you do—do whatever you need to. Just bring her back to me."

Gabe rolled his eyes and stared upriver toward the abandoned Tri-Delta Plant around the bend. He peered at Brandi's lifeless corpse and contemplated. His father, his wife Yolanda, Frannie Fitzgerald, Jonathan Dekker, Jameson Parker years ago. And now Brandi Conrad. Gabe smirked.

"Wh—what's so funny?"

Staring at the scorched hills on the opposing banks of the Acheron, Gabe prophesized. "There's so much death in a place where people live forever."

Nick didn't have time to scrutinize his suddenly analytical brother's statements. "Please, Gabe."

Gabe shook his head.

"Why? Why won't you?"

"It's not that I won't. I can't. Not anymore."

"Yes, you can."

"No, Nick. I can't."

"You can, you have to. Look, see? It's Br—Br—"

Gabe noticed Luke on the shore aimlessly kicking at pebbles. His own son wouldn't even look at him. And now his brother was down on his knees, pleading and begging like a wretched weak excuse of a man. Gabe was losing patience. "I came to clear up a few things over there," he claimed while pointing across the river. "I didn't want to run into you. Not today, not ever."

Nick was breathless, almost hyperventilating. "I'm begging you, Gabe. What more do you want from me?"

"What I wanted from you was for you to stay here thirty years ago and not have all this dumped on me. And now, now you want something from me?" Gabe scoffed. "You know what, brother? Even if I *could*, I wouldn't."

Nick spluttered. "I'm not asking for forever. I'm not asking for a year. Or a week. Just—Gabe, just five more minutes with her. Just five—three minutes. *Please*."

"Go home, Nick. Go and get the hell out of my town."

Head bowed, Nick drew his eyes away from his brother and gazed down at Brandi. He tousled her hair and caressed her face. Her skin felt cold. Nick sobbed louder. Gabe was of no help and so he looked around for anyone else. Or anything.

While scanning his surroundings, he spotted the blinking

lights atop Aliquippa Mountain. Right. Left. Right. Left. Ticking away the minutes, one second at a time.

Chapter 39

Nick was dead.

His heart may have been pumping blood, neurons may have been firing across the synapses in his brain and his lungs may have been inflating and deflating. But for all intents and purposes, Nick was dead. On the inside.

He sat in the drab-colored room and once again found himself waiting. With his left ankle over his right knee, he drummed his fingers on his leg and sized up the other patients. An elderly man moaned and groaned as he found no relief in the uncomfortable chair. His wife sat next to him, staring, wondering how much time they had left together. A frail woman with a few white hairs who topped out at ninety pounds nodded off. Her daughter, perhaps granddaughter, leaned forward and replaced the breathing apparatus that had slipped from the woman's nostrils. A husband and wife clutched each other's hands tightly while their child played with a toy, moving triangular shaped animals up and down steel bars, wearing a bandana that covered a bald head resulting from radiation. Nick couldn't discern the gender of the child.

Uncertainty and fear hung in the air like a guillotine about to slice through life. The patients and their loved ones sat and silently prayed for good news. They all hoped for the same thing—more time.

When the door opened, all sets of eyes eagerly moved toward the nurse. Looking at her clipboard, she flipped one page forward, then two more back. "Nick Harrison," she called out.

Just for spite, Nick sat there and didn't utter a sound.

Louder. "Nick Harrison!"

Incredible. He'd been coming for over a year, his third visit in six weeks since returning home from Avalon Hills. And still, they mispronounced his name. Was it really *that* difficult a name?

"Nick Harrison!"

"Garrison?"

She frowned, double checked the name. Rather than apologizing, she simply asked, "That's you?"

Nick didn't answer verbally. Instead, he stood up.

"This way, sir."

Nick followed the nurse through a labyrinth of narrow corridors. She stopped and stuck out her arm like she was displaying a new car he'd just won. "Need to check your weight."

Nick obliged.

"One ninety four," she announced. "Up four pounds." She turned and walked away. Nick assumed that was his cue to follow.

Now in the exam room, he sat. She went down the list of his current meds. He confirmed he was still taking most of them, a few he was not. She took his blood pressure. "One twenty-six over eighty-two. Almost perfect."

Nick nodded.

"And why are we seeing the doctor today?"

We? "I'm here 'cause it's my follow-up appointment. You're here 'cause you need a paycheck."

The nurse wasn't sure how to take that so she half-smiled. "He'll be right in."

Nick sat alone in the exam room and waited.

Fifteen minutes passed before Dr. Rajagopal walked in with a flurry. "Hello, Nick. How are you?"

Nick accepted the handshake. "You're the doctor. You tell me."

The doctor laughed louder than needed. He lowered himself onto a small stool and rolled closer to Nick. He thumbed through the reports, nodding as he did. He made sure Nick could not see what was written. Nick always found that curious. They were *his* medical records. What the hell was so top secret?

Dr. Rajagopal contorted his face in a strange way, his lips turned so far right it was as if he was trying to kiss his own ear.

He raised his eyebrows. He massaged his chin, scratched his head.

Guy does everything but talk to me. "So?"

"I—" The doctor started to speak, then stopped and laughed in an amused way.

Jesus Christ. Spit it out already. Nick prodded. "Yes?"

"I've been an oncologist for many, many years, Nick," Rajagopal began as he continued flipping papers. "I—well, not just me but all my fellow doctors like to think we know it all. But every once in a while something comes along that throws us for a loop."

"Uh huh."

"I really don't know what to say."

"About?"

Rajagopal examined the file for a beat before closing it with fanfare. His question stunned Nick. "Do you believe in God?"

"I guess. If and when I need to, sure."

The doctor smiled. "I don't like to use the word miracle. It's such a cliché. But really, I'm not sure how else to describe this."

He rolled alongside Nick and displayed the reports for Nick to review. He presented various pages, pointed at numbers from numerous tests before Nick's trip back home, and matched them against recent tests Nick had undergone since returning. Nick underwent a battery of exams. CAT scans, PET scans, MRIs and even the seemingly outdated good ol' fashioned X-rays.

"I consulted with three of my peers, all oncologists here in Phoenix, about your case. I even went as far to contact my old roommate from Stanford who now is affiliated with the Cleveland Clinic." Rajagopal shrugged. "As weird as this sounds, your glioblastoma appears to be gone. No traces at all. It's as if the brain tumor was never there or somehow healed itself." He leaned in, whispered, "A miracle."

Nick was not surprised to hear this. "Gone?"

"Completely." The doctor raised his hands, opened, and closed his fists. "Poof. Gone. The results of all the tests we performed on you since returning from back east are one hundred percent clear. The brain tumor is no more. What's your home town again?"

"Avalon Hills."

"Avalon Hills," repeated the doctor committing the name to memory. "There must be something in the water."

Nick simply nodded. "Must be."

"If you wouldn't mind, I'd like to send you for more tests. We realized it cleared up. But I'd sure like to find out how. And why."

"Not necessary, but thanks."

"It could be beneficial," the oncologist argued. "Think about it. I'm not saying immediately. You've been through a lot lately. Whenever you feel up to it."

"I'll think about it."

The doctor closed the file, placed it on his lap and looked strangely at Nick.

"Something wrong?"

The doctor struggled to find the right words. "May I be candid?"

"Definitely."

"I'm a doctor, not a psychiatrist," he began, "so I may be way off base with my assumption, but I thought you'd be happier."

"Happier?"

"Frankly, yes. I've got a waiting room filled with patients who would be thrilled to hear these kinds of results. Yet, you seem, what's the word? Disappointed?"

Nick feigned a smile and tried to blow it off. "Guess it just hasn't sunk in yet."

"When it does, you'll realize what a gift this is. You have a second chance at life."

Second chance. "Mm-hmm."

Rajagopal offered a cautious smile and then patted Nick on his knee with his own file. As he stood and started making his way out of the room, he stated, "I'd like to see you in two months for a follow-up."

"Okay."

The doctor opened the door and had one foot in the hall-way.

"Doctor Rajagopal?"

He turned, faced Nick. The concerned expression on his patient's face caused him to close the door. "Yes?"

It was now Nick who struggled for the proper words. "What do you think happens after we die?"

"Pardon?"

"After we die? You're a cancer specialist. You see death a lot. What do you think happens?"

Rajagopal tried to blow it off with political correctness. "Every religion believes something different. I think it's important for everyone to come to terms with it on their own volition. What I believe, what works for me, would not work for you. Everyone has different—"

Nick rose, searching for an answer. "What do *you* believe?"

Since political correctness accomplished nothing, he tried humor. "You're asking if I believe we all become angels and float around playing the harp?"

"No."

"Are we reunited with those we've loved?"

Nick shrugged. "I guess. I'm asking—I'm asking if you think we wind up in the afterlife with the one we are *supposed* to wind up with, even if it didn't work out that way in this life."

"That's over my pay grade. I'll see you in two months." And he walked away, leaving Nick without an answer.

Chapter 40

Nick pulled into his complex, drove around to his apartment, and sent a two word text: *I'm Here*. The response was immediate: *Comin'*.

He angled his head and watched the door to his apartment open. Luke was the first one out. He greeted Nick with a wave, then stuck his head back in. "C'mon, we're gonna miss the flight!"

Nick's heart skipped a beat. For just a second, a flash, the wink of an eye, he envisioned this is how it *could've* been. Coming home and picking up Luke and Brandi on their way for dinner or to a ballgame. Doing what families do. He swallowed hard and felt his eyes water.

He stared longingly at the open door. Perhaps if he wished hard enough, Brandi would appear. Sure, it was impossible. There was no way. But one thing Nick learned six weeks ago in Avalon Hills was that sometimes the impossible becomes possible.

He continued staring. Under his breath, he whispered, hoping for a miracle. "C'mon, Brandi, c'mon."

"I'm here, I'm here."

"Jeez, Dawn! Move your ass."

Suitcase in hand, Dawn practically skipped to the car. "Hey, Nick."

"Hey, Dawn," he replied, hoping to hide the disappointment.

ↄ∘ↄ

Nick just couldn't catch a break. For the first time he could recall, traffic in Phoenix was light. He'd be at the airport quicker than hoped for. That meant he didn't have much time to say what he wanted. Still, he waited a little longer.

He checked the rear view and saw Luke and Dawn sitting close. Their bodies snuggled against each other as they prepared to face their future together. *Young and in love.* Nick smiled solemnly.

Unlike Nick, life moved quickly for Luke. After Brandi died in her sleep, in Nick's arms, he returned to Phoenix. With nothing for him in Avalon Hills, Luke came along. His mom was gone. Although he didn't fear his father, Gabe, coming after him to even some score, Luke felt it was time to move on, time to start life over. He took up in Nick's extra bedroom.

Dawn decided to quit her job at The Bradshaw south of Avalon Hills and leave for the west to be with a man she loved. Or at least was attracted to. A week after Nick and Luke were in Phoenix, Dawn arrived and moved in to the extra bedroom with him.

Luke quickly secured a job in a tattoo parlor just down the street in Mesa. One late night he saw an infomercial for a graphic arts institute up in Seattle. He applied, sent samples of his work, and got accepted. Unlike Nick, Luke was moving on with his life. Good for him. As his mom boasted proudly, he was a good kid.

Luke Conrad's life was going fast. Nick's, regrettably, was moving at a snail's pace.

"Hey, Luke," Nick called out to the back seat.

"Yeah, dude?"

"I…um…I just want to say your mom would be proud of you."

Luke leaned forward and clamped his hand around his uncle's shoulder. "Thanks, man. I appreciate that."

Twenty minutes later, Nick pulled to the passenger drop-off curb at Sky Harbor Airport. Doors opened. Nick popped the trunk. Luke pulled both suitcases out and led the procession to the sidewalk. "Hey, baby," Luke began, "Mind giving us a few?"

"Not at all." Dawn kissed Luke open mouthed and squeezed his ass for good measure. "I'll be inside." She then turned to Nick. Nick stuck out his hand but received a gentle kiss on the cheek. "Thanks for everything," Dawn uttered in his ear.

Nick whispered back. "Take care of him. That's my girl's son."

Dawn waved goodbye and bounded into the terminal. Nick and Luke stood awkwardly on the sidewalk. Luke appeared uneasy. Nick rocked on the balls of his feet. They said nothing. Then they spoke at the same time. Then they stopped. And laughed.

"What do you think?" Nick inquired.

"About?"

Nick threw his chin toward the terminal. "About Dawn? Is she the right one?"

"Jeez, dude. Are you channeling my mom?"

"No, no," Nick forced a smile. In spite of metal protrusions sprouting from Luke's face, every orifice in sight pierced, covered in tattoos, and an obelisk on his head, Nick was really going to miss this kid. "Just wondering what your plans are."

"Don't have any. Plans suck. I'm just going to go with it."

Go with it? Now who's channeling Brandi? "Unasked for advice?"

"Let me have it."

"She seems like a sweet girl. And if she is the right one, good. If she's not the right one, then okay, too. But when you find the right one, you grab her and never ever let her go. Never. Trust me, I know."

Luke nodded. "You got it." He hesitated. "I'm guessing you're not walking us in, huh?"

Nick waggled his head. "Nah, never been good at saying goodbye."

Luke grinned. "Don't get all weepy on me, man."

"I'm not!"

"Dude, you are."

Nick dabbed his eye just to prove Luke wrong. Unfortunately, Luke was right.

"You gonna be all right, Uncle Nick?"

"I'll be fine."

Luke could see Nick was full of shit. "Listen. I'll be back for Thanksgiving. Three and a half months."

Nick grinned. His mom was coming also. He already decided that's when he'd break the news and introduce her to her grandson.

Unsure how to say farewell, Nick scanned the sidewalk. Travelers raced into the airport fearful of missing their flights. Others came out, lugging suitcases and hailing cabs. Nick's jaw dropped when he saw the jet black hair.

Tunnel vision. Everything around him blurred. No horns honked, no exhaust fumes from idling cars, no screaming children, or cheerful relatives reconnecting. The world came to a stop when he saw her.

Same hair style.

Same height.

Same body type.

Brandi?

She stood twenty yards away, looking across the road as if searching for someone. She didn't see Nick. Through the parting crowd, Nick noticed her wearing skintight faded blue jeans and a leopard print top. She made a visor with her hand and continued peering off.

"Brandi."

"Huh?" Luke furrowed a brow and followed Nick's sightline.

Nick took a step toward her. It couldn't be. He knew it was impossible. But yet, here she was. As she always told him *seeing is believing*. Twenty yards away.

"Uncle Nick?"

"Brandi..." Nick murmured.

She smiled at someone approaching. She waved joyfully and threw her head back in her trademark silent laugh.

"Brandi. Oh God! It's her."

Nick had only managed a few steps when his shoulder was clutched by Luke.

She leaped into the arms of another man and they twirled like two figurines in a music box.

"Danny!"

"Julie!"

Nick heard Luke whisper, "It's not my mom."

Nick pursed his lips and shot a sorrowful look toward the

heavens. When he turned back around to face Luke, his eyes were tearing up. "I fucked up, Luke."

"How? How did you fuck up?"

"I should've let it go. I never should've started."

"Man," Luke began. "How could you know?"

Nick didn't need to hear it but Luke spoke anyway. "Whatever healing powers combined by the mixture of chemicals at Tri-Delta would eventually dry up anyway. It wasn't a bottomless pit. There was no limitless amount. Maybe it would've dried up in three days, maybe three years. Who knows? But your brother—and my father—screwed it up for everyone. He smashed all those barrels and, with them, the magical powers. Anyone on that other side of the Acheron would've died anyway."

"I should've known," Nick insisted.

"Man, c'mon. Don't blame yourself. That river was filled with some sort of, hell, I don't know, protective barrier or something that kept everyone alive. Even if Gabe hadn't torched the whole place, they would've died anyway."

"And your mom?"

"What about my mom? You did what your heart told you to. And that's never a bad thing."

"I—I should've—" Nick stammered softly, blaming himself. Although he broke Brandi out, it was tantamount to fighting the laws of the universe, opposing fate, altering destiny. Those people had died. How could Nick have known that once they'd be removed from the safety across the Acheron their time would be limited?

What exactly caused Brandi to die? The same thing that caused Jonathan Decker to die when he escaped and attempted to reunite with his wife. The same thing that caused Aunt Martha to die two days after being reunited with Hank. They were meant to stay put.

Was he that different from Gabe? Indirectly, Nick had transformed himself into a plain God. "I should've known," he reiterated meekly.

"You want me to get bumped to a later flight so we can talk?"

Nick sniffled. "No, you go. Go live your life."

"I'll call you when we get in."

Nick extended his arm. Instead, he found Luke wrapping his arms around him. The bulky kid bear hugged him and even lifted him off the ground. "You take care of yourself."

"You too, Luke."

"Uncle Nick?"

"Yeah?"

"Thanks."

"For what?"

"You tried to give my mom her life back. At least you tried. But in the process you gave me one. I was heading down a bad road had I stayed there. I don't want to get all sentimental and crap but dude, you may not have saved my mom. But you saved me. I'll make you *both* proud of me."

"You already have made us proud." Nick shuffled his way to his car.

Just before getting in, he heard Luke call out to him. "You'll be okay?"

Nick feigned a smile. "I'll live."

⌀⌀⌀

With the resonance of jet engines thundering overhead and people heading off to other destinations, Nick departed Sky Harbor. He opted for side streets rather than the freeway. With no one waiting at home, he was in no hurry to get anywhere.

Eventually this fog that clouded him would lift. He'd ultimately get back in the game, start dating again. And yes, maybe even fall in love. But no one would ever replace the one he was destined for.

He just hoped time would not erase these memories. He wanted them to last until…until he would see her again.

Perhaps, Nick thought, he'd start going to church. Maybe some priest or minister or preacher or rabbi could answer the question Dr. Rajagopal could not. *What happens when we die?*

Would he see her again? He didn't know. But he had to believe he would. He needed to believe it. To keep his sanity he had to have faith that when it was time, he'd be reunited with her. Maybe not in this life, but in the next one. Nick realized he would mark off the days, one by one, until he could hold her again.

He brought his car to a stop at the traffic signal. He held his chin in his hand and gazed around. A sedan pulled up along-side. In the back, he could see two children wrestling over a toy. The husband was fiddling with the radio. The wife, a woman with jet black hair, angled and shouted at her kids to keep it down.

Nick pulled his gaze away from the family and looked forward through the windshield. Rising from the center of town was Camelback Mountain. Nick had lived here so long he was accustomed to the rock formation that jutted from the earth. He looked to the summit and did a double take.

Maybe it always had been there and he never noticed. Or perhaps it was new. Atop the peak were two TV towers. Side by side, they alternated blinking. Right. Left. Right. Left. Marking the passage of time in one second intervals.

Thirty blinks. Thirty seconds passed. Thirty seconds of his life slipped away just like that. Thirty seconds closer to eventually being reunited with Brandi.

Nick eyed the traffic signal, impatiently waiting to move forward. Next to him, the man behind the wheel threw out his arms impatiently at the endless red light.

Nick faced forward, stared at the red beacon.

And waited…

About the Author

Ever since he was little, Rob Silverman had two dreams. One was to play right field, the other was to be a writer. Then, in the blink of an eye, he was middle aged and with the chances of making the majors gone, he focused on his other dream.

Since 2008, he's been writing for a popular baseball website. An avid reader, he spends his spare time yelling at his TV during Baseball season, listening to Bruce Springsteen and classic rock from the '80s, re-watching all six seasons of *LOST* and finding somewhere to sit when one of his spoiled dogs won't get out of his favorite chair.

Born and raised in New York City, he graduated from UNLV and now lives in southern Nevada.